ENDURANCE

Pinnacle Thrillers by J. A. KONRATH

The List

Origin

Endurance

ENDURANCE

J. A. KONRATH

PINNACLE BOOKS
Kensington Publishing Corp.
www.kensingtonbooks.com

PINNACLE BOOKS are published by

Kensington Publishing Corp.
119 West 40th Street
New York, NY 10018

All Kensington titles, imprints, and distributed lines are available at special quantity discounts for bulk purchases for sales promotions, premiums, fund-raising, educational, or institutional use. Special book excerpts or customized printings can also be created to fit specific needs. For details, write or phone the office of the Kensington sales manager: Kensington Publishing Corp., 119 West 40th Street, New York, NY 10018, attn: Sales Department; phone 1-800-221-2647.

This book is a work of fiction. Names, characters, businesses, organizations, places, events, and incidents either are the product of the author's imagination or are used fictitiously. Any resemblance to actual persons, living or dead, events, or locales is entirely coincidental.

ISBN-13: 978-0-7860-4276-0
ISBN-10: 0-7860-4276-1

First Pinnacle premium mass market printing: May 2019

10 9 8 7 6 5 4 3 2 1

Printed in the United States of America

We inflame wild beasts with the smell of blood,
and then innocently wonder at the wave of brutal appetite
that sweeps the land as a consequence.
—MARK TWAIN

Maria unlocked the door to her room and was greeted by Abraham Lincoln.

The poster was yellowed with age, the edges tattered, and it hung directly over the queen-size bed where the headboard would normally be. The adjoining walls were papered with postcards, all of them boasting various pictures and portraits of Lincoln. The single light in the room came from a floor lamp, the shade decorated with a collage of faded newspaper clippings, all featuring—big surprise—Lincoln.

So that's why the crazy old proprietor called it the Lincoln Bedroom.

Maria pulled her suitcase in behind her, placed the room key on a scarred, old dresser, and turned the dead bolt. The door, like the lock, was heavy, solid. As reassuring as that was, this room still gave her the creeps. In fact, everything about this bed-and-breakfast gave her the creeps, from its remote and impossible-to-find location, to its run-down facade, to its eccentric decorations and menagerie of odd odors. But Maria didn't have a choice. The hotel in town had overbooked, and this seemed to be the last room available in the entire state of West Virginia.

Iron Woman had become quite the popular event, with worldwide media coverage, and apparently they'd given her room reservation to some reporter. Which was ironic, because Maria was a registered contestant, and without contestants, there wouldn't be any need for reporters. The reporter was the one who should have been staying in the Lincoln Bedroom, with its bizarre decor and its strange smell of sandalwood mixed with spoiled milk.

Maria sighed. It didn't matter. All that mattered was a good night's sleep after more than twelve hours on the road. She'd missed her late-night workout—this inn didn't have an exercise room—so the best she could hope for was a five-mile run in the morning before getting back to the event hotel, which assured her it would have a room available tomorrow.

Actually, the hotel room will be ready later today.

A glance at the Lincoln clock on the nightstand showed it was past two in the morning.

She had promised to let Felix know when she got in, and pulled her cell phone out of her jeans, her thumbs a blur on the keyboard.

F—U R probably asleep. I M @ a creepy B&B, not the hotel. Long story, but it's free. That = more $$$ to spend on our honeymoon. WTL8R. TTFN, H2CUS, luv U—M.

Maria circled the room, holding her cell over her head, trying to find a signal while the floorboards creaked underfoot. When a single bar appeared, she sent the text message and walked to the poster. She placed her cell on the nightstand as a reminder to charge it before she went to sleep, hefted her suitcase onto the bed, and dug inside, freeing her makeup bag and taking it to the bathroom. She flipped on the light switch and was rewarded with the sight of President Lincoln's face on the toilet seat cover.

"I'll never look at a five-dollar bill the same again,"

she said, but her tone was without mirth. Rather than amusing, she was finding this whole Lincoln thing creepy.

Maria shut the door behind her—more out of habit than modesty—lifted the lid, undid her jeans, and sat down, the cold seat raising goose bumps on her tan thighs. She yawned, big and wide, as the long day caught up with her.

The bathroom, like the bedroom, was tiny. The sink was crowded next to the shower stall, and if Maria were a few inches taller her knees would touch the opposing wall. Hanging on that wall was a framed painting of Lincoln. A head-and-shoulders portrait of his younger years, before he had the famous beard.

His ultrarealistic eyes seemed to be staring right at her.

"Pervert," Maria whispered.

Lincoln didn't reply.

Voices came through the wall. The same two men Maria had heard while checking in, arguing about some sports game, repeating the same points over and over. She listened to the floorboards creak and wondered if the men would keep it up all night, disturbing her sleep. The thought was quickly dismissed. At that moment, Maria was so tired she could have dozed through a Metallica concert.

She finished peeing, flushed, then turned on the faucet. The water was rust colored. Last week Maria had read an article about waterborne bacteria, and she elected to brush her teeth with something safer. She turned off the water and set her toothbrush on the sink. Then she opened the bathroom door, picked her suitcase up off the floor, and placed it on the bed. Maria pulled out a half-empty bottle of Evian and was two steps to the bathroom when she froze.

Didn't I already put the suitcase on the bed?

A flush of adrenaline made Maria turn, her heart racing. She stared at the suitcase like it was a hostile creature, and then she hurried to the front door and eyed the knob.

Still locked. The key was where she'd left it, on the dresser.

Maria spun around, taking everything in. A small desk and chair were tucked in the corner of the room. The bed had a beige comforter and a matching dust ruffle, and it seemed undisturbed. The closet door was open, revealing an empty space. Tan curtains covered the window on the adjacent wall.

The curtains were fluttering.

Almost like someone is hiding behind them.

Her first instinct was to run, but common sense kicked in. She was on the second floor. It was doubtful someone had come in through the window and moved her luggage. A more likely explanation was she'd put the suitcase on the floor herself and was too tired to remember it. The curtains probably jerked because the window was open and a breeze was blowing in.

"You're exhausted," she said aloud. "You're imagining things."

But Maria was sure she put the suitcase on the bed. She'd put it on its side and unzipped it to get her makeup bag. She was *sure* of it.

Maybe it fell off?

But how could it fall and land perfectly on its wheels? And why didn't I hear it fall?

She stared at the suitcase again. It was heavy; packed alongside her clothes was an entire case of bottled water, a result of her recent germ phobia. The suitcase would have made noise hitting the floor. But all Maria heard from the bathroom was those men arguing, and . . .

"The creaking," she said aloud. "I heard the floors creaking."

What if the creaking didn't come from the room next door?

What if the creaking came from her room—from someone walking around?

Maria felt goose bumps break out on her arms.

What if that someone is still here?

She paused, unsure of what to do next. Her feet felt heavy. Her mouth became so dry her tongue stuck to her teeth. Maria knew the odds were high that her paranoia was the result of exhaustion. She also knew there was practically a zero likelihood someone had come into her room just to move her suitcase.

And yet . . .

Maria clenched and unclenched her hands, eyes locking on the curtains. She made a decision.

I need to check.

She took a deep breath, let it out slow. Then she crept toward the window. The curtains were still, and Maria wondered if she'd imagined the fluttering. No light came through them even though they were thin. Not surprising— the inn was way out in the boonies, not another building for miles, and the tall pine trees obscured the moon and stars.

Either that, or someone is crouching on the window-sill, blocking the light.

Maria swallowed, knowing she was psyching herself out, feeling the same kind of adrenaline tingles she got before a race.

Upstairs, the arguing abruptly ceased, midword. The

room became deathly quiet, the only sound Maria's timid footfalls, creaking on the hardwood floor.

The smell of rot in the room got stronger the closer she got to the window.

Could someone really be behind the curtains, ready to pounce?

Maria felt like she was nine years old again, playing hide-and-seek with her younger brother, Cameron. He loved to jump out and scream *Boo!* at her, making her scream. For an absurd moment, she could picture Cam behind that curtain, hands raised, ready to leap out and grab her. One of her few pleasant childhood memories of Cam.

Then she pictured something else grabbing her. A filthy, hairy, insane maniac with a rusty knife.

Maria shook her head, trying to dispel the thought.

The thought wouldn't leave.

"Get a grip," she whispered. "There's nothing there."

She was two feet away when the curtains moved again. And again.

Like someone was poking them from the other side.

Maria flinched, jerking backward.

It's just the wind.

It's got to be.

Right?

"It's the wind," she said through her clenched jaw.

The wind. Nothing more. Certainly not some creep climbing into my room.

But, what if . . . ?

She thought about the pepper spray in her suitcase. Then she thought about just getting the hell out of there. Maria wished Felix were here with her. He'd find this whole situation ridiculously funny.

You compete in triathlons and you're too chicken to check a window?

No. I'm not chicken. I'm not afraid of anything.

But she got the pepper spray anyway, holding it out ahead of her like a talisman to ward off evil. She paused in front of the window, the curtains still.

"Do it."

Maria didn't move.

"Just do it."

Maria set her jaw and in one quick motion swept back the curtains—

—revealing bricks where the glass should have been.

She stared for a moment, confused, then felt a cool breeze on her arm.

There. In the corner. A hole in the mortar, letting the air in.

Maria let out an abrupt laugh. It sounded hollow in the tiny room. She gave the bricks a tentative push, just to make sure they were real and didn't swing on hinges or anything. They were cold to the touch, as hard as stone could be.

Only a ghost could have gotten through that. And Maria didn't believe in ghosts. Life had enough scary things in it without having to make stuff up.

She let the curtain fall and thought of Cameron again. About the things he'd gone through. That was real horror. Not the wind blowing some curtains in a run-down, hillbilly bed-and-breakfast.

Maria hadn't seen Cam in a few weeks, because of her training regimen. She promised herself she would visit the hospital, right after the event. Maybe Felix would come with, even though Cam seemed to creep him out.

He'll do it anyway. Because he loves me.

Again, she wished Felix were here. He promised to be at the race on Saturday. Promised to rub her sore muscles afterward.

She glanced down at her left hand, at the pear-shaped diamond on her ring finger. Yellow, her favorite color. Sometimes hours would go by and she'd forget it was there, even though she'd only been wearing it for less than a week. Looking at it never failed to bring a smile.

Maria walked past the bed, glanced at the knob on the front door to make sure it was still locked, and mused about how she'd gotten herself all worked up over nothing.

She was heading back to the bathroom when she saw movement out of the corner of her eye.

The dust ruffle on the bed was fluttering.

Like something had disturbed it.

Something that had just crawled underneath.

Maria paused, standing stock-still. The fear kicked in again like an energy drink, and she could feel her heart in her neck as she tried to swallow.

There is NOT *some man under my bed.*

And yet . . .

Far-fetched as it may be, there was probably enough room for someone to fit under there. The bed was high up off the floor on its frame, with plenty of space for a man to slip underneath. *A filthy man with a rusty knife?*

Maria gave her head a shake.

It's the wind again.

No, it can't be. This side of the bed isn't facing the window.

A rat?

Could be a rat.

"I came in fourth in Iron Woman last year. I'm not afraid of a little rat."

Maria got on her hands and knees and began to crawl over to the bed.

What if there's a man under there?

There won't be.

But what if there is? What if he grabs me when I lift the dust ruffle?

"Then I'll squirt him in the eyes and kick his ass," she said to herself.

Maria reached for the fabric, aiming her pepper spray with her other hand.

I'll do it on three.

One . . .

Two . . .

Three!

Maria jerked up the dust ruffle.

No one grabbed her. The space under the bed was vacant, except for a small plume of dust that she waved away. Maria let the ruffle drop, and her shoulders drooped in a big sigh.

"I really need to get some rest."

Maria got to her feet, wondering when she'd last slept. She quickly calculated she'd been awake for over twenty hours. That was probably enough to make anyone a little jumpy.

She padded back to the bathroom, reaching for her toothbrush on the sink, picturing her head on the pillow, the covers all around her.

Her toothbrush was gone.

Maria checked under the sink and in her makeup bag.

It was nowhere to be found.

She stared at the Lincoln poster. He stared back, his expression grim.

This isn't exhaustion. Someone is messing with me.

"Screw the free room," she said, picking up the bag. "I'm out of here."

Maria rushed to the bed, reaching for her cell phone on the nightstand.

Her phone wasn't there.

In its place was something else. Something small and brownish.

Maria let out a squeal, jumping back.

This can't actually be happening. It all has to be some sort of joke.

She stared at the brown thing like it would jump up and grab her.

Is it real? It looks shriveled and old.

Some stupid Halloween prop?

Then she smelled it. An odor of decay that invaded her nose and mouth and made her gag.

"It's real. Oh my God . . . it's real."

Someone put a severed human ear in my room.

She ran to the door, and the knob twisted without her unlocking it. Maria tugged it inward, raising her pepper spray to dose anyone standing there.

The hallway was empty. Dark and quiet.

She hurried to the stairs, passing doors with the names Theodore Roosevelt, Harry S. Truman, and Millard Fillmore. Over the winding staircase was a gigantic poster of Mount Rushmore. Maria took the stairs two at a time, sprinting as soon as her feet hit the ground floor. She flew past the dining room, and the living room with its artificial fireplace, and ran up to the front door, turning the knob and throwing her weight against it.

Her shoulder bounced off, painfully. Maria twisted the knob the other way, giving it a second push.

No good. The door won't budge.

She tried pulling, with equal results.

Swearing, Maria searched for a dead bolt, a latch, a doorstop, or some other clue why the door wasn't opening. The only lock on the door was on the knob, and that spun freely. She ground her molars together and gave it another firm shoulder-butt.

It was like slamming into concrete. The door didn't even shake in its jamb.

"Hey! Girly!"

The words shook Maria like a blow. A male voice, coming from somewhere behind her. She spun around, her muscles all bunching up.

"Yeah, I'm talkin' to y'all, ya pretty thang. We gonna have some fun, we are."

The voice was raspy and mean, dripping with country twang. But she couldn't spot where it was coming from. The foyer, and the living room to the right, looked empty except for the furniture. The overhead chandelier, made from dusty deer antlers, cast crazy, crooked shadows over everything. The shadows undulated, due to the artificial fireplace, a plastic log flickering electric orange.

"Who's there?" Maria demanded, her pepper spray held out at arm's length, her index finger on the spray button and ready to press.

No one answered.

There were many places he could be hiding. Behind the sofa. Around any number of corners. Tucked next to the large bookcase. Behind the larger-than-life-size statue of George Washington, holding a sign that said WELCOME TO THE RUSHMORE INN. Or even up the stairs, beyond her line of sight.

Maria kept her back to the wall and moved slowly to the right, her eyes sweeping the area, scanning for any kind of movement. She yearned to run, to hide, but there was nowhere to go. Behind her, she felt the drapes of one of the windows. She quickly turned around, parting the fabric, seeking out the window latch.

But, like the Lincoln Bedroom, there was no glass there. Only bricks, hidden from view on the outside by closed wooden shutters that she'd thought quaint when she first pulled in.

This house is like a prison.

That thought was followed by one even more distressing.

I'm not their first victim. They've done this before.

Oh, Jesus, they've done this before.

Maria clutched the pepper spray in both hands, but she couldn't keep it steady. She was so terrified, her legs were trembling—a first for her. A nervous giggle escaped her lips, but it came out more like a whimper. Taking a big breath, she screamed, "Help me!"

The house carried her plea, bounced it around, then swallowed it up.

A moment later she heard, "*Help me!*"

But it wasn't her echo. It was a male falsetto, mocking her voice.

Coming from the stairs.

"*Help me!*" Another voice. Coming from the living room.

"*Help me!*" This one even closer, from a closet door less than ten feet away.

"*Help me.*" The last one was low-pitched. Quiet.

Coming from right next to her.

The statue of Washington.

It smiled at her, its crooked teeth announcing it wasn't a statue at all.

The incredibly large man dropped the WELCOME sign and lunged, both arms outstretched.

Maria pressed the button on the pepper spray.

The jet missed him by several feet, and his hand brushed her shirt.

She danced away from his grasp and then barreled toward the stairs as the closet door crashed open and someone burst out. Someone big and fat and . . .

Sweet Lord, what was wrong with his body?

Maria pulled her eyes away and attacked the stairs with every bit of her energy. The hundreds of hours she spent training paid off, and she climbed so quickly the man— *Don't look at his horrible face*—on the second floor couldn't react in time to grab her. She ducked past, inhaling a stench of body odor and rot, heading for the only other room she knew to be occupied, the one with the two men arguing sports.

And they were still arguing, behind the door labeled THEODORE ROOSEVELT. Maria threw herself into the room without knocking, slamming and locking the door behind her.

"You've got to help—"

The lights were on, but the room was empty. Maria looked for the voices, which hadn't abated, and quickly focused on the nightstand next to the bed. Sitting on top was an old reel-to-reel tape recorder. The voices of the arguing men droned through its speakers in an endless loop.

A trick. To distract her. Make her feel like she wasn't alone.

Or maybe the purpose of the recording was to lure her into this room.

Then the tape recorder, and the lights, abruptly went off.

Maria froze. She heard someone crying, and with no small surprise realized the sound was coming from her. Dropping onto all fours, she crawled toward the bed. This room was laid out the same way as the Lincoln room, and she quickly bumped against the dust ruffle, brought her legs in front of her, and eased underneath on her belly, feetfirst, keeping her head poking out so she could listen.

At first she couldn't hear anything above her heart hammering in her ears and her own shallow panting. She forced her breathing to slow down, sucking in air through her nose, blowing it out softly through her puffed cheeks.

Then she heard the footsteps. From the hallway. Getting closer. First one set, slow and deliberate, each footfall sounding like a thunderclap. Then another set, equally heavy, running up fast.

Both of them stopped at the door.

"I think the girly is in here."

"That's Teddy's room. We can't go in."

"But she's in there. It's bleedin' time."

Maria heard the doorknob turn. She scooted farther under the bed, the dust ruffle covering her hair.

"You shouldn't do that. You really shouldn't do that."

The door creaked, inching open. Maria saw a beam of light sliver through the crack. It widened until she could see two huge figures silhouetted in the doorway. They each held flashlights.

"The one that catches her, bleeds her first. Them's the rules."

"I ain't goin' in. You shouldn't, neither."

"Shuddup. This girly is mine."

"It's Teddy's room."

"Shuddup!"

The man dressed in the George Washington outfit shone his light on the other man's face. Maria put her hand in her mouth and bit down so she didn't scream. His face was . . . *dear God* . . . it was . . .

"Watch my eyes!"

"I said shuddup!"

"I'm tellin' on you!"

"Hey! Don't!"

The door abruptly closed, and both sets of footsteps retreated up the hall, down the stairs.

Maria's whole body shivered like she was freezing to death. Terror locked her muscles and she couldn't move. But she had to move. She had to find some kind of way out of there.

Were all the windows bricked over? Maybe some of them weren't. Maybe she could get out of a window, climb down somehow. Or get up on the roof. The roof sounded a lot better than waiting around for those freaks to come back.

Maria heard something soft. Faint. Nearby.

Some kind of scratching sound.

She concentrated on listening, but couldn't hear anything above her own labored gasping. She took a deep breath, held it in.

And could still hear the breathing.

Raspy, wet breathing.

Right next to her.

Someone else is under the bed.

"I'm Teddy."

His voice was deep, rough, and hearing it that close scared Maria so badly her bladder let loose.

"I'm gonna bleed you, girly girl. Bleed you nice and long."

Then something grabbed Maria's legs, and she screamed louder than she'd ever screamed in her life, screamed louder than she'd ever thought possible, kicking and clawing as she was dragged down through the trap-door in the floor.

ONE YEAR LATER

"Why don't you go with your grandmother?" Mom said, wiping the sweat from her forehead and replacing it with a streak of grime. "Take JD for a walk."

Kelly Pillsbury frowned at her mother, who'd been trying to change the flat tire for more than ten minutes now. The last nut refused to come off. Each of the women had taken a turn with the tire iron, but the nut was rusted on tight. Grandma was the one who suggested a squirt of WD-40. Now they were all waiting around for the lubricant to soak in, loosen the nut up, so they could get back on the road.

"I'm cool," Kelly said.

She took a furtive glance at the wilderness around her. More trees than she'd ever seen, covering the hills and mountains in every direction. It was gorgeous, and being out here made Kelly forget her established role as a sullen tween.

Make that *teen*. She was turning thirteen in only three days.

Something caught her eye at the tree line, alongside the winding road. A quick streak that looked like a man.

A man darting behind some bushes.

But it had been too big for a man. A bear, maybe?

No. Bears don't wear overalls.

Kelly squinted into the woods, but the figure didn't reappear. She listened for a moment, and heard only the faint *click click click* of the wind spinning the rear wheels of their three bikes, bolted to the rack on the Audi's roof.

After a moment, Kelly believed she'd imagined the figure, that her eyes were playing tricks on her after such a long road trip.

Who would be way out here in the middle of nowhere anyway? We left modern civilization two hours ago, the last time we stopped for gas.

She looked back at her iPod and unpaused her game, *Zombie Apocalypse*, on level 64, with only one quarter of her health left. Kelly had never beaten level 65, and she'd been playing the game for more than a month.

"Kelly?" her mom said.

"Huh?"

"That wasn't a suggestion."

"What?" Mom was seriously breaking her concentration.

"Go help Florence walk the dog."

Kelly flicked the touch screen, pausing again. Mom had her bare arms folded, her muscles popping up like a man's. Kelly subconsciously checked her own arms. She prided herself in being strong, but she never wanted to look like that. *Never.* Muscles on women were gross.

"Grandma's doing fine."

The women both looked at Grandma. The sixty-five-year-old was tugging on JD's leash. JD was sitting on the road, licking himself between his legs. At over a hundred pounds, the German shepherd weighed about as much as Grandma did.

"Kelly. Don't make me say it again." Mom lowered her voice. "Give her a chance. Please. For me."

Kelly sighed loudly and rolled her eyes, even though Mom never said *please*. Then Kelly tucked her iPod into her fanny pack and stalked over to Grandma and the dog. It was bad enough that Grandma was coming to live with them after the Iron Woman race, but Mom had also insisted Kelly give up her room and move into the much smaller third bedroom.

Totally unfair.

Kelly didn't understand why Grandma was moving in anyway. She and Mom had some kind of falling-out years ago, after Dad died, and Kelly hadn't seen her grandmother since she was six. She had no idea why they'd been out of touch for so long, but now here they were, pretending to care about each other.

One big happy.

"Stubborn, isn't he?" Grandma let the leash go slack. Like Kelly, she was dressed in jogging shorts and a loose tee, though even at her ancient age, Grandma filled the clothes out better. "I don't think he likes me."

"He only walks for me and Mom. If he didn't like you, you'd know. He'd be growling and the hair would stand up on his back. C'mere, JD."

At the command, JD's ears pricked up and he pranced over to Kelly, the leash pulling out of Grandma's hand. He bumped his massive head into Kelly's hip and gave her arm a lick. He then switched to licking the scab on her knee—a training injury from a few days ago.

Grandma walked up to them. She wasn't as muscular as Mom, and just a bit shorter, but the resemblance was amazing. When the three of them stood next to each other, it was like looking at the same woman at different stages of her life. Each of them also wore their blond hair the same way, in a ponytail, though Grandma's was mostly gray.

"Want to go north?" Grandma said, pointing her chin over Kelly's shoulder.

"I hear a waterfall. We could go check it out."

"I don't hear anything."

"You will, as we get closer. Come on."

Grandma moved at an easy jog, cutting across the road, into the thick trees. Kelly lived her whole life in southern Illinois, flat as a bowling alley with no flora taller than cornstalks. West Virginia, with its mountains and forests, seemed like a different country. It was beautiful, but Kelly refused to admit it aloud, sticking her nose back in her iPod whenever Mom or Grandma pointed out something pretty during the long drive. She didn't want to give either of them the satisfaction, still sore about the bedroom thing, which Mom sprung on her when they picked Grandma up at the airport yesterday.

Why didn't Mom give up her room to Grandma? It was all a bunch of BS.

No, not BS. It was straight-up bullshit.

Just thinking about the swear word made Kelly feel older. She frowned, then followed her grandmother.

Ten steps into the woods, Kelly felt like she'd been swallowed. The trees were everywhere, and she lost all sense of direction. Grandma weaved through the forest like a jackrabbit, her pace increasing, and Kelly began to fall behind.

"Slow down! JD can't keep up!"

In fact, JD was doing fine. Kelly was also doing fine, at least in the stamina department. She'd trained for seven months for the triathlon and was enormously proud to be the youngest contestant this year. But Kelly was used to running on asphalt, not rocky wilderness. Her steps alternated between jagged outcroppings and soft dirt that sucked at her gym shoes. Kelly spent so much time watching her footing she was afraid Grandma would get too far ahead and disappear.

"Don't look at your feet."

Kelly startled, coming to a stop. Somehow Grandma had materialized right in front of her.

"I'm gonna break my ankle."

"Look into my eyes, Kelly."

Kelly did as instructed. Grandma's eyes were blue, like hers and Mom's, but set in a valley of deep wrinkles. Kelly couldn't remember Grandma ever smiling. Not that she was a mean woman. But she was serious all the time.

"Can you see my hand?" Grandma asked.

Kelly glanced down at Grandma's wriggling fingers.

"No, Kelly. Keep looking at me while you do it."

Kelly sighed, then stared at Grandma again.

"Keeping your eyes on mine, can you see my hand?"

Kelly couldn't see it, at least not clearly. But she could make out an indistinct blur.

"I guess."

"What am I doing?"

"Wiggling your fingers."

"Good. Now watch me."

Grandma took a step back and stood with her legs apart, her hands at waist level, one in front of the other. She quickly raised her arms up over her head, then brought each hand around in a circle. They met again at her beltline, palms out. The entire time, her gaze was locked onto Kelly.

"What's that?" Kelly asked.

"The beginning of a kata called *Kushanku*. It helps improve your peripheral vision. The goal is to be able to see your hands while looking straight ahead."

"What's the point?"

"To be aware of everything around you and not just what's in front of you."

"So?"

"So then you'll know if someone does this."

Kelly felt wind on her cheek. She looked, and saw Grandma's palm an inch away from slapping her ear. Kelly hadn't seen Grandma's hand move at all.

JD growled, baring his teeth.

"Shush," Grandma said. "Be nice."

The dog whined, then sat down and began licking himself again.

"Can you teach me how to do that?" Kelly asked. "To hit that fast?"

"It's up to your mother. She never really warmed up to the martial arts."

"Show me that kata thing again."

"Kushanku."

Grandma repeated the move. Kelly handed over the leash and tried it. She could just barely make out her hands at the very edge of sight.

"I can see them."

She also thought she saw something else. Something moving in the woods. Kelly remembered the man she'd seen earlier, but kept her eyes on Grandma, as instructed. Besides, if there was a man in the forest, JD would be barking.

That is, if JD could keep his snout out of his own crotch for more than ten seconds.

"Good. Now use your peripheral vision when you're running over the rocks, so you don't have to keep your head down. Keep your eyes ahead of you, but not your entire focus."

"I can try."

Grandma took off, JD running alongside her. Kelly trailed behind, doing as Grandma said, and found she could move much quicker. She looked around for the man in the overalls, but saw only foliage.

Kelly smiled, relaxing a little. The summer breeze smelled like pine trees and wildflowers, and she enjoyed the stretch and pull in her hamstrings and quads. It was a brief run, barely even a warm-up, before Kelly caught up to Grandma on a crest.

"Hey," Kelly said. "JD let you walk him."

Grandma wasn't even out of breath. "Can you hear it now?"

"What?"

"Listen."

Kelly heard it. A hissing, splashing sound.

"The waterfall?"

Grandma nodded. "Which direction is it in?"

"I can't tell."

"Close your eyes. Open your ears."

Kelly shut her eyes and listened. The sound seemed to be coming from no particular direction.

"Try turning around. Tune out everything else."

Kelly shifted slightly. She spun in a slow circle, eventually locking in on the direction of the water. When she opened her eyes, she was grinning.

"It's this way," Kelly said, bounding off into the woods.

She jogged down a hill, around a bend, and then to a clearing, skidding to a stop because the ground simply ended. Kelly felt her stomach sink, staring down off the side of a sheer cliff. She wasn't good with heights, and even though she could swim three hundred laps in the school pool she was terrified of diving boards. Standing on ledges just wasn't her thing.

Then she saw the waterfall.

It was gigantic, at least fifty feet high. The vertigo made her back up two steps.

"Lovely," Grandma said.

Kelly hadn't even heard the old woman come up beside her.

"I don't really like heights."

"Your eyes can make you afraid of things you shouldn't be afraid of. Are you standing on solid ground?"

"Yeah."

"What do you think you should trust more, your eyes, or the solid ground?"

"The ground."

"So trust the ground and let your eyes enjoy the view."

Kelly trusted the ground and stared at the waterfall. A fine mist hovered overhead and made a double rainbow in the rays of the setting sun. It was prettier than a post-card and not so scary anymore.

"Is this what Vietnam looked like?" Kelly asked. Then she immediately regretted it. According to Mom, Grandma never talked about the war. Kelly knew she was there for four years as a combat nurse, but that was all.

"Parts of it. Parts of it were so beautiful it hurt."

"Is that where you learned that kung fu stuff?"

"It's karate. And no, I learned that after my tour ended. Let's go back, see how Letti is doing with that tire. Can you find the way?"

"I dunno. I don't think so."

"Try it. Maybe you'll surprise yourself. If you get confused, see if you can spot any of our footprints. The ground is soft and we made quite a few."

Grandma's eyes were serious, but kind.

"How come you never smile?" Kelly asked. She watched Grandma's eyes get hard again and regretted the question.

"It happened during the war," Grandma said. "They shot my smile off."

What? They shot her smile off? Then Grandma winked.

Kelly grinned, took a final, unsteady glance at the waterfall, then bounded back into the woods. Nothing looked particularly familiar, but she managed to spot a footprint so she knew she was on the right track, even though the footprint seemed rather large. Then she recognized a big tree she'd passed earlier, and she altered her course, picking up speed and growing more confident.

Abruptly, something snagged her shoulder, pulling her off her feet. Kelly landed on her butt, hard, and someone covered her mouth before she could yell out.

"Shh." Grandma was kneeling next to her, her hand over Kelly's face. "Stay calm."

Kelly didn't understand what was happening, and she was about to protest, when she noticed JD. The dog was crouching down, ready to pounce, his teeth bared. All the hair on the dog's neck stood out like spikes. Kelly followed the animal's gaze and saw—

—trees. Nothing but trees.

Then something moved. Ever so slightly, but enough for Kelly to distinguish the body from the surrounding foliage.

It was a man, hiding behind a giant oak. The man she'd seen earlier, the one in the overalls. He was incredibly tall, wearing a plaid shirt and a baseball cap. There was something wrong—something horribly wrong—with his face. And his eyes . . .

His eyes look red.

The man stared right at Kelly, and she'd never been more frightened in her life.

JD barked, making Kelly jerk in surprise.

"Hello," Grandma said to the stranger. "We were looking at the waterfall. I hope we're not trespassing on your property. If so, we're sorry." Grandma didn't sound sorry. She sounded tough as a barrel of hammers.

The man continued to stare. He didn't move. He didn't even blink.

What happened to his face?

"We'll be on our way."

JD barked again, then began to growl.

"Easy, boy. We don't want you biting any more strangers."

JD had never bitten anyone. But Kelly understood why Grandma said that; it might scare the man off.

But the man didn't look scared. He simply shifted from one leg to the other, revealing something he was holding in his hand.

Oh shit.

That's a shotgun.

"Let's go," Grandma whispered. "Fast."

Kelly didn't have to be told twice. The two of them sprinted, JD alongside, down the hill in a zigzag pattern. Kelly kept expecting to hear a gunshot, and could almost feel a cold area between her shoulder blades where she was sure the bullet would hit. Mom had what she called a varmint gun, a small .22 she used to scare off the raccoons who liked to get into the garbage cans. Kelly knew the damage that could do.

This man's gun was a lot bigger.

Not soon enough, they broke through the tree line and were back on the road.

Kelly looked left, then right, and couldn't see their car.

Had the man gotten Mom?

"This way," Grandma said. "Over the crest."

Grandma's strides were long, and Kelly matched her. On the asphalt she had a lot more confidence, the hard road under her feet solid and familiar. She sprinted ahead, feeling her muscles stretch, JD easily matching pace as he galloped alongside. The hill was a gradual incline, tough on the shins, and after two hundred meters her breath came faster.

Is this the right way? What if Grandma is wrong? What if Mom isn't over the crest?

She took a quick glance over her shoulder, but the strange man wasn't behind them.

What was wrong with his face? It was all messed up.

They were almost to the top of the hill now. Ten steps. Five steps. Kelly willed her mom to be there. Not only there, but with the tire already fixed so they could get the hell away from here. Kelly pulled even farther in front, reaching the crest, staring down on the winding road and—

Nothing. Mom and the car weren't there.

Then JD took off, pulling the leash out of Kelly's hand, jerking her forward and almost making her fall. He tore ahead, running around the bend, out of sight.

Kelly glanced at Grandma, who was matching her pace. The old woman stared back, her face solemn.

"The car . . ." Kelly sputtered.

"It's ahead."

"JD . . ."

"Ahead."

Kelly felt like crying. "I'm . . . scared."

"Use it. Everyone gets scared. Don't let it paralyze you. Your body, or your mind."

Kelly lengthened her stride again; a dangerous move since they were going downhill. If she hit some loose gravel or stumbled somehow at this speed, it would cause more damage than just a skinned knee.

"Kelly. Slow down."

But Kelly didn't slow down. Her feet pressed against the street faster and faster, and Kelly became off-balance on the decline. She pitched forward, envisioning her chin cracking against the pavement, her face scraping down to the teeth and cheekbones, her knees breaking and head bursting—

"Kelly!"

Grandma caught Kelly's shirt, steadying her. Kelly took a few more unsteady steps and then slowed down enough to keep her balance.

They pushed through the turn, Kelly hoping she'd see Mom and the car and JD, fearing she'd see the strange man with the gun.

But there was nothing ahead but empty road.

"We went . . . the wrong . . . way," Kelly said between pants. She began to slow down even more.

"Keep running."

Kelly wished she'd paid more attention on the car ride up. None of this seemed familiar. The road. The woods. The mountains. It all looked the same.

"Is this . . ." she said, gasping, "the right road?"

"Yes."

"But . . ."

"Don't talk. Run."

Grandma pulled in front. Kelly fell back five paces,

thinking Grandma was wrong, thinking about turning
around and going the other way.

Then they rounded another turn and Kelly saw their car.

JD left Mom's side and came sprinting over to Kelly.
He knew not to jump on her and instead doubled back
and ran with her until they reached the car.

"I changed the tire. Did you and Grandma enjoy—"
Mom squinted at Kelly. "Babe, are you okay?"

"There was a man." Kelly huffed and puffed. "His face
was messed up. He had a gun."

Grandma coasted to a stop alongside them.

"Florence? What happened?"

Mom hadn't called Grandma *Mom* since Dad died.

Grandma blew out a deep breath. "I'm not sure. Could
have been a hunter. Could have been some hillbilly pro-
tecting his whiskey still. Scary-looking fellow, wasn't
he, Kelly?"

"Did he threaten you?" Mom asked.

Grandma shook her head. "Kept his gun down. Didn't
say a word. Might not be used to talking, though. He had
a severe harelip, probably a cleft palate. Talking would
be difficult."

"Should we call the police?"

"For having a gun in West Virginia? They'd laugh us
off the phone."

"Are you okay, Kelly?"

Kelly felt like crying, and Mom showing concern
made the emotion even stronger. But she sucked it in, got
her breathing under control.

I'm almost a teenager. Teenagers don't cry.

"I'm fine."

"Are you sure?"

Grandma folded her arms. "She said she's fine, Letti. Kelly's almost a teenager. Quit treating her like a child."

Kelly matched Grandma's pose, taking strength from it. "Yeah, Mom. Now, can we get going?"

Mom made a face, then looked at her watch. "We've got another forty minutes before we get to the bed-and-breakfast. Do you need to pee?"

Kelly rolled her eyes. "No."

"Are you sure?"

"Jeez, Mom." She walked over to the car and climbed into the backseat.

Surprisingly, Grandma got in next to her.

"Let's let JD ride shotgun. I'd like to see that game you're playing on your iPod."

"Uh, sure."

As Mom pulled back onto the road, Kelly showed Grandma *Zombie Apocalypse*.

"It's really hard. I can't get past level 65."

"Sure you can," Grandma said. "You just haven't yet."

Kelly attacked the level with a frenzy. For some reason, more than anything, she wanted to prove Grandma right.

"I'm sorry, Miss Novachek. All of our rooms are booked."

Deb Novachek kept her anger in check. She was an expert at that.

"But I have a reservation. I confirmed it yesterday."

The concierge looked pained. He was a tall, pasty man with a bad hairpiece that looked like an animal was perched on his head. His name tag read FRANKLIN. "I realize that. And I humbly apologize for the inconvenience. We overbooked. Your room will be available tomorrow morning, and we'll upgrade you to a suite at no extra cost."

"That's not good enough. Tomorrow is the pre-event briefing. I have to be there early."

Deb fleetingly considered playing the *special needs* card, but she knew she'd sleep in her car before she did that. Hell, she'd sleep on the street with a newspaper blanket before she asked for preferential treatment.

"I really wish there was something I could do. I'm very sorry."

"I'd like to speak to the manager."

"Miss Novachek, I am the manager. I'll not only upgrade you to a suite tomorrow, but we'd be happy to pay for it to make up for the inconvenience."

"That doesn't do me any good tonight."

Deb felt like crossing her arms, but resisted. It messed with her balance.

"Unfortunately, this seems to happen every year at triathlon time. Every hotel and motel in town is filled to capacity."

Deb frowned. "Could I room with another contestant staying here?"

Franklin reached for the phone. "That would be up to them. If you give me a name, I can connect you."

"I don't know anyone here. This is my first time at Iron Woman."

"I'm sorry. I can't just start randomly calling guests." He put the receiver down and tapped his pale chin, apparently thinking. "You know, there is a bed-and-breakfast, forty miles out of town. It's so out of the way, it probably has some rooms available. Would you like me to check for you?"

Deb took a deep breath, let it out slow. "Yes. Please."

"I'll need to find the number. I'll be right back."

Franklin waddled off. Deb turned away from the check-in counter and faced the lobby. It was crammed full of people. Some of them spectators. Several of them reporters, complete with video cameras and microphones. A few of the women were obviously athletes, and Deb considered approaching some of them, asking if they'd like to share a room. But she didn't move.

Deb valued her privacy. Social situations were painfully awkward for her.

Which is why she quickly turned away when she saw the man staring.

Men stared at her all the time. So did women. And kids. Even animals did, somehow able to sense something was wrong with her.

But this man wasn't gawking. He had a playful smile on his face, and his eyes crinkled when she caught him looking.

This wasn't a gawker. This was a flirt.

Deb preferred the gawkers. She unconsciously glanced down at her cosmetic legs. They were covered by sweat-pants. Unless someone was paying close attention, they couldn't tell, even when she was walking.

"Hello."

The voice startled her, and she turned around. Mr. Flirt was in her personal space, less than a foot away from her, a sly grin on his face. Deb noted his breath smelled like cinnamon, and he was even cuter up close. Strong chin with a bit of stubble. A roman nose. Neatly cut hair, dark and parted on the side. Sort of like a younger George Clooney.

"Can I help you?" Deb's voice came out clipped, and a bit squeaky.

"Are you Debra Novachek?"

"Who wants to know?"

"Mal Deiter. *Sporting Digest*. My office has been in touch."

He offered his hand.

So he's not a flirt. He's a reporter. Which means he knows about my legs.

Deb didn't know if that made it less awkward or more awkward. For some reason, she had pictured a woman interviewing her. Or some pudgy old man.

Not someone good-looking.

Good-looking guys made her nervous.

"Nice to meet you, Mr. Deiter." She took his hand and shook it hard, businesslike, then quickly pulled away. "They seem to be having some trouble finding me a room here."

"I'm sorry to hear that."

"If you're really sorry, you can give me your room."

"I would, Ms. Novachek, if I had one. But I'm already doubled up with my photographer." He pointed to a portly man with a very large camera in his hands, shooting people in the lobby. "That's Rudy. Great talent, but a terrible roommate. He snores so loudly he can loosen your fillings. I'm going to wind up on the lobby sofa if I want to get any rest tonight."

He smiled, and it was a dynamite smile. Deb wondered why he worked for a magazine when he had a face for TV. She decided against asking, not wanting to compliment him and risk it sounding like a come-on.

Not that Deb could even remember what it was like coming on to a guy.

The manager returned. "The Rushmore Inn does have a few rooms left for tonight. I took the liberty of making you a reservation and drawing you a map. We're also covering the cost of your room there. It will be free of charge."

Deb bit back thanking him, instead saying, "I have a GPS. I don't need a map."

He pushed the paper toward her. "It's really out of the way. I doubt the Inn, or even the road, is on the GPS."

"How long will it take to get there?"

"An hour. Maybe an hour and a half at the most."

Deb clenched her jaw. Her mood worsened when she saw the cute reporter furtively eyeing her legs.

She slapped her hand on the map and picked it up.

"Again, we really apologize for this inconvenience." The manager smiled, but this time it seemed more cruel than sympathetic. "I hope to see y'all tomorrow, Miss Novachek."

Deb raised an eye at the manager's sarcastic tone. She let it slide, instead turning to the reporter.

"I'm sorry, Mr. Deiter. This isn't going to work."

"Call me Mal."

"Mal, I know we were going to do the interview tonight over dinner, but I won't have time. It seems I just lost three hours."

"You still have to eat, don't you?"

"Hopefully, I can pick something up on the way to the inn. I didn't figure on an extra ninety-minute drive tonight."

The fat photographer, Rudy, had come over and was snapping Deb's picture.

This annoyed her. She hadn't checked her hair or her makeup.

Not that they want pictures of my face. My face isn't the reason for the interview.

"Ms. Novachek, this is Rudy."

"Ma'am." Rudy held out a chubby hand. It was moist when Deb shook it.

"Nice to meet you, Rudy, but it looks like you guys will have to find some other subject for your story."

"We've got other subjects," Rudy said. "But you're the big one. You came first in your age group in the Denver triathlon, and third overall. You're a tremendous athlete, Ms. Novachek. Especially considering the loss of your legs. I've heard you have different prosthetic legs for each part of the event. Do you have some with fins for the swimming portion?"

Rudy was talking loud enough to attract the attention of others in the room.

Deb felt every eye on her, but managed to keep her voice steady.

"I don't wear my legs for the swimming portion. I wouldn't want anyone to think I had an unfair advantage. And now, if you'll excuse me."

Deb shoved the map into her fanny pack and began to walk away from the counter.

"But we want you for the cover . . ." Rudy said.

She willed herself not to run. These weren't her running legs, and it was easy to catch her toes on things. The thought of the fat guy snapping her photo when she was flat on her face was too much to bear. "Ms. Novachek . . . please . . ."

The reporter was next to her, his expression concerned.

"I'm sorry, Mr. Deiter—"

"Mal."

"—I'm simply not going to have time."

"I could ride with you to the inn. He said the Rushmore, right? I was actually going to take a cab there, anyway. That's where the Pillsburys are staying. They're my other interview."

"I only have a two-seater."

"It would just be me. Rudy will stay here. He's actually a nice guy. A bit blunt, but not a mean bone in his body. I hope he didn't offend you."

"Not at all."

That was the truth. Nothing offended Deb these days. And she prided herself that she was also beyond embarrassment. Since she lost her legs, Deb had gotten so accustomed to her condition that she was mostly oblivious to other people's reaction to her. Hell, when she jogged around town, she often stopped to let kids touch her running prosthetics.

So why am I so anxious to get away right now?

She knew the reason.

It's because he's attractive. Talking to handsome guys makes me feel inferior, inadequate.

Incomplete.

But am I strong enough to deal with it?

Deb took a calming breath, let it out slow.

Yes. Yes, I am.

"Please, Ms. Novachek. I feel like we've gotten off on the wrong foot . . ."

Deb stopped and shot him a look. He seemed confused for a moment, and then he turned such a bright shade of red she thought he might pop.

"Oh . . . jeez . . . look, I really didn't mean to say *foot* . . ."

She let him squirm for a moment, because he was cute doing so. Then she let him off the hook.

"It's okay. I put my foot in my mouth all the time. Want to see me take it off and do it right now?"

He looked mortified, then noticed her grin and burst out laughing.

Deb allowed herself a small smile. It felt pretty good.

"Ms. Novachek, I have a feeling this is going to be a great interview."

Deb had that feeling, too. "Call me Deb."

"Thank you, Deb." He offered his hand again.

This time, when she took it, she didn't squeeze as hard. Or pull away as fast.

"Look, Deb, I don't want to impose, but the desk clerk said they had several rooms, and since all of my interviews are at the same inn, it makes sense for me to stay there as well. Do you mind if I grab my suitcase from my room? I know you're in a hurry but I haven't even unpacked yet. It'll just take a second."

"Sure, Mal. I'm parked right outside the lobby. It's the red Corvette."

"Thanks. I'll be two minutes, tops."

He gently disengaged his hand, then quickly walked over to Rudy and exchanged a few words. Deb turned to go to her car and caught a glimpse of the manager again. He was looking straight at her and seemed to be saying something.

To me?

No. He was talking on the phone. He smiled at her, then shot her with his thumb and index finger.

Asshole.

Deb turned, slow and easy, and headed through the lobby, to the revolving doors.

Revolving doors were tough to navigate in her cosmetic legs. So were stairs and ramps. Ladders were the worst of all, and the one time she tried to climb one, she fell and sprained her wrist.

There are no handicaps. Only challenges.

But why does every simple thing have to be a challenge?

Back when she was still doing the Internet dating thing, one of her prospects actually had the guts to ask what it felt like, trying to walk on prosthetics.

"Ever have your foot fall asleep then try to walk?" she'd responded.

It was a good analogy, but not perfect. It explained the lack of sensation, and how taking away that sensation made it very hard to judge where to place your feet. But it didn't cover the balance difficulties. Deb spent over a year in thrice-daily physical therapy to get to where she could walk again, and another two years to be able to run, which required a whole new set of challenges.

She approached the revolving door warily, timed it right, then took some awkward little hops to get in, holding the door for support. When she made it through she let out a little sigh of relief—falling in a revolving door was *the worst.*

Her Vette was where she'd parked it, in the drop-off zone. Deb fished out the keys and hit the alarm, unlocking the doors. Then she maneuvered into the front seat, adjusted her fanny pack so she wasn't sitting against it, and took the portable GPS out of the glove compartment.

The creepy manager was right. Her Garmin couldn't find the name of the inn, or the road it was on. She programmed in the spot where it was supposed to be and stuck the unit up on the dashboard, then fought the urge to check herself in the mirror.

After ten seconds she gave in, flipping down the sun visor, meeting her own gaze.

No crud in the eyes. Her brown hair, with red and blond

streaks, was a bit poofy and windblown from the ride up, but the layers looked natural and were hassle-free, just like a three-hundred-dollar haircut should be. The touch of blush and pink eye shadow—applied at home in D.C. on the off chance the reporter spotted her in the lobby—were still in place. Deb touched up her lip gloss with just a dab of wet red, and judged herself okay.

Deb knew she was pretty. She just wished she were whole.

She fidgeted, waiting for Mal. He looked to be late twenties, maybe early thirties. Only a few years older than her. Deb hadn't seen a wedding ring on his finger, but that didn't mean much. At their age, all the good-looking ones were either spoken for or gay.

Not that it mattered. The only man Deb had been with since the accident was Scott, and it had been awful with him and not something she ever cared to repeat.

Another minute crawled by, and Deb began to wonder if Mal had changed his mind. She'd gone on a blind date last year, and the guy had gotten up to go to the bathroom at the restaurant and never came back. It was right after he'd gotten a little frisky with his flirting and had cupped her knee, feeling the prosthetic leg below it.

This isn't a date. It's an interview. And he already knows you have no legs.

She wondered if Mal, or Rudy, would want to see her bare stumps for the article. That would be a *no way*. The only one who had ever seen them was her doctor, and the only other person who would ever see them would be her undertaker.

Someone knocked on the hood, startling her. Mal leaned over the driver's side door.

"Can you pop the trunk?"

Deb hit the button, then had a moment of panic realizing what he'd see.

It doesn't matter. He'll see your prosthetic legs during the competition anyway.

She braced herself for his comments when he sat down next to her, but all he said was, "Thanks again for the ride, and the interview. Please let me pay for gas."

"If you insist. But this beast doesn't get very good mileage."

"I can imagine. I drive a Prius. But I always wanted a Corvette."

"Me, too." She smiled. "Buckle up for safety."

Deb started the car, engaging the hand clutch on the gear shift, and squeezed the gas lever on the steering wheel. The tires squealed, pinning Mal into his seat, and the car peeled away from the lobby entrance and onto the main road.

Almost immediately Deb squeezed the brakes, skidding to a stop as someone darted into the street ahead of her—

THWAK!

—the dark figure slapped the hood of her car, spun, then scurried away in a limping crouch. He disappeared into the bushes alongside the road, into the woods.

"Holy shit," Mal said.

Deb blew out her cheeks, the adrenaline making her hands shake.

"Did I hit him?"

"I dunno. He was huge."

"All I saw was long, white hair. But an old man couldn't move that fast."

"Did you see his eyes?"

Deb nodded, then shuddered.

"They were red," Mal said. "I swear they were red."

After taking a few more seconds to compose herself, Deb pulled onto the side of the road and parked the car.

"It wasn't your fault," Mal said. "He jumped out of the bushes right in front of you."

"If I hit him, it's my fault. I have to check."

"I'll go with you."

Deb undid her seat belt and pulled herself out of the Vette. It was dusk, but looked even darker because the sun had dipped below the tree line. The town of Monk Creek wasn't exactly a town, per se. It was more like a collection of a few motels, some scattered stores, and a loose group of homes interspersed along the mountainside and woods in a thirty-square-mile area. The hotel was packed, but once you stepped off the property you were smack-dab in the middle of the wilderness.

Deb squinted into the brush just off the shoulder of the road, where the man had disappeared. If he'd been hurt, he couldn't have gotten far.

"Hello?" she called.

No one answered. A strong breeze kicked up, blowing Deb's hair into her eyes and making her widen her stance so she didn't tip over.

"Anyone there? Are you okay?"

She watched the breeze make the bushes sway, back and forth, like they were waving at her.

Deb peered at the ground, at the slight slope leading into the woods. In her Cheetah Flex sprinting legs she could bounce down there, no problem. In her cosmetic legs, chances were high she'd be on her ass after a few steps.

"I'll go check," Mal said, a penlight in his hand.

Deb frowned, began to protest, but he was already halfway down the embankment, pushing into the brush.

She waited, feeling her stomach go sour.

What if I hurt him? What if he's badly hurt?

What if he's dead?

The thought of killing another human being—it would be too much to live with. She cursed herself for showing off in the car, accelerating so fast. Since her accident, Deb prided herself in paying extra attention, avoiding mistakes and screwups, because she realized how precious, and precarious, life was.

Deb walked over to the front of the Vette, checking the fender for dings. Or blood.

All she found was a decent dent in the hood, from when the man slapped it.

Had he slapped it out of anger? Or to steady himself because I hit him?

Then she noticed the blood. Hard to discern against the red paint job, but it was there.

Quite a bit of it.

Deb felt herself getting ready to vomit, when someone yelled, "Uh!"

Mal?

She went back to the shoulder, squinting into the gathering darkness. No sign at all of Mal, or the man. The wind continued to blow the bushes to and fro, to and fro.

"Mal?" she called.

Mal didn't answer.

Deb tried louder. "Mal!"

A faint sound caught on the breeze. Something high-pitched.

Is that giggling?

Deb considered going to the trunk, putting on her

running legs to make it easier, and then decided *screw it* and began to make her way down the slope.

Just as she reached the bottom, something lunged out of the bushes at her. Deb couldn't react quickly enough, and her balance was thrown off. She landed hard on her backside.

"Mal!"

Mal's eyes were wide. And his pants—they were covered in blood.

Deb positioned herself onto her knees. Getting up off the ground in her cosmetic legs was difficult, so she reached for Mal, wrapping her fingers in his belt to steady herself.

"Deb . . ."

"Call an ambulance, Mal," she said, grabbing his penlight and pushing into the bushes.

"Deb, don't go in there. It's—"

Deb didn't hear the next thing he said. Once past the bush, her senses were overloaded with the stench, and the sight, of blood.

A ridiculous amount of blood.

It soaked the ground and drenched the surrounding foliage.

But it was more than just blood. It was bits of tissue. Sinew. Organs.

The spectacle overtook her, and she stumbled forward, losing her footing on something slippery, falling forward into a wet loop of intestines.

Deb recoiled, squealing, pushing herself away, bumping into a severed head with . . .

Antlers.

It's a deer.

Jesus Christ, it's just a deer.

Then someone grasped her shoulder.

Deb turned around, the scream building in her chest, and saw Mal above her.

"Looks like we both need a dry cleaner. I slipped, too."

He offered his hands, and she used them to pull herself up.

"I didn't hit a deer. I'm sure of it."

Mal's face was kind. "I know."

"It was a man."

"I know. We both saw it."

Deb played the light over the carnage. Deer parts were everywhere.

"Did that guy do this?"

Mal nodded. "I think he killed the deer and was skinning it."

"There's blood on the hood of my car."

"Deer blood, probably. Maybe he didn't have a hunting license, heard you pulling up, thought it was the game warden. Hell, it might not even be hunting season, for all I know."

"So I didn't hurt him?"

"I don't see him anywhere. If you hurt him, he'd be nearby, don't you think?" Deb shined the light on the deer head, wincing as she did.

"When skinning a buck, is it normal to cut the eyes out?"

"No. It's not. Let me see the light." Mal took it, moved in closer. "The ears are gone, too. So's the tongue."

"That's disgusting."

Mal pointed the light at her. "I think we should go. Right now."

Deb didn't like his tone. He sounded scared. When he took her arm, she didn't protest, and when he put his hands on her hips to help her up the embankment she cared more about haste than dignity or modesty.

"I've got water in the trunk. We can clean up."

Mal shook his head. "Not here. Not now. Let's get out of here."

"What's going on, Mal? You're freaking me out a little. And it's not like this situation isn't already freaky enough."

"It's Monk Creek. It has a history. When I was researching this article, I read up on it. Things have happened in this town. Bad things."

"Like what?"

Mal looked over his shoulder into the darkness, then back at Deb. "I'll tell you in the car. Please. Let's go."

The breeze kicked up, and Deb heard it again, faint but unmistakable.

Giggling.

It took less than ten seconds for them to get into the car, lock the doors, and get the hell out of there.

"Buck and a half."

The bartender was overweight, unshaven, and his apron bore stains from days before, stains that were easy to see even in the low lighting of the smoky, shitkicker bar.

Felix Richter slapped a ten next to the can of Miller High Life. The bartender reached for it, but Felix's finger kept it pressed to the bar countertop.

"I'm looking for a bed-and-breakfast in these parts."

The bartender spit tobacco juice into an ashtray. "Then get yourself a map, boy."

"This one isn't on any maps. It's called the Rushmore Inn."

The man sitting next to Felix—stereotypical redneck

hunter type—leaned closer. Felix ignored him, watching the bartender, searching his eyes for any sign of recognition.

"Never heard of it."

If the bartender was lying, he was good at it. Felix had become pretty good at spotting liars. He'd talked to more people in the last year than he had in his previous twenty-six.

Still keeping his finger on the bill, Felix tugged a worn photo from the breast pocket of his flannel shirt. He held it up.

"Seen her before?"

"Can't say that I have."

"Maybe it would help if you looked at the goddamn picture."

The bartender's eyes flitted to the photo, then back to Felix. "Don't recall," he said, spitting again.

"I'll pay for the information." Felix dropped his voice. "I have a lot more money."

"Then buy yourself some swabs to clean out your ears. I never saw the girl before."

Felix let him take the ten. Then he flipped the picture around and stared at it.

Like always, seeing her face made his jaw get tight. Her voice played in his head, even though her last words to him had been an acronym-filled text.

Felix—you're probably asleep. I'm at a creepy B&B, not the hotel. Long story, but it's free. That equals more money to spend on our honeymoon.

We'll talk later. Ta-ta for now, hope to see you soon, love you, Maria.

He thought about looking at his phone to read the

message again, for the ten thousandth time. Then he thought about calling her, just to hear her voice mail message. He kept paying her monthly cell bill even though the account hadn't been used in twelve months.

The barkeep brought back his change. Felix took it, left the beer untouched, and got up to leave.

How many bars had it been so far? Fifty? Sixty? Add in the restaurants, the gas stations, the motels, the homes, and it was well over a hundred he'd visited.

Not too many left.

And then what? Give up? Finally have her declared dead and give her the funeral her parents have been pleading for since Christmas?

No. Felix wasn't going to give up on Maria. Ever. When he'd asked questions at every shop and residence within a hundred square miles, he'd start over at the top of the list.

Someone had to know where the Rushmore Inn was.

If the Rushmore Inn even exists.

Felix stepped out into the night, rolling his head on his neck, loosening up the tension in his shoulders. The bar parking lot wasn't paved, and the gravel crunched underfoot like freshly fallen snow.

He looked out over the road, into the dark forest.

The woman I love is in there. Somewhere.

After Maria went missing, he'd tried all the conventional methods of getting her back. The police. The FBI. Hanging flyers. Offering a reward for information. Even hiring a private detective.

The only thing he'd accomplished was getting fired from his job, which turned out to be a good thing. It freed him up to investigate full-time.

Unfortunately, his unemployment checks were just

about ready to run out, and the only lead he'd uncovered in all of his searching and questioning was a vague reference by an old drunk to a bed-and-breakfast called the Rushmore Inn.

"Supposedly it's been in these parts forever, but no one knows where it actually is. Or those that know, don't tell. It's like one of them Roach Motels. People check in, but they don't check out."

Felix questioned him further, but his answers became increasingly incoherent. Drunken mumblings of strange rituals and birth defects. The old woman who lived in a shoe. Something to do with blood types. He eventually passed out in mid-ramble, right at the bar. When Felix went to visit him the next day, having written down his address from his driver's license, the old man wasn't there.

He turned up that afternoon. The state trooper said it was a car accident. But Felix had seen the supposed crash site. The blood trail went on for almost a quarter of a mile. Like someone had tied a rope around the old guy and taken him for a drag.

Felix took a big gulp of West Virginia air. It smelled clean and fresh, but there was a sour note beneath it. Felix hated the country. He hated the trees, and the mountains, and the clear sky, and the beautiful sunsets. If he ever found Maria, he'd never leave the city again.

When, he corrected himself. *When I find Maria.* Not *if.*

He climbed into his pickup; a purchase meant to help him blend in with the locals, like his flannel shirts and work boots and unshaven face. Digging out the area map, he drew an *X* through *Mel's Tavern*. The map contained so many *X*'s it was getting tough to see the roads.

A knock on the driver's side window startled Felix. He

looked up, saw a man standing next to his truck. The hunter from the bar.

He was older than Felix, maybe midthirties, and in no danger of ever winning a beauty pageant. Tall and pudgy, like he'd never lost his baby fat, sporting a plump, almost feminine face, which had a strange appearance to it that Felix realized was a complete lack of facial hair. No stubble. No eyebrows. Not even eyelashes. In contrast, the black hair on his head looked like a wig.

Felix unrolled the window with one hand. The other he stuck under his seat, finding his 9 mm Beretta.

"Heard you talkin' 'bout the Rushmore Inn," the hairless guy said. "You payin' for information?"

"Top dollar."

The man looked around, uneasy. His denim overalls were splotched with brown stains. "This ain't a good place to talk. You stayin' nearby?"

Felix considered what to say. He decided on the truth, since the chance of learning something outweighed the potential danger.

"Place called the Cozynook Motel. Outside of Slatyfork."

"What room?"

Did he really want the hunter to know his room number? What about Cameron?

The hell with Cameron.

"One-ten."

"I can come by, hour or so."

Felix tried to play it cool. Maybe the hunter knew something. Or maybe he just wanted to round up some buddies, drop by, and rob him. In these parts, apparently, strangers weren't missed.

"I'm looking for this woman," he said, flashing Maria's picture. "Have you seen her?"

The hunter studied the picture. Felix studied his eyes.

"She one of them try-atha-leets?"

"You've seen her?"

The hunter shrugged. "All kinda look the same. But if she was at the Rushmore, she probably got in some deep shit. I'll come by later, we talk some more."

If he did have information, Felix didn't plan on leaving him out of his sight. He'd done that once before, and the guy wound up a thousand-yard smear on highway 39.

"I was planning on checking out tonight," Felix lied. "If you have something to tell me, we could take a walk in the woods."

The hunter shook his head. "Woods ain't safe round here."

"How about we take a ride, then? Drive around for a bit?"

"Maybe. What's your blood type?"

Felix blinked. "Excuse me?"

"Blood type. You know. Type A, type B, type O." *What the hell kind of question is that?*

Then he remembered the old drunk said something about blood types.

Was there a connection?

"I'm A. A positive."

The hunter sucked on his lower lip, then blew it out. "Okay. We can take a ride."

The big man walked around the front of the truck, and Felix noted the large hunting knife strapped to his leg. When he climbed in, the cab bounced from his weight.

All of a sudden this seemed like a very bad idea.

"We drivin' or what?"

Felix had to let go of the gun to turn the ignition. His initial feeling of hope was replaced by uneasiness. This guy was so big his head touched the ceiling.

"What's your name?" Felix asked.

The hunter grunted. "I'm John."

"Do you know where the Rushmore Inn is, John?"

"Not here. I'll tell you when we're moving."

"Why? Are you afraid?"

John leaned over, his brown eyes slightly crossing. His breath was warm and smelled like decay. "Damn right I'm afraid. And you should be, too." Then he smiled, revealing brown, crooked teeth and gums that looked like raw hamburger. "Y'all should be scared as hell."

She has the dream. Again.

In it, the man has two heads and three arms. His second head is smaller, misshapen, with a mouth crammed full of crooked teeth.

He climbs on top of her, one head giggling, the other drooling.

Others watch.

Other monsters.

A man whose fingers are fused together, like flippers. The bushy unibrow dividing his oversized forehead makes him look Neanderthal. He has a tiny nose and tiny ears, out of proportion with his large face. He claps his flippers, applauding the show.

Another man with a pointed head, thin on the top and bulbous on the bottom, like an eggplant. He hops from foot to foot, anxiously awaiting his turn.

One man has a split down the middle of his face, as if someone hit him in the nose and mouth with an ax. He snorts through the combined nose/mouth opening, spit and snot spraying.

Another man, naked and disgustingly obese, is propped up in an old, rusty wheelchair. Instead of knees, he has tiny, baby feet attached to his thighs.

His right arm is also no larger than a baby's. It's waving at her as he smiles.

There are others. Many others. Many that are even worse.

She doesn't scream. They like it when she screams.

Instead, she clenches her fists, her fingernails digging into her palms, her teeth biting her own tongue, willing herself to wake up.

Her eyes open wide.

The creatures are still there.

This isn't a dream.

She's been awake all along.

Letti Pillsbury glanced in the rearview mirror at her mother and daughter in the backseat, huddled over the video game. It made her feel both happy and sad, and more than a little dishonest. But she and Florence had agreed not to tell Kelly until after the Iron Woman event.

One thing at a time.

She shifted her eyes back to the road and then to the map. It wasn't a real map. In fact, it looked like a photocopy of a hand drawing, and a poorly done one at that. Letti had called the inn yesterday and spoken to the female proprietor to get better directions.

"Ten-point-six miles southwest down 219 once you pass 55. The road isn't marked, so use your odometer. It's on the right. We're so looking forward to having y'all."

The odometer was creeping up on 10.5, but there was nothing out here but hills and forest, and it was getting increasingly more difficult to see as the sun went down. Letti questioned, not for the first time, her decision to stay this far away from the competition, instead of at the event hotel. But money was tight and would only get tighter, and when the Rushmore Inn brochure arrived in the mail, stating they'd won free rooms, she couldn't pass it up. Letti didn't even remember entering the contest, but apparently she'd checked some box while filling out the extensive paperwork for the competition. The inn was really out of the way, but even if it had the worst amenities in the history of bed-and-breakfasts, it was still a lifesaver.

Letti slowed down, squinting into the trees, looking for the road. At first, the endless forest and jutting mountains had taken her breath away with their beauty. But after hours of the spectacular view, she began to feel intimidated. Letti hoped the race course was clearly marked, because if one of them got lost in this wilderness, they'd be lost forever.

When the odometer hit the magic number, Letti rolled onto the narrow shoulder and coasted to a stop.

"Are we here?" Kelly said, poking her head up through the space in the front seats and giving JD a pat.

Letti checked the numbers again. Then she rechecked the map.

"According to this, yes. But there's nothing here."

"There." Kelly pointed. "See the tire tracks?"

Letti followed her daughter's finger and saw two barely visible tracks, almost completely hidden by weeds, leading into the forest between a small gap in the trees.

"That's not a road," Florence said. "That's not even a trail."

"It matches up to the map. And look."

Letti pointed to a tiny sign, hanging from a tree. It read RUSHMORE INN.

"Why would they paint the sign green?" Florence asked. "It blends in to the trees. And it's so small."

Letti turned the wheel and pressed the gas.

"Letti, you can't be serious. What if we get stuck?"

"We're driving an Audi. It's all-wheel drive."

Florence clucked her tongue—something she did when she was displeased. "Let's go back into town. I'm sure there are other rooms available. I'll pay for it."

Letti bristled at her mother's words, and any doubts she had about this road vanished, replaced by anger. *Pay for it?* Now Letti was determined to see this through, even if they had to drive over a logjam to do it.

The Audi's tires dug in and performed as advertised, traversing the bumps, divots, and rocks without getting stuck. But the suspension left something to be desired, the shocks bouncing them around like a carnival ride.

Twenty yards into the woods the sun disappeared, forcing Letti to flick on her brights. Though overgrown, the path was relatively straight, and no trees or large obstacles got in their way.

Boy, it's dark.

In southern Illinois, on the Great Plains, even a moonless night was starlit. But this was like swimming in ink. Letti had the window cracked open, and she could practically feel the darkness seeping in.

Then the car jolted, the front end tilting downward. Letti whacked her head against the steering wheel, causing the horn to honk, and JD bounced against the dashboard, uttering a surprised yelp.

Letti pushed herself back into her seat, but the car

still canted on an angle, like they were driving down a steep hill.

"Mom?"

"We went into a hole, or a ditch, or something. Are you both okay?"

JD hopped onto Letti's seat, his big paws between her legs. He growled at the driver's side window.

"JD! Down!"

The growl became a sharp bark, and the dog's entire body tensed. Letti stared where JD was looking, out into the woods. She saw only blackness.

"JD? What's wrong, boy?"

Kelly patted his head, her voice full of concern. "There's something out there, Mom. He senses it."

Letti put a hand on his collar. JD was baring his teeth, and he stood rigid as a statue, his hackles up. The last time she'd seen the dog act this way was a few months ago, when someone tried to break into their house at three a.m. It turned out to be their drunken neighbor, mistaking their house for his. JD had gone Cujo at the intrusion, leaping at the door with such force he'd knocked out the security window.

She certainly didn't want a repeat of that right now.

Letti pressed the brake and shifted the Audi into reverse, giving it a little gas.

The wheels whirred, but they remained stuck.

"I can't see anything out there," Florence said, her nose pressed to the glass.

"It's like staring into a grave at midnight."

Letti gave it a little more gas, shouldering JD aside and watching the RPM gauge jump.

The car still didn't move. She wondered if the Audi

was on its undercarriage, the wheels off the ground. She would have to go check, see if she could—

JD barked again, clipped and loud, surprising the shit out of her.

"JD! Down!"

Letti gave the dog a rough shove, pushing him off her lap and back into his seat. Then she reached for the door handle.

"Letti!" Florence yelled in her ear. "Don't get out of the car!"

Her mother never raised her voice. Ever. Not even when Letti was a child. So hearing it now felt like a slap. Letti recovered quickly, turning around in her seat to look at her.

"What's the problem, Florence?"

"There's something out there," Florence said.

"JD has never been in the woods before. It's probably a rabbit. Or a deer."

"Or a bear." Florence looked solemn.

"You're being ridiculous."

"Indulge an old woman. Turn off the car and the headlights for a minute."

Letti sighed. "Florence . . ."

"Please. What can it hurt?"

Kelly leaned forward. "What if it's that guy with the gun, Mom?"

"We're a long way from him, Kelly."

"What if it is a bear?"

"Then hopefully he'll help us get unstuck."

No one laughed. Sighing, Letti flipped off the ignition and killed the lights.

It seemed even darker now. Darker, and unnaturally quiet. Letti couldn't see her hand in front of her face.

Then a light came on in the backseat.

Kelly. Holding up her iPod, its screen bright white.

"Turn that off, dear. With no light, our eyes can adjust to the darkness."

Dear? Florence never called me dear.

Letti chided herself. She wasn't in competition with her daughter.

The light went off. Everyone waited. Letti wasn't scared. She never got scared. It was a useless emotion, like guilt, and worry. Even if there was a bear out there, the thing to do was deal with it, not hide from it like frightened children.

"Have we waited long enough, Florence?"

"Shh. I hear something."

"What?"

"Right next to the car."

Letti felt the gooseflesh rise on her arms.

"Are the doors locked?" Florence whispered.

Against all common sense, Letti lowered her voice as well. "Why? A bear is going to pull open the door?"

"I don't think it's a bear," Florence said. "I think it's something else."

Letti found the lock button, flicked it twice to make sure. Then she pressed her face to the window, trying to peer outside. Slowly, her eyes began to adapt, and she could see her breath fogging up the glass.

Letti wiped it off with her palm.

It didn't wipe off.

She rubbed harder, her flesh squeaking on the window.

The condensation stayed there. And as she squinted at it, she watched the fog get bigger.

Hold on . . . it's not on the inside.

It's on the outside.

Someone has their face against my window.

JD went crazy, jumping fully on top of Letti, his claws digging into her thighs, barking and scratching at the glass in full-on attack mode. Letti's face was buried in his muzzle, fur getting up her nose. She gave the dog a rough shove, turned the ignition, threw it into gear, and jammed on the accelerator.

The engine whined, then the wheels found purchase and the Audi lurched forward, climbing out of the ditch, bouncing its occupants against the ceiling, JD falling into the passenger seat. Letti cut the wheel hard to the right so the rear didn't get stuck, and all four tires bit into the dirt as she fishtailed. She flipped on the brights, gasping as something darted behind a tree only a few feet away from them.

A man?

Pretty big for a man.

"Mom!"

Letti saw it, too; a tree, dead ahead. She wrestled with the wheel, guiding the Audi back onto the trail, the tree trunk banging against the side mirror and shearing it off.

Twenty yards later, the woods suddenly opened up into a clearing. Letti hit the brakes, skidding to avoid smashing into the front porch of the large house that seemed to appear out of nowhere.

Then there was a massive *BANG!* as the front tire popped.

After five miles of driving, the stench of blood began to make Deb sick, and she pulled the Vette over on the side of the road to clean up.

"I have bottled water, some towels, in the trunk," she

said, the first words spoken since they'd left the butchered deer. "I also have some plastic garbage bags."

"You come equipped," Mal said.

"It's a triathlete thing. Never know when you'll be swimming or have to hydrate."

They got out of the car, walked around to the rear. Mal pulled out his suitcase, and Deb pulled hers. She was thinking the same thing he probably was: in the darkness, the only way to change clothes was next to the light from the trunk. She watched him struggle for a moment with what to do, and then she pulled her bloody tee shirt up over her head, revealing her neon sports bra.

"Would you like some privacy?" he asked.

Deb loosened the drawstring on her sweatpants. "I wear a bikini when I compete. There's nothing you'll see here that you won't see there."

She rested her butt against the bumper, then tugged down her pants. Removing them from her legs was awkward, but Deb favored flared cuffs, making the process easier. When she was finished, she stood in her bra and panties, expecting Mal to be staring at her prosthetic legs.

Instead, Deb caught him staring at her breasts, which made her feel wonderfully normal. She tried not to smirk, reaching into the trunk for a water bottle and a towel as he began to unbutton his shirt. Deb cleaned herself off as best she could. When she glanced at Mal again, he was in his boxer briefs. It was obvious he worked out.

"Can you toss me a water bottle?"

Deb thought, staring at his chiseled abs, about asking him if he needed help. But that was totally inappropriate, especially after what they'd just been through. Instead, she went with something banal.

"Do you run?"

"Yeah. Not like you, though. Never competed in anything. After five miles I feel like puking."

"Everyone feels like puking after five miles. It's called *hitting the wall*. You have to run through it."

"That's why you're the athlete, and I'm the reporter. Once I hit the wall, I curl up and start crying."

"I do that, too. But only after the race."

Deb took a long pull from the water bottle, then dumped the remainder on her prosthetics. Her cosmetic legs, as opposed to her sports legs, were flesh colored and shaped like real calves, the outer skin latex. Inside each was a titanium bar, which attached to a complicated spring-joint mechanism that functioned as ankles. Her high-top Nikes were specially made to snap on to the ends. Every so often, Deb toyed with the idea of getting a custom pair of stiletto boots. She missed high heels. But walking was enough of a challenge without an extra three inches.

Except for the flesh-colored Velcro straps just below her knees where the prosthetics began, the legs looked real, even close up. But they got dirty very easily and were a pain to clean. The dried-on blood was proving especially tough, and Deb was worried if she rubbed too hard, she'd rip the latex.

"Maybe this will help." Mal tugged a bottle out of his suitcase and held it up. Grey Goose vodka.

"Apparently you come equipped, too."

"I travel a lot, and hate paying twelve dollars for martinis at the hotel bar."

"I'm not sure getting drunk will help get the bloodstains out."

He shook his head and walked over, kneeling down between Deb's legs.

"Do you mind?" he asked.

Deb didn't mind at all. She watched as he poured some alcohol onto a clean part of his towel and then rubbed her prosthetics with it. For the briefest of moments, Deb could almost feel his touch on her missing legs, her brain linking his actions with remembered sensations. She shivered, and told herself it was because of the night breeze and not anything else.

"I think I can take it from here," she said, holding her hand out for the vodka.

He looked up like a guy ready to propose marriage, which was something Deb knew she'd never see. The tiny flirtatious spark she'd felt a moment ago became resentment. At herself. At her legs. And at Mal, for daring to treat her like a normal person.

Scott, her boyfriend once upon a time, didn't react well to the loss of her legs. It freaked him out, and he didn't act the same after the amputations. He alternated between treating her like a fragile China doll that might break and acting like she was deformed. The one time they tried to have sex, and the comments he made, were so upsetting she dumped him right there and hadn't been with a man since.

She'd dated again, eventually, after getting through rehab on her own. But in Deb's experience, all men were in one of two groups. Those that wished she had legs, and those freakazoids who had a thing for women without legs. Deb made the mistake of joining an amputee forum on the Internet, and later an online dating service. In both cases, the only men she attracted were weirdos with a stump fetish.

Mal, treating her like she was 100 percent normal, was messing with her head.

Deb wasn't normal. She never would be. And if he didn't stop staring at her with that sly grin, she was going to smack him.

"I said I got it, Mal. Back off."

He raised his hands in supplication and quickly retreated.

Deb took a big swig from the bottle, feeling it burn down her throat, coming to rest like a hot coal in her belly.

Damn him for being cute, and damn him for being nice.

She poured more vodka on her towel and began swabbing her legs again. The alcohol worked fine at dissolving the blood. It also got rid of the blood caked under her fingernails, which was important, considering she paid a hundred bucks to get them done. Still, she couldn't wait to find this stupid inn and get into a bathtub.

Deb hoped it had bathtubs. She wasn't good with showers.

Mal seemed to take the rejection in stride, hopping on one foot to get his fresh jeans on. Deb went with a pair of nylon snap pants, the kind basketball players used. They had snap-on buttons along the outside and inside of each leg, so they could be torn off quickly. That was a nice function, but Deb preferred them for the opposite reason; she could put them on by using the snaps rather than stepping into them.

"Have you done any climbing since the accident?"

She shot him a look. "Speaking of non sequiturs. Are we starting the interview now?"

Mal was buttoning up his shirt, another light blue one. "I figured we have three things we could be talking about. The deer."

Deb shook her head. "I'm not sure I'm ready for that yet."

"Me, neither. That leaves the interview, and getting

personal. And I assume, by the way you told me to back off, you aren't all that interested in getting personal."

Deb capped the bottle and tossed it to him, perhaps a bit too hard. "No, I haven't done any rock climbing since I lost my legs."

She shivered again, and this time she was positive it was the night air. Deb pulled a hoodie out of her suitcase and wrestled that over her head.

"Is the accident too difficult to talk about?"

His voice had a hint of challenge. Deb relaxed a notch.

"Not at all." *The only thing that scares me is flirting.*

She threw the wet, bloody towel and the empty water bottle into the trunk and watched Mal muscle his suitcase up and place it next to her sports legs.

"You've got three pairs of prosthetics in here," Mal said. "What are each of them for?"

An easy question. Deb got asked a lot about her various legs.

"The ones that look like skis bent into question marks, those are my Cheetah Flex-Sprints. They're made of carbon fiber, curved backward the same way the legs of a gazelle are curved, which transfers energy better than a human knee and ankle."

He reached for one and asked, "May I?"

"Sure."

He picked up the Cheetah. "Wow, they're light."

"Try to bend it."

Mal placed the rubber tread attached to the curved bottom in one hand, and the stump cup in the other. It really did resemble an upside-down question mark, and when Deb wore them she thought she looked like a satyr— a woman with the legs of a goat.

Mal flexed, and the leg bent slightly.

"Strong," he said. "And springy."

"Very springy. With a running start, I can jump high enough to slam-dunk a basketball."

"What about these?" he said, replacing the Cheetah with a titanium bar with a clip on the end.

"I call those my Long John Silvers."

"Because they're silver?"

"That, and they look like old pirate peg legs. The clip onto the bottom of the pylon hooks on my bike pedals. They're shit to walk in, but function the same way as a tibia does, without any spring. Direct energy transfer from my thigh to the pedal."

"Now, you said you don't wear your prosthetics while swimming."

"I actually have a pair for swimming, with fins on the feet, but they're for training and recreation and I left them at home."

"So what are these?"

He picked up another leg. Like the Cheetah, it was a thin band, wide as a ski. But it wasn't as curvy. Rather than a question mark, it looked more like the letter *L*. And instead of a rubber tread foot, this one ended in a rubber knob with small metal spikes. Sort of like the bottom toe of the *L* had a sea urchin on the tip.

Mal touched a spike. "Let me guess. These are what you use when you're fighting in gladiator tournaments?"

"Rock climbing legs. Specially made."

Mal raised an eyebrow. "I thought you don't climb rocks anymore."

Deb stared over his shoulder. She couldn't be sure, but she thought she caught some kind of movement behind him, down the embankment.

Something big and dark.

"Let's get out of here," Deb said.

Mal put the leg back and shut the trunk. Deb climbed back into the driver's seat and started the car, peeling out back onto the highway.

"I'm a reporter, so I have to ask these questions," Mal said. "But I don't want to overstep my bounds."

Deb checked her rearview mirror. Nothing there. "Go ahead. No question is off-limits."

"Do you mind if I record this?"

"Not at all."

Mal flipped on the overhead light and dug a mini-recorder out of his pocket.

It was about the size of a cell phone.

"Okay. Why have climbing legs if you don't climb anymore?"

Deb felt the goose bumps on her arms, but she managed to shrug convincingly. "Because I'll climb again. Someday. I just haven't fit it into my schedule yet."

"Are you scared?"

She glanced at him. He wasn't mocking her, wasn't judging her, and he had a notepad in his hand, jotting things down.

"How much do you know about my accident?" Deb asked.

Mal flipped to an earlier page in his notebook. "You were solo climbing in the New River Gorge in Fayetteville, West Virginia. Not too far from here. The rock you were hanging on came loose, and you fell thirty feet, shattering both your legs. You had to crawl three miles to safety."

Mal's facts were actually wrong, on several points. But Deb chose to correct him on only a few, and keep the most important one to herself.

"I crawled two-point-seven miles, not three. I went back and measured it. And I actually fell closer to sixty feet, but the first thirty were a gradual slide down an angled rock face. That first part probably only took five or six seconds. But it felt a lot longer."

"I can imagine."

Deb looked at him. "Can you? Can you really? I was on my belly, face pressed against the mountain, arms and legs spread out, trying to find some sort of grip, some kind of toehold, so I wouldn't slide over the edge. But the rock face was sheer. As flat and smooth as glass. I skidded down it slowly—even slower than a child on a park slide. But I couldn't slow down, couldn't stop my gradual descent. You know, six seconds is usually nothing. Hell, I've been talking longer than six seconds. But as I was sliding, heading toward the edge, I had time to think. I had time to actually think about my own death. About what it would mean."

Mal leaned in closer. "What would it mean?"

Deb stared ahead, into the blackness of the open road, and felt herself shiver.

"It would mean nothing. I was going to die for no reason at all." She let out a clipped, humorless laugh. "The whole point of my life was to be a cautionary tale for other rock climbers to make sure you use pitons."

"You weren't using pitons?"

"I was hammering my first piton in when . . . the rock gave way." Mal wrote something down.

"Can you talk about what happened after the fall?"

The memory was hazy, like trying to recall a dream or a hallucination. But parts of it stuck out. Parts of it felt like they'd been burned into her head with a branding iron.

"It didn't hurt at first. I remember waking up, confused

about where I was. Then I saw my legs, both of them bent backward. It looked like I had two extra knees, and the bones were jutting out the front of my shins. You know, I actually tried to pull one out? I thought I'd landed on a stick, and it was poking out of me. Instead, it was my tibia. I tried to yank out my own tibia."

Mal cleared his throat. "That's . . . horrible."

"I was in shock, and I still wasn't feeling any pain. But then I started crawling. That's when it really got horrible."

"Because the pain hit?"

"It hit. Hard. As I was pulling myself to my car, dragging my legs behind me, I kept catching my tibia bones on things. Rocks. Branches. I actually got snagged on a dead squirrel and pulled that along with me for about a hundred yards."

Deb could remember the crawling. The pain. The horror. The desperation. Because she knew, if she got to the car, the worst was yet to come. She hoped he wouldn't ask about that part.

"I was also losing blood, getting dizzy. I'd tied my shirt around my knees to stop the bleeding, but I was still leaving a trail. And some local wildlife took notice."

Mal looked up from his notepad. "A coyote? Bear?"

Deb shivered again. It was really getting cold. "Cougar."

"I didn't think there were mountain lions in West Virginia."

"It followed me. I saw it up close. At first I thought I was hallucinating. But I wasn't. Had to be close to two hundred pounds."

Deb could remember how it stared at her. How it snarled. How it smelled. She would never forget its musky, pungent scent. Or its broken tail, bent in several places like a zigzag.

"Did it attack?"

She subconsciously touched the scars on her side. The cat had pounced on her, batting her with its massive paw, the claws hooking into her flesh. It did this several times. Playing with her. Taking its time. It even lazily groomed itself between strikes, its merciless yellow eyes following her as she tried to scrabble away.

"It treated me like I was a mouse. I would crawl a few feet, and it would drag me back. Like it was all a game."

"How did you get away?"

"It was futile. Eventually I stopped trying and just closed my eyes and waited for it to kill me. But it didn't. Maybe it had already eaten. When I looked for it, it was gone. Then I continued on, to the car."

"How did you drive? I mean, you couldn't use your legs, right?" *So much for him not asking.*

"Cell phones don't always work in the mountains. Mine didn't. And I couldn't put any weight at all on my legs, but I couldn't press the pedals with my hands and still see where I was going. So . . ." Deb let her voice trail off.

"So?"

"What would you have done?"

"I dunno. Looked for a tree branch, something long to press the gas."

"There was a mountain lion outside the car."

"Tire iron?"

"In the trunk. I could barely get myself into the driver's seat. I couldn't have pulled myself into my trunk."

"I give up. What did you do?"

"I put my foot over the gas, grabbed my tibia, and pressed down on it."

Mal set his writing pad in his lap. "That's . . . that's just . . ."

"Disgusting? Repulsive? The most terrible thing you've ever heard?"

"That's the *bravest* thing I've ever heard. You're one helluva woman, Deb Novachek."

Deb looked at Mal. He was beaming at her. Then she opened her window a crack, because it had gotten kind of warm in the car.

"Look for a dirt road, on your right," she said, happy to change the subject.

"According to my GPS, it should be coming up."

After a few hundred yards, Mal said, "Is that it?"

Deb squeezed the brake bar and peered where Mal was pointing. Rather than a road, there were two faint tire tracks that led into the woods.

"It can't be."

"There's a sign. On that tree."

The sign was half the size of a pizza box, painted green with a large white arrow. It read RUSHMORE INN – ¼ MILE. Deb didn't mind quaint and rustic. But backwoods and hidden weren't a good match.

"You're kidding me." She frowned. "How is anyone supposed to see that?"

"Maybe they like their privacy."

"Maybe they don't like guests. It's not even permanent. It's hanging on a rope."

And it was swinging, even though the wind had stopped.

Almost like it was hung there just a moment ago.

"The weeds are tamped down," Mal said. "Looks like someone drove down there recently."

"Never to be seen again."

"Are you actually nervous about this?"

Deb didn't answer.

"Come on. How bad can it be?"

"You're asking the wrong girl."

Mal shrugged. "Well, I'm tired and I need a shower, and there's no place else to go, so let's give it a shot. What do you say?"

Deb didn't like it. She didn't like the fact that it wasn't on the map. She didn't like the creepy manager who suggested the place. And she didn't like Mal's sudden enthusiasm for driving off the main road and into the woods.

What do I know about Mal anyway?

She hadn't asked him for ID or credentials. He smooth-talked his way into her car, and now he had her out here, all alone, in the middle of bumblefuck. Hell, maybe there was no inn at all. Maybe this was some scheme Mal cooked up with that manager guy.

Then a very bad thought hit her.

What if that strange man who slapped the hood hadn't done that to the deer?

What if Mal had done it?

Mal was covered in blood. And he had a few minutes from the time he left the car to the time she saw him . . .

"You look freaked out," Mal said. He reached out to touch her arm, and she flinched away.

"Let's keep our hands to ourselves, okay?"

He backed off, fast. "No problem. Do you want me to hike over there, check it out first?"

If this was all part of his plan to abduct her, what was to stop him from lying and saying everything was fine?

She stared at him. Hard. He was cute, charming, and seemed to be bending over backward to accommodate her.

Of course, all of those same things could have been said about Ted Bundy.

"Let's go back to the hotel, Deb. I'll grab Rudy, and you can have our room. That's what I should have done in the first place. Then I could have interviewed you over dinner, and we wouldn't have almost hit that guy, gotten soaked in deer blood, and then wound up here, on the set of *Texas Chainsaw Massacre 8*."

It was funny, but she kept a straight face without much difficulty. "Do you have a press pass?"

"Sure."

"Can I see it?"

Mal seemed to study her, then he reached for his back pocket. He pursed his lips.

"My wallet is in the trunk. In my other pants. Look, if you're still mad about me touching your prosthetic legs, I was just trying to be friendly. I knew I was going to ask some hard questions, and I didn't want you to think I was a jerk."

So he hadn't been flirting. He'd been softening her up before the interrogation.

Deb went from paranoid to hurt.

That's when the rear tire exploded with the sound of a thunderclap.

Deb's eyes went wide as Mal lunged at her, his expression crazed as his fingers wrapped around her neck.

Felix hadn't ever dwelt on the necessity of good hygiene, but its importance overwhelmed him when John climbed into his truck.

The hunter reeked.

It was a pungent stench; body odor, sour milk, and

some sort of perfume that smelled like the soap his father used. *Sandalwood.* Felix tried breathing through his mouth, but it left a lingering taste on his tongue, so he opened his window and inhaled the air coming in.

"Am I going the right way?" he asked quickly before turning back to the window.

John didn't answer. Felix flipped on the interior light. John's eyelids were drooping, and his jaw hung slack as he stared straight ahead.

"John? Are we going in the right direction?"

"Huh?"

"The Rushmore Inn. Is this the right road?"

John scratched his hairless cheek with dirty finger-nails. "Yeah. It's right up here. Pull over."

"Where? Here?"

"Yeah."

There were no crossroads. No buildings. It was just highway and forest.

"There's nothing here, John."

"Driveway is hard to see."

John still had that vacant look on his face. Felix wondered if the guy was crazy. Or taking some sort of drugs. But on the off chance that John was telling the truth, Felix pulled the Chevy off the road and onto the grass.

"Okay, now what do—"

The hunting knife was at Felix's throat so fast he felt it before he saw it, the blade pressing against his Adam's apple, forcing him against the headrest.

"Here's what we gonna do, Mr. Type A. You gonna climb out, slow and easy, and then we takin' a little walk in the woods. Your blood ain't no good, so I won't have no problem spillin' it."

The knife was incredibly sharp. Felix could feel the sting when it lightly broke his skin. Like a long papercut. John's other massive hand was tangled in Felix's hair, cupping his head like a basketball.

Fear smothered Felix like a wet blanket.

When Felix was able to speak, his voice was hoarse, barely audible. "My money is in my wallet. In my back pocket."

"This ain't about money, shit-brain. This is about poking your nose in what's none of your goddamn business. Now, get out of the truck."

The knife sawed forward, giving Felix another, deeper cut. He thought about his Beretta, just under his seat. It might as well have been a hundred miles away. There was no way for him to reach it without his throat being slit.

Every system in Felix's body went haywire. He got very hot, which was incongruous with his shivering. His bladder seemed to get smaller, tighter. His stomach churned, and his bowels were ready to burst. His breath came out in quick pants, making him even more light-headed.

This isn't happening. It's not happening.

Please don't let this be happening.

He felt around for the door handle, thinking that maybe he'd have a chance to run when he stepped out of the truck, depending on how tight a grip John kept on him.

John kept his grip tight as a vise. He pulled on Felix's head, keeping it at waist level, as he followed Felix out the door.

"Let's mosey on into the middle of the road. Won't no one mind a big pool of blood there. It'll look like a deer got hisself hit."

John tugged him away from the car. Felix's heart was pounding so hard it hurt, and at the same time he was finding it difficult to walk. Mixed in with the terror was a sense of detachment. Like it was happening to someone else.

Am I really about to die?

He'd never thought much about death before, and certainly never thought this was how his life would end. He wondered if he should be concentrating on something important. Or praying. Or looking back over his life and trying, in his very last seconds, to make sense of it all.

But all he could focus on was the knife.

"Unlike some of my kin, I don't take no pleasure in killin'. Momma says it's on account I'm too soft. But I done some bad things. And right now, I reckon I'm gonna do some of those bad things to you."

Felix heard someone say, "Please, don't," and realized it was coming from him.

"I gotta. Maybe Momma won't think I'm no softy no more if'n I bring her your head. But heads don't come off easy. Takes lots of cuttin' and hackin'. I 'spect you'll feel most of it."

"Please . . ."

"On your knees, boy."

Felix was forced down in the headlight beams. He stared at John's waist, smelled his body odor, and realized these were the last sensations he'd ever experience.

Except for pain.

How will it feel when he cuts into my throat? Will it hurt a lot? Will I choke on blood?

Will John slit my neck, or dig the tip of the blade in?

What's in a throat, anyway?

Jugular vein.

Carotid artery.

Adam's apple.

The cartilage part. What was that called?

The trachea.

How will it feel when he pokes through the trachea?

How about when he goes even deeper?

Will the pain stop when he severs my spine?

Felix felt like sobbing. He didn't want his last thought to be about the pain to come. He wanted it to be about something more important. He wanted it to be about Maria.

He pictured her face. Her eyes. Her smile.

He wanted so badly to see her, one last time.

I'm so, so sorry, baby. I failed you.

"What happened to her?" Felix croaked.

"Them questions is what got you into trouble, boy. You still asking 'em?"

"I have to know." Felix swallowed. "Please."

John snorted and spat. "We bled her. Same as the others. Nice and slow. Not fast, like you're gonna be. Just try not to splash any on my new truck."

Rage overtook Felix, burning away the blanket of fear, filling his veins with electricity.

"If'n you take a deep breath, maybe you'll be able to look round for a bit after I get your head off."

Felix lashed out with his fist, connecting with John's crotch, feeling his hand sink in while simultaneously trying to twist away from the knife.

John grunted, jerking to the side, dragging the tip of the blade across Felix's chin and cutting to the bone. Felix flinched away, but John's hand was too big, his hold too tight. He cut again, the jagged back of the hunting knife catching Felix across his scalp. Felix reached out with both hands, his fingers wrapping around the cruel, sharp steel.

John bent down and pulled. Felix felt it cut into his fingers, but he refused to let go. He swung his head upward, fast. His scalp rammed into John's chin, snapping the larger man's head backward.

John jerked up to his full height, did a half turn, then fell like a redwood, banging his forehead into the asphalt when he hit the road, his knife clattering beside him.

The pain hit Felix all at once. His neck. His head. His fingers.

Oh, Christ, my fingers.

He held them up but couldn't see much in the dark except for blood. Then he reverted back to self-preservation and scurried over to the knife. He was able to pick it up, albeit painfully, and then slowly approached John.

The giant's eyes were closed. Felix heard a low, rumbling sound, and he realized John was snoring.

Is he faking it?

Felix placed a foot on the hunter's shoulder, shoved him from his side onto his back. In the high beams, he could make out the growing knot on John's forehead.

Felix could also make out the injuries to his hands. It looked like he'd stuck them in a blender.

Seeing the cuts made them hurt even more. Felix hurried to the car, threw the knife in the backseat, tucked the 9 mm into his waistband, and then dug the first aid kit out of the rear compartment where he kept his car jack and toolbox. He slathered his hands with a full tube of Neosporin, then began to wind them with gauze. Halfway into wrapping his right hand he had to stop and redo it, leaving his index finger free so he could still shoot the gun if needed.

Then Felix yanked out his toolbox, searching through it until he found the handcuffs. An impulse purchase he'd made at the same time he'd bought the gun, on the off chance he might run into whoever had done Maria harm.

He stuck the keys in his front pocket and rolled the big man onto his belly—a difficult task with someone so heavy. The cuffs just barely fit around his thick wrists. Then Felix managed, with even more difficulty, to pull his cell phone out of his pocket.

Felix used his index finger to dial 9 and 1. Then he paused.

John hadn't said Maria was dead.

What if she was still alive?

And what if John could take him to her?

"It's a police matter," Felix said aloud.

But what if the cops couldn't get John to talk? What if they weren't persuasive enough?

Felix stared at the snoring giant.

The man who knows what happened to Maria. The man who sliced up my face and fingers. The man who almost cut off my head.

Felix hit the *end call* button and tucked the phone away.

I'll get him to talk.

Felix walked over to John and gave him a hard kick in the ribs to make sure he was still out. The hunter didn't so much as flinch. Then Felix collapsed into the driver's seat and adjusted the mirror to look at his injuries.

It was ugly.

His shirt was soaked to the skin with blood. His head looked like he'd dunked it in the stuff, and his hair was plastered to his scalp. Not quite as bad as Sissy Spacek at the end of *Carrie*, but damn close.

Felix mopped away the blood with a stack of paper napkins acquired during his last trip to McDonald's,

paying special attention to wiping off his eyes, where the
blood stung like chlorine.

His chin seemed to be the more serious injury; gentle
manipulation revealed the jawbone in the slit. Stitches
were needed, but Felix could barely hold the gun, much
less a suture. Luckily, in his toolbox was a tube of cyano-
acrylate. *Superglue*. Felix pinched the ends of the wound
together and ran a seam of glue across it. The gel set immediately, knitting the edges, forming a tough scab.

The scalp was more complicated, both hard to see and
reach. Not worrying about the mess he was making of his
hair, Felix alternated between a napkin compress and
dabs of glue until the bleeding got under control.

Now, what to do about John?

The Cozynook Motel was the best bet. Even though it
was full occupancy, each of the rooms had a back patio,
facing the woods. Felix could pull the truck around, load
John into the room without anyone seeing.

And what about Cameron?

Felix buried the thought. Maria's brother would either
go along with this or he wouldn't. But he wouldn't tell
anyone. Not after what Felix had done for him.

All that was left to do was figure out how to load John
into Felix's truck. He walked over and grabbed the man's
leg, attempting to drag him.

No good. John had to weigh three hundred pounds.
Felix was strong, and he maintained his exercise regimen
even during his obsession with finding Maria. But unless
he had a ramp and a dolly, or a block and tackle, there
was no way he could get John into the flatbed.

That left one alternative. John had to get in himself.

Felix knelt next to the big man's head, a gun in one
hand, a vial of ammonium carbonate from the first aid kit

in the other. He held the smelling salts under John's nostrils until the man's eyes popped open and he twisted away from the fumes.

"Momma?" he moaned.

"I'm not your momma, asshole."

John blinked, then sucked in his lower lip. The fear displayed on his round, hairless face made him look like an overgrown child.

"Am I bleedin'? Sweet Jezus, am I cut anywheres?"

Something caught Felix's attention. Up on the crest of the hill, on the road leading up the mountain.

Headlights.

Someone was coming. Fast.

"Get up. You're coming with me."

"My head hurts. Is my head cut?"

Felix's gaze flitted back to the approaching car. Thirty seconds until it arrived. Maybe less.

"You're not bleeding."

"You sure?"

Felix brought the gun up. "You have five seconds to get to your feet, or you will be bleeding. I'll blow your fucking knee off."

"Don't! Aw Gawd, please don't . . ."

"Get up."

John tried to get his legs under him, but he was too big and heavy.

The car zoomed within a few hundred yards of them.

Felix shoved the gun in his waistband and winced as he pulled on John's armpit, helping the man get to his knees.

"Into the back of the truck. Move your ass."

The car was almost upon them now. In just a few seconds they would be in the driver's headlights. Felix rushed back to his truck and killed his own headlights and the interior light and then hurried back to John, who was standing in the middle of the road with his mouth open, looking terrified.

"In the fucking truck!" Felix jammed the gun into the hunter's ribs, prodding him toward the back end. He pulled down the tailgate door, climbing onto the flatbed with John.

"Stay down! Don't fucking move!"

Felix held his breath. John shook next to him.

The giant was sobbing.

The headlights approached. Felix could make out the shape of the car. A sedan. Square headlights. Something on the roof of it.

A hunting rack?

No. Sirens.

It's a police car.

And it's slowing down.

Felix tightened his grip on the Beretta, wondering what he would do if the car stopped. He could tell the truth, say he was trying to dial 911 but couldn't get a cell phone signal.

But then the cops would have John. What if they couldn't make him talk?

Where would that leave Maria?

Or worse, what if they knew John? What if all the townies were drinking buddies? Maybe Felix was the one who'd wind up in jail.

Felix listened to the car slow down and watched the cop's headlights throw shadows over the flatbed. He placed his finger on the trigger of the Beretta.

They're not going to take John.

The police car cruised by, then sped off down the highway, into the distance.

Felix breathed again. He climbed out of the bed, going around to the cab to get a bungee cord.

"What're you gonna do to me?" John whimpered.

"Shut up."

"You sure I ain't bleedin'?"

"I said shut up!"

Felix whipped John in the head with the bungee. Then he wound it around John's legs and threw a tarp over him.

Next Felix spent a few minutes cleaning himself off, stripping off his shirt and using the melted ice from the extra large cup of cola he'd bought hours ago to pour over his face and neck. The blood had begun to dry and wasn't coming off easily, but with a new shirt and a baseball cap he wouldn't get a second look from any other drivers he passed.

"Where you takin' me?" John said, his voice quavering.

"We're going to have a nice, long talk about Maria."

"You better let me go. Or you're gonna get in big trouble."

"You're the one who's in trouble, asshole."

"If'n you hurt me, you'll never get your girl back."

Felix's heart leapt up to his throat.

Is Maria really still alive? Or is this inbred son of a bitch just saying that to save his own neck?

I'll find out the truth. So help me, I'll find out everything this redneck has ever done, going all the way back to his toddler years.

Felix cracked an ugly, hysterical smile, uttered a noise somewhere between a chortle and a sob, and then pulled onto the highway.

* * *

She doesn't know what day it is. Or what month it is.

By how long her hair has grown, she knows she's been here a long time.

Ten months? A year?

Longer?

The depression is impossible to overcome. It's even worse than the fear. Even worse than the abuse. Even worse than the—

She doesn't want to think about that last thing. But it will happen again.

Soon. Very soon. She's due.

Escape is impossible. The door is solid iron, set in concrete. She isn't allowed anything that can be used as a weapon. Not a pencil. Not even a spoon.

She once tried to hide a chicken bone in her cell. She was going to sharpen it, use it against them.

It was discovered. The consequences were horrible.

Resistance is met with punishment. Beatings. Food being withheld.

And worse. Much worse.

She used to have nightmares. Of them. A few in particular. The crueler ones. The sicker ones.

Now it's all one big nightmare.

For a while she stopped eating. Wanted to die.

They tied her to a chair, stuck a tube down her throat, one end attached to a meat grinder, and force-fed her. Along with the grain and hamburger, they ground up a rat in there as well.

A live rat. Blood, fur, bones, squeals, and all. From the grinder, straight to her belly.

She ate her meals after that.

Her cell has a dirt floor. A metal door. A mattress. A hand pump for water, though the water tastes strange. An aluminum chamber pot. And books. They let her have books. Some old paperbacks. And a lot of nonfiction. About Presidents. It's tough to read, because the single overhead bulb is only twenty-five watts, but she makes do.

She exercises every day. It helps pass the time. Helps keep her sane.

But she isn't sure how much longer she'll be able to cling to sanity.

She's lost weight and isn't quite sure how she's still alive. How she's been able to survive what they keep doing to her.

There are others down there with her. Other prisoners. She isn't sure of the number. At least three. Possibly more. Talking is met with swift punishment. Whenever she's taken from the cell, it's with a hood over her head so she can't see.

But she knows there are others. She's whispered to a few. Befriended some without ever seeing their faces. Men and women in nearby cells.

But they never stay for long.

Maybe they were moved. Maybe they even escaped.

But she knows what really happened to them.

This place is a slaughterhouse. And no one gets out alive.

Once, she heard a baby crying. The sound made her weep.

Weep for the child. Weep for its poor mother.

Weep for herself.

She had resigned herself to never having kids. Spat her condition in their ugly faces.

They tried anyway. They keep trying.

In the beginning, she was grateful for not being able to conceive.

Now she almost wishes she could. Just to connect with another human being.

To hold a baby, just for a moment. To hold anyone at all.

She wants so to see her family. Hell, to see herself. She hasn't looked in a mirror for so very long.

And the sun. She'd give anything to see the sun again.

She tries to maintain hygiene. They give her soap. She washes herself with the cold well water from the pump. Washes the few articles of clothing she has. They give her toothpaste but no toothbrush. She uses her finger.

Escape is impossible. Resistance is met with violence.

But there's always the possibility of rescue.

Her hope has dimmed as the months have dragged by. But it isn't fully dead yet. There's still a tiny flicker of hope left.

Because she knows that he's looking for her. She knows he'll never give up.

And when he comes, she wants to be ready.

So she tries to stay healthy. Tries to hang on. Tries to endure it all.

But she realizes, deep down, she won't last much longer.

There aren't as many prisoners. That means they're using her, more and more.

It won't be long before they use her all up. The scars on her arms attest to that.

She does another set of push-ups, her fingernails filthy from the dirt floor.

Drinks some water, wincing at the taste. It makes her light-headed. Dizzy.

Then she hears the footsteps.

They're coming. Again.

She tries not to cry. She needs to save her strength. There's nothing she can do to stop it.

The tears come anyway.

Then her cell door opens, and the endless nightmare is about to get horribly worse.

JD was going nuts, scratching at the front windshield and barking so fast and loud Florence wondered how the animal was able to breathe. The older woman reached forward into the front seat and grabbed his collar.

"Down, boy!"

The German shepherd whined, then sat. The night was dark and quiet and seemed to press down on their car.

"What happened, Grandma?"

Florence patted Kelly's leg. "Front tire blew out."

"How? Did we hit something?"

"I'm not sure, dear."

It was an odd blowout, for sure. Their previous flat was the result of running over a nail, causing a slow leak. This was more like an explosion.

Almost as if . . .

The knock on their window made all three women jump. A flashlight beam hit Florence in the eyes, forcing her to squint. The dog went supernova, pouncing toward the beam and the figure who controlled it, slobber splattering all over the passenger-side window.

"Are y'all okay in there?"

Letti hit the interior light, and Florence stared out at the woman who asked the question. The stranger was tall, easily over six feet, built like a linebacker.

It was too dark and she stood too far away to make out anything else.

"JD, shush!" Letti said.

JD kept barking.

Florence tapped the dog on the head. "JD!"

The dog shut up, but its lips remained curled in a snarl. Letti hit the power window, opening it a crack.

"Welcome to the Rushmore Inn," the large woman said. Her voice was unusually high for someone so big. "Y'all must be the Pillsburys. We been expecting you. I'm the owner. Can I help with any of your luggage?"

The woman put her round face near the window and smiled, revealing a set of gigantic dentures. It looked like she had a mouth full of Chiclets. This close, Florence saw the crow's-feet, the neck wattle, and guessed her to be midsixties. She wore a blue floral print dress that had a lace collar and looked antique. Her gray hair couldn't be described as a beehive, but it was twisted and piled up on top of her head pretty high, hair-sprayed into a helmet. Perched on top, of all things, was a pillbox hat, the kind made famous by Jackie O.

But the thing that really caught Florence's attention was the woman's eyes. Big and brown and bulging like a frog's. The mouth might have been smiling wide, but the eyes seemed vacant.

Letti turned around and looked at Florence, both women exchanging an expression of doubt. But before Florence could say anything, Letti told Kelly to put on JD's leash, and then she opened the door.

Florence got out of the car and found herself standing face-to-face with the innkeeper. Well, face-to-bust anyway. The woman had at least six inches on Florence.

"I'm Eleanor Roosevelt," she said in a singsong,

Southern belle voice. "My grandfather was second cousin to Theodore Roosevelt, the twenty-sixth President of the United States. But, of course, I was named after Mrs. Franklin Delano Roosevelt. FDR was the only President to serve three terms in the White House."

Her bug eyes blinked, and she offered a fake smile and her hand. Florence shook it and found herself in a power struggle of who could squeeze harder.

Eleanor's hand was large, meaty, and she had formidable strength. But Florence had been sticking to a strict exercise routine for more than forty years and could knock off a hundred fingertip push-ups without breaking a sweat. Though she didn't have leverage on her side, her fingers had the power to crush a soup can.

The two women remained locked like that for several seconds, neither of them betraying anything in their faces.

"And you are?" Eleanor asked, her voice steady as her grip increased.

"Florence. I'm not named after anybody. I find it refreshing to be my own person."

Eleanor tilted her head to the side. "You look to be about my age, Florence. Are you certain you're fit enough to compete in Iron Woman? It would be a shame if you keeled over from a heart attack. Do you remember when President Dwight D. Eisenhower had a heart attack in 1955?"

"I never liked Ike."

Eleanor's eyes narrowed, and she released Florence's hand, wiping it on her bulging stomach. "Yes. Well, then. It's certainly a pleasure to meet you." She turned. "And you must be Letti. I spoke with you on the phone. I'm Eleanor Roosevelt. My grandfather was second cousin to

Theodore Roosevelt, the twenty-sixth President of the United States."

"I caught that earlier. Nice to meet you, Eleanor."

Florence watched as Eleanor tried to mash Letti's hand, and was pleased when Eleanor let out a yelp at her daughter's strength.

That-a-girl, Letti.

Eleanor couldn't pull her hand away quickly enough.

"We seem to have run over something in your driveway and gotten a flat tire," Letti said, her face betraying nothing.

Eleanor clucked her tongue. "Yes. It happens a lot out here. We try to keep the driveway clear, but there are sharp rocks everywhere."

Letti folded her arms—her victory pose. "We lost our spare on the trip up. Do you have the number of a garage around here? Someone who sells tires?"

"Absolutely. But no one will come out here this late. It will have to wait until tomorrow."

"We have to check in at the race tomorrow morning," Letti said.

"Not a problem. I can have one of my boys take you into town."

"We have three bikes we need to take with."

"We have a truck. It will be fine."

Florence thought she saw something—a shadow— over Eleanor's shoulder.

It disappeared behind the inn.

"Do you have many animals in these parts?" Florence asked.

Eleanor lowered her voice an octave. "All sorts of nasty things run around in these woods. Bear. Wild boar.

Even mountain lions. All the more reason for us to go inside. Come on, now. Y'all must be exhausted after your long trip. From Illinois, isn't it? The Land of Lincoln? Just follow me."

Eleanor walked off, taking big strides. Florence shot her daughter a look and saw Letti grin. Her daughter was amused by Eleanor. Florence wasn't amused so much as disturbed. Something wasn't right about that woman. Something that went beyond mere eccentricity.

They unpacked the trunk, Eleanor not making good on her promise to help them. Florence shouldered hers and Kelly's backpacks, then stared into the woods. While the foliage and scent were different, the atmosphere eerily mirrored the jungles of Vietnam. The quiet. The stillness. The darkness that seemed to seep into your very pores. After a lifetime of traveling and missionary work, Florence still wasn't comfortable in the wilderness. She'd borne witness to countless cases of man's inhumanity to his fellow man. But that was a known danger. The woods whispered of the unknown. Of unseen things that wanted to eat you.

Letti and Florence hefted their gear over to the inn, Kelly in tow with JD. Eleanor stood on the porch with her creepy smile, holding the door open. The building itself was three stories, made of logs. Wooden shutters covered the windows. The roof was hard to see, as not a single exterior lamp was on.

"Welcome to the Rushmore Inn," Eleanor said again. The woman apparently liked to repeat herself.

Upon stepping inside, all the creepy feelings Florence had toward Eleanor tripled. The interior—lit by murky, low-watt bulbs—was a cross between a museum and a

junk shop. Presidential memorabilia decorated the walls
and furniture in a most haphazard way. Paintings. Posters.
Newspapers. Photos. Election signs and buttons. Rather
than charming, the effect was overwhelming. Florence
tried to find something, anything, that didn't have a President's name or image on it. Her eyes fixed on a plain
white ashtray. Being curious, she looked closer. Inside
were the smiling faces of Richard and Pat Nixon.

"This just went from quirk to fetish," she whispered
to Letti.

"She's way past fetish. This is full-blown psychosis."

Florence also noted a strange odor in the house. Beneath the strong scent of incense were notes of body
odor, and something else. A rotting smell, like carna-
tions gone bad.

"I see you admiring the decorations," Eleanor said, her
arms making grand, sweeping gestures.

"It's very presidential," Letti said, barely containing
her smirk.

"Indeed." Eleanor's face took on a solemn cast. "Presidents are the most important people in the world. They're
like royalty. After all, what could be more important than
running a country? All that power. All that responsibility.
As Americans, we should proudly revere our Presidents,
for they're so much better than we are."

"Didn't Jefferson say all men are created equal?" Florence asked.

"Presidents are more than mere men. They're born to
lead. Did you know all forty-three Presidents have carried
European royal bloodlines? Thirty-four of them are genetic descendants of the French ruler Charlemagne.
Nineteen are related to England's Edward the Third."

Eleanor produced a handkerchief from the cuff of her long-sleeved dress and mopped at the sweat on her neck.

"If you go back far enough, everyone is descended from the same people," Letti said.

"Of course they are, dear. Adam and Eve. But only a small minority of these descendants have carried the royal bloodline and were fit enough to lead nations. I have to ask . . . is Letti short for Leticia?"

"Loretta."

"Too bad. Leticia Tyler was married to our tenth President, John Tyler. Not a very dynamic first lady, and a cripple at the end of her years. But she had eight children. Only seven survived. How many have you had?"

"Just Kelly."

Eleanor fanned her face with the handkerchief, a dainty movement incongruous with her massive frame. "Only one child? Such a shame. God told us to be fruitful and multiply. Did you know there was a woman in the eighteenth century who had sixty-nine children? She gave birth to sixteen pairs of twins, seven sets of triplets, and four sets of quadruplets. How blessed her family must have been."

"I'm surprised her uterus didn't run off and hide," Letti said.

Eleanor turned to Florence. "How sad that both of us are past our childbearing years, isn't it, Florence? It would be so lovely to have a few more."

"I only needed one because I did it right the first time," Florence said. Out of the corner of her eye she caught her daughter smiling.

Eleanor turned her attention to Kelly.

"But this young lady here. She has many children in

her future. Her breasts are just coming in. I can picture them, swollen with milk. Ready to suckle her young."

"Yuck," Kelly said. "If I have kids, they're getting formula."

Florence didn't like the woman talking to her grand-daughter. Letti didn't seem to like it, either, and put a protective hand on Kelly's shoulder. Eleanor apparently didn't notice, and moved closer to the girl.

"And what's your name, precious one?"

"I'm Kelly. This is JD."

JD was staring at Eleanor like she was a rabbit he was ready to chase.

"And what does JD stand for?"

"Jack Daniels. Mom named him. We got him when my dad died."

"He looks very protective of you. How old is he?"

"Eleven."

"Our thirty-fifth President, John F. Kennedy, had a German shepherd named Clipper. Such a good-looking animal." Eleanor tucked her handkerchief away and went *tsk tsk tsk.* "Too bad JD is near the end of his life. Shepherds don't live much longer than eleven years." Kelly's eyes got wide.

"We really do appreciate the free rooms," Letti said, stepping between Kelly and Eleanor. Florence noted the forced smile on her daughter's face.

"We're very tired, so if you could please show them to us."

Eleanor raised up her nose, as if she just smelled something she didn't like. "Of course. Please follow me."

The large woman strolled past the living room and up the stairs, moving at a quick clip. Florence and Letti, hauling the bags, had to march double time to catch up. Like the walls, the stairs were made of naked wood, the banisters iron. There was a gap between the opposing flights, so it was possible to look straight up between them and see the roof. The stairway was slathered with more presidential stuff, including a large poster of Mount Rushmore. When they reached the second floor, Eleanor was standing in front of a closed door, tapping her foot. Her boots were vintage like her dress, black leather with hooks for the laces.

"This is the Abraham Lincoln Bedroom. It will be perfect for Kelly. You other ladies are on the third floor." She handed Kelly a key, then began walking back to the stairs.

Letti voiced her objection before Florence could. "We'd like to all stay on the same floor, if possible," she called to Eleanor's back.

Eleanor turned and offered a mirthless smile. "That's impossible. I'm afraid I haven't made up any of the other rooms."

"I'll take this one," Florence offered.

Kelly already had the key in the door and had opened it. The light was on, and as expected, Lincoln memorabilia was the dominating motif.

"This room is cool! I did a school report on Lincoln. Remember, Mom?"

"I'd feel better if you stayed in a room next to me or Grandma."

"Aw, c'mon. I'll be fine. JD will be with me."

"I'm a fan of Lincoln, too, dear," Florence said. "I was actually at Ford's Theatre when he was shot. Other than that, it was a pretty good play."

Kelly pouted. Florence considered correcting her on her pouting—pouting wasn't a useful habit to pick up—but she wasn't going to usurp Letti's authority and start making rules. That had been one of many conditions Florence had agreed to when she asked to move in with them. In truth, if Letti had asked that Florence wear a bag on her head and never speak again, she would have agreed to that as well. Repairing her relationship with her daughter, and building one with her granddaughter, were the most important things in her life.

Funny how priorities change when circumstances change.

"You should room next to Mom," Kelly told her. "It will give you a chance to patch things up."

Florence gave Letti a look that said, *Did you tell her?* and Letti gave her the same look right back.

"I'm not stupid," Kelly said, putting her hands on her hips. "I don't know what the deal is between both of you, but now is a good time to work it out. I'll be in here with JD, eating granola bars and playing with my iPod. G'night."

Kelly smiled brightly, stepped into the Lincoln Bedroom with the dog, and shut the door behind her. Florence heard the lock turn.

"She takes after you," Florence said.

Letti folded her arms. "Meaning she never listens?"

"Meaning she's strong willed and a smart observer."

"I don't have all day." This from Eleanor, still waiting at the stairs.

Letti pursed her lips and walked after the woman. Florence followed.

After another flight of stairs, and another poster of

Mount Rushmore, the women arrived on the third floor. More low lighting. More odd memorabilia on the walls.

This woman must spend all of her free time on eBay.

"Letti, this is the Grover Cleveland room. I believe you'll find it quite comfortable. And for you, Florence, the Ulysses S. Grant room, right next door."

"Thank you, Eleanor."

Eleanor handed her the key, but hung on to the key ring.

"If you're hungry tonight, the kitchen is on the first floor. There's food in the icebox. I made cupcakes earlier. But be careful walking the halls. Rumor has it the inn is haunted. This property used to be a tobacco plantation. The owners had six slaves, and they treated them harshly. Lashings. Thumb screws. Are you familiar with strappado? They would tie a rope around a slave's wrists, fasten it to this iron banister right here. It's actually a gate. See?"

Eleanor touched the railing, unlatching it. It swung inward on hinges, revealing the twenty-five-foot drop to the first floor.

"When the slave fell, the rope would pull taut and dislocate his shoulders."

"Charming," Florence said, her voice flat.

"Legend says one slave, after his fifth drop, lost both of his arms when they ripped from his sockets. He's said to roam the hallways at night, looking for his missing limbs. One wonders what infraction he committed to deserve such treatment. Or why his owner would risk the loss. After all, slaves cost money." Eleanor closed the gate. "Did you know twelve of our Presidents were slave owners?"

"Thank you again," Florence said, giving the key a

hard tug and freeing it from Eleanor's grasp. "We need to be in town at eight a.m. for the race sign-in and walk-through. Are you sure your son won't mind giving us a ride? I'm guessing we'll need to leave by seven."

Eleanor offered a big-toothed smile. "He won't mind at all. I can have breakfast ready for y'all at six-thirty."

"Are there other guests?" Letti asked.

"At the moment, no. But we're expecting more later tonight."

Florence couldn't understand how this place stayed in business. "Is it the slow season?"

Eleanor's bug eyes became wide. "Not at all. We're just very particular when it comes to who we invite into our little inn."

"You must get a lot of repeat business, then."

"You wouldn't believe it. After their first night, some of the guests never want to leave." She winked, then performed a clumsy curtsy. "Good night, ladies. See you soon."

The innkeeper waddled off. They watched her descend the stairs, giving the iron railing an affectionate pat.

"I don't like that woman, this inn, or the surrounding area," Florence said.

"But you can't beat the price." Letti put her key in the lock.

"Tell me again how you found this place?"

"They mailed me a letter, saying all of us won a free three-night stay."

Florence shook her head. "But how do they benefit from that? It's not like all the other guests here are making up for it. This place is dead as a tomb."

Letti swung her door open. "We discussed this already.

No matter how crummy the place was, we were going to stay. It's saving us a lot of money, Florence. And you know we need the money for—"

"For me. I know, Letti." Florence put a hand on her daughter's, which was resting on the doorknob. She lowered her voice. "We really need to talk about your husband . . ."

Letti pulled her hand away. "One of the rules is we're not going to talk about that."

"Kelly is right. If we don't discuss it, if you don't understand me, how will you ever forgive me?"

"Where in our deal does it say I have to forgive you?"

Letti pushed the door open and went into her room, slamming it in Florence's face.

Do I deserve that?

I don't know. Maybe I do. Maybe Letti has been right all along.

But that doesn't mean I would have done things any differently.

Or would I have?

Florence sighed. She'd raised a girl who was just as hardheaded as she was. Hopefully Letti wouldn't make the same mistakes with Kelly that Florence had made with her.

Florence padded to the Grant Bedroom, opened the door, and stepped inside, feeling the space.

It didn't feel right.

The lights were already on, illuminating the expected Ulysses S. Grant decorations plastered everywhere. Somehow Eleanor had managed to find President Grant curtains, and a bedspread that looked like a giant fifty-dollar bill. But it wasn't the Grant motif that gave Florence pause.

It was the sense that she wasn't alone in the room.

Florence believed, and had been proven correct on dozens of occasions, that she could sense when others were nearby. It wasn't any ESP baloney, or any supernatural trick. Many animals had some sort of proximity sense, alerting them to when prey or predators were close. Bats. Sharks. Whales and dolphins. Dogs. It was well within the scope of nature to sense other living creatures near you, without sight, sound, or touch. The same way you could sense when someone was looking at you from across a room, or sense that the door was about to open.

Everyone had this ability, to one degree or another. Florence felt that she honed hers through a lifetime of traveling to different environments, coupled with her interest in meditation and the martial arts.

Different places felt different, in a way beyond what the five senses could report.

And in this room, Florence felt like she was being watched.

But they weren't friendly eyes watching her.

They feel more like hunter's eyes.

The last time she'd had this feeling was during the war. She'd been with the third field hospital, 85th Evac, in Qui Nhon. The conditions had been primitive. Surgery in tents. Not enough equipment. Always low on medicine. After a full morning of plucking slugs out of a boy's legs without antiseptic or rubber gloves, she'd gone to the latrine to wash the blood out from under her fingernails, and some instinct made her duck. A second later, a sniper's bullet passed over her head, killing the nurse in line ahead of her.

Florence had felt him.

Just like she felt someone now.

She took in the room, her eyes sweeping over it slowly. It was small, tidy, smelled strange like the rest of the house. There was a bed. Dresser. Bathroom.

Window. Door.

A closet door.

Is that what I'm feeling? Someone in the closet?

Florence moved to the door, slow and cautious. Her left hand reached for the knob. Her right hand drew back in a fist.

She hesitated.

What if there is someone in there?

For all of her adult life, Florence took pride from her ability to take care of herself. No matter the situation, she could handle it.

But now? At my age? In my condition?

Running earlier with Kelly had been difficult and hiding her pain had been impossible. The only reason Kelly didn't notice was because she'd been so scared.

Florence let her fist open. If there was someone in the closet, she wanted something with a little more heft than her fist. The lamp next to the bed would pack a bigger wallop.

Florence picked it up. It was a standard ceramic table lamp, maybe five pounds, the cylindrical shade boasting a glued-on picture of Grant's face.

Then she raised the lamp up with one hand and grabbed the knob with the other.

Ready or not . . .

She yanked the door open and stared.

Staring back was nothing but empty clothes hangers.

Florence blew out a deep breath and set the lamp back down.

But she still felt like she was in someone's crosshairs.

Under the bed?

Florence eyed it. Queen-size. A large frame, up off the floor on casters.

She watched it for a moment, looking for movement.

It remained absolutely still.

Maybe it's paranoia. Maybe my proximity sense is just one more thing that's failing on me.

Or maybe there is someone under there.

Florence swallowed, then took a deep breath.

Only one way to find out.

She slowly crouched down, reaching for the dust ruffle on the bed.

"Florence?"

Florence jerked her head around, saw her daughter standing in the doorway.

"Letti?"

Letti folded her arms and leaned against the jamb. "Okay. Let's talk."

Deb lashed out, striking Mal in the chin as his hands locked around her throat.

"Down!" he yelled.

He pulled her head toward him, toward his lap, his arms incredibly strong. The seat belt gave some slack then locked up, keeping her in her seat. She made another fist, chopping at his balls, missing and whacking his thigh.

"Someone is shooting at us!" Mal said, catching her wrists.

She paused for a moment. Mal released her, pressing the catch on his seat belt, kneeling down on the floor mat, and then reaching for her again. Deb processed what he said.

The tire blowout. Did someone shoot the tire?

Deb killed the engine and the headlights. Then she hit the seat belt button, draping herself over the armrest, the gearshift digging into her belly.

"Are you sure?"

His voice was low, harsh. "I used to be a cop. That was gunfire. Someone took out our wheel. Stay below the window."

Deb tried to press herself into the bucket seats. Mal opened the passenger door and spilled out onto the road.

"Come out this way." Mal beckoned for her. "He's on your side."

Deb pulled herself toward him, and he grabbed her hands. She moved a few inches, then stopped cold.

My leg is stuck on something.

She wiggled her pelvis, trying to turn her knee. But without being able to feel her foot, she had no way to know what it was stuck on or how to free it.

Mal tugged harder, wrenching her shoulders.

"Hold on," she ordered. "Let go a sec . . ."

He complied, and she tore at her snap pants, her fingers ripping at the Velcro strap. Then she hit the release nozzle, breaking the suction between her stump and the prosthetic's socket. She reached for Mal again, and he tugged her roughly, yanking her out of the car and into his arms. They fell, Mal onto his back, Deb landing on top, her chest crushing into his, their faces inches from each other.

"What do we do?" she whispered.

"I don't know where the shot came from. I'm going to wait for him to fire again, then try to flank him."

Deb pulled away, trying to get off him, and her empty pant cuff caught on something. To keep from falling over, she straddled his waist.

"I thought you didn't like me," Mal said.

"Are you always such a smart-ass in life-or-death situations?"

"Your hair smells nice."

"Jesus." Deb shook her head and twisted around, freeing the cuff from the hinge of the car door. Then she rolled off Mal and sat with her back to the fender.

Mal eased the car door closed and sat next to her. The night was dark and silent. Even the crickets had ceased their song.

A minute passed. Then another. Deb's eyes slowly adjusted. The orange hunter's moon overhead, pinned in a sky of stars, made it easier to see.

"Think he's still there?" Deb asked.

"I dunno."

"Can't he circle around and shoot us?"

"Yes."

Deb frowned. "Weren't we safer in the car?"

"Probably." Mal leaned closer. "But now I'm wondering why he didn't shoot us instead of the tire."

They waited for another minute. Doubt took root in Deb's head, then began to grow.

"Are you sure that was a gunshot and not just a blow-out?" she asked.

"Yes. Pretty sure."

"Pretty sure?"

"Mostly sure."

Deb squinted at him. "Have you ever had a blowout before?"

"No. But I know a gunshot when I hear it."

"How do you know a tire blowing up doesn't sound like a gunshot?"

"I know." Mal rubbed his chin. "I think."

Another minute ticked by. Deb was listening so hard she could make out the sounds of the night. The crickets returned. A frog croaked. Miles away, an owl announced itself.

"How sure are you now?" Deb asked.

"Sort of sure."

Deb sighed. Her mistrust of Mal's intentions morphed into mistrust of his instincts. While she no longer felt he was a threat, she did think he was wrong about the gunshot. Deb began to crawl around the back of the car.

"Hey!" Mal caught her remaining prosthetic leg. "Where are you going?"

"To search the tire for bullet holes."

"That's probably not a good idea."

"So we just sit here all night?"

"Good point. I'll come with."

Mal crawled up alongside her, their sides touching. The temperature outside had dropped at least ten degrees since the sun went down, and his body heat felt good.

At the rear bumper they both got down on their bellies. Mal produced his penlight and shined it on the tire, revealing a tangle of rubber strips and twisted steel-belted radials.

"Do you see a bullet hole?" Deb asked.

"I can't tell."

"So it could have been just a regular blowout?"

"I guess that's a possibility."

Great.

"So, what now?" Deb asked, her irritation coming through.

Mal dug out his cell phone. "No bars. Want to try your phone?"

Deb got onto her knees, then used the bumper to lift herself up onto one leg.

"What are you doing?" he asked.

Without answering, she hopped up to the driver's side door, opened it up, and hit the trunk release. As she expected, no one took a shot at her. She hopped back, feeling smug, foolish, and irritated all at once. Her side was still warm where Mal had lain next to her.

"You putting on the spare?" Mal asked. He was also standing up, scanning the trees.

"It's a Corvette. There is no spare."

"What? Why not?"

"Each tire has unique treads. They aren't interchangeable. So no spares."

Deb reached into the trunk for her Cheetah prosthetics. They were easier to walk in than her cosmetic legs. Especially if they were going into the woods to look for the inn.

She could guess how hard it would be to find a tow truck in this area at this time of night. That was, if her cell phone even worked. Reception out here was spotty at best.

"Look, Deb, maybe I was wrong. About the gun thing."

"You think?"

"I'm sorry if I freaked you out."

"Apology not accepted."

"Okay, how can I make it up to you?"

"You can carry my suitcase."

She adjusted the silicone end pad in the gel sheath on her stump, then fit it into the custom cup of the running prosthetic. A few presses of the vacuum button and it was formfitting and tight. Then she took off her cosmetic leg and repeated the process. With her Cheetahs on, walking was much easier. She waited for Mal to stare at them. How could he help it? She looked like the Greek god Pan, prancing around on his goat legs. All she needed were horns and a lute.

But Mal was staring at her chest again.

"See anything you like?" she said, her voice dripping with sarcasm.

"Sorry. It's just . . ."

"Just what?"

He shrugged. "I know it isn't professional, me being a reporter. But you're an attractive woman, and I like you."

Deb didn't appreciate how that made her feel. "You're right. That's not professional."

"You think I'm a doofus, don't you?"

"A doofus? How old are we, twelve?"

Mal grabbed their luggage. Deb went to close the trunk, but paused. She didn't want to leave her prosthetics. If the car was towed, she wouldn't be able to compete in Iron Woman without them. So she shoved them all in a duffel bag, then went into the car and grabbed her cosmetic leg, which was caught on the wire pulley system that activated the brake pedal. After putting on the hazard blinkers and locking the door, she was ready to go.

"Let me have the light. I need it to see where I step."

Mal handed it over. They walked off the highway and

onto the dirt. Deb flashed the beam at the RUSHMORE INN sign, with its arrow pointing ahead.

I don't like this. I don't like this at all.

But she knew they had to try it out, or else spend an uncomfortable night in the Vette and face exactly the same problem in the morning. That was out of the question. If Deb missed the check-in, she missed the race.

"So what exactly is it about me that you don't like?" Mal asked.

"Insecure much?"

"That's the thing. I'm not insecure at all. But people usually like me."

Mal shined the light on the forest floor, sidestepping a dead branch. The trail was easy to follow, even though it couldn't be called a road.

"Cockiness isn't attractive," she said.

"Am I cocky? I thought I was just confident. Maybe not as confident as you . . ."

Deb stopped and hit him with the light. "And what is that supposed to mean?"

"I'm just surprised you're letting me carry your suitcase."

"Are you saying I can't accept help?"

"I'm saying you're superwoman. I expected you to strap the car to your shoulders and run it back into town."

"That's a pretty insensit—"

Deb stopped midsentence. An odor had penetrated her nose and tongue. A distinctive odor, rank and musky.

It awoke a deep-seated fear in Deb. A primeval fear.

A familiar fear.

I know that smell.

Deb swept the beam around them, frantically looking for the source.

"What's wrong?"

She opened her mouth, but the words stuck in her throat.

Can it be? Jesus, no . . .

"Deb? What is it?"

With great effort she managed to get the two words out.

"Mountain lion," Deb whispered as her light came to rest on a bush, reflecting off a pair of deadly yellow eyes.

The ride to the Cozynook Motel was nerve jangling. Felix spent most of the trip looking in the rearview mirror. Checking to make sure John stayed under the tarp. Checking to see if the cop car was following him. Checking his own reflection to verify this was all really happening. His mind kept flitting between the fear of getting caught and the hope that maybe fate would intervene and stop him from doing what he was planning on doing.

Whenever he became too distracted, he tried to focus on Maria. The chance that she was alive meant he had to take this risk. Felix swore he'd do anything to get her back. Including going to jail. Including hurting someone who had something to do with her disappearance.

"We bled her. Same as the others. Nice and slow."

Felix glanced at the Beretta on the dashboard. He would make John talk.

He'd make that big son of a bitch talk until his lips fell off.

The motel parking lot was full, probably the only time of year that happened. The one-story building was laid out in an L shape, its twelve rooms all side by side, guests' parking spaces by their front doors. Earlier that day, Felix and Cameron had visited everyone staying there, showing Maria's picture, asking questions. No one knew anything. But unlike most of the townies, the visitors were at least sympathetic.

The people who lived in the area were another story. Not that they were mean, or even particularly cold. A better word for them was *distant*. Over the past twelve months, Felix had talked to dozens of Monk Creek residents. He was usually met with a warm smile or a nod, but once he started asking questions their demeanor would change. Felix originally thought it was because small towns were private, wary of talking to strangers.

But now he suspected differently. Now he saw a big conspiracy of silence.

There was something going on in Monk Creek no one wanted to discuss.

And John had something to do with it.

Felix drove past the parking lot, onto the unkempt grass alongside the building. He pulled the truck around the back, into a copse of trees behind his room. Once parked, Felix turned off the ignition, wincing as his ruined fingers removed the keys. Then he waited in the darkness, listening to the night, second-guessing himself for the last time.

I can still go to the cops, turn him in. John tried to kill me. I haven't broken any laws.

Yet.

Felix considered starting the truck again. Taking John to the police was the only legal, and moral, course of action. The police had more resources, more manpower. Maybe trying to get John to talk would endanger Maria.

But what if the cops don't believe me? What if John's lawyer tells him not to say anything? What if John is well-known in the community? What if he's friends with the police?

Felix couldn't risk John not talking.

The only way to know the truth is to get it from John myself.

Felix grabbed the gun on the dash, opened the door, and climbed out of the truck. He walked around to the flatbed and rapped John on the heel with the butt of his Beretta. John squealed in fright.

"Out. Now."

"Please don' hurt me."

Felix hit him again, harder. John moaned and began to inchworm backward out of the truck on his knees and chest. Felix grabbed the large man's cuffed wrists and helped him off the tailgate, onto his feet.

The night had gotten colder, the cool breeze pinching Felix's wounds. John's face was glossy with sweat, reflecting the light from Felix's bathroom window. Felix removed the bungee cords wrapped around John's legs and led him to the back porch; a poured slab of concrete with two weathered resin chairs facing the woods. He tried the patio door.

Locked.

Felix squinted through the split in the curtains, saw Cameron lying on the made bed, watching TV. He knocked lightly, and whispered. "Cam, it's me. Open up."

Cam's head jerked at the sound, and a moment later he sprang off the mattress and opened the door. The younger man was dressed for bed, in boxer shorts and a tee shirt, but he still wore those black leather gloves. Felix had never seen Cam take the gloves off, even in the sweltering West Virginia summer when temperatures peaked at 103.

"You got one," Cam said, his eyes getting big when he noticed John. Cam's voice was high and raspy, as if he'd never finished the last few weeks of puberty, even though he'd just turned twenty. "Christ, Felix. You're covered with blood."

"Get the rope," Felix said.

Cam did as instructed, and Felix lead a docile John to a battered desk chair, which creaked under his weight as he sat down. When Cam brought the nylon clothesline, he secured John's body and feet while Felix covered him with the gun.

"You don' wanna do this," John said.

Cam stepped away, looking startled.

"Cam . . ." Felix said. He knew Cam's history, knew that he might not be able to handle what was about to happen. "Maybe you should wait in the—"

Cam's hand shot out, slapping John across the face. It sounded like a firecracker going off in the small room.

"Where's my sister, you son of a bitch!"

Cam raised his hand again, but Felix grabbed his arm, wincing at the pain in his injured fingers. He looked into Cam's eyes, saw them crackling with fire.

This is a bad, bad idea.

"Easy, kid," Felix said, trying to keep his voice even. "John wants to cooperate. Don't you, John?"

John eyed the floor, saying nothing.

"Does he know where Maria is?" Cam caught Felix's forearm and squeezed.

He was strong for his slight build.

"Maybe." Felix tugged his arm away. "I'm not sure."

Cam grabbed John's ears, forcing his head up. "Where is she? Where's my sister?"

"You better let me go." John looked close to crying again. "Y'all be in big trouble if'n you don't let me go."

Cam stared hard, and something flashed across his face.

Is that a smile?

"Can you count, you big, fat redneck?" Cam asked. "Because I'm going to count to ten. And if you don't tell me where Maria is, I'm going to kill you."

Felix felt like he swallowed a bucket of ice. He knew why Cam was in the hospital. Knew what Cam was accused of doing.

Accused of. Never proven.

Still, it was enough to get him committed.

"Cam," Felix cleared his throat. "Let's go in the other room, talk this over."

Cam ignored him, walking around to the back of John's chair. "I bet you're so slow and dumb you count on your fingers, don't you? Here, let me help you count."

John's lips began to tremble.

"Cam . . ." Felix said. This situation was spiraling way out of control.

"One," Cam counted.

CRACK.

It sounded like a branch snapping. But it wasn't wood. Felix knew that Cam had just broken one of John's fingers.

John's face turned bright red, and Felix saw the scream building up in his throat. He managed to grab a dirty sock from the floor and shove it into John's open mouth a second after the howl began. The sound went on and on, and Felix had never heard anything so pitiable, so awful, in his entire life. It made him sick, all the way down to a cellular level. Like Felix's entire body had become rotten, making him want to crawl out of his skin and go hide.

But Cam wasn't finished.

"Two."

Another snap. John thrashed his head back and forth,

the tendons in his neck sticking out, his throat vibrating with muffled cries.

Felix's stomach clenched like a fist. He stumbled into the bathroom, dropping the gun in the sink, vomit spewing up and spraying the toilet. He sunk to his knees and held the bowl, trembling. The steely resolve of a year-long search seeped out of Felix's body, replaced by pain, fear, and regret over what was happening.

I have to stop this. Now.

But John's a killer. He had something to do with Maria's disappearance.

He's also a human being.

A human being who tried to kill me.

So that means we can torture him?

He may still have Maria.

That last thought gave Felix the strength to stand up and return to the bedroom, albeit on wobbly legs. John was thrashing back and forth, his muffled screams making the hair on Felix's neck stand up. Cam hyperextended another one of the man's fingers, twirling it around and around like he was stirring a cookie batter.

"Cam." The spectacle before Felix was surreal.

"I got this, Felix." Cam grinned at him. "Least I can do, since you busted me out of the loony bin."

Cam grabbed another finger, and Felix yelled, "Enough!"

Cam's head shot up, looking like a teenager scolded for bad grades.

"Back off," Felix ordered. His voice was shaky, but he held Cam's gaze until the younger man slunk away.

Felix glanced quickly at John's hands—most of his fingers were stuck out at odd angles—and walked around to face him. John was bright red, his face wet with tears.

Felix yanked the sock out of his mouth and was rewarded with a soul-wrenching moan.

"Am . . . am I bleedin'?" John said.

Felix swallowed. "Not yet. But if you don't answer my questions, my partner is going to start cutting off your fingers. Do you understand?" John nodded, his chin trembling. Felix leaned down over him.

"Tell me, John. Is Maria alive?"

John stared, but stayed quiet. Drool leaked out of the corner of his mouth. Felix had once jammed a finger catching a football, and it hurt like hell. To have five broken fingers, misshapen and manhandled, must have been unbearable.

"Answer me. Is Maria alive?"

"You . . . hurt me bad," John cried.

Felix felt his stomach turning again. But he managed to keep it under control when he said, "Cam, go out to the truck and get this bastard's hunting knife."

Cam nodded and hurried off. Felix considered his prisoner. Maybe John didn't want to talk, because he thought if he did, he'd be killed. Killed because he was no longer useful. Or killed in retribution for the things he'd done to Maria.

"I'm not going to kill you," Felix said. He knew it sounded hollow. Lame. But the alternative was letting Cam start slicing off fingers; something Cam seemed disturbingly eager to do. This was a slippery slope, and unless Felix could convince John he'd live through this, the situation would get a lot messier.

Could I allow Cam to keep hurting John?

Felix closed his eyes. He saw Maria's face. If John had something to do with her disappearance, Felix would let

Cam roast the guy over hot coals in order to get answers. Felix could have a crisis of conscious after John talked.

If John talked.

"Got it," Cam said, hurrying back in. "Man, this knife is wicked."

John began to blubber uncontrollably at the sight of Cam, and Felix felt ready to do the same.

Be strong. It's for Maria.

Cam positioned himself behind John.

"Don't cut me . . . please don't cut me." He knew it sounded hollow.

"I just want to know what happened to my fiancée," Felix said. He forced himself to maintain eye contact.

"He's . . . he's gonna cut my fingers off."

"Not if you tell me the truth. If you tell me the truth, I promise he won't cut you. We won't hurt you anymore if you tell me." He crouched down, staring into John's face. "Is Maria still alive?"

John's lips trembled, but he stayed silent.

Anger surged up in Felix like the vomit had moments ago, and the last vestiges of sanity left him as he reared back and slapped John across the face, hard as he could.

"Goddammit, tell me!"

John's whispered answer was the most important thing anyone had ever said to Felix.

"Your woman is . . . alive."

Maria allows herself to be led out of her cell by George. He's one of the largest of her captors, close to seven feet tall, and among the most sadistic. He's not as deformed as the others, though his head is a little too big for his body, and his arms are too long, like a gorilla. The cattle prod he has in his hand is used for amusement as much as persuasion.

But today George seems distant. He straps on her ball gag without saying a word, and the nudge he gives her with the stick lacks electricity.

He puts the black cloth bag over her head, grabs her elbow, and leads her through the underground tunnels. As usual, Maria counts her steps. The first dozen times, they'd been clever, having her walk in circles. All the better to keep her disoriented. But lately they'd slipped into a routine. At exactly 115 paces, they come to the door to the Room.

She hears the door open, feels George push her from behind. Maria's legs lock. As terrible as her captivity has been, her times in the Room were the low points. What happens in the Room goes beyond pain, beyond sickness, beyond desperation.

What happens in the Room is an abomination.

George nudges her, but she still refuses to enter. She braces herself, expecting the jolt, anticipating the hurt.

But it doesn't come. Instead, she's shoved inside, many hands grabbing her, pulling her to the chair, strapping her down. Then the bag is pulled off her head, and Maria stares into the bulging eyes of Eleanor Roosevelt. She's surrounded by a menagerie of freaks. Practically all of them. Deformed, twisted, grotesque, some half-naked, some fully nude. They form a large circle around Maria, smiling, drooling, grunting.

Eleanor holds a cupcake in her hand, a lit candle jabbed into the pink frosting.

"Happy anniversary, child. Today, you've been with us a whole year."

As the words sink in, Eleanor blows out the candle. The freaks—those who have two normal hands—begin to clap. There are hoots. Howls. Giggles.

Maria sobs. She fights her bonds. Fights with every last bit of her strength, even as she realizes that Felix will never save her, that she'll never get out of this hell alive, that these subhuman monstrosities are going to use her all up until there's nothing left.

Maria watches George sit in the opposing chair. It's his turn today; the apparent reason for his lethargy. She watches Jimmy—his eyes crossed and the pale hump on his back protruding through the split in his filthy lab coat—wheel the machine forward.

Maria screams when the needle goes in.

Kelly's fascination with the Lincoln Bedroom lasted all of six minutes, and then she was lying in bed, tackling *Zombie Apocalypse* on her iPod. With Grandma watching, she'd finally beaten level 65, though it had taken up all of her shotgun ammo. Now she was on level 70, fighting a boss who was three times her character's size, with a stomach so fat it looked like he'd eaten ten other fat guys.

Kelly strafed him with the machine gun, circling his rotund body while dodging the green acid he kept puking at her. She got his health down to only a few red bars, and then one of his lumbering minions grabbed her, turning her into a pile of ash.

Retry? the game asked.

"Hell, yeah."

She adjusted the pillow she was on, took the last bite of a chocolate chip granola bar, and prepared to kick some fat zombie ass.

Then JD growled.

Kelly glanced at her dog. The hair on his muzzle was sticking straight out, and his lips were raised in a snarl. His defensive stance. But he wasn't focused on her. He wasn't focused on the front door, either.

JD was staring at the closet.

That's strange.

"JD. Come."

Kelly patted the mattress beside her. At home, the German shepherd wasn't allowed on the bed, but Mom couldn't bitch about what she didn't know.

JD didn't move. He growled again, hunkering down like he was ready to pounce.

Kelly studied the closet door. She'd checked inside earlier, while exploring the room, and had found it empty. But the way JD was snarling, he obviously didn't think it was empty anymore.

Could there be something in the closet?

The thought of it was creepy, and made Kelly shiver.

"What is it, boy?" she asked. A pointless question—it wasn't like JD was going to answer.

But he did answer, in his way. He stared at her and whined.

The only time Kelly ever heard JD whine was when she accidentally slammed his tail in the patio door. That's what he looked like now—eyes wide, ears flat, tail drooping under his hind legs. Like he was hurt.

Or scared.

That's stupid. Dogs don't get scared.

Do they?

Kelly stared at the closet door again. She'd been pretty engrossed by her game. Could someone have snuck past her and gotten into the closet?

No. JD would have noticed.

Maybe it wasn't a person. Maybe an animal had crawled in there, through the walls. They'd had a racoon in the house before, up in the attic. JD used to bark like crazy when he heard it.

But JD wasn't barking now. He was growling and whining.

Some other type of animal, maybe?

A few seconds ago, the closet had been just a boring, old closet. But now, with how JD was acting, it was actually beginning to freak her out.

She thought about the hunter by the waterfall, the one with the messed-up face. After beating level 65, she'd used her iPod to Google *cleft palate*. That led her to a site about birth defects, and some of the images were among the most horrible Kelly had ever seen. On one hand, it must have been awful for the poor people who had to live with those deformities. On the other hand, there was something so instantly repulsive about those images, Kelly had to stop looking at them.

Could that hunter guy be in my closet?

Kelly pictured him standing behind the door, waiting silently for her to go to sleep. So he could sneak up on her and kiss her with that disgusting mouth.

Kiss her, and worse.

Kelly had never kissed a guy. Not even on the cheek. She didn't want her first to be that awful man.

I'm imagining things. He's not in the closet.

He can't be.

Right?

"Come here, JD." Kelly said it softly.

JD didn't come. He looked at her, then back at the closet.

Kelly set her iPod on the nightstand and swung her feet over the edge of the bed. She held her breath, listening for any sounds that could be coming from the closet—

—and heard someone cough.

JD barked once and lunged at the closet door, scratching at the knob. Kelly quickly stood up and backed away, to the bathroom. The wooden floor was cool under her bare feet, and she felt nearly naked in her sleep tee shirt, even though it had three-quarter sleeves and hung past her knees.

The shepherd continued his attack on the doorknob, even biting it, and though JD had never been able to open a door before, Kelly had an unrealistic belief that he might this time.

"JD, come."

The dog glanced at her.

"Come. Now."

He trotted over, tongue hanging out, tail wagging. Kelly patted his head, surprised by how reassuring it felt. Then she knelt down and hugged his neck, both of them eyeing the door.

The seconds ticked by. Kelly began to wonder if she'd imagined the cough.

Could it have been something else?

Old houses made noises. There were water pipes, and furnaces, and any number of things that made sound. At home, when Mom flushed the toilet, Kelly could hear it from the basement.

Maybe it wasn't a cough. Maybe someone upstairs had turned on the shower.

Or maybe someone *did* cough, but it came from the room next door, not the closet.

JD pressed his cold nose into Kelly's neck, making her flinch. She stood up.

I should open the door to check.

While Kelly didn't consider herself a tomboy, she was far from a sissy. Kelly preferred Slipknot to Hannah Montana, and would much rather watch the *Saw* movies than *High School Musical*. She could pick up snakes and frogs without screaming, unlike other girls in her class, and during a sleepover was the only one who could spend a full two minutes in the pitch-dark bathroom with the Ouiji board Sue Ellen Wilcox's brother swore was possessed by Satan. The only irrational thing that scared Kelly was heights.

Is being afraid of the closet irrational? Or common sense?

"It's irrational," Kelly said. Her mother loved the word *irrational*. And if she were there right now, she'd march over to the closet and show Kelly how irrational her fears were.

Drawing on that, Kelly walked toward the door.

The floor creaked under her feet. Though only a few yards separated her from the closet, it seemed like it took a very long time for her to get there. Each step closer increased Kelly's apprehension. When she finally reached out and touched the knob, her throat felt like there was a walnut stuck in it she was unable to swallow.

Just open the door.

She tightened her grip, but still hesitated.

What if I open it, and the hunter is standing there?

Kelly looked back at JD. He'd stayed next to the bathroom, still as a picture.

Maybe I should listen at the door first.

The girl carefully placed her ear against the cool, rough wood. Again she held her breath, listening for sounds.

A few seconds passed.

Kelly heard nothing.

Mom's voice appeared in Kelly's head, like it did whenever she stepped onto a diving board. *"You're being irrational, Kelly. What's the worst that can happen?"*

Crack my head open and drown?

Or in this case, get attacked by a crazy, birth-defected redneck?

Maybe pushing a chair up against the door was a better idea than opening it. Kelly saw a small desk and chair, tucked into the corner of the room. She could brace the chair up under the knob, so nothing could get out of the closet.

No. I'll never get to sleep unless I check. It's a big day tomorrow. I can't spend the night with one eye open, waiting for a monster man to break out and attack me.

Kelly turned the knob—

—yanked the door open—

—and saw—

"Nothing," Kelly said, blowing out a big breath. She turned around to glare at her dog. "JD, you're one dumb—"

A creaking noise came from inside the closet, so close Kelly could practically touch it. She startled, jumping backward, eyes focusing on . . . *an empty closet.*

So what made that noise?

Curiosity won out over fear, and Kelly crept back toward the closet. It was a small space, no more than five feet wide and deep. At eye level, bisecting the space, was a metal bar, where two wire hangers hung.

Is one of the hangers swinging?

Kelly couldn't tell. If there was movement, it was slight, and might have happened when she opened the door. She stepped closer, sticking her head inside the closet. There was no overhead light, and it was tough to make out any details beyond the three walls. Kelly went back to the bed, picked up her iPod, and switched it on. One of her apps was simply a bright white screen that functioned as a night-light. She shined it all over the closet, not exactly sure what she was looking for, but finding something unusual on the floor.

A straw of hay.

Not unusual by itself. But the odd thing was its position. The hay seemed to be stuck under the back wall of the closet. Almost like it was caught in a door.

Kelly tentatively pressed her palm against the wooden wall and pushed. The wall didn't budge. She gave it a quick rap with her knuckles.

Hollow. But that might be the room next door.

Kelly crouched down, grasped the straw between her thumb and index finger, and tugged. The hay broke in half, still wedged beneath the wall.

WTF?

Then something nudged her from behind.

Kelly yelped, scrambling forward, turning around to face JD.

"Bad dog," she said, though he really didn't do anything worthy of scolding.

The comment didn't seem to bother the canine. He

brushed past Kelly, sniffing the floor, and his nose locked on to the corner of the closet. He whined and pawed at the wall, finding something that interested him.

Kelly nudged the shepherd aside and pointed her iPod at the space he'd been clawing at. The white screen illuminated a small, wooden knob on the floor. It looked like the top of a broomstick, no taller than two inches. Kelly tried to pick it up, but it was stuck. Instead of pulling, she tried to push.

There was a clicking sound, and the wall Kelly had her shoulder against suddenly moved.

A secret passage.

Before Kelly had a chance to process what was happening, JD darted past her, scratching the wall, pushing it open on an unseen hinge like a big door. Then he charged into the blackness behind the wall, disappearing into the darkness.

"JD!" she yelled after him.

Kelly heard the *click click click* of his toenails on the wooden floor echo away into silence. She squinted into the gap. It was a thin hallway, no more than two feet wide. Unlit, though the iPod allowed her to see that the hall stretched for several yards.

She turned to go tell her mother, then stopped, imagining Mom's lecture.

"You let JD run off? How irresponsible, Kelly."

Mom liked the word *irresponsible* almost as much as *irrational*.

I should still go get her.

But why? I'm almost a teenager. I don't need to go to Mom for everything.

What if someone is in there?

JD barked. He didn't sound very far away.

"JD!" she called again.

He barked once more.

Then he yelped.

The yelp was the deciding factor. Kelly had raised JD since he was a pup. Mom bought him right after Dad died, and Kelly had had quite enough of losing loved ones, thank you very much. If her dog was hurt, she had to go get him. No other way about it.

Kelly quickly put on her jogging pants and her gym shoes and stepped into the gap. It was just wide enough for her to walk normally, rather than sideways, though her shoulders did brush the walls. She moved quickly, her iPod bobbing up and down so she could alternate between watching her footing and looking ahead. The corridor smelled like mildew and dust, with notes of something else beneath it—something that reeked like really bad body odor.

The corridor ended at a right turn. Kelly paused. The iPod light wasn't strong enough to illuminate more than a few feet.

"JD?"

No answer.

I should go get Mom.

Then she heard another yelp. Closer this time.

"I'm coming, JD!"

Kelly rounded the corner, picking up her pace. She held out her free hand and touched the wall, her fingers trailing along rough, unfinished wood, and stopped when she touched something that moved.

Kelly flashed the iPod light at the object. It was a small, square piece of plywood, swinging on a single nail, like a picture frame. She touched the bottom and swiveled it upside down, revealing . . . *a hole. It's a hole in the wall.*

The hole was perhaps the size of a quarter, and there was a faint light coming from it. Kelly's finger probed the outside. She got ready to stick her finger in, then halted.

Bad idea. It could be a rat hole.

But what if it's another secret door?

She poked the tip of her index finger inside, ready to pull it back if she felt anything sharp. Her finger went in to the first knuckle . . . the second knuckle . . .

And then it touched something cold and flat.

Glass?

I guess I have to look.

The hole was high enough for Kelly to have to stand tippy-toed to see through it. She pressed her nose against the wall, the wood smelling really foul, and squinted into the opening.

Kelly saw a toilet. She gasped when she noticed the toilet seat had Lincoln's face on it.

It's the toilet in my room.

Kelly backed away from the peephole, turning to run back to the room. This was bad. This was really bad. That creepy old lady was spying on them, and Kelly had to tell Mom and Grandma.

"Help me."

Kelly paused in midstep. The voice belonged to a girl. A young girl, from the sound of it. Coming from the same direction she'd heard JD yelp.

"Please help me. My name is Alice and I'm scared."

Kelly peered over her shoulder, into the dark. She knew she couldn't leave a little girl behind. Fighting panic, she managed to sound calm when she said, "Where are you, Alice?"

"I'm here. There's a doggy with me. He's hurt."

"How is he hurt, Alice? What happened to my dog?"

"He's limping. His foot is all twisted up."

JD cried out, a pitiful sound that made Kelly want to scream.

"I'll be right there, Alice," she said, racing ahead, frantic with fear and adrenaline, coming to another turn, thinking about poor JD with his paw broken, and then coming to . . . *a dead end*.

Kelly stared at the wall, wondering what to do next, and noticed another hanging square of plywood.

"Alice?"

"I'm stuck in here. Please help me."

The voice was coming from directly behind the wall.

Kelly sidled up to the wall and stretched to look through the peephole. She saw only darkness.

"I can't see you, Alice. Is my dog in there?"

JD yelped again.

Kelly pushed on the wall, but it didn't budge.

"*You need to pull it,*" Alice said.

Kelly had no idea how to pull a flat wall forward, then decided to stick her finger in the hole and try tugging on that. She put it in carefully, gripped the side, and then . . .

"Uhhhhn . . ."

The pain was so sudden, so shocking, that it literally took Kelly's breath away. She tried to yell, but nothing came out, and at the same time she tried to free her finger from the hole and succeeded only in making the pain worse.

Something had her finger. Something sharp and tight that wouldn't let go.

Kelly dropped her iPod. It landed faceup, its gel case working as advertised and absorbing the shock. In the dim light it emitted, Kelly could see that there was blood leaking down her hand. She pulled again, determined to rip her finger off if it would free her, but the agony made her cry out. Kelly beat against the wall with her fist, then kicked the wall, filling her lungs to unleash the mother of all screams.

Then she abruptly stopped when she heard something behind her in the corridor.

Is it JD? Please let it be my dog.

It wasn't her dog.

"I told a lie," Alice said, walking closer. "A bad lie."

Kelly buried the scream, instead starting to cry. "You have to help me, Alice. My finger is stuck."

"My name isn't Alice," the approaching figure said. "It's Grover."

"I don't care what your name is," Kelly said, anger joining up with her pain.

"Alice was Theodore Roosevelt's first daughter," Grover said. "She had pretty hair."

Then Grover stepped into the faint light of the iPod. He stood over six feet tall, and was wearing stained overalls and a faded plaid shirt. His eyes were tiny, too close together. His jaw was big, and it stuck out like Popeye's, but his head got thinner toward the forehead, almost like a Halloween gourd. Perched crookedly on his head was a curly, blond wig.

"Do you think I have pretty hair?" the grown man said, still using the voice of a little girl. He touched one of the curls.

Then he yelped like a hurt dog.

Kelly began to scream, but Grover put a big, rough hand over her mouth and nose, holding it there and giggling *hehehehe* like a five-year-old.

Kelly kicked and punched and struggled to take a breath. But he wouldn't let her.

Mal gripped Deb's arm, first pushing her off-balance, then steadying her. The darkness felt like a weight pressing down on Deb, threatening to push her into the earth.

"Where is it?" he whispered.

"Bushes," Deb said.

She'd seen the deadly, gold eyes of the cougar a second ago, but they'd retreated into the black.

"You sure?" Mal asked. "I don't see anything."

"Smell that?"

Mal sniffed the air. "Rank."

It was an odor Deb would never forget. "Big-cat smell. Back up slowly. And let go of my arm—you're gonna knock me over."

Mal released her. Deb had no problem walking backward in the Cheetah prosthetics on flat land, but the wooded terrain proved difficult. All she could think of was being batted around like a ball of yarn, each swipe of the cat's hooked claws digging into her skin and sending her rolling across the ground. She had scars all over her body from such an experience. In a way, it was even worse than shattering her legs.

Deb was so worried about the mountain lion springing on her, she wasn't paying close enough attention to her footing. Two steps later she was tipping backward, her arms pinwheeling to regain balance.

Mal caught her shoulders, held her steady until she could get her feet under her.

"Thanks," she managed.

"You sure there's a cougar?"

"I'm sure."

"How sure?"

Deb didn't like his doubt. She'd seen the lion's eyes. Seen them as clearly as she was looking into Mal's.

But then, Mal had been pretty sure their tire had been shot out, and he'd apparently been wrong there. So his questioning was no more than . . .

"You must be Deborah Novachek, and that reporter fellow."

The voice came from the same bushes where Deb had seen the cat. It was a female voice, friendly enough.

"You don't happen to see a mountain lion around, do you?" Mal asked.

Deb frowned at him. Mal shrugged.

"A mountain lion?" the woman said. "Heavens, no. Though they are known to hunt in these parts. Y'all had better come inside. I'm Eleanor Roosevelt, the owner of the inn."

Eleanor stepped through the bushes, and Deb played the penlight across her. She was a large woman and carried herself in a strong, sturdy way that belied her advanced age.

"Nice to meet you, Eleanor," Deb began. "Are you sure you—"

"My goodness, young lady. What happened to your legs?"

Mal squeezed her shoulders a bit tighter, as if in reassurance. Deb shrugged him off.

"I lost them in a climbing accident," Deb said. "And I saw a mountain lion just a—"

"Are you sick?" Eleanor interrupted. "We can't allow you inside the inn if you're diseased."

"Rude much?" Mal asked.

Being impolite didn't matter to Deb, especially with a cougar nearby. But now she began to question if she'd seen the cat at all. She took pride in her inner strength, but being in these mountains again brought back some pretty terrible memories. And since no cats seemed to be pouncing on them, perhaps she'd imagined those eyes. The smell might have been something else. A badger, maybe.

"I compete in triathlons," Deb said, her eyes darting around the woods, looking for movement. "And I haven't had so much as a cold in over five years."

The large woman cocked her head to the side, as if considering her. Then her face split into a big-toothed smile. "Well, then, let's get you people inside. Welcome to the Rushmore Inn."

Mal picked up the bags he'd dropped, and Deb followed him through the bushes, one eye on her footing and the other on the forest. The animal smell was gone.

Once past the bushes, a clearing opened up in the woods, revealing a massive, three-story log house. There weren't any lights on the outside, and no light coming through any of the shuttered windows. It was as dark and quiet as the mountains surrounding them.

"Welcome to the Rushmore Inn," Eleanor said again, pulling open the door and holding it while they entered.

The smell inside wasn't bad, exactly, but it wasn't pleasant. Sort of a sour, antiseptic odor mingled with sandalwood incense. But unique as that was, it paled compared to the decor.

"As you can plainly see," Eleanor Roosevelt said, closing and locking the door behind them, "I greatly admire our nation's leaders. They're such important men. You might say I'm a bit obsessed with the subject."

"Yes." Mal nodded, looking around. "You might say that."

He gave Deb a sideways glance, his smirk barely concealed.

"My grandfather was second cousin to Theodore Roosevelt. There's presidential blood in my family. It's a fact I'm particularly proud of, though it isn't without its . . . *challenges*."

Like turning your house into a flea market, Deb thought. But instead of speaking it aloud, she said, "Mrs. Roosevelt, my car is out on the road. It seems we've gotten a flat tire."

Eleanor clucked her tongue. "You'd be surprised how often that happens around here. In the morning we can call the auto repair shop."

"I need to be at the hotel early to . . ."

"My son will take you," Eleanor interrupted. "He has a truck for your bike."

"Already shipped the bike ahead. But the ride would be terrific."

"He'll be leaving early, so be sure to get some rest tonight. Might not be a bad idea to go straight to bed."

"An excellent suggestion," Mal said, raising his eyebrows at Deb.

She ignored him. "Is there any chance we could get something to eat?" Deb asked. "We missed dinner on the ride up."

"The kitchen is back there, down the hall. The icebox is stocked, and you're welcome to help yourselves. I made cupcakes earlier today, and there are a few left. But let me show you to your rooms, first."

Eleanor plodded up the wooden staircase. Deb wasn't a big fan of stairs, but the iron railing looked solid. She followed Mal up, stopping only to admire his trim backside as they ascended. Deb found it amusing that he continued to flirt despite several rebuffs. For a millisecond she entertained what it might be like to date Mal. The fantasy disintegrated when she caught the toe of her Cheetah prosthetic on the top stair. Luckily, she managed to make it to the second floor without a face-plant.

"Deborah, this is the Theodore Roosevelt room," Eleanor said, holding out a key. "One of the finest rooms in the inn."

Deb didn't suppose that meant very much. "Does it have a bathtub?"

"Indeed it does. And for you—I didn't catch your name."

"Mal. Mal Deiter."

"Next door over, Mr. Deiter, is the Harry S. Truman room. While it doesn't have a bathtub, I believe you'll find the walk-in shower most agreeable. And necessary, considering your current appearance."

"We ran into one of the locals, making venison headcheese," Mal said, taking the key. "Is it currently hunting season?"

Eleanor smiled. "There's always something in season around these parts."

"Have the Pillsburys arrived yet? I didn't see any other cars around. I'm a reporter, and I'm supposed to interview them."

"They have, but I'm afraid they turned in for the evening."

"Perhaps I'll get to see them at breakfast."

"Perhaps. If you'll indulge an old woman's fancy, might I ask you a question?"

"Of course."

"I pride myself in being able to guess blood types. You strike me as a type O. Am I correct?"

"Yes, you are."

Eleanor's bulbous eyes lit up. "Would that be positive or negative?"

"Positive."

"You're sure about that?"

Mal winked. "I'm positive."

Eleanor nodded politely. "Thank you, Mr. Deiter." The old lady curtsied. "I trust you'll both have a pleasant night."

Then she waddled off, leaving the two of them befuddled.

"Blood type?" Deb finally asked when the old woman had descended the stairs.

"Maybe she's a vampire," Mal said. "She might have been the creature you saw in the bushes."

"I saw a cougar, Mal. Not an old woman."

"Was it wearing a pillbox hat?"

Deb allowed herself to smile. "Maybe it was. I think it also had a rifle. Perhaps it shot out my tire."

"Touché. I'm going to unpack and grab some food. Meet you in the kitchen in a few?"

"Sure."

Mal handed Deb her bags, then unlocked his door. "See you in a bit."

In keeping with the theme of the inn, the Teddy Roosevelt room was chockfull of creepy presidential memorabilia. Every wall boasted pictures and banners, the lampshades were collage pastiches, and not a single stick of furniture was without a Roosevelt stamp of some

sort. Eleanor had even managed to find Teddy Roosevelt
bedsheets, his cherubic face five feet wide and grinning
like the Cheshire cat.

Deb placed her two suitcases in the closet, next to an
old reel-to-reel tape deck. Since she wouldn't be here for
more than a few hours, it didn't make sense to unpack.
She'd pull out a change of clothes in the morning.

A trip to the bathroom found her appearance to be con-
siderably less than stellar. She applied a bit of lip gloss
from her fanny pack, a bit of mousse to her hair, and used
the hand soap on the sink to get the last of the deer blood
out from her expensive manicured fingernails. A life-size
poster of Roosevelt hung next to the toilet, his eyes seem-
ing to follow her. Deb didn't mind—the old-fashioned
clawfoot bathtub more than made up for the bizarre decorations. She was aching to have a soak. And if she'd been
alone, she would have put off dinner and done just that.

And yet, she found herself leaving the bathroom, and
her room, in order to meet Mal in the kitchen.

*Why am I so anxious to see him again? And why am I
hurrying?*

He's probably not even there yet.

She still descended the stairs quicker than safety
warranted.

To get to the kitchen, she walked through the living
room, getting a startle when she saw the large man standing in the middle of the room.

No, that's not a man.

It was the statue of George Washington, larger than
life and dressed in period clothing. Deb found it oppressive, and gave it a wide berth as she passed.

The walls of the kitchen were lined with ephemera:
magazine covers, newspapers, brochures, campaign signs.

On the picture rail near the ceiling was a line of dinner plates, each bearing faces and quotes of Presidents. Unlike the unusual odor pervading the rest of the house, this room smelled delightfully like baked goods. Deb's enthusiasm sank when she failed to see Mal.

Maybe he's not coming. Maybe he just went to bed.

Then she noticed him peering into the refrigerator and had to suppress her smile.

"There are enough cupcakes in here to feed the entire state of West Virginia," Mal said. "There's also a mystery meat sandwich. Interested?"

"I love meat in all of its permutations."

Mal stacked a plate of cupcakes and the plate with the sandwich on one hand and grabbed a glass carafe of milk and two apples with the other. He bumped the refrigerator door closed with his hip and laid everything out on the dining room table.

"Pretty good balance," Deb said, easing into a chair.

"I waited tables in college. Would madam care to split the sandwich?"

"Madam would like to eat the whole thing. But since you carried up my bags, I guess I'm willing to share."

Mal went to the cupboard and found an extra plate and two glasses. While Deb poured the milk, Mal searched drawers for utensils.

"So you never got around to telling me about the history of Monk Creek," she said, licking the pink frosting on a cupcake. It was buttercream, and very good. "You said you were researching it and discovered some interesting things."

"Indeed I did. You want to hear something really interesting? This woman has dozens of forks and spoons, but not a single knife."

"Not even a butter knife?"

"Not one. I guess you get the whole sandwich after all."

Deb reached into her fanny pack, took out her Bench-made folding knife. She flicked the five-inch blade open with her thumb and cut the sandwich in half. The meat was whitish, piled on high. The lettuce and tomato were still crisp. Eleanor had made this recently.

"Nice piece of cutlery," Mal said, sitting across from Deb.

"I won't be trapped in the woods without a weapon ever again," Deb said, wiping it on her pants.

They each tore into their halves. Deb was surprised by how hungry she was. She was also surprised by the taste of the meat. It wasn't unpleasant. Just unusual.

"Is this chicken?" she asked.

Mal shook his head. "Pheasant."

"You sure?"

"Pretty sure. Dad used to take me hunting, when I was a kid."

"You still go?"

"No. Lost my taste for it."

"Pheasant?"

"Killing animals. I'm not a hypocrite, though. I'm still a voracious carnivore. But not enough to go after it on my own."

Deb took another bite, then sliced into one of the apples. The crisp fruit was a nice complement to the gaminess of the meat.

"So, Monk Creek," she said. "What did you discover in your investigative reporting?"

Mal finished chewing, and swallowed. "The thing I liked best about being a cop was figuring things out. I didn't like the violence, which is why I left the force to study journalism. So while researching this assignment,

I wanted to learn about the history of the region, to use as a background for the interviews. And I found out some pretty strange things."

Deb cut off another hunk of apple. "Such as?"

Mal polished his apple on his shirt and took a bite. "A lot of people disappear in these parts."

When Deb finished chewing she said, "Quantify *a lot*."

"In the past forty years, more than five hundred people."

Deb did the math in her head. "That's only about one a month. Doesn't seem like too many."

"Considering Monk Creek's small population, that's more than ten times the national average."

She wiped some mayo from the corner of her mouth with the back of her hand. "I've climbed the mountains here. It's easy to get lost."

"But the majority of lost people get found. Either alive or dead. These people are gone. Vanished, without a trace. You'd think some of them would have been discovered."

"Odd," Deb agreed. "Does anyone have any theories?"

"That's also strange. No one seems to think it means anything. Because most of the missing people are from different states, there's no joint task force treating this like a single problem. The only unifying factor is the sheriff of Monk Creek. And he's . . . *interesting*."

"In what way?"

"I spoke with him on the phone. Let's just say I'm not convinced all of his cylinders are firing."

"Why would the town hire him?"

"Maybe that's *why* the town hired him."

Deb finished off her sandwich. "So it's a big conspiracy?"

Mal shrugged. "Could be. Could be just a coincidence."

"You come up with anything else?"

"Just one thing. The disappearances began after a specific event in the town's history. There was a pharmaceutical plant that employed almost everyone in the area. It was closed down by the government in the early sixties, and the town began to die out. As the population dropped, the number of missing persons rose dramatically."

Deb set the apple core aside and went back to the cupcake she'd been licking. She peeled off the paper, thinking about five hundred people missing in this area. Missing, presumed dead.

How does something like that happen? Don't these people have families?

Didn't the families know where they were going?

And yet, Deb herself never told anyone she was going mountain climbing that fateful day. One of many rookie mistakes she'd made. If she'd told someone, and had been overdue, maybe they could have sent help.

Deb felt a stab of adrenaline kick up her heart rate.

No one knows where I am now.

Last year, Deb had lost her parents. Mom, to cancer. Dad, to grief over Mom. The tough exterior Deb wore like armor kept anyone from getting close.

So here she was, making the same rookie mistakes all over again.

I'm not mountain climbing, though.

No, I'm at a creepy inn, out in the middle of nowhere.

But this time, there is someone who knows where I am.

She glanced at Mal, who'd taken their plates and was dumping the apple cores and bread crust into the garbage can in the corner of the room. He lifted the can's lid, peered inside, then made a face.

"You okay?" Deb asked.

"Remember when I said the meat was pheasant?" Mal asked.

Deb's stomach turned a slow somersault. "What are you saying?"

"I think I was wrong," Mal said. "It wasn't pheasant at all."

Maria's alive.

The thought stunned Felix. After a year of hoping, despairing, and wondering, to finally have this confirmed was so overpowering he didn't know whether to cheer, laugh, or weep.

"What have you done to her, you son of a bitch?"

Cam pushed Felix aside and grabbed John by his flabby neck. He raised the hunting knife.

"Answer me or I'll scalp you."

Felix reached out, ready to intervene, but John began to babble. It was a rant, mostly incoherent, but obviously sincere.

"Blue blood. It's blue. We all got blue blood. Me 'n' my brothers. Direct line to Charlemagne. Like the Presidents. Ma says it's too pure. Too presidential 'n' strong. We get sick. We need mixin'."

"We bled her. Same as the others. Nice and slow."

"What the hell are you talking about?" Cam said.

But Felix thought he got it. "You need her blood."

Cam looked at him. "Huh?"

"Transfusions," Felix said. He stared at John. "Is that why you're so worried about bleeding?"

"If'n I get cut, it don't stop. Takes too long to heal up."

Cameron shook his head. "No way. I don't believe it."

"It's true," John implored. "We don't hurt her none.

We just use her for bleedin'. And . . ." John's voice trailed off.

"And, what?" Cam said.

John pursed his lips. Cam pointed the hunting knife at Jon's face. An inch from his nose.

"What!"

"And makin' babies," John whispered.

Felix sank to his knees, feeling like someone had punched him. He'd been overwhelmed by emotion after hearing Maria was alive. Now, hearing why Maria had been taken—to be bled and raped by a family of psychos—it was too much to handle.

"Bullshit," Cam said, shaking his head. "You're lying."

"I ain't. I ain't lyin'."

"We'll see."

And then Cam stuck him with the knife. In his right arm, just below the shoulder.

John screamed. High-pitched and loud, like a girl. Cam jammed the sock back into the hunter's mouth, while Felix watched, slack-jawed, as blood began to soak John's shirt.

The giant thrashed, breaking the chair, crashing to the floor. Landing on his broken fingers made him scream even louder, and he rolled onto his side, kicking to get the rope off his legs.

Felix tore off John's sleeve to assess the injury. The knife wound did more than bleed. It gushed with John's heartbeat, pumping out of his body with a *lubdub* rhythm.

"Wild," Cam said. His face twisted into a grin.

Felix pressed his ruined hands to John's wound, then spat out at Cam, "You asshole! If he dies we won't find Maria!"

Cam stuck out his lower lip. "What do I do?"

"My tool kit! In the truck! Get the superglue!"

Cam ran off. John flipped, onto his belly, knocking Felix away. Blood soaked the carpet beneath him. He pulled the sock out of John's mouth and implored, "Where is she?"

"Stop the bleedin' . . . gotta . . . stop the bleedin'."

"Tell me where Maria is, and I'll stop the blood."

"Turn . . ." John mumbled.

"Turn? Turn where?"

"Turnikit . . ."

Shit. John's going to die without giving up where she is.

They'd used all of the rope to tie John up. Felix could have cut off a length, used that, but John was too big to be able to control. Felix's eyes wandered around the room, frantic. They locked on the closet.

Hurrying to it, he grabbed a metal clothes hanger and stretched it in his hands, wincing as he bent back the hook on top. When the wire opened up, he tucked one end under John's armpit. Then Felix brought the two ends together and began to twist the hanger around John's biceps. It was easy at first. But once the wire began to meet with resistance, Felix didn't have enough strength in his mangled fingers to make it tight.

Dammit, where's Cam?

Felix picked up a broken chair leg and jammed that under the wire. He began to turn the leg, like a propeller, cinching the wire tight against John's skin.

John moaned.

The wound still bled.

Gritting his teeth, Felix jammed the sock back into John's mouth and twisted the chair leg even harder.

The hanger pressed deep into John's flabby arm, then

broke the skin. More blood poured out, covering the wire. Felix tried to twist the wire off, and the blood dripped out of the split flesh like a towel being wrung out.

No. No no no no . . .

"John. Listen to me." Felix grabbed John's cheeks, which had grown sickly pale. "You need to tell me where she is."

"Help . . . me."

"I'll help you. But I need you to tell me."

John's eyes glazed over, and he seemed to be looking far away. "Help . . . me . . . Dwight . . ." *Dwight?*

Felix felt the gun press against the back of his head. He knew who Dwight was. The sheriff of Monk Creek had been of no help to Felix during his quest, refusing even the simplest of requests.

"Stand up. Hands over your head. Slow and easy, or I'll have to use force, like I did with your friend outside."

Felix felt his entire world crumbling. He lifted up his hands.

"This man tried to kill me, Sheriff. He's got my fiancée. The one I told you about."

"Is that so?"

The sheriff grabbed Felix's wrist, twisting his arm and forcing him face-first into the blood-soaked carpet. He felt the sheriff put a foot on his back and the handcuff go on.

"You have to believe me," Felix said, his words blowing a bubble of John's blood. "Please."

"We'll get to the truth of this whole situation." The sheriff gave his arm another rough twist, then slapped on the second cuff. "That's for damn sure."

"Help me, Dwight," John said again. His voice had gotten very weak.

"You don't look so good, Johnny. Where's your styptic?"

"I dunno, Dwight. In my truck."

"Shit lot of good it's doin' you there."

Felix turned and looked up at the sheriff. Though not as big as John, Dwight was a large, portly man, with a doughy face and a bald head. He was wearing a brown shirt and green slacks, his badge hanging on his belt next to his gun.

The sheriff knelt next to John and unwound the coat hanger.

"Don't move, dummy. I got to open the wound for this to work."

The sheriff unclipped a knife from his belt and brought the blade next to John's arm.

"Don't . . . move."

With a quick motion, the sheriff jammed the tip into the original wound and cut sideways. John howled, jerking his whole body sideways.

"Goddamn it, John! I almost nicked my finger!"

"It hurts! They broke my fingers, Dwight! They broke all my digits!"

"I gotta expose the goddamn artery."

The blood was really gushing now, almost like a water fountain. Felix watched the sheriff pull a tan package out of his breast pocket. It had *QuikClot* printed on the paper. He tore off a corner and poured white powder into John's wound. John yelped.

"Shush, now. Stop being a baby."

"It burns, Dwight. B-burns bad."

"Hold still. I need to see if I got it all."

John twitched. Felix stared at John's arm. The powder indeed stopped all the bleeding. But there seemed to be another problem.

"Jesus, Dwight! Hurts even worse!"

Felix could see why. The hemostatic agent apparently

had stopped the blood from leaking out, but it hadn't stopped the internal bleeding. John's triceps began to expand, like a balloon.

"I'm gonna have to open you up again, John. Hold on, I got more styptic in the car."

"No! Please, Dwight!"

Without provocation, the sheriff kicked Felix in the side, so hard he actually saw red.

"Now, don't you move none, or I'll make it worse for you," he told Felix.

Then he lumbered off.

My gun. It's in the sink.

Felix pressed his head into the sopping carpet, then pulled his knees up under him. He got to his feet, unsteady, feeling like puking again, and staggered into the bathroom. The Beretta was still there. He backed up against the sink, reaching his cuffed hands behind him, seeking the gun.

The sink was deep, the bowl curved, and every time he touched it, the weapon slid away from him. His fingers, wrapped in bandages, had no feeling in them, and he couldn't see what he was doing over his shoulder.

He felt fresh sweat break out on his forehead, stinging his scalp wound.

Slow and easy, Felix. You can do it.

Nudge.

Miss.

Nudge.

Miss.

He eyed the door, expecting the sheriff to come in any second.

Wait . . . I've got handcuff keys in my front pocket . . .

He'd put them there after cuffing John on the highway.

Felix tried to bring his hands around, but he couldn't even get a finger in his pocket, let along reach for the keys.

No time. Go for the gun.

He backed up to the sink again, stretching his arms.

Concentrate. Reach your hands in deeper.

Felix blinked back tears, held his breath, and locked his right hand around the butt of the gun.

Now what?

He tried to bring the gun around, and shoot forward from the hip, but there wasn't enough play in the cuffs. The best he could do was aim sideways. Felix wasn't a very good shot in ideal conditions. He doubted, with his current stance, he could even hit the wall while standing up against it.

"Now, what do we have here?"

Startled, Felix spun around, pressing the trigger.

The shot missed the sheriff by a good five feet.

However, it didn't miss John. The hunter's head jerked back, and the back of his skull popped off. Brains spilled out like a dropped bowl of oatmeal.

The sheriff was on Felix in three steps, punching him in the jaw, stepping on his neck when he fell, and yanking the gun from his hand.

"Looks like you just went from assault to homicide, boy."

"Sheriff, you have to listen. John has my fiancée. He and his brothers have her someplace."

The sheriff didn't seem to be paying attention. He got on one knee next to John and closed the man's staring eyes.

"Styptic won't fix this one, hoss." He blew out a breath. "Look at all that blood."

"Sheriff . . . listen to me!"

The sheriff's eyes centered on Felix. Felix saw no mercy there.

"No, you listen to me. You're going to get into my car and not speak one more peep, or I'm going to shoot out both your knees. You got that, boy?"

Felix nodded.

The sheriff manhandled Felix to his feet and roughly pulled him out the front door. The squad car was there, and there were several motel guests with their doors open.

"Everyone back inside," the sheriff ordered. "The situation has been taken care of."

The sheriff opened the rear door of his car and shoved Felix into the backseat, next to Cam. Cam's nose was bleeding freely, and his face was the epitome of sullen. He had his hands behind his back; apparently handcuffed, like Felix's.

"Asshole snuck up on me. Probably gonna take me back to the nuthouse. You find out where they're keeping Maria?"

Felix gave his head one quick, brief shake. "John's dead."

"Shouldn't be too hard to find out where he lives."

"What does it matter, Cam? We're fucked."

The car bounced on its shocks as the sheriff climbed in. He adjusted his rearview mirror, looked Felix square in the eyes, and started the car.

When he pulled out onto the road, Felix was confused. He whispered to Cam, "This isn't the way to the police station."

"What are you two hens cluckin' about?" the sheriff demanded.

Felix slunk back in his seat. "Town. It's the other direction."

"I ain't takin' you to town." The sheriff grinned, showing his crooked brown teeth, and Felix felt his mouth go dry. "I got other plans for you boys."

* * *

The machine whirs and clicks, spins and pumps. The IV drains blood out of Maria's right arm, passing it through the siphoning mechanism and pumping it into George. He also has an IV sucking blood out of him, feeding it back into Maria's left arm.

A trade. Blood in, blood out.

This has been done to Maria dozens of times, and it never fails to revolt her. Exchanging blood with these monsters—she thinks of them as monsters rather than human beings—is almost worse than when they climb on top of her. But the revulsion goes beyond the awareness that their diseased blood is in her body. Their blood actually causes her to feel sick.

These freaks are ill. Seriously ill. They bleed from the slightest injury, and the bleeding doesn't stop on its own. If they don't get a transfusion every few weeks, they die.

Maria isn't sure why she's still alive. Apparently whatever disease they have isn't fatal to her. Perhaps she's immune. Perhaps it can't be passed on. Perhaps her body cleans their dirty blood, like some sort of human dialysis machine. However it works, Maria knows that she, and other captives like her, are keeping these mistakes of nature alive.

The process takes a few hours, and it's nearly done. Afterward, the monsters line up, eager for a chance to impregnate her. Maria has tried to tell Eleanor that she can't have children, that her ovaries don't work, but that hasn't stalled their efforts. Eleanor endlessly prattles on about the presidential bloodline, about having heirs, and she has some grotesque, grandiose delusions about her legacy. So convinced of her own importance, Eleanor often lies down alongside Maria and has sex with her own monstrous children and grandchildren in some twisted attempt to produce more monsters.

Though not deformed, Eleanor is the biggest monster of all.

Maria looks around. The freaks are huddled together, grunting at one another. They don't talk much. Some are mentally retarded, from either inbreeding or birth defects or both, and unable to converse. They're missing limbs, or have too many, or their appendages are underdeveloped or in the wrong place. Some have heads that are too large, some too small. Many have harelips. Few of them have hair, and they're all sickly pale and smell sour.

"All done," Eleanor says. She's lifting her dress up over her head. "Let's line up, children. It's time to make babies."

George pulls the transfusion needles from his arms, quickly sealing his wounds with a white powder. He turns to Maria and says, "Me first."

Maria forces down the gorge rising in her throat; vomiting while wearing a ball gag could cause her to choke to death.

George presses the cattle prod to her stomach, then unstraps her feet and hands.

She closes her eyes and thinks of Felix. She imagines him bursting in right now, killing all of the monsters, and taking her away from here.

Will he still want me, after all I've been through?

Of course he will.

It's been a year since she's seen him. Felt his touch. Heard his voice. A long, agonizing, nightmarish year.

George frees her hands, then paws at her pants.

She imagines being with Felix. They're sitting on a porch, drinking lemonade, holding hands. The sun is out. The breeze smells like cut grass.

And since it's a fantasy, she also imagines the child they can't have. A toddler, roaming the lawn, chasing a butterfly, or a dog.

She can even imagine the dog barking.

Maria hears it again, and opens her eyes.

"There's a dog!"

Maria watches as Calvin bursts into the Room. He's the one with the unibrow and the flipper hands, one of which is being nipped at by a German shepherd. Maria is overjoyed to see the animal. She's even more elated when the dog snarls and barks at Eleanor and her monstrous brood, forcing them to back away.

The freaks are terrified. And they should be. A single bite could kill them.

And this dog is big and looks eager to bite.

George, his broad face a mask of fear, pokes at the animal with the cattle prod. The dog takes a quick zap in the muzzle, then darts away. Its lips curl back, exposing long, sharp teeth, and it attacks in a frenzy, biting George's hand five or six times in the blink of an eye.

George screams, dropping the prod. The new blood he's just received bursts out of his hand in all directions, like a Fourth of July firework. He turns, running for Eleanor, dropping to his knees.

"The styptic, Ma! The styptic!"

The dog lunges again, biting at the back of George's thigh, clamping down tight and shaking its head back and forth.

The freaks are in a panic, a wall of misshapen bodies

climbing all over one another in an effort to get away. They're flooding out the exit. Some of them are being trampled. Eleanor looks at George, then at Maria, radiating hate.

"Get the girl!" she yells at her brood.

Maria knows she's terribly outnumbered, and there's a mad dog loose, but she decides then and there to die before she lets them take her back to her cell. She reaches for the dropped cattle prod.

Most of the monsters ignore Eleanor, but a few form a circle around her.

Maria swings the prod, keeping them at bay, turning this way and that way so no one can sneak up behind her. With her free hand she unbuckles the ball gag, lets it fall to the floor. She's light-headed, and the nausea is starting to take hold. Normally, after an ordeal in the Room, she sleeps for a long time. Maria fights the feeling, keeping on the balls of her feet, determined to stay alert.

Someone grabs at her, and she sticks him with the cattle prod. The burst of light and the accompanying sizzle and scream give her strength. She whirls around, stabbing the prod into a creature's bloated face. Then an avalanche of sour flesh rams into her, forcing her to the floor, pinning her under its weight. She twists the prod around, zaps whoever is on top of her. There's a cry, but she's still trapped. There are too many freaks on top of her. She can't move.

She can't even breathe.

Maria grunts, pushing with all of her strength. She's not going to smother. Not now. Not this close to escape. But the fetid, shifting mass of flesh atop her is too heavy to move. Her hair is yanked. A filthy, malformed baby's arm with seven fingers tugs at the corner of her mouth as her face is pressed into the dirt floor.

She tries to suck in some air, but the weight is too much.

I'm sorry, Felix. I tried.

And then, miraculously, the mass shifts. One monster rolls off, screaming. Then another. Maria pushes herself onto her side, gasping for oxygen. She watches as the dog—the beautiful, terrifying dog—tears into another freak, pulling him off her.

They're all scrambling for the door now, dragging their wounded, of which there are many. The dog is on top of the last freak, one with a blockish, Frankenstein head, and hands that look like pincers. The dog's tearing at the monster's throat. Maria looks at the door, trades a hateful glance with Eleanor as she abandons her child and closes it shut.

Maria sits up, clutching the prod in both hands. The dog bites the freak until it stops moving, until a good portion of its neck is hanging limp from the dog's jaws.

The dog shakes its head, releasing its prize. Then it looks at Maria and snarls.

"Good boy," Maria manages to say. Her voice is raspy. She can't remember the last time she's spoken.

The dog hunkers down, the hair on its back standing up. It growls, low and deep, its lips raised and baring teeth.

"Sit," Maria orders.

The dog stalks forward. It's not looking at Maria. It's looking at the cattle prod.

Maria sets it down. "Sit!" she says again.

Incredibly, the dog sits. Its tongue lolls out of its mouth.

"Good dog! Come."

The dog bounds forward, and Maria almost screams when it pounces on her.

But it's a happy pounce, tail wagging. The dog's bloody tongue is warm on Maria's cheek. She grabs its muzzle and hugs it tight. The feeling is so good, so pure, she can't stop the tears from coming.

"Good dog. Can you shake?"

The dog offers its paw. Maria shakes it gladly.

"What's your name, boy?" She fumbles for his collar while he licks her.

"JD. I swear to God, JD, if we get out of this, I'm buying you steak every day for the rest of your life."

JD approves of this, wagging his tail even more.

Maria stands up. She knows Eleanor and her boys will be back, with weapons. Maybe even guns.

She goes to the door, tries the knob. Locked.

Maria slams her shoulder into it. The door is solid. It won't budge.

I can't give up. Not now. Not when I'm this close.

But as Maria looks around the Room, she has no clue how they can escape.

Letti Pillsbury stood in the doorway of the Ulysses S. Grant room, looking at her mother crouch on the floor.

"Do you normally check under the bed every place you sleep?" Letti asked.

"Hmm? No, of course not." Florence stood up, smoothing some imaginary wrinkles from her pants. She looked perturbed, which wasn't something Letti could ever recall seeing.

"Okay, then. You wanted to talk. Let's talk."

The older woman seemed confused, and for a moment

Letti questioned her mother's health. After all, her health was the reason she was moving in with her and Kelly.

"I want you to understand, Letti."

"Understand what, Florence?" Letti crossed her arms, determined not to make it easy for her.

"Why I didn't come to your husband's funeral."

"I know why you didn't come, Florence. You were off in Bosnia or Ethiopia or one of your other *causes*."

"I was in Mumbai. Doing volunteer work, Letti, during the floods. We were saving lives. Peter, bless your husband's heart, was already dead. There wasn't anything I could do for him."

She doesn't get it. Maybe she never will.

"*Peter* didn't need you, Florence. *I* did."

Florence raised an eyebrow. "So you're saying your grief is more important than building a dam that saved three hundred lives?"

Letti refused to let her eyes tear up. "I was devastated. I needed my mother."

"I raised you so you wouldn't need me."

"You're impossible." Letti turned to leave. She felt Florence's hand on her shoulder.

"What do you want me to say, Letti? That I made the wrong choice? You're strong. Always were. Peter's death was a terrible tragedy, but I knew you could handle it. Mumbai needed me more."

This is a waste of time. She'll die before she apologizes. But she's right. I am strong. And I will not cry.

Letti spun around, feeling the scowl take over her face. "If Mumbai is so goddamn important, why didn't you go running there when you were diagnosed with cancer?"

Florence flinched. Letti immediately felt bad for saying it, but she was on a roll.

"You didn't, though. You came to *me*, Florence. Me and Kelly. I thought it was because you wanted to mend fences. To get to know your granddaughter. But money is the real reason, isn't it? You gave away all of yours, helping strangers. Now you need a place to die, and my house is a free hospice."

Florence kept her face calm, but Letti saw something behind it crack. "Oh . . . Letti . . . is that what you think?"

Letti bit her lower lip. She felt the tears coming, but refused to blink. "We needed you, Florence. Kelly and I. And you weren't there. But now you need us, and here we are. Maybe Mumbai built a big statue to Saint Florence for saving their village. But I never wanted to be raised by a saint. I wanted a mom."

"And I wasn't a mother to you." Florence said it as a statement.

"Mothers nurture," Letti said. She felt the tear roll down her cheek. "Mothers support. Mothers show up at the goddamn funeral when their daughters lose their husbands."

Florence said nothing. She just stood there, stoic as ever.

I might as well be talking to a statue.

"It's so important to me for you to understand why I did it, Letti."

"I know why you did it, Florence. But I'll *never* understand it. And I'll never forgive you for it."

Florence opened her mouth, but no sound came out.

Point. Match. Game.

So why did it still feel like losing?

Letti walked out of the room, shutting the door behind her. She went down the hall to the Grover Cleveland room and let herself in. For a moment, she felt like giving in to the tears, crying her eyes out. But she pushed the feeling down. The last time she cried was at Peter's funeral. She'd lost two people that day.

Her husband, and her mother.

Letti wouldn't allow herself to cry over her mother again.

She took a deep breath through her nose, let it out slow through her mouth. Like she'd been taught. All during her youth, Florence had subjected Letti to countless instructors, coaches, and senseis, in countless sports, martial arts, and disciplines. Florence thought dropping Letti off at a dojo or a yoga class was a substitute for parenting. But none of her many teachers could fill the void Letti felt, and none could teach her how to deal with her resentment.

Letti took another slower, deeper breath, letting her heart rate slow down.

The room smelled strange, and the decorations were even more so.

Damn, this is one creepy place.

If Letti hadn't known what Grover Cleveland looked like before coming to this room, she certainly did now. Everywhere she looked, there were pictures and drawings and photos of the chubby, mustached President. He was on the curtains, the walls, the bedspread, the doors, and even the lampshades.

That Eleanor Roosevelt has some issues. Hell, she has a whole subscription.

Letti undressed down to her panties, letting her clothes stay where they fell.

She was exhausted, bone weary, but her mind refused to shut off. Sleep would be elusive.

She considered taking a shower, but standing up for those few extra minutes seemed like a tremendous chore.

And, for some strange reason, she didn't feel comfortable being naked.

Letti crossed her arms across her breasts, considering the feeling. It wasn't shame. Letti had toned her body to be all it could be and was proud of her efforts.

No, what Letti felt was something closer to fear.

What am I afraid of? I'm alone.

Still, she opened her suitcase next to the bed and quickly tugged on a tee shirt. After a quick look around the room, checking for leering boogeymen, she took her toiletry bag into the bathroom and began to brush her teeth.

The bathroom was also funky, both in odor and in decor. The large poster of Grover Cleveland facing the toilet seemed to stare right at her. Letti had an irrational urge to hang a towel over its eyes.

The water from the sink was off-color, and tasted funny, so Letti brushed without swallowing any. She finished quickly and crawled into bed, wrapping herself up in Grover Cleveland sheets. Letti automatically reached for the remote control on the nightstand next to the bed, but didn't see it. And there was an obvious reason why; the room had no TV.

Annoyed, Letti wondered how she'd ever be able to fall asleep. Her normal ritual involved talk shows and infomercials until she couldn't keep her eyes open anymore. The silence in this room was much too loud.

She thought about getting up, going to Kelly's room. Maybe her daughter had a TV. Or maybe she'd let Letti borrow her iPod. YouTube was a sorry substitute for Leno, but it would have to do.

Letti was peeling back the covers when her eyes caught on something sitting on the dresser.

A book.

Been a while since I read a book.

She padded over to it and realized it wasn't a regular book at all. It was a hardbound journal. On its cover, in detailed script, were the words *The Rushmore Inn*.

Letti immediately knew what it was. She'd stayed in bed-and-breakfasts before. The proprietors often left journals in the rooms, so people could document their stay. Curious as to what guests would say about this odd little inn, Letti picked up the journal and climbed back into bed. The first page was written in deliberate, ornate cursive.

> *10/23/1975*
> *The inn is practically hidden out here in the woods, but Henry and I find the accommodations and the proprietor quite charming. Henry hasn't returned from hunting yet. While I hope he had fun, I also hope he doesn't bring any of those ghastly birds home. They're such a mess to prepare. Our vows said nothing about "plucking."*
> *I hear someone downstairs. Maybe it's him. Maybe I'll surprise him by being naked when he comes to bed. He's walking up the hall now. I'm going take off my*

The last sentence just ended there, without punctuation. Letti turned to the next page and found it was ripped out. She began reading the next entry, done in a different hand.

> *May 19, 1979*
> *My second night here. I don't like it. There are strange smells, and right now I hear something moving in the walls. It's another two days before*

*Blake and the other men come back from their
mountain climbing, and I almost wish I went
with them. Marcus's wife has come down with
something. She's slurring her speech like she's
drunk, but she swears she hasn't touched any
liquor, and her breath doesn't smell. I hope Blake
comes back soon.*

Again, more missing pages.
This is pretty creepy stuff.
Letti listened, to see if she heard anything in the
walls. There was nothing but silence. Though she knew
the journal was getting to her, Letti moved on to the
next entry.

*July 24, 1984
I can't believe we found this place. It's so deep
in the woods I don't know how it stays in business.
Especially since our room was free, and we seem
to be the only ones here. My wife thinks it's all
incredibly kitschy. I think it's just weird. If this
new job pans out, I'll make some real money and
take her on a proper honeymoon. But I love her,
so it doesn't matter where we are, as long as
there's a bed. Though last night, I could have
sworn I heard something UNDER the bed.*

Feeling foolish, but also a bit freaked out, Letti peeked
over the side of the bed. She grabbed the dust ruffle with
her hand, set her jaw, and lifted it up.
Nothing.
*Florence would find my paranoia amusing. I need to
get a grip.*

Letti considered putting the journal down, but that would have proved it was scaring her. Instead, she skipped ahead, skimming bits and pieces. It stayed true to the theme. Brief, spooky paragraphs, followed by missing pages.

> *August 14, 1991*
> *Paula is still upset about the "monster" she said she saw in the woods. Something with two heads. I think she's seeing things. We both seem to have the flu, though neither of us has a fever. Can't wait to get out of this place.*

Two pages missing.

> *June 1998*
> *Barry hasn't returned yet. I'm getting worried. I hear noises.*
> *I hope we get the car fixed soon so we can leave.*

Page missing.

> *9/19/02*
> *It's the middle of nowhere. There's no place to run. What am I supposed to do?*

Another page torn out.

> *6/2005*
> *This place is really fucked up. I think we're gonna die here.*

More missing pages. Letti turned to the most recent entry.

> *June 12, 2007*
> *Exhausted. Iron Woman training is both the*
> *hardest and the most rewarding thing I've ever*
> *done. I wish I was at the event hotel, but this isn't*
> *a bad substitute. And you can't beat the price,*
> *even though this place is sort of scary. I____*

The *I* trailed off, making a pen mark that went all the way down to the bottom of the page. Like someone bumped the writer. And on the bottom of the page . . .

Brown stains. Like blood drops.

Letti looked around the room, feeling goose bumps raise up on her arms. This had to be some sort of prank. A gag journal, to amuse the guests.

But Letti wasn't amused. She was seriously weirded out.

I need to check on Kelly.

She was getting ready to toss the journal aside and hop out of bed when a mark on the page caught her eye. A black mark.

Letti turned the page past the final entry and saw a child's handwriting, written in black crayon.

im grover.
this is
My room.

Letti scratched at the printing with her fingernail, getting black wax underneath. The familiar smell of crayon wafted up at her, reminding Letti of when Kelly was younger. But Kelly's childhood printing never looked so . . . *creepy.*

Letti turned to the next page.

Letti's head shot up. She scanned the room, listening for strange sounds, feeling like someone was indeed watching her, and at the same time knowing it was crazy to be thinking that.

It's a joke. A dumb, sick joke. When I see Eleanor again, I'm going to tell that crazy old hag what I think of her stupid little inn.

Letti stared down at the journal again. She touched the top corner of the page, ready to turn it.

Do I really want to keep reading this BS?

No. I should go check on my daughter.

Letti began to close the book, and stopped.

They're only words on paper. I don't need to be afraid of them.

So why am I?

Letti chewed her lower lip, undecided what to do next.

Florence would think I'm a real chicken. She was in a war zone for four years, and I can't even read a silly journal.

Letti turned the page, feeling her breath catch.

im in the
CLOSeT
Letti

Letti sprang out of bed, backpedaling to the opposite side of the room, her eyes glued to the closet.

There's no one in there.

But how do they know my name?

Letti wondered if Kelly somehow had fabricated this, had put the journal in her room. She loved scary movies.

But Kelly hasn't been in this room.

Could she have snuck in while I was talking to Florence?

That seemed a lot more plausible than someone named Grover hiding in the closet.

And if Grover really is in the closet, why would he tell me?

Letti set her jaw.

It's a joke. Stop being a baby.

She marched over to the closet, grabbed the knob, and with no hesitation pulled the door open, staring up at the tall, deformed man with the bloodshot eyes and the crazy smile on his face.

"You're pretty," Grover said in a high voice. "Like Kelly."

Letti froze in shock. As the scream welled up in her throat, Grover grabbed Letti around the back of the head with one huge hand and pressed a wet towel to her face with another.

Letti got over her surprise quickly, and her body went

on autopilot, executing the self-defense moves Florence drilled into her head years ago.

First came a fist to the throat, followed by a heel grind to the instep.

She hit fast and hard, holding her breath, waiting for him to stagger back.

Grover didn't stagger. The punch to his neck missed his Adam's apple, because it wasn't where it should have been. Her hand sunk into doughy neck fat and bounced off harmlessly. Letti's kick was similarly ineffective. Her bare heel bounced off what seemed like steel-toed boots.

She quickly followed up with a knee to the groin, putting her weight behind it.

Her knee connected with . . . nothing.

Along with his other defects, Grover didn't seem to have genitals.

Letti didn't give up yet. Still refusing to breathe in, she cupped her hands and slapped them against Grover's ears, trying to burst his eardrums.

This time Grover did react. He stuck his lower lip out and started to cry, the tears running down his misshapen face. But he didn't let go. Instead, he pulled Letti tight to his body. She continued to punch and kick, but she didn't have any room to swing, and her blows did little damage.

Finally, no longer having a choice, Letti inhaled.

The liquid soaking the towel burned her nose and throat when she sucked it in, and for a moment Letti felt like everything was okay, that she was completely safe, and it was perfectly reasonable to fall asleep right now.

A bit of panic-fueled realization got through—*I'm being drugged*—and she lashed out one more time, reaching for Grover's eyes, smearing the tears on his cheeks.

But before she could gouge them out, the darkness took her.

Mal Deiter stared into the garbage can at the severed head. He debated picking it up, showing it to Deb, but rightfully decided that wasn't in good taste.

"What did I just eat, Mal?" Deb asked, an edge to her voice.

"It wasn't pheasant," Mal replied, eyeing the small beak. "It was partridge."

"You mean like *in a pear tree*?"

"His pear tree days are over."

Mal discarded the remnants of their snack, then closed the lid. He faced Deb and saw she wasn't amused.

Too bad. Deb was an attractive woman, but when she smiled, she was dazzling. So far, Mal hadn't been able to make her smile more than a few times, even though he was trying his damnedest. Deb was too guarded, which was a shame. If she relaxed a bit, Mal knew he could really fall for her. But he doubted Deb would let him get close enough for that to happen.

For the time being, he tried to rein in his feelings and keep things professional. Even guarded, Deb was an interesting person, and he liked being around her. He was already trying to think up some good excuse to call her after the interview ended.

"So what's your impression of our hostess?" Mal said, taking his seat. "I'm thinking about calling the Addams Family, seeing if one of them is missing."

Deb's mouth curled in the faintest smirk, and the lines on her forehead smoothed out.

"You might want to call the White House instead. These decorations are mind-blowing."

"They're unpresidented."

This time Deb actually did smile, full wattage, and it lit up the room.

"Thanks for splitting a partridge sandwich with me, Mal. I think I'm going to turn in. Long day."

Mal racked his brain to come up with some reason to keep talking.

Another interview question? Something more personal? A joke?

Then he saw Deb stifle a yawn with the back of her hand, and realized the proper thing to do was let her get some sleep. She was, after all, competing in a triathlon.

"I'll walk you up."

They took the stairs slowly, silently, but the silence wasn't awkward. When they arrived at Deb's room, Mal felt a tinge of uncertainty, like he'd just been on a date and was unsure if he should try for the kiss.

Deb unlocked her door, then turned and looked up at him. For the briefest of moments, Mal saw in her eyes the same desire he felt.

Should I try it?

Then Deb stuck out her hand.

The good-night handshake. Ugh. That's even worse than the good-night peck on the cheek.

"It's been a pleasure meeting you, Mr. Deiter."

He folded her hand into his. "The pleasure has been all mine, Ms. Novachek. See you in the morning."

Mal let the touch linger. So did Deb. Her eyes were big and her chin was tilted up and all the signals were there, so Mal went for it. He leaned down, parting his lips, and got a face full of hair when she abruptly turned around.

Deb slipped into her room and closed the door behind her, leaving Mal standing there like a dork. He recalled what Deb told him earlier.

"How old are we, twelve?"

He sure felt like it.

Mal let himself into his room. Several dozen Harry S. Trumans stared at him, and they all seemed to be thinking what Mal was thinking.

Smooth move, Casanova.

Mal padded into the bathroom, stripped off his shirt and pants, and took a leak. Then he turned his attention to the shower. Unlike the rest of the room, which was decorated in late-'60s Norman Bates, the shower stood apart by appearing modern. It was a walk-in, with a floor-to-ceiling glass door, and the showerhead was big and chrome and new.

Mal turned the knob to *scald* and stepped inside. The water was rust colored, and smelled medicinal, but the stream was strong and felt good on his body. He opened the little box of soap in the soap dish and worked up a lather. Also in the soap dish was a mini bottle of shampoo. Mal unscrewed the top, dumped the brown contents into his hand, and raised it to his head.

That's when the smell hit him.

A foul, rotten smell, like meat gone bad. He brought his hand to his face, sniffed the shampoo, and almost puked.

It's not shampoo. It's blood. Old, decaying blood.

Revolted, he pawed at his head, trying to get the gunk off. He could feel little pieces—clots—become tangled in his hair. Mal felt his stomach twist again, the partridge sandwich struggling to get out like it still had fluttering wings. Doubling over, Mal took deep breaths, watching gunky, brown blood swirl down the drain. He put a hand on the glass door to steady himself, wiping off a streak of steam—

—and saw someone standing in the bathroom.

Startled, Mal backed into the corner of the shower, watching the figure approach. Once he got over the initial shock, his mind tried to make sense of what was happening.

Deb? Coming back for that good-night kiss?

Another guest, who walked into the wrong room?

Eleanor Roosevelt's son, the one with the truck who was supposed to take them back into town?

Someone trying to do me harm?

Mal hollered above the water spray, "Who's there?"

The person didn't answer. He came up to the door and stood there.

Christ, he's huge.

"Who the hell are you?"

The giant didn't reply.

Mal's heart went into overdrive. This whole situation felt like it was happening to someone else, and it was so far removed from reality that he wasn't sure how to react. That he was naked made the vulnerability even more intense.

"What do you want?"

The man stayed silent, continuing to stare.

"Get the fuck out of here, asshole!"

More silence. More staring.

Mal felt like his legs couldn't support him anymore. He'd been in confrontations before. Shoving matches in bars with men who'd had a few too many. Once, a fistfight in high school, that resulted in a black eye.

But this was something different. Something very bad.

This isn't someone in the wrong room. This is someone who wants to hurt me.

Mal reached up, wiping his palm across the glass so he could see the man's face.

Holy shit! What's wrong with his—

The door jerked open, the giant's hand reaching for Mal's neck. Mal danced under the grab, making a fist, letting it fly.

His fist hit the man in the face—

—and sunk into the gaping hole between his upper lip and his nose.

Mal's knuckles were engulfed in something warm and wet: snot, saliva, or both. He recoiled, pulling his hand out of the giant's harelip, and got shoved back against the shower wall.

Then a wet towel was pushed over Mal's face. When he tried to breathe, his lungs filled with an acrid stench that Mal knew all too well. From his cop days, busting huffers—kids who inhaled chemicals to get high.

Ether. He's trying to knock me . . .

That was Mal's last thought before he spun into unconsciousness.

I should have kissed him.

Deb sat on the Teddy Roosevelt bedspread, staring at the door, willing Mal to knock on it. She had wanted to kiss him. She had really wanted it. But when he went for it she chickened out, no doubt humiliating him.

He's not going to knock. He's not ever going to try it again.

Deb closed her eyes and fell back onto the bed, sighing deeply.

I can run triathlons, but I don't have the guts to kiss a guy I like. Pathetic.

She thought back to Scott, her last boyfriend. He patiently waited during her months of recovery, and when they finally tried to have sex again for the first time since her accident, he couldn't get it up. Her cheeks burned at the memory.

"I'm sorry, Deb. I can't."

"Why, Scott? I'm the same woman."

"You're . . . grotesque."

Mal didn't seem to find her grotesque. And Deb doubted he'd have any sort of problems in bed.

But Deb knew *she* had problems. Body image problems. Mobility problems.

Self-confidence problems.

She wasn't comfortable letting another human being see her bare stumps.

How was she supposed to get completely naked with somebody?

I'm so sick of hating myself.

Deb opened her eyes, struck by an intriguing thought.

I could go to his room.

Not to sleep with him. Deb knew she wasn't ready for that. But she could at least kiss the guy good night.

It had been so long since she'd kissed a guy.

Deb pushed herself off the bed and walked to the door. When her hand rested on the knob, she paused.

Now I've gone from being a chicken to being needy.

She thought about what was worse, cowardice or insecurity, and decided cowardice was worse.

Deb stepped into the hall and walked over to Mal's room. Surprisingly, his door was open a crack.

Is he expecting me?

Deb hesitated again.

Knock? Go back? Or go in?

She knocked lightly.

No answer.

Deb lightly bounced up and down on her Cheetahs, trying to decide her next move. If he left the door open by accident, going in would be a bad move.

But who leaves their door open accidentally?

Deb went inside. Immediately, she realized why he didn't respond when she knocked. She heard the shower and saw steam coming out from under the bathroom door.

He isn't expecting me.

For a moment she debated walking into the bathroom and joining him in the shower. It was purely fantasy—she just wasn't the type to do that, legs or no legs. But she let herself imagine how it would unfold. Maybe she could say something clever, like, *"Is there room for two?"* Or maybe she'd just slip in behind him and start washing his back.

Damn it, I should have just kissed him.

The shower cut off.

I could wait here. Surprise him when he walks out. "Your door was open. I thought maybe we could give that kiss another try."

The bathroom door creaked, pushing outward.

Deb turned fast and got out of there. Heart pounding, she slunk back into her room and locked the door behind her.

"Nice, Deb," she said to herself. "Real mature."

Annoyed with herself, she hobbled into the bathroom to check out the clawfoot tub. Earlier, all she wanted to do was take a nice, hot bubble bath. Deb loved bubble baths. She loved being weightless while immersed in water, and getting the suds high enough to imagine that under them, her body was whole.

But looking at it now, she saw how steep and high the bathtub's edges were. Unlike modern hotels, there was no hand bar or railing next to the tub. That meant getting in and out would involve flopping over the edge. The tile floor was probably cold, and there weren't enough towels to cover it. Then, afterward, Deb would have to put her prosthetics back on to get into bed.

A whole lot of work for a bit of relaxation. Besides, she didn't like that gigantic framed poster of Theodore Roosevelt that faced the toilet.

It seems to be looking right at me.

Deb decided against the bath. She'd get up early, deal with it then. Right now, she just wanted to sleep and try to forget this day ever happened. She took off her fanny pack, placed it on the sink, and pulled out her toothbrush and toothpaste. The water was gross, but she made do. Afterward, she picked up a hand towel and left the bathroom. Then she sat on the edge of the bed and undressed down to her underwear.

I really hate this part.

Deb hit the release valves on her prosthetics, breaking the suction. She eased them off and set the Cheetahs on the floor, next to the bed. Then she rolled down the gel sock, sheathing the vestige of her left calf. A day's worth of accumulated sweat dripped onto the floor. Deb wiped the sheath with the towel and gave it a tentative sniff.

Not too funky. I can get another wear out of it.

She pulled the silicone end pad out of the bottom, dried it off, and repeated the process with the other side, setting the sheaths on the night stand. Then Deb finally looked at her legs.

The amputations were transtibial; below the knee. Her left leg was three inches longer than her right, and both came to tapered ends. Deb hated that they were uneven—it made her feel even more deformed. To make the complete package reach *eleven* on the hideous scale, each leg had raised, ugly scars, from her surgery, and from her cougar injuries. On top of all that, she needed to shave.

Yuck, Deb thought. *I'm a monster.*

She always thought that when she looked at her stumps.

Her skin below each knee was pruned and red. The gel sheet provided cushioning, but Deb sweat so much she got heat rash. The alternative was to wear stump socks, which would wick away sweat just like regular socks did. Unfortunately, the suction of the prosthetics weren't as tight when she wore socks, and Deb didn't want to risk having a leg fall off while in motion. Still, she'd eventually have to come up with some sort of compromise. Even the strongest antiperspirants didn't do much to help.

She draped the towel over her legs, then began to dry her stumps, massaging the muscles.

For half a second she pictured someone else doing the massage. *Mal.*

The fantasy ended with Mal gagging and running away.

"You're . . . grotesque."

"Yes. Yes, I am. And it's my own stupid fault."

Deb considered jumping into the self-pity pool and wallowing around, but she was presently too tired to hate herself. Instead she yawned, then flicked off the light switch next to the bed. The room went dark, and Deb buried her face in the Roosevelt pillowcase, letting her mind blank out.

Less than a minute later, she heard something creak.

Like someone is walking toward the bed.

Deb's eyelids snapped open and she fumbled for the light switch.

The room was empty.

She waited, riding out the adrenaline, her heart dancing a rhumba. But there were no more noises. No one around.

Okay. Old houses creak. No need to get paranoid about it. The door is locked. I'm alone. I need to go back to sleep.

She hit the switch, adjusted the pillow, and rested her head.

Creak, creak, creak.

Closer this time.

The light on once again, Deb sat up in bed. No one was in the room. She wondered if there was some reasonable explanation for this. Maybe the creaks were coming from the floor below. Or next door. Or maybe she was hearing something else that she mistook for footsteps.

But it didn't sound *nearby*. It sounded like it was coming from in the room.

She waited longer this time. Waited for the creaking to come back.

There was only silence.

Deb put her head back down, but she left the light on. If there was another creaking noise, she wanted to be able to see what was causing it.

Is someone messing with me?

Who? I'm alone in here.

After another long minute, she closed her eyes. She let her mind wander, and it found its way back to Mal. Cute guy. Obviously interested. All Deb needed to do was get out of her own way and let things develop. If she stopped second-guessing everything, stopped thinking ten steps ahead, maybe she could actually—

Creak.

Deb opened her eyes, wide.

The creak came from right under my bed.

Moving slowly, she peeked over the edge, half expecting to see some masked psychopath lying on the floor, waiting to spring.

She saw nothing. And that scared the living hell out of her.

My prosthetics are gone.

Deb left them alongside the bed. She was sure of it. She checked the nightstand, saw the gel sheaths were still there.

Maybe I'm brain dead. Maybe I put them on the other side.

Rolling over, Deb peered over the other end of the mattress.

All she saw was bare floor.

Someone took my legs.

Then the bed moved. Just a bit, but enough for Deb to realize what was happening.

The person who took my legs is under the bed.

Deb stared at the closet. She had her cosmetic legs in her case. If she could get to them, strap them on, she'd at least have a chance at getting away.

But how? Ease onto the floor and crawl there? That's at least five yards away. I'll never get there in time.

The bed jerked again. Harder this time. Whoever was under there lifted up the box spring and let it drop.

Then she heard him chuckle. Soft and low.

The fear that overtook Deb was the worst thing she ever

felt. Worse than when she was falling off the mountain. Worse than when she was being stalked by the cougar.

This isn't a mistake. This isn't Mother Nature.

This is a human being deliberately intending to do me harm.

Her mind flashed back to the blowout. Maybe Mal had been right. Maybe someone had shot out the tire, to make sure they couldn't get away.

And maybe that someone was under her bed right now.

What am I supposed to do? Any other person would be able to run away.

Maybe I can talk to him.

Deb's voice was shaking when she said, "Who's there?"

After a terrible silence, a voice directly beneath Deb said, *"I'm Teddy."*

It hit Deb like a slap to the face. She was so frightened she began to shiver.

He was *right* beneath her.

"What . . . what do you want, Teddy?"

No answer.

"Teddy . . . ?"

"I wanna watch you bleed, girl."

Deb put her fist in her mouth, biting on her knuckles so she didn't scream. She cast a frantic glance around the room, looking for some kind of weapon. There was nothing. And she'd left her fanny pack—and her knife—on the bathroom sink.

"I got yer legs," Teddy said. *"You can't get away."*

The fear was overwhelming. What could she do, other than wait there, unable to escape, while this crazy man crept up the side of the bed and climbed on top of her? She might as well have been tied up. Or paralyzed.

How do I run from someone when I can't even stand up?

Mal, Deb thought. *He's right next door.*

"Mal!" she screamed, banging on the wall behind her. "Mal, help!"

"Help me, Mal!" Teddy joined in, using a falsetto. *"Please help me!"*

Deb filled her lungs and yelled as loud as she could, "MAAAAAAL!" Mal didn't answer.

"Your little boyfriend ain't gonna help you, Debbie. Harry already took care a' him."

Teddy pushed the mattress up, so hard and violent that Deb almost rolled off.

"Ready er not, here I come."

She heard a palm slap the wood floor. Summoning up some dregs of courage, Deb peeked over the edge and saw Teddy's hand, sticking out from under the bed. It was large and grimy, the fingernails long and yellowed.

Teddy's thumb was actually two thumbs; at the knuckle it split into a Y shape.

Deb thought about reaching down, grabbing it, trying to break a finger, but she was too scared to move.

Another hand appeared, also with a bifurcated thumb. Then Teddy slowly eased himself out. His hair was brown, matted, a bird's nest of tangles. He turned and stared up at Deb. His face was just as ugly as his hands. Bushy eyebrows. A scraggly beard. One eye bigger than the other, the lens gray with a cataract; the other so deeply bloodshot it looked like a maraschino cherry. Teddy smiled, showing stained, rotten teeth, and Deb caught his pungent odor—stale sweat and sour milk.

"Ain't you a pretty one. Ole Teddy may get hisself a taste 'fore we get to bleedin' you."

Then Teddy pulled himself the rest of the way out from under the bed, and Deb got another shock.

He doesn't have legs.

No, wait. He does.

His overalls ended just below the buttocks, and jutting out of them were two tiny, underdeveloped feet. Like those of a baby.

I have a chance.

I can get away.

Fear gave way to action, and Deb rolled to the opposite side of the bed. She slid off the end, face-first, landing on her hands and knees. Then she peeked under the dust ruffle to see where Teddy was—

—and stared directly into his gray eye, only inches away.

Teddy's hand shot out, grabbing Deb by her hair before she had a chance to flinch. Deb made her fingers stiff and poked at his good eye, jabbing hard.

Teddy howled, releasing her, and Deb crawled like crazy around the bed.

Hall or closet? Hall or closet?

Closet. I can't get away without my legs.

Deb beelined for the closet, her bare knees beating a painful staccato against the hardwood floor. Teddy slid out from under the bed, pushing himself along on his belly, cutting off her route. Then he headed for her, efficiently dragging himself forward in a serpentine manner, like a fish swimming on land.

Deb spun around, scurrying past as his hand reached out. His fingers brushed her thigh, but he couldn't grab on. She frantically tried to figure out where to go next. The closet was blocked. So was the hallway. And Teddy was slithering toward her at a quick clip, a grotesque, hairy snake.

The bathroom? Go for the knife?

No. I'd be trapped in there.

So what the hell can I do?

My Cheetahs. He took them.

Maybe they're under the bed.

She grabbed the post, sliding under the bed, immediately seeing the displaced boards and the hole in the floor. Teddy was reaching for her again, fingers grazing her stump. She caught a quick glimpse of his wide, brown grin, and then Deb pulled herself, face-first, through the trapdoor.

Then she was falling—a sick, familiar feeling that was worse than any pain in the world. Her fear was short-lived, and she quickly banged her arms and head into a recessed floor, only a few feet lower than the one she'd just fallen from. Trying to catch her breath, Deb squinted at her surroundings.

I'm in a crawl space between the first and second levels.

A few yards away was a dim, flickering light.

A candle.

Deb felt around, finding one of her Cheetahs, then the other, and then Teddy was dropping through the trapdoor, landing next to Deb with a *huge* thump.

She swung her prosthetic like a scythe, hard as she could, trying to catch Teddy's face with the blade edge. The blow hit home, the leg vibrating in Deb's hands. Teddy howled, covering up his head. She followed up with two more strikes, trying to pound his face into hamburger. But the Cheetahs were lightweight, not much heft to them, causing only superficial injuries.

Tucking the legs under her arm, Deb crawled toward the candle. It was awkward, and she had to switch from crawling to a sideways shuffle. She sucked in dust and cobwebs, trying to avoid banging her head on various support posts.

Teddy began to chuckle. "Oooo, y'all gonna pay for hittin' me, little girl. Y'all gonna pay dearly."

Deb reached the candle and smacked her palm on top, snuffing out the flame. The blackness was stifling, and the enormity of her situation hit her like a sledgehammer.

I'm trapped in a dark crawl space with a psychotic freak.

She began to hyperventilate, unable to get enough oxygen. That led to wheezing.

I'm too loud. He'll find me.

Deb clamped a hand over her mouth, trying to silence herself. When she was sure she wouldn't pass out, she scooted away from her position, moving quietly. It was slow going. She didn't want to bump into anything or make the floor creak.

After she got some distance between herself and the candle, she began to put on her Cheetahs. Even though her hands were shaking, her years of competing in races paid off and Deb was able to get them on in less than thirty seconds.

Now I need to find an exit.

Deb raised her hands up over her head, feeling above her. She found a beam and began to follow it along its length, crawling as silently as she could.

"Where you goin', Debbie?"

Teddy was close. Very close. To her right. Deb paused, holding her breath, listening for movement.

She didn't hear anything.

He's either sitting still, moving toward me, or moving away from me.

So what's my best option?

Keep going. Don't wait for him to find me.

Deb softly blew out her breath, then continued her trek.

"I get it. Y'all wanna play a game." Teddy had gotten even closer. Almost near enough to reach out and touch.

"A little hide-'n'-seek." She moved faster, feeling a sob well up in her chest.

I can't cry. I need to stay quiet.

"I looooove games, girly girly."

She froze.

Oh, sweet Jesus, he's right in front of me.

"I know all sorts of games. 'Cept I never played none of 'em with a cripple before. You got no legs, just like me. I won't even gotta tie you up to make babies."

He got even nearer. She couldn't see him, but she could sense his mass, feel his body heat.

Can he sense me as well?

"Maybe Momma will even let us get married. She'll make us a big ole wedding cake."

He's so close.

Deb could actually feel his warm breath. It washed across her face like a foul summer wind blowing across a garbage dump. She tilted away, turning her head, crazy with fear that the floor would creak and he'd find her.

I can't see him. That means he can't see me. Stay calm.

"Will y'all marry me, Debbie girl?"

Teddy was close enough to kiss. He had to know she was there. Sweat rolled down Deb's forehead, stinging her eyes. She closed them, willing, *praying*, for Teddy to go away.

"Teddy and Debbie, sittin' in a tree. *K . . . . . I . . . . . .
S . . . . . S . . . . . I . . . . . N . . . . .*"

Deb lashed out before he could say *G*, making her
hand into a claw and raking her hundred-dollar manicure
across his face. He screeched, and she scampered past
him, crawling as fast as she could. She smacked her forehead into a joist, didn't stop to assess the damage, and
continued hurrying until she felt a cool breeze. Air flow
potentially meant an exit. Deb paused, trying to sense its
direction, and adjusted her course.

"The wedding is off, bitch!"

He was right behind her again. Deb plowed ahead,
reaching a wall. She tried to go left, then right. Each way
was blocked off.

Dead end. I'm dead. I . . .

Then her hand touched something solid and familiar.

A ladder rung. This is a ladder.

Ladders were Deb's nemesis, and a large part of the
reason she never tried to mountain climb again. If she
couldn't take ten vertical steps, how was she supposed to
scale a sheer cliff face?

Previous ladder experiences—even with small step
ladders—tended to end badly. And out of all her prosthetics, the Cheetahs were the most ill-suited for ladders.
The backward curve meant she had to push her legs out
behind her to take a step, which was awkward and threw
off her balance.

"Gotcha!"

Teddy grabbed her around the thigh. His grip was iron,
and his fingers palpated her quadriceps, stroking inti-
mately.

Deb screamed, bringing her arm forward, then jamming her elbow back. It connected with his face.

Teddy grunted, releasing his grip. Deb kicked out backward, felt her Cheetah bounce off him. He knocked her prosthetic aside, so hard it almost came off.

He's too fast. Too strong. There's no place to escape.

I need to try the ladder.

Using only her upper body, Deb lifted herself up the first four steps. The darkness was absolute, and she had to work by feel. Grabbing a rung with both hands, she did a chin-up. Then, holding the rung with one arm, she stretched up her other arm for the next rung.

Pull.

Reach.

Grab.

Pull.

Reach.

Grab.

Once she got the rhythm, she ascended quickly. And she no longer heard Teddy behind her. Maybe he—

He's got my leg!

Deb pulled, her arms shaking, but she didn't move an inch.

He's going to drag me down. How long can I hold on for?

Deb hooked her elbow over the rung, waiting for him to tug.

Teddy didn't tug.

Why isn't he pulling?

Deb almost laughed hysterically when she figured it out.

It's not Teddy. My Cheetah is caught on the rung.

The curve of the prosthetics acted like a hook, and it had apparently snagged onto the ladder. Deb lowered herself down a few inches, arched her back, and freed her leg.

But now her adrenaline had run out, and her arms were shaking from the strain. Going up any farther was impossible. She needed to get a foothold, rest for a moment, or else she'd lose her grip.

Deb prodded around with the tips of her Cheetahs, trying to feel for a rung. Her leg found purchase. She tested it, easing herself down. It bore her weight. She stood there on one leg in the darkness, getting her strength back, straining to hear any sound of Teddy.

Where is he?

Maybe he can't climb ladders. Maybe he isn't strong enough.

Maybe he—

Deb almost fell when her foothold moved.

Oh fuck.

I'm standing on him.

She scrambled to get a better grip on the rungs, and then began to ascend again, her tired muscles be damned. Fear gave her speed and strength, and after seven more rungs she reached up for the next and met with a ceiling.

A dead end?

Can't be. Why have a ladder that takes you nowhere?

Holding on with one hand, her chin resting on the top rung, she pushed up with her free palm.

The ceiling moved, because it wasn't a ceiling at all. It was another secret entrance.

Deb pushed it aside, then chinned-up into the open space. There was a thin strip of light at face level, and Deb realized she was looking under a door. She hoisted herself up, pulling herself into this new room. Then she moved the board back and stood on top of it, her head brushing against something.

Coat hangers. I'm in a closet.

Then the door flew open, and Deb was hit in the face so hard it knocked her down.

Felix stared out the rear window of the police cruiser. A tow truck hauling a Corvette passed them going in the opposite direction. It was the only other vehicle he'd seen in the last thirty minutes.

"Where are you taking us?" Cam asked the sheriff.

He'd asked that same question at least a dozen times. The sheriff had yet to answer.

Felix wondered what was happening. Was this going to be some sort of backwoods justice? Take them deep into the woods and beat the shit out of them?

No. The sheriff would have done it already. Why drive for this long? There were plenty of woods around here where no one would hear the screams.

So what does he want?

Felix's mind switched back to Maria. His brief elation that she was still alive had turned into a deep-rooted, sick feeling.

They're raping and bleeding her. They've been doing this for a whole year.

The enormity of the horror she had endured made Felix want to scream.

I have to save her. I have to. I can't let them do this to her for one more day.

But alongside the outrage and the pain, Felix felt a twinge of something shameful. Something he had a hard time facing.

Is she even Maria anymore?

He couldn't shake the image of her, gaunt and gibbering, her mind completely fried because of her ordeal.

What if, when I finally find her, she's a vegetable? What if she's so traumatized she can no longer take care of herself?

Felix clenched his jaw.

Then I learn to change diapers.

I love her. I'm going to save her. Both her body and her mind.

But Felix didn't see how he was going to save anybody, handcuffed in a squad car, being taken someplace other than the police station.

He glanced at Cam. The younger man didn't seem scared. If anything, he seemed hyper.

Not for the first time, Felix questioned whether bringing Cam along was the right decision. On one hand, Cam loved Maria just as much as he did. To leave him languish unjustly in a psychiatric institution was wrong, especially when Felix needed help looking for Cam's sister.

On the other hand, Cam had been in the institution for a reason.

For 95 percent of the time, Cam seemed entirely normal. But every so often Felix would catch him talking to himself and saying some pretty bizarre shit. And several times over the last few months, Cam seemed to zone out completely, even when Felix was yelling in his face.

Then again, if I had his history, maybe I'd zone out, too.

Still, the enthusiasm he showed while breaking John's fingers was definitely not normal. Willingly hurting another human being—even if that person was a kidnapper and a rapist—was really dark stuff.

"We'll be okay," Felix said, more to reassure himself than Cam.

"I don't think so," Cam said. "I think he's taking us somewhere to kill us." The matter-of-fact way Cam said it was chilling.

"He's a police officer. He won't do that."

"He didn't call it in," Cam said. "Didn't report back."

"It's a small town. There's no one to report to."

Cam shook his head. "He's not the only cop in the county. There are others. Murder is still a big deal. But he didn't call anyone. Base. The coroner. Paramedics. That means he's going to get rid of us."

Felix felt himself get very cold. He was mentally and physically a wreck, hurting in a dozen places, his mind alternately torturing and tantalizing him with thoughts of Maria. To think that he was going to die soon was almost too much to handle.

"Don't worry," Cam said. "It's not so bad."

Felix let out a half-insane chuckle. "What's not so bad?"

"Dying," Cam said.

Cam would know.

The police cruiser began to slow down. Felix looked around. Nothing but woods and darkness. A lump formed in his throat.

The lump got even bigger when the cruiser pulled onto the shoulder, into a copse of trees.

"Sheriff," Felix said. "Please. Don't do this."

"Son, I can't begin to describe what a pain in the rear you've been these last few months. Botherin' the locals. Stickin' your nose where it don't belong. All for one little woman." The sheriff stared in the rearview mirror, looking at Felix. "There are other fish in the sea, boy. Didn't your mama ever tell you that?"

"She's alive?"

"Hell, course she's alive. I saw 'er just a few weeks ago. Got my transfusion and dipped my wick in 'er honey-pot. I tell you, she's one sorry piece of tail. Does nothing but lay there and cry. I don't see why you're so damn anxious to get 'er back."

Rage replaced fear. Felix tried to get at the sheriff by ramming his head through the Plexiglas partition between the front and back seats. The only damage he caused was to himself, opening up the cut on his head.

"Careful there, son. Y'all oughta save your strength. Fine-looking young buck like yourself. I don't personally care for none of that sodomite behavior, but to some of my brothers a hole is a hole is a hole. You keep acting so impetuous, you won't last a week with my kin."

Felix sank back in his seat. Of the countless nightmare scenarios he'd dreamed up to explain Maria's disappearance, none were this bad.

The car hit a hump, bouncing Felix and Cam. If only Cam had been on his right side, maybe he could have reached Felix's handcuff keys in his jeans pocket. But Cam was on the left—the wrong side—and he wouldn't be able to dig them out, not with the sheriff eyeballing them every few seconds. And Felix had been stretching since the moment he got into the car, and his hands hadn't even come close.

Not that it mattered. Even if the cuffs were off, the sheriff was still armed. Assuming he and Cam could somehow get out of the cruiser, they wouldn't get far.

The police car stopped. Felix's brain popped and sizzled, trying to figure some way out of this mess. He glanced at Cam. Incredibly, the kid appeared peaceful, like he was going for a ride in the country.

What the hell is wrong with him?

"We're here, fellas. Don't give me no trouble. I get angry, I start breakin' things on y'all. You hear?"

The sheriff got out of the car, gun in hand, and opened the door. Felix got out first, staring into woods so dark he felt like he was being swallowed. There was nothing around, far as he could see. When Cam exited the vehicle, the sheriff took out a flashlight and marched them forward.

Out of nowhere, a gigantic house appeared. Made of logs, surround by tall trees on all sides. Not a single light was on.

Is this the Rushmore Inn?

"The forest rangers don't even know this place exists," the sheriff said. "Got some trees on the roof, so it can't be seen flyin' overhead. Every so often, hunter'll stumble on it. We take care of 'em."

He marched them inside the heavy front door, closed it behind him, and yelled, "Ma! I'm home!"

Felix looked around the room, awed by the decor. U.S. Presidents were everywhere. He was so floored by how odd it was that he almost failed to notice the large old woman lumbering toward them.

"Good evening. I'm Eleanor Roosevelt. Welcome, gentlemen, to the Rushmore Inn." She fussed with her hair, held in place by a white hairnet, then turned to the sheriff. "Dwight? Why didn't you tell me you were bringing guests?"

"Sorry, Ma. This was last-minute." Dwight took off his cowboy hat and held it by the brim, looking solemn. "I'm afraid I got some bad news. These fellas here killed John."

Eleanor blinked her bulbous eyes. "John? My John?"

"'Fraid so. These are the ones I told you about a while ago. The ones looking for the girl. They shot John in the head. Like a dog, Ma. Nuthin' I could do."

"Better than he deserved," Cam said. "You people are scum."

Sheriff Dwight hit Cam in the stomach, dropping him to his knees.

"Mind my momma, boy."

Eleanor placed a hand on her chest. She moaned, a low, keening sound that grew higher and higher in pitch, like a foghorn.

"There, there, Ma." The sheriff patted her shoulder.

Eleanor stopped howling long enough to pull a hand-kerchief out of her robe pocket. She dabbed her eyes, but as far as Felix could tell they were already dry.

"Get me some water to calm my nerves, Dwight. There's a pitcher on the table."

Dwight nodded, heading for the pitcher. Felix flexed his legs.

If he turns his back on me, I'll run at the old woman and . . .

The next thing he knew, Felix was on his knees, teeth clenched in agony. It felt like a pickax hit him in the stomach. He stared up at Eleanor, who was now holding a stick she must have had hidden in her robe.

She touched the stick to Felix's arm, and it hurt worse than if she'd branded it with a hot iron.

It's a cattle prod. But Felix was much more interested in the hand that held it. On Eleanor's pinky.

A yellow diamond ring. Pear shaped.

Maria's engagement ring.

She's here! Maria is here!

"Shame on you," Eleanor said. "Shame on both of

you. John was a good boy. A special boy. He wasn't the brightest bulb in the chandelier, but he loved his momma, and I had big plans for him."

"He was a rapist and a murderer," Cam said.

Eleanor juiced him with the prod, and Cam cried out.

"Not another word out of you, boy. Dwight! Where's my water?"

"Here it is, Ma."

The sheriff handed her a glass of rust-colored liquid, and she drank the whole thing, smacking her lips at the end.

"Not much in the taste department, but wonderful for the nerves. Get my blood kit, Dwight."

"Got it already, Ma."

"Test 'em."

The sheriff knelt down, poking Felix in the hip with something that stung. He did the same thing to Cam. Then he opened up a leather satchel and pulled out some vials of fluid.

He just took our blood samples. He's going to test if we . . .

Jesus, who's that?

A giant had come down the stairs. A giant with a gaping split in his face. He walked up to them and stared at Felix, flicking his tongue out through the hole in his nasal cavity.

"Did you take care of the reporter, Harry?" Eleanor asked.

The giant nodded.

"Where is he?"

"Immmby av imm."

"Jimmy has him?"

He nodded again.

"Good boy. You done your momma proud. Have you heard from Teddy yet?"

Harry shook his head. Eleanor sighed. "He's probably fooling around again. Teddy is a lot like your father. That man was a rascal, never satisfied. Sometimes, your father would mount me four, five times a day." Eleanor fanned her face with her palm.

The sheriff walked over, holding two test tubes.

"The older one, no," he said. "But the younger one's a match."

Eleanor pointed at Cam. "Harry, show that one to his new room."

"Shouldn't he take them both down, Ma?" The sheriff crouched down on his haunches, staring at Felix. "I thought my kin could have a bit of fun with this one."

"There ain't any place for him, Dwight. We're over-booked as it is. Past capacity."

"We could double up."

Eleanor shook her head. "Not safe. When the guests are allowed to mingle, they get ideas about escapin'."

The sheriff grinned, and it was an ugly thing. Felix hadn't noticed before that he had the tiny, rounded teeth of a child.

"I'll cut out his tongue," the sheriff said. "He won't be minglin' with nobody."

Eleanor waggled a finger. "Don't you dare get any blood on my Richard Nixon rug."

"So what do we do with him? Should I just take him out back, put one in the back of his head?"

The sheriff made his hand into a gun and pointed his index finger at Felix.

"No. Give him to Ronald. He ain't been fed proper in a while."

"Yes, Ma."

The sheriff hooked a hand under Felix's armpit, pulling him to his feet.

"And when you're finished up, Dwight, help Grover up in the Grant Bedroom. The old woman in there is the only one left."

The sheriff made a pouty face. "Aw, c'mon, Ma. I gotta get back to the office. I'm working tonight. Can't Ulysses do it?"

"Ulysses is towing a guest's car."

"How about Millard or George?"

"Millard is cleaning up a mess in the transfusion room. One of our permanent guests is holed up in there. She's with a dog that bit George, pretty bad. Millard's going to take care of it, soon as he gets dressed."

Permanent guests?

"You're talking about Maria," Felix said.

Eleanor cocked her head at Felix, then zapped him with the prod. Felix fell onto his knees again.

"I wasn't speaking to you," Eleanor said. "But yes, I was talking about Maria. Big disappointment, that one. I had hopes for grandchildren, but the girl is barren as the Sahara Desert. But don't you get your hopes up, young man. Millard is going to put the poor girl out of my misery. He's very good at that. And it's no loss for us. We have enough new blood to last us for the year."

"You . . . monster," Felix said, bracing himself for another jolt.

But Eleanor didn't prod him again. She just smiled.

"Sometimes, people in power have to do distasteful things for the greater good. Throughout our nation's history, our Presidents have had to do many things that could be considered unsavory. And before them, the kings that passed on their sacred bloodline often made sacrifices for the greater good. Being born to rule is a huge responsibility, and royalty has no need for morality."

Then Eleanor stuck the cattle prod on Felix's chest, pressing him to the floor, holding him there until his entire world was reduced to a blazing pinpoint of pain.

"Get him off my rug and feed him to Ronald," Eleanor said. "Then go help Grover with the old woman."

The sheriff scratched his head. "Shit, Ma, it's just an old lady. Grover can handle—"

Eleanor's hand shot out, fast as a rattlesnake, slapping Sheriff Dwight across the face.

"Dwight D. Eisenhower Roosevelt, don't you swear in this house."

The sheriff looked at his shoes. "Sorry, Ma."

"Besides, you should never underestimate women of later years. They're a lot stronger than you think."

"Yes, Ma." The sheriff hauled Felix to his feet once again. "This is the one that did John. You want to give him a horsewhippin'? I can fetch it for you."

"It's been a frightfully busy day, Dwight. I'm too gosh darn tired to horsewhip anyone right now. Besides, Ronald will deliver a right proper punishment without me."

The sheriff nodded. "As you wish, Ma. And remind me before I go I got somethin' for you in the car."

Eleanor beamed. "Is it the Reagan-Bush '88 banner I've been asking for?"

"It sure is. Found one on Craigslist. Practically brand-new."

She touched the sheriff's red cheek. "Y'all are such a dear boy. When you get off work tonight, come knock on Momma's door. She'll show you how grateful she is."

Eleanor ran her liver-colored tongue over her lower lip.

Felix winced. *I didn't think this could get any more repugnant, and it just did.*

The sheriff set his cowboy hat on a cabinet, opened a drawer, and took out a mining hat. He perched that on his head, turned on the light.

"Move it, boy. Lest I horsewhip you myself."

He prodded Felix out the front door, walking him into the woods. After being inside the house, the forest seemed even darker. Felix eyed the tree line, wondering how far he'd get if he made a run for it.

Best-case scenario, I escape, return, and save Maria and Cam.

Worst case, I get shot. Which sounds preferable to being eaten by Ronald, whoever that is.

Then Felix felt the sheriff grab the chain linking his wrists. Escape was no longer an option.

"Straight ahead. Keep a-moving."

He marched Felix through the trees. They walked for several minutes, not following any particular path Felix could make out. The sheriff's headlamp constantly scanned the foliage in all directions. Like he was afraid of something sneaking up on him. And maybe he was.

They eventually reached an open clearing. The sheriff's light focused on . . .

A cave. With a metal pole sticking into the ground in front of the entrance.

And scattered around the pole . . .

"Jesus Christ," Felix said.

There were bones. Human bones. Dozens and dozens of them, littered about like the aftermath of a plane crash. Skulls and rib cages and pelvises. Femurs and spines. Some dark with age. Some still with strips of bloody flesh clinging to them.

"Shh," the sheriff whispered. "If Ronald is sleeping, you don't wanna wake him up."

The sheriff tapped Felix on the back of the head with his gun, trying to get him to move forward. Felix didn't budge.

"Move it, boy."

"No fucking way."

Then Felix felt the sheriff's hand on his, grabbing three of his mangled fingers.

Oh please, no . . .

Felix heard the bones break before he felt them.

Snap snap snap.

Then the pain hit, making everything Felix had experienced that night pale by comparison.

He opened his mouth to scream, and just as it was leaving his throat the sheriff forced something into his mouth.

A ball gag.

"That's what you did to my brother, John," the sheriff said. "How's it feel, boy? How's it feel to break a man's fingers when he can't fight back?" He grabbed Felix's right hand and repeated the process.

Christ, no . . .

Snap snap snap.

Felix's stomach was empty, but he dry-heaved anyway, bile coming up through his nose.

Using Felix's fingers like a steering wheel, the sheriff guided Felix to the metal pole. He quickly uncuffed his left hand, made Felix hug the pole, and cuffed him again.

"Have fun with Ronald, you sonofabitch."

The sheriff reared back and punched Felix in the gut. Felix dropped to his knees, sobbing, watching as the sheriff scurried off, leaving him alone in the darkness.

Then Felix maneuvered around to face the cave. Though the full moon was shining through the break in the canopy, Felix's eyes hadn't fully adjusted to the dark, and he couldn't see anything. But he could smell it. A rank, foul odor.

Spoiled meat and blood and feces and musk.

The smell of a predator.

The handcuff keys were still in Felix's pocket. And with his hands now cuffed in front of him, they were within his reach.

Felix brought his right hand in front of his face. He didn't want to look at it, but he had to assess the damage. Felix squinted in the darkness, saw his ring finger, middle finger, and index finger, all bent backward at forty-five-degree angles. The bloody bandages he'd put on earlier had begun to drip. Felix tried to move his hand, and a ripple of agony coursed through him, making him want to die to end the pain.

I'll never be able to get those keys out of my pocket.

Then Felix looked up and saw the dim silhouette of something coming out of the cave.

When Kelly opened her eyes, she was lying on dirt.

Am I outside? What's going on?

It all rushed back to her in a flood of images. Going into the closet. Chasing JD. Talking to Alice.

No, not Alice. Alice was really a crazy, freaky man named Grover. He caught me because my finger was . . .

Then the pain hit. Kelly stared at her index finger, saw an ugly, serrated cut around the knuckle. She'd seen an injury like that once before. Back home, one of her classmate was helping his father set fox traps, and one snapped down on him. Kelly figured when she stuck her finger in the peephole, Grover had put a fox trap on it to hold her there.

She bent the digit, wincing, feeling the tears well up but biting them back.

I'll cry later. I need to figure out what's going on.

She tore her eyes away from the injury and studied her surroundings.

Even though Kelly was on dirt, she wasn't outside. She was in some kind of tiny, dark room. The walls were concrete. The door was metal. The only furnishings were a bucket and a water pump.

"Mom! Grandma!"

Her voice echoed around in the enclosed space. She got up and went to the door.

Locked.

"Mom!" Kelly yelled with all of her lung power.

"Who's there?" someone said back. A man. Not far away.

"Help me! I'm locked in here!"

Kelly put her ear to the door.

"I'm locked in, too," the man answered. He didn't sound like he was standing outside. More like he was in a room to the left. She walked over to the wall and cupped her hands together, putting them against her mouth as if she was about to shout. Then she pressed her hands to the wall and said, "Can you hear me?"

Kelly held her ear against the cold concrete and waited for a response.

"Yeah, I can hear you." The man's voice was quiet, but clear.

"Where are we?" she asked.

"We're under the Rushmore Inn, being held in slave cells."

"What do they want with us?"

"They're sick. They want to use our blood for transfusions. And . . ."

Kelly didn't like the way his voice trailed off, like he was about to tell her something and then changed his mind.

"And what?"

"What's your name?"

"I'm Kelly. You?"

"Cam. I came here with my sister's fiancé, Felix. We've been looking for her for a year. We think she's here."

A year? They've been looking for a year?

Kelly shook her head.

No way. I couldn't last a year here.

"Have you seen my mom or grandmother?" she asked, her voice getting higher as panic set in. "Letti and Florence Pillsbury?"

"I haven't seen anyone. Just the guy who brought me down here. Ugly bastard with a split in his face. They need our blood because theirs is bad, or something like that."

Kelly was horrified. "Our blood?"

"I'm O negative. So is my sister. It's pretty rare."

Kelly closed her eyes. She was O negative, too. So were Mom and Grandma.

"What else do they want us for?" she asked.

Cam didn't answer.

"Cam, please, if you know something, tell me. I can handle it."

"They . . . they kidnap women to make babies."

Kelly knew she had to be brave. Mom told her that the

best way to overcome bad situations was to fight the fear and keep a clear head. Emotions weren't useful.

But Kelly felt the tears coming on anyway.

"Kelly? You okay?"

"I'm only twelve years old!" Kelly wailed.

"Jesus. Look, it will all be okay. We'll get out of this. I promise."

"How? What if they've already got Mom and Grandma? No one knows we're here."

"I've been in bad situations before, Kelly. We'll make it."

Kelly lost herself to tears, crying so hard her nose began to run. All the while she heard Cam saying, *"It's okay. It'll be okay."* Over and over again.

She thought of Mom, who'd given the same lecture to Kelly since she was four years old and skinned her knee.

"Be strong. You won't help your situation by crying. Focus on what you need to do to fix it."

Mom was right. I can cry about the pain. Or I can deal with it.

Kelly blew her nose on her sleeve, then asked Cam, "What situations?"

"What?"

"You said you've been in bad situations before."

"It's . . . tough to talk about."

Kelly pressed her ear to the wall. "Please, Cam. I feel like I'm going to crack up. Tell me something hopeful."

Cam didn't answer.

"Please."

"It happened when I was a kid. I was playing in an abandoned house up the street, with my best friend. A man, a drifter, he grabbed us. I was locked in a closet. My friend . . . the man hurt him. Bad. For a long time. It

was so bad, he died. I heard everything. But I managed to get away. I escaped back then, Kelly. I'll escape again. We both will."

"That's . . . awful, Cam."

"Nietzsche said what doesn't kill us makes us stronger. I'm strong, Kelly. And I bet you are, too. We're going to get out of this."

"Be quiet!"

It was a new voice. A woman. Coming from the opposite wall.

"Who's there?" Kelly yelled.

"Shut up!" the woman said. *"We aren't allowed to talk! They do things to us when we talk!"*

"Who are you?" Kelly asked. "What's your name?"

There was a clanging noise, followed by the woman saying, *"No! I wasn't talking! I was telling them not to talk! Please don't hurt me! I'm carrying a baby!"*

It was followed by a scream so raw, so horrifying, that it was the single most frightening thing Kelly had ever heard in her life.

What could make someone scream like that?

Kelly hugged her knees and watched the door. Her nose was running again, but she didn't dare sniffle. She wasn't going to make even the slightest sound.

Please, don't come in.

Please go away.

Please please please go away . . .

When Mal opened his eyes, he was lying naked on a cold, stainless steel table. He recognized the type from his cop days. It was sturdy, able to hold up to five hundred pounds, and had gutters along the edges to catch bodily fluids.

A mortician's table.

He tried to sit up, but there was a strap around his neck. His wrists and ankles were similarly bound, heavy leather and tight buckles.

Mal remembered the shower, the bloody shampoo, then someone grabbing him.

What the hell is going on?

He looked around the room. It was small, but brightly lit, with a large fluorescent lamp overhead. Concrete walls. Two doors. A TV and VCR, resting unevenly on a cardboard box. They were plugged into an extension cord that ran along the dirt floor under the closest door.

Next to the table was a cart, piled high with medical instruments, none of which looked clean. Knives. Saws. Scalpels. Drill bits. Clamps. Needles. And a bowl of white powder.

"The time is ten fifty-two p.m. We'll begin the operation shortly."

Mal followed the voice, saw a man standing at the foot of the table.

It's an honest-to-Christ hunchback.

The hunchback wore a filthy white lab coat, his gnarled spine protruding up through a split in the back. The man also had clubbed feet, and one leg was several inches longer than the other, as judged by the high, clunky soles of his orthopedic shoes. His skull was bulbous, misshapen, hairless, and his cheekbones were uneven.

"What's going on?" Mal said. "Who are you?"

The hunchback raised a camcorder to his chest, pointing it at Mal. He smiled, revealing several missing teeth.

"I'm Jimmy, your surgeon. It appears the patient is awake. Let's make sure."

Jimmy raised a scalpel in his free hand, and before Mal could protest, the hunchback poked him hard in the thigh. The pain was instant and awful.

"Fuck! What the fuck are you doing?!"

"Indeed, the patient is awake and responsive to stimulus."

Jimmy pulled the scalpel free.

"Let me up, you crazy fucker!"

Jimmy set down the camcorder between Mal's legs, then hobbled over to the television. It was an old CRT model with a pull knob for an *on* switch. Snow appeared on the screen, with the accompanying static hiss.

"I understand your concerns," Jimmy said. "Surgery can be a traumatic experience. This tape should answer some of your questions."

Jimmy pressed *play* on the VCR. After a few seconds of white noise and vertical flipping, an image came on.

It showed a woman, strapped to the very same table Mal was lying on.

Jimmy was using a hacksaw to cut off her leg.

Though the sound was turned low, the woman's screaming stabbed Mal in the ears.

The scene cut to a different angle of a different person. An older man. He was begging, beating his bound fists on the table, while Jimmy had a hand inside his stomach cavity.

Next came a close-up of a woman's breast, being filleted off as she thrashed.

"This next one is my favorite," Jimmy said.

On the screen, he was using a spoon to pluck out a man's eyeball.

"Did you hear the *pop* sound when it came out? I can rewind it if you didn't."

Mal squeezed his own eyes closed.

This isn't happening. This can't be happening.

"It's not over yet!" Jimmy whined. He stuck Mal with the scalpel again.

"Keep watching!"

Mal forced his eyes open, one nightmarish image after another searing itself onto his brain. Amputations. Organ removals. Procedures that weren't even remotely medical, like the one involving a power sander.

"Dermabrasion," Jimmy said. "It removes acne."

"You're insane," Mal said. "You're fucking insane."

Jimmy switched off the TV, then stared over Mal's head.

"You have a potty mouth, Mr. Deiter."

Mal looked up, saw Eleanor had walked into the room. She was wearing a robe and a hairnet, a frown creasing her ugly face.

"Eleanor, what the hell—"

Eleanor clamped a hand over his mouth. "Any more foul language and I'll have Jimmy sew your lips together. Understand?"

Mal saw she was serious, and he nodded. Eleanor let her eyes, and her hand, trail down his naked body.

"I see that you keep in shape," she said, drawing a circle around his belly button with her finger. "That's good." Then her hand brushed over his penis, and the sensation was almost as awful as being stabbed with the scalpel.

Mal swallowed, biting back fear. "If you want money . . ."

"We have all the money we need, Mr. Deiter. But thank you for offering."

"Applying styptic to control bleeding," Jimmy said. Mal watched him take a pinch of white powder and press it into his thigh wounds.

He uttered, "Son of a . . ." but managed to stop himself before *bitch* came out.

"Self-control," Eleanor said, tying a medical face mask across her mouth and nose. "I admire that in a man."

"What do you want?" Mal said through gritted teeth.

"What I want, Mr. Deiter, is the same thing I've wanted for forty years, from the first time I felt my eldest child George kick inside my womb." She leaned in closer. "I want one of my sons to become President of the United States."

Mal realized this wasn't some sort of kidnapping scheme or an attempt to frighten him. Eleanor wasn't just eccentric. She was truly out of her góddamn mind.

"All forty-three of our Presidents carry the royal bloodline." Eleanor said. "My family has the very same bloodline, Mr. Deiter. We're Roosevelts. And one day, another Roosevelt will sit in the Oval Office."

Mal pulled at his straps, hard as he could. They didn't give an inch.

"Did you know the term *blue blood* was applied to nobility because those of royal descent tended to have fairer skin, which allowed blue veins to show through?" Eleanor asked. "While having royal blood makes someone like me genetically superior to someone like you, such purity does come with its particular challenges. Anemia and hemophilia are two of them. Phocomelia. Amelia. Porphyria. Achromia. Scoliosis. Alopecia. Thrombocytopenia."

Insanity, Mal mentally added.

"These have plagued royal families for generations.

My sons bear these burdens heroically, as nobility should. But they require regular transfusions in order to remain healthy. Y'all can't buy blood at the corner market, Mr. Deiter. Especially not the rare type we need. When one of my boys becomes President, we'll no doubt have unlimited access to the nation's blood banks. In the meantime, the only way for me to get a regular supply of fresh blood is to acquire it myself."

"You want my blood," Mal stated.

"Goodness no, Mr. Deiter. Your lady friend, Deborah, has the type we require. Yours is no good to us. But you can still be useful. My son Jimmy doesn't have any political aspirations, unfortunately. But he does hope to one day become a doctor. That's a noble calling in itself. And for that, he needs a lot of practice."

Jimmy stuck his face next to Mal's. The whites of his eyes were bloodshot.

"Today I'm going to be practicing amputation. I'm gonna start with your left hand."

For the first time in his adult life, Mal felt like whimpering. He managed to get out, "Please, don't."

"You're a strong man, Mr. Deiter," Eleanor said. "Jimmy's patients don't normally last for more than four or five operations. The record is nine. I bet a healthy young specimen such as you can beat that record."

Jimmy picked up the bone saw from the cart of instruments. "I'm sorry, but we don't have any anesthetic."

Jimmy pulled the face mask up over his nose. Then he put something in his ears. Eleanor did the same.

Earplugs. To block out my screaming.

"Please," Mal said, even though he wasn't heard. "Please don't."

"Don't forget your gloves, Jimmy!" Eleanor yelled. "We don't want you accidentally cutting yourself!"

Jimmy nodded, putting on a pair of bloodstained oven mitts. Then he picked up a scalpel, barely able to grip it. Eleanor held the camcorder. "Please . . ."

The blade touched Mal's arm.

"Knock me out," Mal said. "For God's sake, knock me—"

Then the cutting began, and Mal didn't say anything else coherent.

When Letti opened her eyes, she heard a man screaming.

What's going on?

She looked around, saw she was in some sort of cell. Bare, concrete walls, like a basement. Dirt floor. Completely empty, except for a water pump and a filthy plastic bucket.

Letti sat up. "Kelly! Florence! Are you there!"

"Mom!"

"Kelly!"

Letti rushed to the metal door. Locked.

"Kelly! Are you okay?"

"Mom, we have to be quiet."

"Kelly, what's—"

"Please, Mom! Don't talk anymore! They hurt you if you talk!"

Her daughter sounded terrified. And rightfully so, if she was locked up like Letti was.

The man's screaming rose in pitch, until it became a single high note that Letti felt in her molars.

What are they doing to him?

"Kelly, hang in there, baby. I'm coming."

Letti took a step back from the door. It looked formidable, but it also looked old. Letti could squat lift over five hundred pounds, and she had no doubt she could squat double that with her daughter in danger. She reared back, letting the urgency of the situation take her, and drove her bare foot into the door.

It clanged, and she felt the reverberation all the way to her coccyx.

Letti kicked it again.

And again.

And again.

And again.

And again.

And again.

The door wasn't giving up, but neither was she. Letti took a few steps back, giving her leg a rest, getting ready to charge it with her shoulder.

Then the door swung open.

Standing there, in some kind of padded armor, was the biggest man Letti had ever seen. He was more than a foot taller than she was. Strands of long gray hair hung around his shoulders and poked through the grille of the football helmet he wore.

Letti lowered her shoulder and charged him, aiming at the giant's waist, grunting in satisfaction when she pushed him back several steps.

Just a bit more, and I'll be out of the cell. Then—

Letti felt a knife stick her between the shoulder blades.

She dropped onto her face, crying out in agony. Then the pain stopped, and she realized it wasn't a knife at all. The giant was pinning her down with something.

Letti craned her neck around. Saw the stick he held, blue electric sparks crackling at the tip.

A cattle prod.

"Youse a fighter," the man said. He had a voice like steak sizzling on a hot pan. "I likes fighters."

He juiced her again, and Letti clenched her teeth, refusing to cry out, refusing to let Kelly hear her pain.

Finally, mercifully, the current stopped. Letti could feel the burn mark on her spine. The giant bent down, resting his knee on her neck, forcing her face into the dirt.

"Now, y'all better be quiet," he said, "else I'll stick this prod someplace you won't like."

Letti was hurt, but more angry than scared.

"I'll kill you if you so much as touch my daughter . . ."

The giant laughed. "*Touch* your daughter? Little lady, I'm gonna use up both you and your daughter till there ain't nothin' left. Ole Millard is gonna show you things you never done dreamed of. And you both gonna be mommas to some a' my babies."

With his free hand, the man scooped up dirt and forced it between Letti's lips.

"I own y'all now," he said. "'N' I can do whatever I want with that which is my property. Now keep yer trap shut. I gotta go deal with somethin'."

Millard got off her neck and walked out, so confident in his superiority he showed Letti his back. He locked the door when he left.

Letti sat up, spitting out dirt, clenching and unclenching her fists.

"One more chance, asshole," she said to the empty cell. "Give me one more chance. You won't knock me down again."

* * *

When Maria opened her eyes, she was hugging the German shepherd, burying her face in his muzzle. For the first time in a year, she had a sliver of hope.

However, the hope was fading fast. The door was the same as the one in her cell: solid metal with a heavy lock. Even if she had all day and a sledgehammer, she wouldn't be able to get through it. Eleanor had once mentioned these underground rooms were once the slave quarters for a tobacco farm.

"Not a single slave ever escaped in the decades it operated. Those that tried were beaten, or punished with strappado."

No, rather than focus on escaping, Maria needed to prepare herself when they came back for her. And they had to come back, eventually. They needed the transfusion machine to survive.

The machine.

Without it, they'll die.

Maria let go of JD and stood up, staring at the infernal device. She unplugged it from the extension cord snaking under the door, then squatted down and grabbed the bottom. With a quick lift, she upended the device, grinning as the casing split open.

But she wasn't finished. She pulled off the case and tore into its innards, pulling out parts and wires. Picking up a piece of the housing, she used it as a club, smashing and smashing until every single part was broken. Then she turned her fury on the chair, the one they strapped her and countless others on to in order to bleed them. Maria broke that into bits as well, half crying and half laughing and entirely hysterical.

When she finished, and it lay in ruins around her, she collapsed, hugging her knees, grinning even as the tears streamed down her face.

JD came over, offered his paw.

She held him again, the act of petting an animal allowing her to calm down, to come back to reality.

Then she heard the door lock *snick* open.

JD pulled from her arms, launching himself at the man as the door opened. Maria crab-walked backward, looking for the cattle prod, hoping that the person at the door wasn't—

Millard.

He was the biggest, and meanest, of all Eleanor's children. At least seven feet tall, with broad shoulders and thick wrists. His hair was white, shoulder length, scraggly. And like the others, his eyes were bloodshot all the time, a symptom of one of his many conditions.

Millard went far beyond the casual sadism of George, Dwight, and Teddy, or the simpleminded brutishness of Harry, Grover, and Calvin. Millard was a psychotic animal. He enjoyed hurting things. He lived for it. So much so, that his brothers were all afraid of him. Maria had heard that Millard hunted deer with a knife, and then cut off their legs, one at a time, to see how far they could run. He was the only son Eleanor wouldn't sleep with.

Maria had scars from Millard. She'd only given him three transfusions, and each time he'd come up with new ways to inflict pain during the procedure. Thumbtacks and witch hazel. Matches. A cheese grater and a saltshaker. Nothing that would harm her seriously, but would hurt worse than anything in the world.

As Millard stomped into the room, JD threw himself

at the gigantic man, aiming for the cattle prod clenched in Millard's hand. But Millard seemed fatter than usual, and Maria quickly spotted why.

He's wearing the Ronald suit.

The Ronald suit was made of thick bands of foam. It was used when Millard was dealing with Ronald—no one else had the guts to. There was no way JD would be able to bite through the padding. Even Millard's head was protected, in a black football helmet with a metal grid faceplate, crude white skulls painted on each side.

Maria glanced at her cattle prod, knowing it would be ineffective.

I can't fight him. I have to run.

Millard lifted up his arm, and 120 pounds of dog hung from his padded wrist, refusing to let go. The giant punched the shepherd in the ribs, once, and again. But JD hung on like a champion.

Maria ran at them, holding the cattle prod in front of her like a fencing sword. She thrust it up high, connecting with Millard's faceplate.

Sparks flew. Millard yanked the prod from her but stumbled to the side, allowing an open path to the doorway.

"JD! Come!"

On command JD released the giant's arm. He shot through the door just as she was slamming it on Millard. Incredibly, the key was on a key ring and still in the lock—Millard must not have had any pockets in the Ronald suit. Maria turned the key, locking him in, and then backed away from the door.

It shook, but didn't open. Millard was trapped.

"Nice job, JD. JD?"

Maria looked around. The dog had taken off.

"JD!" she called. "Come!"

Frantic thoughts invaded her mind.

Did I leave him in there with Millard?

No. He got out. I know he got out.

So where is he?

"JD!"

Maria had never seen the hallways down here; they always put a hood on her when she was out of her cell. The corridor walls were stone and concrete, crumbling with age. The floors were dirt. Light came from bare bulbs, hanging from the ceiling by extension cords. The hallway itself was actually more like a tunnel, curving left and right with no logical direction.

"JD!" Maria yelled again. She knew she was due for a complete mental breakdown. A physical one as well—having that freak blood in her always made her woozy afterward. But she had to stay strong, had to keep going. Had to capitalize on the opportunity.

"JD!" she implored, begging the universe for the dog to respond.

"Who's calling for my dog?"

It was a woman's voice, coming from farther down the hall. Maria moved slowly, listening for noises and constantly checking behind her. When she rounded a bend, she saw JD, scratching away at a cell door.

"JD! Good boy!" She patted him on the head.

"Who's there?"

"I'm Maria," she told the woman in the cell. "Is JD your dog?"

"Yeah. Who are you?"

"I'm a prisoner here. Like you. Hold on, let me find the right key."

Maria fussed with Millard's key ring, finding the one for the cell on the third try. Upon opening the door, the dog rushed in, licking at the woman's legs.

She was tall, muscular. A bit dirty, but not a long-time guest.

"I owe your dog several steaks. He saved my—"

"Are those keys?"

Maria nodded. The woman pulled them from Maria's hands and rushed past.

"Hold on," Maria said, hurrying after her. "We need to talk."

"I need to find my daughter. She's locked up in one of these rooms."

"We'll find her," Maria said. "But you need to know what we're dealing with here."

"I know what we're dealing with. Some real sicko freaks. Kelly! Can you hear me?"

"Mom!"

Kelly's mother rushed to the next cell door, fussing with the lock.

"Which key is it? Which goddamn key?"

Maria put a hand on the woman's shoulder. "Lady, you need to calm down a bit."

"Calm down? Do you know what these people have done to us?"

Maria rested her hand on the keys. "Look at me. I've been here a year. I know what these people can do. And if you don't listen to me, we aren't going to get out of here alive."

The woman looked like she was about ready to throw a punch, and Maria wondered if she just should get the hell out of there, leave them behind.

But the punch didn't come. Instead, the woman managed to calm herself down. "I'm Letti. Thank you for opening my door. Can you help me with this one?"

Maria nodded, finding the right key. When she unlocked it, there was an intense mother-daughter-dog reunion. Maria was touched. She hadn't seen a normal person since she'd been abducted, and certainly hadn't felt love like she was currently witnessing. But they needed to get going. There were other prisoners. And Eleanor had guns, and more psycho children.

A lot more.

"We need to go," she said.

Letti seemed reluctant to break the embrace with her daughter, but she did so. "Kelly, this is Maria. She just saved our asses."

"After JD saved mine," Maria said.

Kelly offered Maria her hand. She looked a lot like her mother.

"There are others down here," Kelly said. "A pregnant woman, and a boy named Cam. I think he's your brother."

Maria's breath caught. "Did . . . did you say *Cam*?" Without waiting for an answer, Maria cupped her hands to her mouth and yelled, "Cam!"

"Maria!"

Sprinting across the hall, Maria unlocked the next cell door she came to. Seeing Cam—her brother, Cam—standing there with a lopsided grin on his face, turned her tear ducts into faucets.

When she hugged him, it was so tight he yelped. Maria threatened to fall apart, the sensation was so overwhelming. For a moment this living nightmare faded away, replaced by happy childhood memories of safety, security, and love.

"We found you," Cam said. "Me and Felix. We've been looking all year."

Maria held Cam at arm's length, her eyes getting wide. "Felix? He's here?"

"They took him to see a guy named Ronald."

Ronald? Oh no . . .

"Ronald's not a guy," Maria said. "He's a—"

"Someone help me!"

The female voice came from one cell over. Maria reluctantly let go of Cam and hurried to the next door. The cell's occupant was older, late thirties, dressed in a tattered housedress. Her hair was long, and just as matted as Maria guessed her own hair to be. The bump on her belly was large enough for her to be in her last trimester.

"Oh, thank God," the woman said, falling to her knees and weeping. "I've been praying for so long to get rescued."

But Maria wasn't paying attention. She was thinking of Felix, with Ronald.

I need to get out of here. I need to help him.

"What's your name?" Letti asked the woman.

"Sue Corall."

"Are you alone, Sue? Are there other people with you?"

"My husband, Larry."

"Is your husband here?"

Sue didn't answer, but her eyes glazed over.

"Sue?"

"I . . . I think he's in the next cell. Jimmy . . . the hunchback . . . he . . . he keeps . . ."

Letti took the keys from Maria, who was staring at the cell door across the hallway.

I know that one. That's my cell.

I'll die before I'll let them put me in there again.

"Oh . . . Christ." Letti turned away from the door she just opened. Sue came waddling over, but Letti grabbed her shoulders, refusing to let her see.

"He's my husband!" Sue implored.

"Sue . . . you really don't . . ."

"Let me go!"

Letti allowed the woman to pass, and Maria made the mistake of following her into the room. The odor hit her first; feces and urine and rot.

But seeing was worse than smelling.

"Whoa," Cam said.

Sue's husband was lying on the dirt floor.

At least, what was left of him was.

The man was missing one leg, his left hand, half of his right arm, an ear and an eye. Badly stitched wounds on his torso spoke of other missing parts. His shoulders were also dislocated, cocked out at odd angles.

Strappado. This poor bastard.

Sue shrieked, falling on her knees next to her husband, cradling his head. He moaned at the tender action.

His teeth are gone, too.

Larry said something. Even without teeth, Maria got the gist of it.

"Kill . . . me. Please . . . kill . . . me."

"Help him," Sue cried. "Someone help him."

Maria felt terrible for both of them, but she didn't see how they'd be able to get him out of there. Larry was in too much pain to even turn his head. Besides, Maria had to find Felix, and fast. It could already be too late.

"He wants to die." Everyone looked at Cam, who had come into the room.

He had an oddly serene look on his face.

Sue shook her head. "No. No no no."

"Please . . . kill . . . me."

"We can get you help," Sue implored. "We can get out of here, and get you help. Get you doctors." Sue patted her belly. "This is your baby, Larry. *Yours.* They think it's theirs, but I was pregnant when we came here."

"I . . . want . . . to . . . die. Please . . ."

Sue clenched her fists and beat them against her thighs, moaning.

Cam knelt next to Sue. "You love your husband."

Sue could barely speak through her sobbing. "More . . . more than anything."

"Then you have to let him go."

"No. God, no."

Letti put her arm around Sue's shoulders. Cam stared down at the man. "You want to die?"

Larry nodded.

Maria's stomach bottomed out. She didn't like the direction this was heading.

She said, "Cam . . . ?"

Cam touched Larry's cheek, gave it a gentle caress. And then, with a quick, violent motion, Cam grabbed the man's head and twisted it around 180 degrees.

The *crack* was so loud Maria could taste it.

Sue let out a wretched sound, somewhere between a scream and a sob. Kelly buried her face in Letti's shoulder. JD hunkered down, his muzzle hair standing on edge, baring his teeth at Cam.

Maria was awestruck.

She thought about Cam's past, his ordeal years ago when he and his friend were abducted by a pedophile. Cam hadn't been the most stable child in the world before then, but afterward he'd become withdrawn and quite literally a danger to himself and others. He was committed into a psychiatric institution, given therapy and various drugs, but his condition never seemed to improve. While locked up, he was even accused of doing something unspeakable to another patient, even though it was never proven.

Could Cam—my dear, sweet, little brother Cam—be more disturbed than I ever imagined?

Or was he just being merciful when he snapped that poor man's neck?

"We have to find Felix," Cam said, standing up. "Sis, do you know how to get out of here?"

Maria simply stared at him, unable to reconcile his actions.

"Sis? We need to move before they come for us."

"How many of them are there?" Letti asked.

Maria spoke in a monotone, keeping her eyes on Cam. "A lot. Eleanor, she names each one after a President."

Kelly said, "There have been forty-three Presidents, Mom."

Letti put her hands on her hips. "Are you saying that crazy old bitch has forty-three crazy mutant children running around here?"

Maria thought of that old nursery rhyme, the one Eleanor was fond of repeating.

There was an old woman who lived in a shoe.

She had so many children, she didn't know what to do.

"I think she's only had around twenty," Maria said. "But she brings women in here. Gets them pregnant. Some of the babies don't survive. Birth defects. And she kills the baby girls. Says no girl will ever be President."

Letti gripped Maria's arms. "How many are we talking here, Maria?"

"Including the children?" Maria said.

"Yes. Including the children."

Maria closed her eyes, doing a mental count. "From what I've seen, there are more than fifty."

* * *

Florence stared at the woman sitting on the floor of her closet—the women she'd just hit in the face—and instantly recognized who it was.

"You're Deborah Novachek."

Florence knew her because she was perhaps the most famous athlete competing in Iron Woman.

Deb looked like hell, filthy and frazzled, and now bleeding from her nose.

She stared up at Florence and then kicked out one of her prosthetic legs.

Florence sidestepped the kick and spread out her palms.

"Easy. Take it easy. I didn't mean to hit you, but I didn't expect you to be in my closet. My name is Florence Pillsbury. I'm a triathlete, too. Are you in trouble?"

Florence watched as Deb processed this. The poor girl was shaking all over. "Trapdoors. Secret passages. Someone got into my room. A freak, with red eyes. He's chasing me."

Florence immediately helped the girl up.

"Are you hurt? Who got into your room, dear?"

"We've got to get out of here. We've got to—"

The knock at the door cut Deb off. Both women stared at it.

Florence asked, "Who is it?"

"This is Sheriff Dwight, of the Monk Creek Police Department. Can you open up for a moment, ma'am?"

"Sher—"

Florence clamped her hand over Deb's mouth, cutting her off. This didn't feel right.

"Just a second," Florence called. Then she whispered to Deb, "I've got a weird feeling. Go hide under the bed."

Deb shook her head. "No way in hell."

"The bathroom, then."

"He's the sheriff."

"There's something in his voice I don't like. Please hide while I talk to him."

Deb chewed her lower lip. Then she nodded and walked to the bathroom, bouncing on her curved prosthetics.

"Mrs. Pillsbury?" the sheriff said, knocking again. "Please open the door. It's about your granddaughter."

When Florence saw Deb was locked in the bathroom, she went to answer her door.

The sheriff was a tall man, plump, pasty, wearing an ill-fitting police uniform. His hat was askew on his head. There was also something funny about his eyes. The edges were bright red.

They're bloodshot. He's wearing contact lenses to hide it.

"What about my granddaughter, Sheriff?" Florence opened the door only a few inches and kept her foot planted behind it, like a doorstop.

"You need to come with us."

Us? But he's alone. Unless . . .

Florence craned her neck back, trying to see around the sheriff. She caught a glimpse of a man behind him. A tall man, in overalls. He had a large jaw and a rounded forehead that came to a point. Having done missionary work around the world and seen countless impoverished and disabled people, Florence recognized the man's condition as microcephaly. He was what circus sideshows called a *pinhead*.

Not a person normally associated with law enforcement.

Florence's uneasy feeling about this inn quadrupled

when Deb showed up in her closet, but now it was off the charts. She realized her whole family was in danger.

Okay, now that I know the threat, I can deal with it.

Florence took a deep breath, centered herself, then stepped away from the door.

The men burst in. The microcephalic clapped his hands together and giggled, and the sheriff offered a mean grin, showing that dental hygiene wasn't one of his top priorities.

"Granny, that was a big mistake."

He hitched up his belt and rested his hand on the butt of his gun, striking a rehearsed pose that was probably meant to intimidate.

Florence wasn't intimidated. With her right hand, she struck the sheriff's jaw, driving his head upward. With her left, she shoved his wrist away from his holster and snagged his gun.

"Don't move," she said, backing away. "Don't either of you—"

"Get her, Grover!" the sheriff yelled.

Grover either always followed orders, or he was mentally impaired and didn't recognize the threat of a gun. It didn't matter either way to Florence. The microcephalic was twice her weight, and if he grabbed her it was over.

She shot him twice in the chest, and he fell like a redwood, crashing into the floor with a *thump* almost as loud as the gunfire.

Then she turned the revolver on the sheriff.

"Where's my family?"

The sheriff's eyes got wide, revealing more of their red-rimmed edges.

"Granny, put down the gun."

"My family. Or I shoot you like I shot him."

The sheriff cast a quick glance at his fallen partner.

"We got 'em. Ain't no way you gettin' 'em back."

"How many people are holding them?"

He stayed silent. She pulled back the hammer on the revolver.

"How many?"

"A lot more than the four bullets you got left, Granny. You got no idea what's goin' on."

From the bathroom, Deb screamed.

Then Grover grabbed Florence's ankle.

Felix stared, slack-jawed, at the figure slinking out of the cave. Its golden eyes caught the moonlight and glinted.

Ronald isn't a man. He's a mountain lion.

A surge of adrenaline temporarily overrode the pain in Felix's tortured fingers, and he pawed at his pocket, trying to get at the handcuff keys. He slipped his shattered index finger into his jeans, pushed down, and screamed when his finger bent the wrong way.

He withdrew the finger, his whole body shaking in raw agony.

Ronald cocked his head to the side and padded closer, in no obvious hurry. Felix knew he needed to focus on the keys, but he was transfixed by the cat as it approached. The musk smell got stronger, and Ronald's tail—broken in several places and shaped like a jagged lightning bolt— swished back and forth. It was strangely beautiful, almost hypnotic.

Then the cougar hissed, revealing three-inch fangs, snapping Felix back into reality.

Handcuffs. Focus on my handcuffs.

Felix tried his unbroken pinky. Wincing, he slid it into his pocket, but couldn't get down deep enough to grab the keys. He could just barely touch the metal ring with his fingertip, but couldn't hook his pinky around them.

Ronald stalked closer to Felix, head down, eyes shining. The beast was huge, easily over two hundred pounds. Each paw was bigger than Felix's face.

Ignore the pain. Get the keys.

Grunting, Felix forced his pinky in deeper, bending his ring finger back, the broken phalange bones grinding against one another, his previous knife wound splitting open.

Almost . . . almost . . .

Too much. The pain overtook him, and the world swirled away. Felix's vision dimmed at the edges, the darkness forming a tunnel that got smaller and smaller until he blacked out.

Felix awoke on his knees, hugging the pole, his face warm. He opened his eyes—

—and saw Ronald only inches away, his hot, feline breath blowing onto Felix's face.

Felix felt the scream welling up, and then the cat's massive paw shot out, catching his pelvis, spinning Felix around the pole by his cuffed wrists.

This seemed to amuse the cougar, because he batted Felix in the other direction, like a tetherball. Felix felt the rents in his hips, where the claws hooked flesh through the denim.

My hips?

Oh no . . . my pocket . . .

He chanced a look down at his bloody, ripped jeans.

Are the keys still in there?

Felix patted the material, feeling warm blood and torn

fabric. The pain was twofold, both his ruined fingers and the gouges in his hip seemed to be in a contest for which hurt more. But there, under the heel of his hand—

The keys. And they're poking through the denim.

Using his pinky and his thumb, he pinched the protruding handcuff key—

—and Ronald bit into Felix's foot.

The bite wasn't full force, the cat's teeth not even penetrating the shoe. But the pressure caused a muscle cramp.

He's playing with me.

The cougar tugged Felix, pulling him across the ground, forcing his hand away from his pocket as his body extended.

Did I get the keys?

I can't tell! I can't see!

And then Felix was fully stretched out, his cuffs around the pole, his body pulled taught by Ronald's grip.

Do I have the goddamn keys?!?!

He squinted into the darkness, saw the key ring wrapped around his thumb.

Ronald continued to pull. The cuffs cut into Felix's wrists. The pressure on his foot got worse, twisting Felix's ankle. His spine screamed, joints reaching their limits, sockets beginning to separate, cartilage threatening to tear.

He's pulling me in half.

I'm so sorry, Maria. I tried. I love you so very much.

And then the cat released him.

Not stopping to celebrate his luck, Felix scrambled back to the pole, getting it between him and the mountain lion. Then, using his teeth and his lips and his two unbroken fingers, he managed to fit the key into handcuff lock—

—just as Ronald swiped at him again with his huge paw.

Felix's world spun, and he rolled and rolled and came to rest on his back, staring up at the orange hunter's moon. He wiped his sleeve across his face, clearing some blood from his eyes.

The cuffs. They're off.

I'm free!

Felix didn't bother to look for Ronald. He got to his feet, fighting ten different kinds of pain, and scrambled into the woods. When he left the clearing, the tree canopy covered the moon, making it impossible to see. Felix ran blind, his mangled fingers bumping off of trees, and continued to forge ahead until he saw a light in the distance, a light coming up exceedingly fast.

It's a tow truck.

That was Felix's last thought before the truck plowed into him.

Mal stared at his hand. Jimmy was dangling it up over Mal's face.

"The operation has been a success," Jimmy said. "The patient has survived."

Mal turned his head to see the stump of his wrist, one of the pointy bones still sticking out through the flesh. It wasn't bleeding anymore—a quick dip in the white powder clotted the wound within seconds. But the pain was still there.

The pain went deeper than just Mal's nerve endings firing off signals. The pain was also mental. The memory of what this monster had done to him—cutting the skin, snipping the muscles with scissors, using a hammer and chisel to get through the bone—that would haunt him for as long as he survived. Mal's begging and pleading had devolved into incoherent bawling. Staring at the monster who had done this to him, the monster who gleefully held up his severed hand like a prize fish he'd just caught, was almost more agonizing than the physical hurt.

"Excellent work, my boy," Eleanor said, setting down the camcorder. "Momma has to go check on the guests upstairs. But you might want to give your patient another examination." Eleanor looked at Mal and smiled. "I think he may have some cancer in his feet."

Eleanor patted Mal on the cheek, then waddled off, leaving through one of the operating room's two doors.

"Foot cancer?" Jimmy said, his expression grim. "That's a very serious condition. We'll have to begin treatment immediately."

Jimmy went to the instrument table, gripping a hacksaw in his oven mitt.

Mal cringed away, starting to babble again, knowing it wouldn't do any good.

And then his arm, bloody and missing a hand, slipped out of the leather strap binding his wrist.

Without thinking, Mal thrust his traumatized arm at Jimmy as he inspected his saw, jabbing his protruding ulna bone into the hunchback's neck.

The pain was otherworldly. But the bone—sharp as a splinter from the chisel—cut deep into Jimmy's flesh.

Jimmy grunted, stumbling backward, pressing both mitts to his wound. The blood gushed right through them.

"Laceration . . . to the . . . . internal jugular vein . . . Need . . . QuikClot . . . to stop the bleeding . . ."

Jimmy reached for the bowl of powder on the instrument cart. Mal, his vision red with agony, thrust out and knocked the bowl away, upending it onto the floor. A plume of white dust hung in the air, then settled.

"Gone . . ." Jimmy's red eyes grew wide. He stared at Mal. "You . . . knocked it over . . . The styptic . . ."

One of the hunchback's hands stayed pressed to his pumping neck wound.

The other picked up a scalpel.

Mal watched him stagger forward, the scalpel raised.

"You're a doctor!" Mal managed to say. "You can stitch yourself up!"

Jimmy halted his advance. "Stitch . . . ?"

"You can do it! You can sew up your wound! There's a needle on the cart!"

Jimmy looked at the scalpel again, and Mal was sure the crazy son of a bitch was going to plunge it right into his heart.

But Jimmy didn't. He dropped the scalpel, shook off the oven mitts, and grabbed the large, curved, surgical suture. He lifted the needle up, the thread dangling down, and stared at it.

"Do it," Mal said. "Stitch up your neck. You can fix it. You're a doctor."

Jimmy nodded several times. "I'm . . . a doctor."

Then he pinched the wound closed with his free hand and gouged the needle into his skin.

"Keep going," Mal said. "You can do it. In and out, just like that."

Jimmy pierced his flesh, again and again, showing a fair amount of enthusiasm. But enthusiasm didn't replace skill, and after six stitches the wound was still gushing.

He'd also sewn his fingers to his neck.

"That's it!" Mal said. He felt both ready to laugh hysterically and sob at the same time. He shook away both emotions, forcing himself to stay in the moment. "You're doing it, Dr. Jimmy! A few more stitches and you're done!" Jimmy lasted one more stitch. Then he dropped onto his face.

Mal let out a breath, his head resting back onto the table. He closed his eyes.

It's over.

Now I need to get out of here.

Maybe I can escape.

Maybe I can even find a doctor to reattach my hand.

It's over.

The worst is over.

Then his eyes went wide with panic when he heard the door open.

Deb stole a glance at the framed poster of Ulysses S. Grant facing the toilet as she hid in Florence's bathroom. Like the poster in the Roosevelt room, it seemed to be looking right at her.

Then she stared at the door, straining to hear what was happening.

"Granny, that was a big mistake."

Florence was in trouble.

What do I do? Go out there and try to help?

Anything is better than waiting in here for them to find me.

Deb flinched when she heard the gunshots. Two, in rapid succession.

Jesus, did they kill her?

"Hi there, girly girly."

Deb spun around.

The poster of Grant was yawing open on hinges, and Teddy was slinking out into the bathroom through a hole in the wall.

He flopped onto the floor, reaching his hideous, double-thumbed hands for her, grabbing her prosthetics.

Deb cast a frantic look around, seeking some kind of weapon. There was nothing. Just a sink, a toilet, and a shower. She lashed out at the poster, trying to break the glass.

Plastic. The covering is plastic.

Teddy began to pull himself up her artificial legs, groping at her underwear.

"How 'bout you 'n' Teddy get familiar on the floor right here, girly?"

Deb felt herself losing balance, tipping forward. She reached for the toilet to steady herself, her hands slipping on the cistern cover.

The heavy, porcelain cistern cover.

She snatched it off the toilet tank, a flat slab of stone that weighed at least eight pounds. Without thinking, she slammed it down onto Teddy's head.

Once.

Twice.

Three times.

One the fourth strike, the cover cracked in half. Deb raised the broken piece, ready to bring it down again.

She didn't have to. Teddy's skull looked like a kicked pumpkin. His bloodshot eyes—popping from their sockets from the beating—stared at her accusingly. Deb pushed him aside, sliding his body across the spreading lake of blood, reaching for the door behind her, stumbling out of the bathroom to see—

BANG!

—a third gunshot, Florence shooting a man on the floor in the head—

BANG!

—the older woman fluidly bringing the pistol around

and pulling the trigger as the sheriff lunged at her, shooting him in the stomach. He dropped to his knees, clutching his gut.

"Deborah? Are you okay?" Florence asked, keeping her eyes on the sheriff.

"Teddy . . . he got into the bathroom. He crawled through the walls. There are secret passages everywhere."

"Come over here. I've got some jogging shorts and a sweater in my suitcase. Put them on."

Deb looked at herself, half naked, and sought out the suitcase next to the bed, making sure she kept far away from the dust ruffle.

The sheriff groaned. "Lordy, you got me good, Granny."

"The next one goes through your head, Sheriff. If you don't want to end up like Grover here, tell me where my family is and how many people are guarding them."

The sheriff shook his head. "Don' matter none. I'm dead anyway. Wasted all my styptic on John."

"That's not a fatal wound."

The sheriff grinned. "It is for me. So you can take that gun and shove it up your ass, old woman. I ain't tellin' you shit."

Deb sat on the floor, fighting to get the shorts up over her Cheetahs.

When she heard the sheriff yelp, she looked up and saw Florence grinding her heel into the man's stomach wound.

"Let's get something straight right now," Florence said. "I've seen some terrible things in my life. Things I promised I'd never do, no matter how desperate I got. But if you keep me from my family, I'll break that promise and make your last moments on earth absolutely unbearable. Now, I'll ask you once more, and then I'm going to stick my finger in that bullet hole and pull your guts out. Where is my family and how many people are guarding them?"

The sheriff made a grunting noise. Wincing, he said, "Rot in hell, you old bag."

Deb's mouth fell open as she watched Florence drop to one knee and jab her index finger into the sheriff's stomach.

The sheriff thrashed for a moment and then made good on both of his promises; he refused to talk, and he died.

Florence's eyes went wide. She felt his neck. "He shouldn't be dead. I was a combat nurse. It wasn't a fatal wound."

"Look at all the blood," Deb said, pointing.

There was a large pool of red on the floor around the sheriff. Pints of the stuff. A similar amount surrounded Grover.

"Styptic," Florence said. "That stops bleeding." She wiped her finger off on the sheriff's sleeve. "They're hemophiliacs. Their blood doesn't clot on its own."

"Teddy said something about needing my blood."

Florence shot her a look. "Are you O negative?"

Deb nodded.

"So am I. So are my daughter and granddaughter. Did you get the room for free?"

"Yeah."

Florence wiped her finger off on the sheriff's sleeve. "So did we. When we filled out the applications for Iron Woman, we listed our blood types. O negative is rare. Less than seven percent of the population has it."

"What are you saying?"

"They lured us here for our blood."

It was so ghastly, so unreal, Deb didn't want to believe it.

Florence touched one of the sheriff's open eyes. She plucked off a contact lens, exposing an eyeball as blood-shot as Teddy's.

"Besides hemophilia, they're also anemic. They may have other blood disorders as well. Without regular trans-fusions, they'll die."

"That's fine by me." Deb tugged on a sweater. "Does he have any more bullets?"

Florence checked his belt. "No. But he's got a knife." Florence offered the switchblade to Deb.

"I've got one in my room. I need to go back upstairs to look for my friend Mal."

"I'm looking for my daughter and her daughter. Letti and Kelly. I'll start on this floor, you start upstairs. If you find anything, yell."

Deb nodded. "You do the same."

Florence stood up. "Both of these men were big, strong. I'm guessing there are others. But a deep cut ought to stop them, even kill them."

"Shouldn't we call someone?"

Florence pointed at the sheriff. "Who? The police?"

Deb had no answer for that. "Do you have a car?"

"No. Flat tire. But now I'm thinking they shot the tire out. It sounded like a gunshot."

"Us, too. That's what Mal said. A gunshot."

"When you find him, get out to the road, see if you can flag down a car for help. But be careful. We don't know how many of them there are. Talking to Eleanor, I get the feeling there might be a lot. And she obviously has outside help, if she was able to see our triathlon applications."

Deb nodded. "I know one of them. An asshole desk

clerk back at the event hotel. He's the one who sent me here."

Florence frowned. "Maybe we should stick together."

"We can cover more ground by splitting up. And we may not have a lot of time."

Florence seemed to consider it, then held out her hand. "Good luck."

Deb shook it. "You, too."

They held their grip for a moment, and Deb sensed a finality there. She wondered if she'd ever see the older woman again.

Then Deb walked out of Florence's room. The hallway was empty, silent. She took the stairs slowly, holding the handrail. Previously, the inn had seemed kitschy and somewhat amusing. Now it was downright ominous. The floors, the walls, the ceilings—Deb could imagine secret passages and trapdoors everywhere she looked. This entire building was a fun house straight out of hell. Mal's words of the many disappearances over the years kept echoing in Deb's mind. Five hundred people had gone missing in this area, and this place was no doubt the reason why.

Eleanor and her family have been operating with impunity for decades.

How big has her clan become?

"So big it needed the blood of five hundred people," Deb whispered to herself.

She made it down the stairs without any freaks popping out at her, and approached the Theodore Roosevelt room.

Will it be locked? I left my key inside.

The knob turned. She hesitated.

Is someone in my room?

Deb considered going back upstairs, asking Florence for help.

Just run in, grab the knife. It will only take three seconds.

Deb braced herself, bending her knees, leaning slightly forward.

I'll go on three.

One . . .

Two . . .

Three!

She shoved open the door—the room looked empty—took four quick steps and ran to the bathroom—also empty—reached for her fanny pack on the sink—dug out her knife—flicked open the blade.

So far so good.

Next stop, the closet. Deb wasn't going to leave her prosthetics in there. It would take weeks to get replacements made, and she needed to have spares on her in case something happened to the Cheetahs.

The closet door was closed. She approached it slowly, tightening her grip on the folding knife. Placing her ear against the door, she held her breath, listening for any sounds.

There was only silence.

She shifted from one leg to the other. Without her gel socks, the sockets on the prosthetics were starting to chafe, because they no longer had a perfect fit.

I'll snag them after I grab my legs.

Deb opened the closet door.

Two naked men were sitting on the closet floor, going through her suitcase, throwing her clothes everywhere. They had bulbous, bald heads, and crooked mouths. One had three nostrils. The other had an empty hole where his nose should be. The whites of their eyes were stop-light red.

Before Deb was even able to gasp, three hands reached out at her, grabbing her Cheetahs, pulling them out from under her so she fell onto her ass.

Deb kicked out, trying to pull away, but the two men were already crawling on her, pawing at her thighs, her hips, her chest.

And that's when Deb realized, to her horror, that it wasn't two bodies on top of her.

It's one body with two different heads.

Kelly felt sick. Sick and scared and hurt and overwhelmed and most of all, young. She felt more like a first grader than a teenager.

She looked at Mom, who was in a heated conversation with Maria about which way to go. The pregnant woman, Sue, stood there like a zombie, completely zoned out. JD was sniffing around, waiting for someone to tell him what to do. The only one who seemed to be okay was Cam. He leaned against the wall, arms crossed, looking vaguely bored.

I wish I could act more like him.

Kelly was racked with worry. Even though she was out of that horrible cell, they were still trapped in these tunnels. And according to Maria, there were a lot of bad people who lived here. Kelly knew that even if they got away, they wouldn't have anywhere to go. They were in the middle of the woods. The car didn't work. Maria and Sue and Larry had been here for a long time and hadn't been able to escape.

What if we're trapped here forever?

"Mom?" Kelly said.

"In a second, Kelly."

Kelly wished Grandma was with them. Mom was strong, but Grandma was strong in a different kind of way. She was calmer, more rational. Though Kelly didn't know her grandmother very well, she knew that if anyone could get them out of this situation, Grandma could.

"You okay?"

Kelly glanced up at Cam, who had moved next to her.

"Yeah," she managed.

"You're very brave," Cam said.

"You think so?" Kelly hugged herself. "I'm scared out of my freakin' mind."

"We're all scared, Kelly."

"Even you?"

Cam nodded.

"Even when you . . . broke that man's neck?"

Cam glanced away. "Yeah. That was scary. But he was hurting bad and wanted to die, so I did him a favor. Besides, death isn't so bad."

"How do you know?"

Cam took off one of his leather gloves and showed Kelly his wrist. It was covered with scars.

"After my friend died, I killed myself."

"You mean you tried to kill yourself," Kelly corrected.

"No. I succeeded. I was actually dead for two and a half minutes before they revived me."

Cam held out his arm, so Kelly could touch it. The scars were creepy, but kind of cool, too. She ran a finger across one, surprised by how bumpy it was.

"What did it feel like?" she asked. "To die?"

Cam shrugged, tugging his glove back on. "It was like going to sleep."

"It wasn't scary?"

"There are a lot scarier things than dying, Kelly."

"Like what?"

Cam stared at her. "Like living."

Kelly decided she liked Cam. She liked his straight talk and how open he was.

He's also kind of cute.

"We're going this way," Mom said. "C'mon, Kelly."

Kelly began to follow.

Cam thinks I'm brave. How do brave girls act around cute guys?

Without second-guessing herself, she reached out and took Cam's hand.

When she felt him squeeze it back, Kelly wasn't as scared as she was before.

As expected, Letti's room was empty. Florence found the secret entrance in the back of Letti's closet and considered going in.

Not yet. I should check all the other rooms first.

Florence was still shaken up by what she'd done to the sheriff. After witnessing suffering, misery, and man's inhumanity to man on six continents, Florence would have bet her life she'd never do something so atrocious.

And yet, she'd done it without even hesitating.

Because they have my family.

It put things into perspective. In a big way.

If I'm ready to throw out my ideals and morals for the people I love, why did I spend so much of my life helping strangers?

For the first time ever, she understood why Letti was so mad at her for missing her husband's funeral. The realization was like a splash of ice water in the face.

I blew it. I'm so sorry, Letti. I'll make it up to you. I swear I will.

Exiting the Grover Cleveland room, she crept quietly down the hallway and moved one door over to Lyndon B. Johnson.

Never did care for LBJ. Let's see if anyone is home.

She put her hand on the knob and found it to be unlocked. Moments ago she'd double-checked the sheriff's Colt revolver and made sure there were two bullets left, one under the hammer. Florence held it at her side and went into the room fast, putting both hands on the gun so it couldn't be knocked away.

There wasn't a bed. No desk or dresser, either. The room had an eerie, pink glow to it, coming from three china cabinets along the rear wall.

Florence had seen some things in her day. Some terrible things.

This was one of the worst.

Back when she was a child, a traveling carnival came to town. Her father paid a nickel extra so they could get into the freak show tent. Florence cringed at the sight of deformed people, some of them real, some fake. A human torso. A woman with bird feathers. An ape man. A fellow who stuck skewers through his cheek and tongue. A woman who ate glass. But the thing that stood out the most in her juvenile brain—the thing that scared her more than anything else—was a jar.

"It's a pickled punk," her father had said.

Florence later learned that was a carny term for a baby with birth defects, preserved in formaldehyde. That particular child had four legs and a harelip.

Florence now faced an entire wall of deformed babies in jars, lit from behind. Traces of blood in the preservation fluid made the jars give off a soft, red glow.

My God. There are dozens of them.

Babies with multiple limbs. Babies with no limbs. Some had organs on the outside. Some had feet where the arms should be. Some had flippers like seals. Some were completely covered in fine hair. Some were tiny, their umbilical cords still attached, no more than embryos. Others filled their jars completely, their malformed little bodies crammed inside.

There were misshapen heads, distended bellies, twisted spines, shrunken limbs. Every way the human genome could be perverted was on display.

There were even a few that looked perfectly healthy.

Before Florence tore her eyes away, she noticed a commonality among them all. The overwhelming majority were females. Each jar had a handwritten label, listing names and birthdays.

They're all named after first ladies.

You poor, poor things.

Florence wondered how many of them died naturally and how many were killed on purpose. She brushed a tear from her eye, then left the room quietly, as if she might disturb them.

After taking a moment to compose herself, Florence pressed onward. The Warren G. Harding Bedroom was next. Again, the door was open. Florence went in fast, entering a dark room. She paused, listening.

Snoring. Loud snoring.

Florence felt for the light switch along the wall, flipping it on.

"Ma?"

The man on the bed was massive. His head—double normal size—looked eerily similar to the Elephant Man's from that black-and-white movie, his forehead bulging out in large bumps, his cheekbones uneven and making his mouth crooked. His torso and legs were also malformed, twisted and lumpy, as round as tree trunks.

Proteus syndrome, Florence knew. She'd seen it in South Africa. *His body won't stop growing.*

But unlike gigantism, where a person grew in relative proportion, Proteus meant that different parts grew at different speeds. The overall effect was like making a figure out of clay, then squeezing some parts and adding more clay to others.

"You ain't Ma."

Warren—Florence assumed that was his name—rolled out of bed with surprising speed. His bare feet, swollen as big as Thanksgiving turkeys, slammed onto the floor.

He had to weigh over four hundred pounds, and his gigantic head lolled to the side when he stood up. But Warren was able to walk.

And he was walking toward Florence.

She raised her pistol. "I need to know where my family is."

He moved closer. With each step, the floor shook. He wore a bedsheet wrapped over his shoulder like a toga.

"Youse pretty."

Warren stuck out his tongue, licking his huge, flabby lips. A line of drool slid down his crooked chin.

"Don't come any closer."

"Youse wanna make babies with Warren?"

Florence aimed at his head.

"One more step, I'll shoot."

Warren took one more step.

Florence made good on her threat.

The two shots hit him in his oversized forehead.

Warren lunged at her, moving so fast Florence barely had time to dive to the side.

His skull is too thick. The bullets bounced off the bone.
The giant turned around and faced her.

"Warren's head hurts," he said. Then his eyes got narrow. "Now Warren gonna make you hurt, too."

Mal placed the pointed end of his exposed ulna against his throat, ready to kill himself before he let any more freaks operate on him.

But when the door opened, it wasn't Eleanor or her monstrous brood.

It's a dog.

A German shepherd, tail wagging. It put its front paws on the embalming table and licked Mal's face.

"JD! Oh, Jesus . . ."

Mal watched a blond woman enter the room, followed by several others. The blonde wore a tee shirt, but no pants or shoes. A younger version of her—obviously her daughter—followed, holding hands with a boy wearing black leather gloves. A pregnant woman with a thousand-yard stare followed, clutching her belly. The last person in was a woman in a tattered jogging outfit. She had limp hair and hollow eyes and looked like she'd lived through a war.

They immediately went about unstrapping him, bombarding him with multiple questions.

"Who are you?"

"What happened?"

"Are you okay?"

"Where's Eleanor?"

"Where's the exit?"

"What's your name?"

"I'm Mal," he said. The pain in his wrist was bad, but

bearable. He sat up, and the movement made him woozy. The older blonde put a hand on his shoulder to steady him.

"Do you know how to get out of here, Mal?"

"I think so. But I need a favor first."

"What?"

"Your dog has something that belongs to me."

The woman snapped her head around and pointed. "JD! Drop it!"

The German shepherd opened his jaws, and Mal's hand flopped onto the ground. The blonde picked it up without hesitation.

"I'm so sorry."

"Pleased to meet you," Mal said, "since we already seem to be shaking hands."

The woman set the hand down next to Mal. Then she took a roll of gauze from the instrument tray and began to wrap it around Mal's stump. "I'm Letti."

"I know. I was supposed to interview you and your family." Mal blinked twice, trying to keep it together. "Where's Florence?"

"I don't know."

"Have you seen a woman with no legs? Her name is Deb?"

Letti shook her head. Mal eyed the other people in the room. He recognized the girl, Letti's daughter, and the thin woman. She was also an Iron Woman triathlete, a high-ranked contender who vanished last year before the competition. Maria somebody.

Apparently, I've discovered the reason for all the disappearances in the area.

Though close to being in shock, Mal was still enough

of a reporter to recognize what a terrific story this would make.

If we get out of here alive.

"I think my clothes are in a pile over there."

Kelly turned away while Letti and Maria helped him get off the table and dress. Mal's cell phone was still in his pants pocket. He tried it.

No signal. And why would there be? We're under-ground.

Letti found a plastic bag for his hand. She placed his severed appendage inside and tied the bag to his belt.

"Thanks. There's another door," Mal said. "Far end of the room. That's where Eleanor went. I think it's the way out."

Everyone loaded up on surgical tools—scalpels, knives, saws, cannulas—filling hands and pockets. Then they walked to the door, giving the corpse of Jimmy a wide berth. Letti let JD go through first.

"Clear," she said.

They shuffled through the doorway, one by one. Rather than the exit, this was another room. It was large, a few hundred square feet. Concrete walls. Dirt floor, but muddy in parts. In the corner was a hole in the ground, several pipes leading into it. A pump and two water heaters stood next to the hole.

The rest of the room was packed, floor to ceiling, with cardboard boxes.

Dozens and dozens of them, many of them crumbling and moldy.

Mal squinted at the nearest box.

DruTech Pharmaceuticals—Contergan.

He touched the cardboard and his finger went right through it, like tissue paper. Powder spilled out. Mal stared at the floor and saw a great deal of the powder mixing with the dirt. Near the water pump, there was so much powder it had turned the mud a lighter color.

"What's Distoval?" Kelly said, staring at a box.

"Distoval is another name for Contergan," Mal said. He'd just read about this very subject when researching the history of Monk Creek. "It was a sedative, developed in the 1950s in Germany. They thought it was a wonder drug. DruTech was the company set to manufacture it in the U.S. But the FDA didn't approve it. DruTech lost a fortune and closed up their factory in town. They were supposed to dispose of their supply. I guess they paid off Eleanor, and it ended up here."

"Why wasn't it approved?" Letti asked.

"You probably know it by its other name. Billy Joel even mentioned it in a song."

"Thalidomide," Sue whispered.

Mal nodded, which made him slightly dizzy. He knew he was rambling, but it helped him feel grounded. "It caused massive birth defects. Real freaky stuff. Pregnant women taking it gave birth to children with some pretty terrible deformities." Mal pointed to the well. "And it's apparently gotten into the inn's water supply. The drugs have seeped into the ground. Anyone pregnant drinking from that well will . . . oh shit."

Mal's addled brain remembered the woman who very obviously was with child.

"Are you saying"—the woman was gently rubbing her belly—"that my baby . . ."

"We don't know that." Letti went over to her. "We don't know for sure, Sue. We'll get you to a doctor when we get out of here."

"But . . . this is Larry's baby. It's supposed to be normal."

Letti patted Sue's hair. "There's nothing we can do about it now, Sue. Let's focus on getting out of here."

"I can't have one of those freaks growing inside me. I can't."

Mal had been feeling pretty terrible before, but now he felt like curling up into a ball and dying.

"There's the door," Cam said. "Maybe that's the way out."

Cam led Kelly, by the hand, to the exit. Letti and JD followed.

"I'm so sorry," Mal said to Sue.

"They did things to me," Sue said. "Horrible things. I can't have my baby be like that."

"I'm sure it will be okay," Mal lied.

Sue nodded. She and Mal walked toward the door, and then Sue broke off, heading for the well.

"Wait! Don't!"

The pregnant woman gave him a sad, backward glance, then jumped into the hole. Two seconds later, there was a splash.

"Help!" Mal shouted. "Help us!"

Letti and Maria hurried over.

"She jumped in. She just jumped in."

The three of them formed a ring around the well, staring down into the blackness.

"Sue!" Letti called.

Sue didn't reply. There were no splashing noises. No sounds of struggling.

Just bubbles.

The bubbles of someone letting all the air out of her lungs and sinking.

Aw, Jesus, what have I done?

"It's not your fault," Letti said. "She would have found out eventually."

Mal continued to stare into the well. Jumping in didn't seem like a bad idea, actually.

"We need you," Letti said, taking his good arm. "I know you've been through a lot, but we need to stick together to get out of here."

"We can't," Mal said. "We can't get away."

"Yes, we can."

Mal pulled away. "They've been killing people for over forty years. More than five hundred people. No one has ever escaped to tell the world about it."

"Then we'll be the first."

Mal stared into Letti's eyes. They were strong, determined. Like Deb's eyes.

Deb.

I have to find Deb.

"I guess I could lend a hand," Mal said. "One, at least."

He allowed Letti and Maria to lead him to the door. The next room was another storage area, thalidomide boxes stacked everywhere. There were three other doors, not including the one they came through.

"Kelly?" Letti said, looking around. "Kelly!"

But Kelly, the dog, and the boy were gone.

Felix opened his eyes to blurry, swirling lights. He took a breath and winced—add several broken ribs to his grocery list of things that hurt. Blinking, he realized he was on his back, lying in the woods. The two lights he saw were headlights, coming from a vehicle a dozen yards away.

The memories came to him in snippets.

. . . accidentally shooting John in the head . . .

. . . being taken here in a police car . . .

. . . the cougar attack . . .

. . . getting hit by the tow truck . . .

The tow truck.

Felix knew the tow truck was part of this whole night-mare. He needed to get away from it. Far away.

Biting his lower lip so the whimpering wasn't too loud, Felix managed to turn onto his side. There wasn't a single part of his body that didn't throb.

A stick broke, nearby. Someone walking through the underbrush.

Ronald? Or the tow truck driver, Ulysses?

Felix looked around, saw he was near a depression in the ground filled with dead leaves and pine needles. He rolled to it, squeezing his eyes shut against the pain, coming to a rest on his back because he couldn't breathe while on his stomach with his ribs hurting so badly. Then he put a stick in his mouth to bite down on and used his mangled hands to scoop dirt and dead foliage onto him-self, trying to cover his body completely.

The sound got closer. It was steady, rhythmic.

Footsteps.

If Felix had any doubt it was Ulysses coming for him, those doubts were laid to rest when he heard, "Don' make me come find you, little man. You make me hunt around, it'll be worse on ya."

If Felix had any sense of humor left, he might have laughed at the irony.

Like things could get worse.

The footsteps got closer. Felix peeked up through the pine needles on his face, waiting for Ulysses to approach.

That's when he noticed his cell phone.

He'd had it in his jeans pocket. It must have come out when he was hit by the truck, or when he was rolling. The tiny green light, indicating the phone was on, blinked like a homing beacon.

If Ulysses sees that phone . . .

Just then, Ulysses walked into the clearing.

He was big, every bit as big as John. Thick in the shoulders and the chest. A head as massive as a tree stump. Felix could make out only his silhouette in the moonlight, but he could see Ulysses was carrying something long and curved.

A crowbar.

Felix quickly reached out his hand, slapping his palm over his cell phone, covering the green light.

Then there was a burst of red. Ulysses had lit a flare.

The red glow illuminated the large man's facial deformity. The right side of his face bulged out like he had a baseball under his skin. This stretched out his mouth, making it almost twice as wide as normal. Ulysses looked like he could swallow an orange, whole.

Felix stared, impotent, as the man stalked closer. Soon he was three steps away . . . Two steps . . . One step.

Please no, oh please don't step on . . .

MY HAND!

Ulysses's work boot crunched down on Felix's broken hand, prompting a pain so intense Felix had to gnash his teeth so he didn't scream.

"Y'all put a dent in my truck," Ulysses said, staring into the woods.

Get off my hand! Get off!

"When I find you, I'm gonna beat out that dent with your skull."

GETOFFGETOFFGETOFF!!!

Ulysses hacked and spat, hitting Felix on the cheek. Felix squeezed his eyes shut, feeling the spit slide down into his ear, knowing he couldn't hold the scream in any longer.

Then Ulysses abruptly walked on, into the forest, the red flare growing dimmer and eventually disappearing.

With tremendous effort, Felix got up onto his knees and, using his thumb and pinky, shoved the cell phone back into his pocket.

The inn. I need to go back to the inn and find Maria.

But with his mangled hands, he knew he was practically useless. He couldn't hold a weapon. He couldn't even open a door.

Are my fingers broken? Or just dislocated?

Squinting in the moonlight, he studied his bent digits. The bends and twists were primarily around the knuckles. But, incredibly, the two fingers Ulysses had stepped on looked better than before.

Maybe I can bend them all back.

He brought his right hand up to his mouth, ready to stick his finger inside.

Just bite down, and let gravity do the rest.

But Felix didn't bite down. On the list of things he didn't want to do, trying to fix his fingers ranked slightly above pouring gasoline on his head and setting his hair on fire.

Just do it.

Felix didn't move.

Do it! For Maria!

He clamped his teeth down, hard, and then quickly dropped his wrist.

SNAP!

A sob escaped him, and his whole body shook. But his index finger did seem to be better. Even semifunctional.

Three more to go.

He switched hands, raising the left one to his face, when he noticed a firefly in the bushes, glinting yellow. The firefly also had a mate, a few inches away.

Then the fireflies blinked, and Felix realized he wasn't staring at fireflies.

He was looking into the eyes of the mountain lion.

Deb didn't hesitate. With her folding knife in a death grip, she hacked away at the throat of the nearest Siamese twin, cutting and slashing until she hit bone and they crawled off her, spraying geysers of blood.

When they got to the bed, the twins sat up. The duo shared the same two legs, but at the chest they forked into two halves. A single, underdeveloped arm jutted out of their sternum just below the split. The head on the left-hand side was limp, nodding forward, eyes rolled up. The left arm was similarly slack.

"Andrew?" the other head said, staring at his dead twin. "What's wrong, Andrew?"

He slapped the slack head, repeatedly. Deb gawked, the horrible image too much for her to handle. She scooted away from them, snagging the bag with her prosthetic legs from the closet.

"You killed Andrew!" the other twin cried. He attempted to lunge at Deb, but only half of his body worked.

As he pathetically tried to drag himself forward, Deb crawled to the nearest wall and pulled herself up.

The blood soaking her sweater was warm, and the stench was making her sick. She stripped down to her tee shirt and shorts, and headed into the hallway. More than anything else, she wanted to run outside, get as far away from this awful house as possible. But she wasn't going to leave Mal behind. Somehow, she knew he'd give her the same consideration if the roles were reversed.

The next room over had ABRAHAM LINCOLN stenciled on the door.

Brandishing the knife, Deb went in quick, feeling along the wall for the light switch. When she flipped it on, all she saw was lots of creepy Lincoln decor.

But the room was empty of people.

Next came Calvin Coolidge. Like every door so far, it was unlocked, making Deb wonder if any of the locks actually worked. Testing her theory, she turned the lock on the knob and then twisted it.

It doesn't lock at all.

Again she stepped into a dark room, reaching for the light switch next to the doorway—

—touching the man who was standing there.

Deb recoiled, pulling away, backpedaling into the hall. Her ass hit the banister, and for a crazy moment she thought she was going to flip over it and tumble down to the first floor. She lowered her center of gravity by doing the splits, her Cheetah prosthetics splaying out as she sat on her ass.

Whomever she accidentally touched walked out of the dark room, into the light of the hallway. He had a large brow ridge, bisected with a single bushy eyebrow, on a head that was big and flattish on top. His arms were longer than they should have been, and his fingers were fused together in a triangle shape, like the flippers of a walrus. His other hand had a bloody bandage wrapped around it.

But the most repulsive thing of all was his torso. He had no shirt, and his pale, hairless chest was pocked with dozens of—

Nipples. He's covered with nipples.

The freak opened his mouth and made a noise that was a lot like the honking of a Canada goose. Then he lunged.

Deb thrust her blade at him, but he batted it aside with his bandaged hand, sending it skittering across the floor. She tried to scurry after the knife, but the curved fiberglass of her Cheetahs slipped across the wood floor. The only traction on her prosthetics were the rubber treads, but in a sitting position the bottoms were bent upward like the ends of a *W*.

Calvin honked again, getting his arms around her, nipples poking at her face and eyes. Deb tried to turn, to get onto her hands and knees, but his grip was too strong.

Behind her, the banister creaked, then shifted.

Calvin backed up, apparently afraid of breaking it and falling over. Deb took the opportunity to lunge for the knife, tapping it with her fingertips, sending it spinning toward the railing.

Don't fall! Don't fall!

The knife handle teeter-tottered over the ledge then righted itself. Deb stretched farther, trying to snag it, and then her head was yanked back by her hair. But it felt like more than just pulling. It also felt wet.

She turned her head, trying to peripherally see what was happening.

He's biting my hair.

Deb tried to push against the floor, but her prosthetics couldn't get a purchase. Then her eyes flitted to her bag, the strap still around her shoulder.

She reached for it.

Calvin's hands moved down, encircling her neck, and Deb thought he was going to strangle her. But the pervert lowered his hands, reaching for her breasts instead.

Bad move.

Deb tugged down the zipper on her suitcase and freed one of her prosthetic mountain climbing legs—the one with the spikes on the toe.

Calvin got the spiked end in the eye.

He honked again, rolling off her, slapping both hands to his face.

Deb grabbed the knife and pulled herself upright, ready to fight back. But the strange, heaving sounds Calvin made had a familiar, rhythmic pattern that made her pause.

He's crying. Like a little kid.

While Deb was deciding what to do next, Calvin let out a mighty roar and tackled her, both of them flying over the railing, crashing to the floor twelve feet below.

Florence spent a lifetime studying the martial arts to become more in touch with her body, her surroundings, and her spirituality. But along the path to enlightenment, she also learned how to fight.

The two shots to the head didn't even slow down the monstrous Warren, with his massive skull and elephantine legs. But Florence also had a knife. She moved easily and fluidly toward the stampeding giant, dropped her left shoulder, and rolled up to him, thrusting the sheriff's blade deep into his inner thigh. Florence twisted the knife, intending to sever the body's largest artery, the femoral. Battlefield triage in Vietnam had shown her how quickly an injury like that proved fatal.

Incredibly, Warren swatted her aside, like she was a pesky fly. Florence moved with the blow, deflecting most of its force, and faced him on all fours, still clutching the knife. She waited for him to drop.

He didn't. His leg was bleeding, but not gushing like she'd expected.

His thigh is so thick I missed the artery.

"You stabbed Warren," Warren said.

"And I'll do it again unless Warren leaves me alone."

Florence eyed the door. She probably had a chance to get away. But Warren would no doubt follow, and alert others to what was going on.

It's self-defense, Florence told herself. *I'm not actively trying to kill a man.*

But Florence knew Warren had to die if she was going to find Letti and Kelly.

Strangely, she was okay with that.

"How many brothers do you have, Warren?"

Warren plodded over to the dresser, picking up a packet. He tore it open and slapped white powder onto his thigh and forehead. The bleeding stopped almost immediately.

The styptic the sheriff mentioned.

"Warren has lots of brothers."

"How many is lots?"

He turned to face her. "Lots."

"Your brothers have my daughter and granddaughter. I want to know where they are."

Warren took a step toward her, spreading out his arms. "In the slave cellar. Where y'all're gonna be."

"Warren, if you go back to bed and promise not to tell anyone, I won't kill you."

Warren made a low, throaty sound that Florence figured out was laughter.

"Warren is big 'n' strong. You ain't gonna kill Warren."

He reached out his hands. They were so swollen and distorted they looked less like hands and more like balloons with sausages sticking out of them. Florence gracefully sidestepped his attempted grab, clutched one of his fingers, and drew the blade across the underside of his wrist, cutting as deep as she could.

The blood came out like a lawn sprinkler turned on. Warren howled, turning to reach for the styptic. Florence changed her grip on the knife and stabbed him through his grossly deformed big toe, pinning his foot to the floor. Then she backed out of his range.

Warren tried to reach for the knife handle, but his stomach was so distended he couldn't bend down low enough. It took him less than a minute to bleed to death, and Florence was surprised by how detached she felt watching him.

Then she stumbled into the bathroom and puked her guts out into the sink.

Good. For a second I thought I'd stopped being human.

Still queasy, Florence retrieved the knife and crept out of the room and into the hallway, almost bumping into a man with no arms. Her mind flashed back to Eleanor's words.

"Legend says one slave, after his fifth drop, lost both of his arms when they ripped from his sockets. He's said

to roam the hallways at night, looking for his missing limbs."

But this was no ghost of a slave. This was another of Eleanor's perverted brood. And while he didn't have arms, he did have hands. Underdeveloped baby hands, sticking directly out of his shoulders.

With a bowlegged gait he lumbered toward Florence, and his mouth seemed too small for his overabundance of teeth, which jutted crookedly from his lips in all directions.

"Don't come any closer," Florence said.

Like Warren, this one didn't heed her warning. He came up fast, kicking at her chest, knocking Florence onto her back. One of his filthy feet pinned her wrist to the floor, and he actually gripped the knife with his toes, trying to wrestle it away from Florence.

She made a fist and punched upward, connecting between his legs. He groaned, doubling over, giving Florence easy access to his neck. She raised the knife.

The red sluiced down like hot, sticky rain.

Getting out from under him, Florence heard a thump. She crawled to the railing and looked down.

Deb, and a man, were sprawled out on the first floor. There was a growing pool of blood, and neither one was moving.

Then Florence heard a door open. Followed by a few others.

She did a slow turn, taking everything in, and saw she was surrounded by freaks.

When JD took off through the open door, Kelly followed. The smell hit her first. A rotten, putrid smell. It reminded her of the time she was taking out the garbage and one of the bags broke open, spilling out the remains of a chicken dinner from a week ago.

There's something dead in this room.

But Kelly couldn't see what it was. Unlike the other rooms in these underground tunnels, this one had no overhead lightbulbs.

Then the door behind her slammed shut, cutting off the little light that had been filtering in.

"JD?"

The dog didn't come. Kelly took a few steps forward, hands out in front of her so she didn't run into anything in the darkness.

Her fingers brushed something.

Something moist.

She recoiled, and strong arms grabbed her from behind. Before she had a chance to scream, the man clutching her said, "Kelly?"

"Cam?"

Kelly was still afraid, but he kept his hands on her shoulders, and that felt kind of nice. She felt her face get warm.

He's way too old for me. He's got to be at least nineteen or twenty.

Still, he is *cute. And I* am *almost a teenager.*

"I can't find JD," Kelly said, trying to keep her voice strong.

"Hold on. I have a lighter in my pocket."

A flame appeared in front of Kelly, illuminating Cam's outstretched arm, along with—

"Oh wow . . ."

The room was filled with suitcases. A maze of suitcases, stacked floor to ceiling. Some of them looked really old and were moldering in the dampness.

Others looked so new they could have been purchased yesterday.

"How many do you think there are?" Kelly asked.

"I dunno. Hundreds."

"Do you think . . . ?" Kelly let the sentence trail off, not wanting to speak her thoughts out loud.

"Yeah. I think each one came from a person these psychos murdered."

Kelly shivered. "I don't like this place. We need to find my dog. He ran in here."

"I know. I saw you and followed . . ."

The flame went off. Kelly pressed herself tighter against Cam.

"Sorry," he said, flicking the lighter back on. "Thumb slipped. Let's see what's around that stack."

Cam walked around Kelly, taking the lead, and she was sort of sorry he wasn't holding her anymore. She followed close, a single step behind him. The lighter flame cast wild, flickering shadows, making the heaps of luggage seem like they were swaying.

They rounded the corner, and the smell got worse. Kelly put her hand over her mouth and nose.

"What's that awful—"

The light went out again.

"Kelly," Cam said. "I want you to do me a favor, okay?"

Kelly didn't like his tone. He sounded scared. "What?"

"Take my hand and close your eyes."

"Why, Cam? What's—"

"Trust me. You don't want to see this. Just keep them closed until I say it's okay."

"Cam, you're freaking me out."

"Just do it. Please."

Kelly believed after everything she'd already been

through today, there was nothing else that could scare her. But when Cam said *please*, she gave in.

Besides, I get to hold his hand.

"Okay."

Kelly closed her eyes, and Cam's gloved hand encircled hers. They walked slowly, the smell getting almost unbearable. Cam made a gagging sound, and Kelly had to press her shirt against her face.

What could possibly smell this bad?

"We should go back for my mom," Kelly said. She instantly regretted speaking, because the rotten stench got on her tongue.

"We will. But I feel a draft up ahead. I think it's a way out. Unh!"

Cam's hand pulled from hers, and she was left standing there alone. Her eyes sprung open.

"Cam?"

"I tripped, Kelly. Keep your eyes closed."

But she didn't. And when the light went on, she saw what Cam had tripped over.

A dead body.

The whole room was filled with dead people.

"Kelly!" Letti called out.

Three doors. Which one did she go through?

Letti hurried to the first door, knocking over a soggy cardboard box, spilling pills onto the dirt floor. She tugged open the door and gasped.

There were a bunch of people standing in the room.

But her brain told her something was amiss, that these weren't people. She stared a moment longer and saw that they were all elaborately dressed, some in period clothing. And none of them were moving.

Even stranger, most of them were recognizable.

"Wax figures," Mal said. "I guess there's no room for them in the house."

Naturally, each wax figure depicted a U.S. President. They looked old, and far from pristine. Most were covered in dust and cobwebs. Some had broken limbs and cracked faces. The Richard Nixon closest to Letti was missing his nose.

"Kelly!" Letti yelled again. She took a step forward, toward a particularly ugly statue of George Washington in colonial dress, but someone held her back.

"Hold on," Maria said, easing in front of her. She held up a scalpel she'd taken from the operating room and whispered in Letti's ear, "I've seen this trick before."

Moving quickly, Maria stuck the scalpel into Washington's belly.

The statue—which wasn't a statue at all—howled and lashed out at her.

Four other statues followed suit, coming to life and closing in. Maria backed up, bumping into Letti, and they both hightailed it out the door they'd come in, slamming it behind them. Letti braced her shoulder against the wood.

"Check the other doors! We have to get out of here!"

Mal opened the one on the right. "It's dark. I can't see anything."

The door shuddered. Letti removed the cannula—a large, sharp metal tube she'd grabbed from the instrument cart—from her back pocket and speared it into the doorjamb like a dead bolt. It wouldn't hold for long. Maria checked the far door. "There's a ladder. Come on!"

The trio ran to the ladder. It was made of metal bars,

old and rusty, ascending into darkness. Mal went up first, moving damn quick for a man with only one hand. Maria followed.

The door to the statue room burst open, and a bleeding, pissed-off George Washington stumbled through. He was followed by a large, stout woman wearing a pillbox hat.

"You can't get away, Loretta," Eleanor said. "No guests ever leave."

Letti considered running at the woman, perhaps taking her as some kind of hostage. But four of her large brood filed out of the room behind her, so Letti turned and climbed up the ladder. At each rung, she expected someone to grab her ankles, pull her back down. But it didn't happen. No one even seemed to be chasing her.

When she reached the top, she understood why. The ladder led to another doorway, which opened up into the main floor of the Rushmore Inn, where there were more than a dozen freaks waiting for her.

Felix didn't move. He didn't dare breathe. The mountain lion was less than a foot away, its golden eyes staring Felix right in the face. The cat's ears flattened against its head and the beast roared in unmistakable wildcat style, baring its sharp, thick fangs.

I'm about to die, and there's not a thing I can do about it.

But Ronald wasn't ready to kill Felix. Not yet.

Ronald wanted to play with his food first.

A paw shot out, clipping Felix in the head, the blow dizzying. Felix rolled, crying out, not caring anymore if he was heard or not. He had no idea how much punishment a man could take and still survive, but he knew he was near his limit.

The cougar pounced, landing next to Felix, and gave him another swat. It tore Felix's shirt, and the skin underneath.

Felix tried to feebly scramble away, and Ronald's claw hooked into his leg, pulling him back. He tried once more, and the cat did the same thing.

Enough. I'm done. It's finished.

Felix rolled onto his back, staring up at the full moon peeking through the trees. He realized it would be the last thing he ever saw.

Such a shame. He wanted his last sight to be the woman he'd fought so desperately to save.

I love you, Maria.

And then Ronald's warm mouth closed around Felix's neck.

The first thing Deb saw when she opened her eyes was a swirling, spinning jumble of motes. They danced in her vision, making it hard to focus.

She shook her head, trying to get her bearings, and realized four things in rapid succession.

I fell on top of Calvin, and he's bloody and completely still, and I think he's dead.

My nose hurts, and I have a headache, but I don't think I sustained any major damage.

I lost my knife, but I still have my prosthetic leg bag around my shoulder.

I'm surrounded by freaks.

The last thought jolted her back to the here and now. Deb pushed herself up off Calvin, struggling to get her

Cheetahs under her. The bottom skids kept slipping on the widening spread of blood.

Coming at her from the left side were: a man with one long arm and a very short arm, his skull so misshapen and massive he wore a neck brace to support it; a set of parasitic twins, the smaller, deformed brother's head and hands sticking out of the hip of his host; a morbidly obese man with two extra hands jutting from his chest; and a man without a shirt, exposing lumpy growths all over his body that looked a lot like pink coral.

On her right side, Deb was confronted by: a man with a spine so twisted he walked on all fours; a tall, long-limbed teenager whose eyes were too close together, bloody acne covering his face like a crust; two more men like Grover, with flippers for hands and deformed skulls; and a gigantic, muscular hulk who didn't appear to have any neck.

Deb grabbed her dropped mountain climbing leg, which was lying next to her. Then she crawled out of the blood pool. Her prosthetics were still too slippery to stand up. She assumed a kneeling position, raising the artificial leg like a weapon, realizing she had no chance at all of getting away.

The pimply teenager reached for her, his hands stained with dried blood—probably from picking at his face. His reach was so long Deb was unable to hit him even as his spidery fingers encircled her throat.

And then the teen's head jerked to the side. His eyes—mere millimeters apart—crossed. He flopped to the side, his head bouncing off the floor.

Coming in behind him, someone else reached out for Deb.

Florence.

"Give me your hand," she said.

With the older woman's help, Deb was able to stand up. Once Deb was vertical, Florence lashed out her foot, catching a freak in the jaw, knocking him away.

Deb followed Florence through the hole she'd made in the wall of attackers, walking carefully because her treads were wet. The tiny burst of optimism spurred by Florence's rescue attempt faded quickly when Deb realized there was no place to run.

We can't get away. There are too many of them.

Florence didn't seem deterred by this. She kicked and punched like Jackie Chan's grandmother, and for the moment the freaks gave her a wide berth.

"We should try for the front door," Deb said. They were now standing back to back, both of them swinging at the surrounding horde.

"I'm not leaving without my family."

Someone crawled up to Deb, someone with stunted legs like Teddy's. He grabbed Deb's Cheetah, pulling her off-balance. Deb smacked him in the face with her mountain climbing leg, the spiked end flaying off a few layers of skin. "Deb!"

She looked up, at a door that opened behind the staircase.

Mal!

He looked like hell, and was missing his left hand, and they were both probably doomed, but damned if he didn't smile when she met his eyes.

Following him through the door were two women. One looked like a younger version of Florence. The other was thin and disheveled but brandishing a scalpel like she wanted to cut the whole world's throat.

Our odds just got a tiny bit better.

Mal pushed his way through Eleanor's children, reaching Deb, giving her a quick, gentle caress on her cheek before he wielded a scalpel of his own and began slashing at the oncoming wave of freaks.

For a moment they held their own, and Deb thought they might actually have a chance.

But more of the brood came down the stairs, shuffling toward them like zombies. And even more, dressed in antique clothing, came through the door under the staircase.

How many of them can there be?

Then Deb saw something that could be the game changer.

Eleanor is here.

The matriarch stood next to the stairs, arms folded, looking smug.

It's like chess. If you capture the king, the rest of the pieces stop attacking.

Deb headed for Eleanor, swinging her mountain climbing leg like a club, clearing a path. Eleanor saw Deb approach and must have sensed her intent, because she hurried up the stairs. Deb wasn't good on stairs, but she got ready to follow, to hunt down the old woman and put an end to this madness.

Apparently, someone else had the same idea. Shoving Deb aside, the thin woman with the scalpel tore upstairs after Eleanor. Deb fell over and found herself being pawed and groped on all sides by losers in the genetic lottery.

"We have to go back to the basement!" Mal yelled. "We can't hold them off up here!"

Someone pulled Deb's arm—Florence again. She dragged Deb across the floor, to the doorway under the staircase. Mal and Florence's daughter followed. The door led to a small room the size of a closet, an iron ladder descending into the floor. Deb's hopes sank even lower.

I'm even worse on ladders than I am on stairs.

"You go first," she told Florence.

Florence hesitated. "Can you manage?"

"If I don't, gravity will."

Florence sped down the ladder. Her daughter was next, leaving Deb alone with Mal. The freaks closed in, shuffling en masse like a giant wave about to wash up against them.

"Ladies first," Mal said.

"You go."

"No time to argue."

"I . . . I can't."

Deb knew she would need to scoot down backward, feel around for the rungs. It was dark, and she had no idea how high the ladder was. Mal could go faster, even with one hand. He should—

And then Mal shoved her. Deb teetered, stepping backward, her leg missing the floor and dropping into the hole.

She fell, crying out, insane with panic, and then something snagged her hand and stopped her.

Mal. Holding on to me from above.

"Catch her!" Mal yelled.

Then he let go of Deb's hand, and once again the crazy panic feeling took over, staying with her even as four strong arms broke her fall.

Rather than feeling relief at still being alive, Deb stared up at the ladder above her, willing for Mal to come down.

He didn't.

"Mal!" she yelled. "MAL!"

There was an unbearable silence.

Then Mal began to scream.

* * *

Kelly couldn't quite comprehend what she was seeing. The dead were stacked around her like cords of firewood, almost as high as the ceiling. Most were disheveled, their skin shrunken and mummified. Others were practically skeletal. They towered on either side, threatening to topple over and bury Kelly in an avalanche of corpses.

Cam got to his feet and kicked something aside. The object rolled away into the darkness, but not before Deb could make out its long hair and two hollowed-out eye sockets.

He just kicked a human head.

"The flame is blowing toward me," Cam said. "There's a way out."

"We need to get Mom."

"I think I see your dog."

Cam hurried ahead. Kelly had to follow, or else be left in total darkness. She reached her arms out in front of her, not wanting to bump into anything while chasing Cam, and then felt a sharp pain in her heel just above her gym shoe, like she'd caught it in something.

She immediately lifted her leg up, reaching for her calf—

—touching something greasy and furry. Something that squirmed when her fingers touched its pointy nose.

Oh my God, it's a rat!

Kelly had held rats before; one of her friends had a rat as a pet. But that one was tame and cute, and this one was biting her ankle.

She stabbed at the creature with her scalpel. It dropped off, squealing, just as Kelly felt another one run up her other leg. She jabbed that one as well, but then there were more of them, running over her feet, bumping into her from all directions. The scalpel wasn't enough.

"Cam!"

Kelly ran forward, wanting more than anything to get the hell away from there, and then she was pressed up against the pile of corpses, her face mashing into some-one long dead. Thick dust—*dead flesh?*—rained down on Kelly, getting in her eyes and nose.

"Cam!" she said, and then bent over and vomited when a flake of something putrescent landed in her mouth.

More squealing, and then there was light again and Cam appeared, stomping on rats, breaking their backs and kicking them aside. He took Kelly under the arm and said, "Hurry! I found your dog!"

They stumbled through the corpse maze, rats on their heels, and then Kelly felt a fresh, clean breeze on her face. The smell was glorious. She glimpsed the full moon in the distance, through a barred iron gateway which was pushed open. There, next to a tree—

"JD!"

The dog didn't look at her. He was hunched down, his teeth bared, staring at something in the dark.

Kelly began to run to him, but Cam caught her shirt, holding her back.

"Wait," Cam whispered.

A moment later, Kelly understood Cam's caution.

Slinking out of the woods, approaching her dog, was a mountain lion.

If it's the last thing I do in my life, I'm going to kill that bitch.

Maria headed for the staircase after Eleanor, but a familiar figure blocked her way.

George.

His powdered wig was on crooked, and the Revolutionary War uniform he wore was stained with blood splotches and gunky styptic.

"I din't get to stick it to y'all earlier. But you ain't gettin' away this time."

He reached for her, his lips curled in a snarl. Maria let him grab her, pull her close.

How about I stick it to you instead, asshole?

And then she rammed the scalpel so far into his bloodshot eyeball the tip touched the back of his skull.

George crumpled to the floor. Maria pulled out the scalpel, which came free with a sucking/slurping sound, then darted up the stairs. For a fat old lady, Eleanor could move like a gazelle. Though Maria had done her best to maintain an exercise regimen in captivity, she knew she was malnourished, and the transfused blood in her system zapped her energy even further. By the time Maria got to the third floor, she was winded, and Eleanor had disappeared into one of the rooms.

Maria began with the closest one, Zachary Taylor.

Immediately on entering, Maria was gut-punched by emotion.

Cribs. There are half a dozen baby cribs.

And some of the babies are cooing.

Maria's mind flashed back to when she first realized she was serious about Felix. She hadn't ever planned a future with a man before, and for the first time she had to share an intimate, personal, and ultimately shameful admission.

"I want to have kids with you. But I can't. I have this medical condition. I'll never be able to bear children."

Felix's response was one of the best things anyone ever said to her.

"Then after we get married, we'll adopt, and some lucky kid will get to have the best mother in the world."

Seeing all of these cradles made Maria's heart catch in her throat. How many times, lying on the dirt floor of her cell, had she dreamed of one day holding a baby? Of playing peekaboo? Of changing its little diapers and tickling its little chin?

Slowly, reverently, Maria approached the nearest crib, peeking over the side.

She immediately recoiled. The child had bug eyes and an obscenely large mouth, which was currently wrapped around a piece of raw chicken. It looked up at Maria and hissed, baring pointed teeth.

Unable to stop herself, she checked the next crib. The child had something on its face that looked like a beak, and it was gnawing on its own foot, drawing blood.

The next one was a set of Siamese twins, joined at the face and sharing the same center eye. They saw her and made a sound like a cat being stepped on. The next one—

Perfect. This baby is absolutely perfect.

Fine, brown hair. Wide, expressive eyes. The cutest little nose. The child saw Maria and cooed, reaching out a chubby hand. She held out her finger, letting the baby grasp it, and for a moment Maria forget where she was, and who she was, and all the horrors of the past year, along with her current situation, vanished from her mind.

You're so precious.

Then, from behind her, Maria heard the unmistakable sound of a shotgun racking. Without even thinking, Maria snatched up the baby and spun around.

Eleanor had the gun pointed at her. Maria raised the scalpel.

"Drop it, or I'll kill the baby," she lied.

Eleanor smiled. "Go ahead. She ain't one of mine. Came with a couple who stayed here a few weeks back. Her parents didn't properly adjust to our accommodations, and they're no longer with us. But that little girl is the right blood type. Plannin' on bleedin' her when she gets a wee bit older. Then let my boys have some fun. But I can live with the loss."

Someone came into the room behind Eleanor. Harry, whose harelip was so severe it practically reached his eyebrows.

What do I do?

What can I do?

Nothing. I can't do a damn thing.

"Either kill the child or set 'er down," Eleanor said. "Either way, you ain't goin' nowhere."

Maria took a deep breath, then let it out slow. She went to put the girl back in its crib, but the infant clung to Maria's shirt collar, refusing to be put down. When Maria disentangled her perfect little fingers and laid her on her back, the baby began to cry.

"Shh," Maria said, tears welling up. "It's okay, little one. It's going to be okay."

But Maria knew it wouldn't be.

Then Eleanor stomped over and hit Maria in the stomach with the butt of the shotgun. Maria crumpled to the floor.

"I saw what you did to my transfuser machine," Eleanor said. "It'll take me a week to get another one delivered. You're gonna pay for that, little lady. Pay dearly. I'm gonna punish you the old-fashioned way."

But Maria wasn't listening. She was looking up at the crib, realizing that was the last time in her life she'd ever get to hold a baby.

Then Harry grabbed her.

Letti shoved the woman with the artificial legs aside, reaching out her arms to catch Mal, who was screaming as he fell. He came down face-first, but Letti was ready for it, keeping her back straight, bending her knees, grasping him tight just inches before his head cracked against the ground.

"We have to go," Florence said. "Now."

She was right. Eleanor's brood was coming down the ladder.

The four of them hurried into the next room, shutting the door behind them. Letti, Florence, and the legless woman—Letti remembered that Mal called her *Deb*—began to stack boxes against the door, moving as fast as they could.

"Where's Kelly?" Florence asked.

"She disappeared with JD and Cam."

"They must have gone through here," Mal said, poking his head into the room with the suitcases. "Maybe they found an exit."

Letti hefted a particularly heavy box of pills, dropping it on the pile. "Okay, let's go. Right now. Come on, Florence."

"No," Florence said.

Letti stopped and stared at her mother. "What do you mean, *no*?"

Florence came up to Letti and did something completely out of character.

She held her daughter's hands.

She hasn't done that since I was a kid.

"Someone has to stay here and hold them off so you can get away," Florence said.

Letti shook her head. "No way. We don't have time for this. You're coming with us."

Florence smiled, but it was a sad smile.

Oh no. This isn't happening. She isn't going to do what I think she's going to do.

"I'm sorry. I'm so, so sorry, Letti. I was stubborn. I thought I knew better. But the fact is, you're more important to me than anyone else on the planet. I wish I realized that sooner."

"We can do this later, Florence."

"There's not going to be a later, Letti. Not for me."

Letti took her hands back, folding her arms across her chest. "If you stay here, then I'm staying with you."

Florence shook her head. "You need to be there for your daughter, Letti. Like I should have been there for you. I'm sorry I wasn't at your husband's funeral. It's my biggest regret."

A lump grew in Letti's throat.

I waited so long to hear her say those words. But not here. Not now.

"Florence . . ."

"Tell Kelly I'm sorry I wasn't a bigger part of her childhood. And I'm sorry I won't get to see her grow up into the amazing woman I know she's going to become, because she has you as a mother."

Letti's eyes got glassy. "No. You can tell her that yourself, when we all get out of here."

The door shook, toppling some of the boxes.

"I'm not going to get out of here, Letti." Florence said.

"But you are. And you're going to live a long, wonderful life, taking care of my granddaughter."

She's not doing this. Don't let her be doing this.

"Florence . . . please . . ."

Florence touched Letti's cheek, wiped away a tear.

"Of all the things I've done, Letti. All the soldiers I helped to heal. All the hungry I helped to feed. The vaccines I gave. The dams I built. The villages I helped to save. Of all the things I'm proud of, the thing I'm proudest of most of all is you. You're the best thing I've ever done with my life, Letti." The tears came fast now.

"Oh . . . *Mom* . . ."

"I love you so much."

"I love you, too, Mom."

They hugged. A final, desperate, loving hug.

"I always wanted to grow up to be just like you," Letti said, sniffling.

"You grew up to be even better."

More boxes toppled, and the door opened a crack.

"Let's go!" Deb implored.

Mal nodded his head in agreement. "We really gotta get out of here."

Letti tried one more time. "Mom . . . please . . . don't do this."

Florence gently pushed her away. Then she winked.

"It beats dying of cancer. Now, go find Kelly and let your old mother kick some ass."

The door opened halfway, and the freaks began to slide through. Letti watched Mom turn around and face them, knife in hand, standing tall and proud.

Then Letti followed Mal and Deb through the door,

not looking back, not able to see even if she did because her eyes were blurred with tears.

Kelly had seen big cats before, at the zoo. Lions and tigers and cheetahs. But she'd never seen one in the open, without some sort of barrier to protect her.

JD was a large dog, over a hundred pounds. But he was friendly and never killed a single thing, not even the rabbits and ducks that hung around their house.

The cougar was almost twice as big as Kelly's German shepherd. Big and muscular and wild. It looked like it could bite JD's head off.

"We need to run," Cam said, taking Kelly's arm.

"Not without my dog. JD!"

Cam put his hand over Kelly's mouth. He whispered, "Do you want that thing chasing us? Let's go."

Cam pulled on Kelly, but she resisted.

I won't leave JD behind.

The mountain lion slunk closer to the dog, ears flat against its head. JD growled, then charged, biting the cat on the paw.

The cat rolled, cuffing JD across the muzzle, sending him rolling into the woods. The German shepherd whimpered, and the cat stared at Kelly, right in the eyes. It made Kelly's stomach do flip-flops.

Cam's right. We should run.

She and Cam took off, sprinting away from the creature, heading for a copse of trees. When they reached them, Kelly hid behind a thick one, sneaking a glance behind her.

The mountain lion was bounding toward them.

Kelly gasped, feeling just an instant jolt of terror that she couldn't move.

Then, out of the bushes—

JD!

The dog slammed into the cat's side, clamping its jaws onto the larger animal's neck. They rolled in a tangle of limbs, teeth, and claws, JD growling, the cougar roaring.

Then JD yelped, and was still.

JD! Oh no . . .

The cat shook its head, then once again looked in Kelly's direction.

Kelly took Cam's hand, and they ran like hell.

It was dark, and they couldn't see where they were going. Kelly's feet kept slipping, and branches whipped at her face and hands. She stumbled a lot and fell twice. Her finger still hurt. So did her heel, where the rat bit her. But she ignored the pain. She ignored everything except the overwhelming desire to get as far away as possible.

Kelly wasn't sure how far or how long they ran, but Cam got winded before she did. Then Kelly took the lead, urging him on. They darted through the trees, plowed through bushes, traversed a deep ditch, and eventually the ground became rockier and they began to run uphill.

"I can't," Cam finally said, heaving. "I need to rest."

"It might still be behind us."

Kelly knew cheetahs could run over sixty miles per hour. She didn't know the land speed of cougars, but she knew they were faster than humans.

"Just gimme a minute," Cam said. "My lungs are gonna pop."

Kelly stared into the forest, listening for movement. She closed her eyes to tune in better. There were normal forest sounds. Crickets. An owl. Some kind of night bird, chirping. And something else.

Running water. A brook, or a maybe a river.

"Do cougars track by scent?" she asked.

"What? I dunno."

"Come on."

Taking Cam's hand, she dragged him toward the sound. It wasn't easy to pinpoint, and she had to stop often to listen. Eventually, they made it to the bank of a brook. The water was black, maybe fifteen feet wide. She had no idea how deep it was, but it didn't seem to be moving very fast.

"We need to get across," Kelly said.

"It's probably freezing. It's coming down from the mountains."

"It will wash off our scent. And I don't think cougars can swim. Right?"

"I thought they could, but they just don't like water. But you're right. We'll be safer on the other side."

Pleased that Cam agreed with her, they made their way down the slippery bank. Kelly thought about taking off her gym shoes so they wouldn't get wet, but there could be sharp rocks at the bottom of the creek. She chose to keep them on and plunged her foot into the dark water.

The temperature made her gasp. The weather was nice, probably around seventy, and Kelly wasn't chilly even though she wore only jogging pants and an over-sized tee shirt. But the stream felt like stepping into a bucket of ice.

"Is it cold?" Cam asked.

"Real cold."

"Then let's move fast. The less time in the water, the better."

Once again Cam grabbed her hand, and he led her into the water. Each step she took, the water climbed a few inches, and each inch made Kelly catch her breath. By the middle of the stream she was waist-deep and starting to shiver.

"Almost there," Cam said. "You can do it."

The bottom was muddy and sucked at her shoes. The current was also much stronger than it looked, and Kelly could feel it beginning to push her away from Cam. She clung tightly to his glove, afraid she was going to lose her grip. If Cam let go, she'd get washed away.

There are waterfalls around. I saw one. I'm a strong swimmer, but how long would I last trying to swim up-stream? What if—

Then her footing slipped and she fell forward in the water, dunking her face, dropping her scalpel, sure she was going to be carried off.

But Cam held on. He pulled her past the deep part, and Kelly managed to stand up again. Cam continued to guide her along until they were climbing up the opposite bank.

They sat down on the dirt. Wet. Shaking. Exhausted.

"Thanks," she managed.

As pumped up as Kelly was, she still yawned. She had no idea what time it was, but it had to be getting close to dawn.

"We need to keep going," Cam said.

"I'm freezing."

"Come on."

They trudged another hundred yards into the woods, but Kelly was getting colder rather than warmer. Her teeth began to chatter.

"I'll build a fire," Cam said.

Kelly shook her head. "Those men might see it. Or the cougar."

"We need to warm up or we'll get hypothermia. Come here."

She went to Cam, and they sat down next to a large boulder. Cam put his arm around her, holding her close.

It warmed Kelly up. But it did more than that. For the first time in hours, she felt safe.

"What about my family?" she asked, her face against Cam's neck.

"We'll find them in the morning."

"And JD?"

"I dunno. Maybe he's okay. Did you see the cat kill him?"

"No."

"Then maybe he got away. He saved our lives, Kelly."

She hoped Cam was right. And then, on a wild impulse, she gave him a quick kiss on the cheek.

The first boy I ever kissed.

"What's that for?" Cam asked.

"For keeping me safe."

Then Kelly closed her eyes. She was cold, frightened, hurt, worried out of her mind for those she loved. But resting on Cam's shoulder, his strong arm around her, Kelly somehow was able to fall asleep.

Florence Pillsbury had seen death. She'd seen it up close and personal. Messy, terrible death. Quiet, peaceful death. Death by war and disease and famine and disaster.

She didn't fear death. Death was part of life.

Florence knew she'd had a good life. She'd seen things.

Done things. Raised a terrific daughter. Lived to the fullest, and cherished every day.

Now, it had all come down to this. All of her years of work, and wisdom, and experience, were reduced to this one, penultimate moment.

I will not let any of these bastards get my family.

The first freak lurched forward, waving his arms, howling through a deformed mouth.

Florence drove her knife into his throat.

Two more came.

She slashed at their faces, their hands. Kicked one away. Stabbed the other in the heart.

Three more came.

Another jab in the throat. A punch in the face. A kick between the legs. Two more swipes of the blade.

Three more came.

Florence backed up. She bent down, took a handful of dirt, threw it in their faces. Slashed one. Punched one. Kicked one. Stabbed another that had gotten back up.

Four more came.

Florence hacked and poked and pushed, and their precious blood poured from their wounds.

You won't get my family.

The freaks formed a half circle around Florence, closing in. Some had weapons. Knives. Sticks. A pitchfork.

Florence advanced, hyperfocused, letting one of them stab her in the arm so she could slash his throat and take his knife. With blades in both hands, she backed them up, cutting off the fingers that reached for her, poking at them superficially, hoping their hemophilia would prove fatal.

And the bodies began to pile up. Five. Seven. Ten.

But more kept coming. A seemingly endless army of

mutants. Florence was finding it harder to lift her injured arm. She chanced a look and saw the wound was bad.

Then the pitchfork hit her in the stomach.

Florence dropped both knives, grabbing the handle of the pitchfork, pulling it away from its owner. She spun it around, jabbing everything that moved. The horde backed away, staying out of range. There were still at least a dozen left.

Florence advanced again, but felt something rip in her belly. She knew what it meant.

My injury is fatal.

I'm dead.

I don't have long left.

The old woman ground her teeth together.

But you still won't get my family.

More freaks came in. With more weapons.

Florence limped into the fray. She kicked until she had no energy to kick anymore. She jabbed at everything that moved, jabbed as her insides burned and twisted, jabbed until her entire universe was reduced to one overpowering thought:

YOU! WILL! NOT! GET! MY! FAMILY!

And they fell. One by one they fell. Eleanor's terrible progeny. The killers of countless innocents. Florence stabbed and stabbed and stabbed, and then she upgraded the pitchfork to a machete and chopped at the monsters until there was nothing left but a gigantic pile of lifeless, misshapen flesh.

Then, clutching her stomach, Florence collapsed onto the ground.

She was light-headed. And cold. So cold.

The first symptoms of shock.

But it's okay. I did it.

They're safe.

My family is safe.

Good-bye, Letti.

Good-bye, Kelly.

I love you both so very much.

"Well, lookee what we got here."

Florence glanced up. The man who spoke was massive, wearing some sort of padded body suit. Long gray hair poked through the football helmet on his head.

"Y'all do this by yourself, old lady? *Shee-it.* Momma gonna be upset. Now she gonna have to start all over again."

The man reached down and took the machete from Florence. She didn't have the strength to fight him.

"You must be one tough ole bird. Y'all know what we do to old birds round these parts? We cut off their heads 'n' cook 'em up in a soup." The man cackled, raising the machete.

"What's your name?" Florence asked. It took practically the last of her energy to speak.

"Millard Fillmore Roosevelt," he said proudly.

"Well, Millard Fillmore Roosevelt. I have a daughter. Her name is Letti."

Florence smiled at the man. "And my Letti is going to fuck you up so bad your momma won't recognize your dead body."

And then Florence laughed. She laughed so deeply and heartily that she didn't feel a thing when Millard chopped off her head.

* * *

Letti was torn between worrying about her mother, worrying about her daughter, and worrying about herself.

Mal led the way through the luggage maze, using his cell phone's screen to illuminate the pathway. The smell started off bad and then got worse. Letti held her nose and stepped carefully; she didn't have shoes on.

Kelly got away. And any second now, Mom will be coming up behind us.

Irrational as it was, she kept repeating it in her head, over and over.

"Are you okay?" Deb, the one with the artificial legs, whispered to Letti.

"I'll manage."

"You're Letti, right? I'm Deb. Your mother was a very brave woman."

Letti noted Deb's use of the past tense, but she didn't contradict it.

"I have to find my daughter."

"We'll find her."

We'll find her any second now.

"Oh shit," Mal called back to them. "Ladies, we've got a lot of dead bodies up here. And some rats."

Letti looked down at her bare feet.

"How many rats?" Letti asked.

She found out a moment later. They stampeded her way, covering the ground like a moving, squealing blanket. Letti tried to stay calm, but once the first one ran over her naked toes she freaked out and began to run forward. Within seconds, she caught up to Mal, who was so startled by her he dropped his phone.

The room blinked into darkness. A rat hopped onto Letti's calf, and she flung it off, backing away, stepping on—

"Jesus!"

The pain rocketed up through Letti's foot, making her fall onto her butt.

The rats swarmed on her.

Little feet and greasy fur and rubbery tails soon covered every inch of her body. They climbed up her shirt. They got in her hair. Letti squeezed her eyes and mouth closed and kept absolutely still, even though her every nerve told her to start screaming and slapping them off.

Don't attack them, and they won't bite.

It seemed like an eternity, but the rats eventually climbed off, continuing on their way. Except for the one tangled in her hair. Letti bit her lower lip and grabbed it behind the head. Then she gently pulled it free and tossed it into the darkness.

The cell phone light came back on, and Mal knelt next to her.

"Oh shit."

"I've got something in my foot," Letti said.

He shined the phone's screen at her legs, and Letti saw what she'd stepped on.

A skeletal hand. One of the finger bones is sticking through my arch.

"I got it," Deb said. Without warning, she yanked the old bone free.

Letti bled like wine being poured.

"Can you make it?" Deb asked.

"Do I have a choice?"

"Bring the light over here, Mal."

Mal came over, pointing his phone at the wall of suitcases.

But they weren't suitcases anymore.

They were corpses. Stacked up everywhere. A wall of decaying human beings.

Letti flexed her toes, and winced. It felt like there was something still stuck in there. The thought that a fingernail, or part of a bone, was still in her foot was worse than being trampled by rats.

How strange the rodents just ran past like that. Almost as if something were chasing them . . .

Deb found an older body—a man dressed in a moldering suit—and began to untie the laces on his shoes. When she tried to pull off the shoe, the foot came with it.

Letti appreciated her efforts, but, *yuck*.

Deb managed to empty out the shoe and she threw it, and a holey, smelly sock, at Letti's feet. Letti tied the sock around her wound. The old leather shoe was big enough to fit over the makeshift bandage, but when she tied it the laces broke off. She managed to make a good knot, and then Deb tossed her its partner.

"Come on," Deb said.

She and Mal helped Letti up. When she took her first step, she felt like crying. It hurt worse than childbirth. Letti thought about telling them to go on ahead of her, but then remembered Kelly and willingly bore the pain.

"There's a gate," Mal said. "Right up ahead."

Letti limped forward. A gate meant Kelly got out. Maybe she was nearby.

Maybe she was—

"Oh shit."

That's apparently Mal's catchphrase.

"What is—?"

"Shh!" Mal hissed. "We need to go back. Fast."

Letti shook her head. She wasn't going back in that house, ever. She was going to find her daughter. Pushing past Mal, she shoved the wrought iron gate, welcoming the cool night air.

That's when she saw it.

A mountain lion.

It was big, and in the moonlight Deb could see the blood on its face.

That must be what the rats were running from.

Letti backed up, but the lion had already noticed her. It dropped low to the ground, stalking forward, taking its time. Letti tried to close the gate, but it had no latch. The cat was going to get in and slaughter them all.

"Hold this," Mal said, handing Letti the cell and pushing her aside. Then he reached for something on his belt.

The plastic bag with his severed hand in it.

"Here, kitty kitty kitty," Mal said. "I've got a treat for you."

Then he threw the bag into the woods.

Incredibly, the cat bounded after it, vanishing into the underbrush.

"Well," Mal said. "I guess that came in handy."

Then the trio ran like crazy in the opposite direction, blending into the forest, dodging trees and rocks and bushes. Each step was agony for Letti.

Pain, compounded by uncertainty for Kelly.

The cougar had blood on its face. Had it gotten my little girl?

They ran until Deb tripped, falling onto her suitcase. Letti helped her up.

"Can you make it?" Letti asked.

"Do I have a choice?"

They trekked onward. Letti knew that she might be getting close to Kelly, or might be getting farther away from her. She had to know which.

"Hold up," she told Mal and Deb. "I have to call for my daughter."

"We'll help," Mal said.

Even though Letti was exhausted, frazzled, and in pain, the gesture touched her.

"If you do, it will give away our position."

"Then we fight," Deb said. "Your mother gave us a chance. The least we can do is help you."

Letti nodded her thanks. Then she cupped her hands to the side of her mouth and yelled, "Kelly!"

Mal and Deb joined in. They yelled and yelled and yelled into the woods until their voices were raw.

The woods didn't answer.

Maria woke up when her cell door opened. She'd spent the last few hours lying on the dirt floor, drifting in and out of troubled sleep. Because she anticipated what was coming, she'd been weighing the pros and cons of suicide. But even if she had a way to end her own life, Maria ultimately knew she wouldn't take it.

I'm a fighter. I'm going to fight to the very end.

Maria looked up as Harry and Eleanor entered. Harry had a cattle prod.

Eleanor had a shotgun.

"It's punishment time," Eleanor said. She was wearing another one of her ridiculous Jackie O style outfits, with a matching pink hat, and appeared positively jubilant. "You've caused quite a bit of trouble, little missy. It's gonna take years for us to recover. But us Roosevelts are survivors. We'll make do. Unlike this fella."

Eleanor tossed something at her. Something brown and squarish.

A wallet.

If it was possible for Maria's heart to sink even lower, it did. She reached for the wallet, hands shaking, and flipped it open, seeing Felix's driver's license picture staring back at her.

"Ronald et him up. That was all he left."

The tears came, fast and hard.

"Millard's gone out after your brother. Should be bringin' him back soon. You know those fellas spent a whole year lookin' for you? Year of their lives, just to find your sorry soul. What a waste."

Harry, giggling wetly, bent down to grab her. Slobber and snot ran out the triangular hole in his face. Maria backed away and got the cattle prod jammed into her ribs for her resistance. She doubled over, falling to her knees.

"Now, y'all are gonna walk nice and quiet like a proper lady, or Harry is gonna break your knees and carry you."

Do I want to be complicit in this? Maybe I should let him break my knees.

No. What's coming is horrible enough.

Maria stood up. She walked, stoically, out of her cell, through the hall. The room with the thalidomide boxes was littered with the bodies of Eleanor's children. It smelled like blood, offal, and shit. Swarms of buzzing flies hung in the air like a black cloud. Maria stared at the faces of the dead, recognizing each of her tormentors, but found no joy or peace in their destruction.

They got what they deserved. But it won't bring Felix back, and it won't save me.

At the thought of Felix, she began to cry again.

They led Maria up the ladder and through the house, where even more of the dead were strewn about. She marched up the stairs slowly, as if she were on her way to the gallows.

But this is even worse than a hangman's noose.

Maria was frightened. More frightened than she'd been anytime in the last year. Of all the horrible things they'd done to her, this would be the worst. But she refused to show Eleanor any fear. She wouldn't beg. She wouldn't bargain or plead. When the time came, she'd spit right in that bitch's face.

Finally, they reached the third floor. Maria saw the long chains, with the cuffs, attached to the metal banister.

Strappado.

They were going to attach the chains to her arms, then drop her twenty feet. It would dislocate her shoulders, arms, and wrists, tearing muscles, ripping tendons. Maria remembered when they did this to poor Larry, Sue's husband. He screamed for weeks afterward.

"I'm thinking of a number from one to ten," Eleanor said, her bug eyes glinting. "Guess what it is?"

Maria said nothing, refusing to play Eleanor's sick game.

"It's ten," Eleanor said. "That's how many times we're going to drop you. You're a thin girl, so it shouldn't be fatal. But I bet dollars to donuts that after the second drop, y'all will wish it was."

Maria cleared her throat and hocked a good one right into Eleanor's eyes.

Eleanor pawed at her face, wiping the spit away. "Let's make it eleven," she said. "Harry, put the chains on her."

The harelip stuck his tongue through his nostril hole and nodded. Maria made a fist and punched Eleanor in the nose, grabbing onto the shotgun's barrel. Before she could wrestle it away, Harry was behind her, grasping Maria in a suffocating bear hug.

Eleanor touched her nose, saw blood on her fingers. She quickly removed a packet of QuikClot from her pocket and shoved some of the powder up her nostrils. When the bleeding had stopped, she got in Maria's face. "For that, your last drop will be from your ankles." Then Eleanor reached down for the chains.

Kelly woke up and saw the sun peeking through the trees. She was cold and damp and in the forest, and her ankle and finger hurt like crazy, but her first thought was a positive one.

I'm still alive.

That brief moment of elation was wiped away by panic when she saw Cam was missing. Kelly looked around the woods, but he wasn't anywhere around.

"Cam!" she yelled.

She stood up, her vertebra crackling, and did a slow 360-degree turn.

Maybe he went to find water. Kelly couldn't remember ever being so thirsty.

Or maybe . . .

Maybe they got him.

That thought made her skin crawl. She didn't want to be out here, all alone.

"Cam! Where are you!"

"Hey, Kelly."

Startled, Kelly spun around toward the voice. It was Cam. He had a weird look on his face, one that made him seem like a completely different person.

"I was scared," she said, walking toward him.

"Me, too."

And then his shoulders drooped and he began to cry. Kelly went to him, giving him a hug, feeling his whole body shake with his sobs.

"We're going to get out of this," she said, patting his back. "We'll find my family, we'll find your sister, and we'll get to a road. It's all going to be okay."

Cam put his arms around her. "I keep hearing the screaming."

Kelly wasn't sure what he meant, but there had been a lot of screaming lately.

"It's over now."

Cam shoved her away. "No, it's not! I still hear it!"

Kelly was a bit shocked by how hard he pushed her. He almost knocked her over.

"Take it easy, Cam. There's no one screaming right now."

He put his face in his hands. "Yes, there is."

Kelly listened. She heard normal forest sounds, but no screaming.

"Cam, there's really nobody screaming."

Cam squatted, hugging his knees. He began to rock back and forth.

"I hear it," he said. "I know it's not real, but I hear it anyway. I just want to make it stop."

"What are you talking about?"

Cam got a faraway look in his eyes.

"We were fourteen," he said. "Me and my friend. When we went into that abandoned house. The autopsy report stated he was stabbed more than a hundred and thirty times. None of them were fatal. My best friend died of blood loss. I . . . I can hear his screams sometimes. Not just in my dreams. But when I'm awake. Like now. Sometimes I hear him. Screaming. Begging to be let go."

He's losing it. The poor guy is losing it.

She walked up to Cam, softly put her hand on his shoulder. "It wasn't your fault. You were locked in the closet."

His face drained of color. He appeared terrified. "Do you know what it's like to hear screaming all the time, Kelly?"

"You can't blame yourself, Cam." She rubbed his back.

"Sure I can. I could have done something. I could have stopped it."

Kelly squatted down next to him. "You were just a kid. What were you supposed to do?"

"I can hear the screaming right now." Cam cast a frantic glance into the woods. "I can hear him, like he's right next to me. Begging to live. And then, after a while, begging to die." He put his knuckle in his mouth. "It took him such a long time to die."

Kelly wasn't sure what to do. He was supposed to be the adult, not her. Lost in the woods, being chased by freaks and a mountain lion, wasn't a good time to have a nervous breakdown.

"That's over, Cam. Now you're here with me. You need to be strong. And we need to go find help."

Cam looked at Kelly like he hadn't realized she'd been there. "There's no help. Not for him." A darkness came over his face. "And not for you."

"Stop it, Cam. You're scaring me."

"That's what my best friend said," Cam said. "After I tied him up."

Kelly felt the world start to spin. She thought Cam was just stressed, freaking out because of everything that had happened. Maybe having some kind of flashback.

But now she knew different.

"You killed him," she whispered.

Cam didn't say anything.

"Did you kill your friend, Cam?"

"I blamed it on a stranger. Said I was locked in the closet. I think the police suspected me, but no one could prove anything. I wore gloves. Brought along an extra set of clothes."

"Why?" Kelly asked, backing away. She really didn't want to know. She just wanted some time to get some distance between them.

"To see if I could get away with it. And I did. But even after he died, I could still hear his screams. They were so loud, I couldn't sleep. I tried to kill myself, but the screaming still wouldn't go away. So I did it again, with someone else. In the institution. I thought maybe if I killed another person, my friend would have some company and finally shut the fuck up. But that didn't work, either. So now I'm thinking something else."

He's a psycho.

But Kelly was too frightened to move.

"What are you thinking, Cam?" Kelly asked, her voice cracking.

Cam pulled a scalpel from his back pocket. "I'm thinking, third time is a charm."

He lunged at her, grabbing Kelly's arm, poking her in the shoulder with the blade.

Kelly screamed like she'd never screamed before in her life.

"That's how he screamed," Cam said.

Then he poked her again.

* * *

Deb, who'd been in a dozen triathlons and three marathons, had never been so tired. They'd spent the entire night calling for Letti's daughter, and she was practically hoarse. Each step she took was agonizing. Without the gel socks, her prosthetics chafed at her skin. It felt like everything below her pelvis was one giant blister, getting rubbed with sand.

Mal looked equally disheveled. She knew how traumatic losing a limb was, both physically and emotionally. That he'd managed to keep going, and even retain a sense of humor, showed Deb what a hell of a guy he really was.

He'd noticed her grimacing earlier and had offered to shoulder her suitcase with her extra legs in it.

"I don't need you to give me a hand," Deb had told him.

Mal had laughed at that, and when Deb realized what she said, she was mortified.

"It's okay. It makes up for my *gotten off on the wrong foot* comment when we met."

And he took her bag. Just lost a limb, and he took her bag.

If we get out of this alive, I may have to rethink my no-dating rule.

Letti was the one who appeared most distraught of all. She continued pushing forward, even with a drastic limp, stopping every minute to shout her daughter's name.

Deb knew it was counterproductive at this point. Kelly wasn't answering. And undoubtedly both that cougar, and the remainder of Eleanor's wacko family, could locate them without much difficulty. But neither she nor Mal told Letti to stop.

If it were my kid, I wouldn't stop, either.

Deb had no idea how far they'd traveled, because the woods all looked the same. It became a little easier as the sun came up, but after so many trees and rocks it all just blended together.

"At least it's a pretty view," Mal said, coming up beside Deb. "Check out those mountains."

Deb rolled her eyes. "If you've seen one mountain, you've seen . . . oh my God."

"What?"

"I *have* seen this mountain. I've seen this mountain, from this very spot."

Deb stopped, looking around. She knew, as long as she lived, she'd always remember this spot.

This is where the mountain lion attacked me. I crawled through this area, with two broken legs.

"What are you saying, Deb?"

"Up ahead, just around that bend. The cliff."

"The one you . . . ?"

"Yeah."

"So there's a road around here. Right?"

Deb shook her head. "I had a Jeep. I'd taken it down a trail. The trail is two miles away, but the main road is five more miles."

"Seven miles? That's a long hike. Do you think you can still find the trail?"

"I don't have to. After my accident, the county built a lookout platform on top of the mountain I fell from. There might be someone there right now. If not, they for sure have a radio. Direct line to the ranger station."

Mal was nodding enthusiastically. "We could contact them. They'd pick us up."

They'd tried using Mal's phone to call for help, but that had led nowhere. Even though they found a cell signal and managed to contact the authorities, no one knew where the Rushmore Inn was. Apparently, triangulating a cell phone signal only worked when there were multiple cell towers. Out here, there was only one, and no way to pinpoint their location.

Mal had argued with various people and managed to get the forest rangers to agree to send out a helicopter and look for them.

They hadn't seen any helicopter. And shortly after that conversation, Mal's phone battery died.

He attempted it once more, digging the phone out of his pocket. It wouldn't even power on. Deb tried taking out the battery, rubbing some saliva on the contact points—a trick that often worked on flashlight batteries. It didn't work on cell phones.

"No problem," Mal said. "We'll just get to the lookout tower."

That's when they heard the scream.

It was so far away, it echoed. But Deb could tell it was from a girl.

"It's Kelly," Letti said, limping up to them. "Kelly! Kelly, it's Mom!"

If that was Kelly, she didn't respond.

"KELLY!"

"Letti," Mal said, touching her arm. "We're near a ranger lookout station. We can get help."

If Letti heard him, she didn't show it. Instead, she went limping off into the woods.

"Letti!" Mal yelled after her. "We can get help!"

The forest swallowed her up.

"Should we go after her?" Mal asked.

Deb shook her head. "We know our location. There's a ranger station nearby. The best way we can help her is to get to the authorities."

"How far is this station?"

"Maybe a few hundred yards. But . . ."

"But what?"

"It's about seventy feet up the mountain, Mal."

"It's a lookout tower, right? Maybe if we get to the base of the mountain, they'll see us."

Deb agreed it was their best shot. "Okay. Let's go."

Having a plan reenergized Deb, and she was able to ignore the pain in her legs. But when they finally reached the mountain, she was hit by a wave of vertigo and had to sit down.

It was massive. A giant shelf of solid, grayish-tan rock. There were some outcroppings, a few seams, a patch of dirt here and there where some bushes managed to take root. But it was steeper than she remembered, and bigger.

The old memories came stomping back. She could see the sheer place where she slipped off. The spot where she landed. The mountain bent and tilted in her vision like it was falling on top of Deb, about to bury her forever.

"There's the base," Mal said, pointing at a tiny cabin perched on a shelf of the mountainside. "Hey! We're down here!" He waved his arms, trying to get a response.

No response came.

Mal walked to the mountainside, where the rock met the soil. He placed a foot on the stone, tried for a hand-hold, and got up about eight inches before slipping back down.

It was impossible to mountain climb in the leather dress shoes he wore. And it was doubly impossible to climb with only one hand.

Mal, his expression grim, came back over to Deb. She knew what he was thinking.

"I know," Deb said. "But I can't."

"You're superwoman, remember? You've even got your mountain climbing legs."

Mal patted the suitcase. Deb rubbed her face with her hands.

"You don't understand, Mal."

"Deb, it's okay to be scared. But you can do this. I've seen how you can handle yourself."

"Mal . . ."

"The other time, it was just a fluke. A freak accident. You can make it this time. You can—"

"It wasn't an accident!" Deb said, harsher than she meant to. "It was my fault!"

Mal waited. Deb took a big breath and sighed.

Time to tell the truth.

"I was cocky," she began. "I knew I was a good climber. I knew I could climb this mountain with my eyes closed. So I thought I'd challenge myself. Remember I told you I was hammering in my first piton when I started to slide?"

Mal nodded.

"Look up there." She pointed at the mountain. "See that angled shelf? That's where I fell from. I should have used two or three pitons just to get up to that point. But I was cocky."

"So when you tried to hammer in your first piton the rock gave way . . ."

"Don't you get it, Mal? I didn't use *any* pitons. No ropes. No harnesses. No helmet. I tried to free climb. And I did it without a partner, and without telling anyone where I was. I came here alone, with no gear. It was my own goddamn fault I fell. Not an accident. The rock didn't give way. I just slipped. It was pure stupidity. I was a fucking fool."

She waited for Mal's reaction. His judgment. His disapproval.

He's got to think I'm as big an idiot as I think I am.

But Mal's expression didn't change. And he didn't say anything. He simply kneeled down and opened up her suitcase.

Deb shook her head. "I can't do it, Mal."

He took out her mountain climbing legs. The ones she'd never used, except to bash Eleanor's freaks in the face.

"Mal, I fell off with two good legs. I can't climb that as a cripple."

"You're the strongest person I ever met, Deb."

"I'm an idiot who ruined my life."

"You're an amazing woman. And you're going to climb that mountain, get that radio, and save the day."

He handed her one of the legs. She threw it back at him.

"Don't you see I can't do this!"

"I'm a writer," Mal said. "You're an athlete. If I can learn to type one-handed, you can climb this mountain with no legs."

"And what if I fall off again?"

"Then I'll catch you." Mal winked. "This time you didn't come alone."

Deb didn't know whether to cry, scream, or kiss him. She settled for saying, "Gimme the damn legs."

When she pulled off the Cheetahs they were filled with sweat. Her skin was mottled and blistered and bleeding in some places. But, oddly enough, she didn't care that Mal saw. After laying her soul bare, him seeing her stumps wasn't that big a deal.

Besides, he wasn't looking at her legs. He was looking at her chest again.

"If I make it, you owe me dinner," she said.

"When you make it, I'll take you to Rome. I'll even spring for two rooms so you won't have to share one with me."

Deb looked into his eyes, saw trust and acceptance and obvious affection, and decided that he wouldn't need a separate room.

"Deal," she said.

Then she put on the mountain climbing legs. Unlike the Cheetahs, which were curved, these were L shaped, more like a regular leg and foot. But at the toe were rubber balls with tiny metal spikes sticking out of them. Supposedly for good grip and traction. She didn't know for sure, because the only time she'd ever worn them was during her fitting.

Deb pressed the suction button, sucking out the air from the stump cups so they adhered to her skin. It hurt, but better dealing with pain than dealing with one slipping off.

Mal held out his hand and helped her up. When she found her balance he continued to hold her.

"You can do it," he said.

She nodded, let out a slow breath, and stared at the mountain.

It seemed to have gotten even bigger.

Deb gently disengaged from Mal, then hobbled over to the mountainside. The legs were crap to walk in, but once she got her first toehold they performed as advertised.

She hugged the mountain closely, embracing it, becoming a part of it. She didn't look down. Didn't look up. She looked in the moment, for the next hand grip, the next foot position, the next stable rest point. After a dozen feet up, she found the seam she'd used to get to the shelf and climbed it just as well as she had when she had legs.

It was all so automatic, all so comfortable, that Deb almost forgot her fear.

Then she reached the angled face. The one she slid off. And Deb froze.

I remember sliding down this. I remember the terror. I remember the certainty I'd die. I remember hating myself for making such a stupid mistake.

But most of all, I remember the pain when I fell.

"You can do it!" Mal called from below.

Can I? Can I really?

Maybe I can.

Gritting her teeth, Deb hoisted herself onto the sheer face. The angle didn't seem very steep. That's why she'd been so cocksure before.

Deb reached up, found a tiny protruding nub, and latched her fingers on to it.

One inch at a time, she pulled herself up that shelf. She always made sure at least two limbs had good grips. It was slow going, but effective. She was getting close to reaching a bunch of bushes jutting from the rock face. Once there, she could rest for a minute. Then it would be a pretty easy climb up to the ranger station.

Two feet away now.

Eighteen inches.

A foot.

Deb reached up, ready to grasp a crooked branch, to test to see if it would hold her weight.

The crooked branch moved.

Deb's jaw dropped.

That's not a branch.

I know what that is.

It's a tail.

A crooked tail.

The tail swished and then moved away. It was replaced by a triangular head and two golden eyes.

The cougar.

The cougar with the zigzag tail.

The same one that almost killed me when I fell.

She gasped.

Jesus Christ. It's come back to finish the job.

And then Deb lost her grip and began to slide down the face of the mountain.

"Hey! Boy! Y'all think you a squirrel, hidin' up in that tree?" Felix opened his eyes to a world of pain.

His fingers. His head. His ribs. His hips. His back. Just about every square inch of him hurt. Breathing hurt. Moving hurt. Even thinking hurt.

Plus, he was in a tree.

He looked around, saw he was wedged in the V of a big oak. It was bright outside, the morning sun blinding, and Felix's memories of last night were hazy. But he did recall the cougar, tugging him by his shirt collar, pulling until Felix couldn't breathe anymore.

I must have passed out, and he stashed me in this tree.

Felix knew that other big cats often dragged their prey into trees to keep it from other predators and scavengers. Apparently mountain lions did, too.

"I'm talkin' to ya, boy!"

The tree shook. Felix chanced a look down. Though he'd seen him before only in silhouette, he recognized Ulysses, the tow truck driver. The large man was prettier in the dark. His large, squarish head had a nose that was crooked by about forty-five degrees, making it look like it wasn't completely screwed on. His eyes were also uneven, one higher than the other. He resembled a Picasso.

Ulysses beat the tree trunk with his crowbar once more.

"I been looking all god-dang night for y'all. Getcher ass down here, boy."

Felix didn't think that was a good idea. In fact, he was content to stay up here for the rest of his life. Felix was at least ten feet high, and Ulysses was far too big to climb up after him.

"'Kay. You asked for it."

The big man waddled off. Felix wondered what he was going to do.

Light the tree on fire? Chop it down?

The giant returned with a long length of chain. He wrapped it around the tree trunk and secured it with a heavy padlock.

"*Tim-ber*, asshole."

Then Felix watched him walk over to his truck.

Oh no.

Felix stared down at the ground. A painful drop if he was completely healthy. In his current condition, the fall would be intolerable.

But it beats being dragged behind a tow truck.

Ulysses gunned his engine. Felix realized that the longer he waited, the less courage he would have, so he pressed his mangled hands against the branch, whimpered at the pain in his ribs as he unwedged himself, and then plummeted to the earth.

Hitting the ground was like falling into hell. The pain reached such dizzying heights that it was all he could think about, the only sensation he felt.

Then there was a tremendous cracking sound, like the world was breaking in half, and Felix opened his bleary eyes and saw the tree splitting at the base, dropping down on top of him.

His last remnants of survival instinct kicked in, and Felix rolled away before he was crushed, momentum taking him down into a ditch filled with high grass as the tree was tugged past.

Made it. They haven't killed me yet.

He was dimly aware of the fallen tree slowing down and coming to a stop and a truck door slamming shut. Ulysses was coming to inspect his work.

Gotta get up. Gotta get away.

Miraculously, Felix made it to his feet. He kept low, stumbling past Ulysses as the large man assessed the damage he'd done.

"Where in the heck are ya, boy?"

You want to know where I am? I'm getting into your truck, asshole.

The door handle gave Felix some trouble. The gearshift was even harder.

But he was so used to being in pain at this point that a little more didn't matter.

He hit the accelerator and slammed the tow truck into reverse, backing over Ulysses before the giant even had a chance to turn around. Felix's head bounced against the top of the cab as the rear tire rolled over the bastard's body. Not willing to take any chances, Felix stomped on the clutch, shifted into first gear, and ran Ulysses over again, dragging him a dozen yards. Then he tugged on the emergency brake and got out to see the carnage.

And carnage there was. All that was left of Ulysses

was a mashed leg and an impressive length of intestines, stretching out at least twenty feet.

Felix then turned his attention to the Rushmore Inn, crouching like some prehistoric monster in the forest, waiting to pounce. He half walked, half stumbled to the front entrance, trying to get the knob to work. The door wouldn't budge.

But that didn't deter Felix. He knew how to get inside.

And once inside, he was going to kill every son of a bitch he saw.

"Kelly!"

Letti's throat was so raw from yelling that she was perilously close to losing her voice. But beyond that initial scream, she hadn't heard anything else from her daughter.

Terrible thoughts fueled Letti forward.

Was Kelly hurt? Dying? Dead?

Had they caught her?

What if I don't get there in time?

What if I don't find her at all?

"Kelly!"

Letti limped up a gradual incline. Her foot hadn't stopped bleeding since she'd stepped on that finger bone, and the ill-fitting dead man's shoes had scraped her heels raw. She tried to keep an eye on the ground, looking for some sort of footprints or trail, but the woods all looked the same to her. Maybe Kelly had gone this way. Maybe she was in an entirely different direction.

"Kelly!"

"Dang, yer a loud one."

Letti jerked her head around.

Millard.

He wasn't wearing the football helmet or padded suit anymore. Now he was dressed pure redneck, in bibs and a plaid flannel shirt. His eyes were fire-engine red, and his long gray hair blew crazily around his twisted face.

"Someone wants to say howdy," Millard said. He raised up a blood-soaked pillowcase and dumped the contents on the ground.

Oh . . . Jesus . . . no!

Florence's head bounced in the dirt.

"Mom . . ." Letti whispered.

Millard raised a cattle prod. "And that ain't nuthin' compared to what I gonna—"

Letti pivoted her hips, whipped her leg around, and kicked the tall man in the chin. Millard staggered back, and Letti followed up with a punt between his legs that must have knocked his balls up into his skull.

She didn't stop there. The years of martial arts training her mother had subjected her to were unleashed in an explosion of raw fury. She broke the giant's nose. His cheekbone. His nose again. Ruptured an eardrum. Knocked out two teeth. Knocked out three more teeth. Broke his nose again. Hit his eye so hard it instantly swelled shut.

But the sick son of a bitch didn't go down.

In fact, he seemed to be enjoying it.

I'm going to beat this man to death. I'm going to keep hitting him until my hands and feet are broken. I'm going to—

Millard trapped her leg between his arm and his side on her last kick, and then pulled Letti onto her back.

She squirmed. She twisted. But this man was too big, too strong. And he was still holding the cattle prod.

He zapped her in the belly, making Letti curl up into a fetal position.

"Ain't you a wildcat?" Millard said. He smiled, blood leaking through the gaps in his missing teeth. "Old Millard's good at tamin' wildcats."

He raised the cattle prod like a club, aiming for Letti's head. She got her arm up in time.

At first she thought the *snap!* she heard was the prod breaking in half.

Then the pain hit, and she realized it wasn't the prod at all.

Letti clutched her broken arm to her chest, feeling both sick and unable to breathe.

"All this violence done got me excited," Millard said.

He spit out some blood, tossed the cattle prod aside, and then began unbuttoning his overalls.

The second time Cam stabbed her with the scalpel, Kelly turned and ran. The terrain was rough and rocky, and the woods were thick. She could hear Cam only a few steps behind her, following the path she made through the underbrush, making a sound that was part giggling, part crying.

The woods are too thick. The ground is too uneven. I can't get away from him.

She misstepped, tripping over a tree root, and Cam swooped on top of her, poking her a third time, in the thigh. Then he let her up, let her keep running.

Kelly realized he wasn't trying to kill her. Not right away. He was just going to keep jabbing her with that scalpel.

"The autopsy report stated he was stabbed more than

a hundred and thirty times. None of them were fatal. My best friend died of blood loss."

This scared Kelly even more, made her even more frantic. She tried to watch her footing so she didn't trip again, but she didn't move fast enough and Cam came up behind her, poking her in the back.

It hurt. Every stab hurt worse than a bee sting.

I'm not going to get away. He's going to keep doing this until my whole body is bleeding.

Kelly didn't know where to focus her attention—on her footing or on Cam.

She stumbled again.

He jabbed her a fifth time.

Kelly didn't see how she could get away. He was stronger. He had a weapon. It was too hard to run in the forest. Cam would just keep stabbing her and stabbing her until—

"Be aware of everything around you, and not just what's in front of you."

It was Grandma's voice. The thought was so strong that Kelly felt like Grandma was right next to her, reminding her of what she'd said earlier.

"Use your peripheral vision when you're running over the rocks, so you don't have to keep your head down. Keep your eyes ahead of you, but not your entire focus."

Kelly forced herself to take everything in, not just the ground in front of her.

She remembered the trick Grandma taught her, how to see using the whole eye.

Incredibly, the running became easier. She found her footing without having to slow down, and each step was solid and sure. Listening behind her, Kelly could tell she was pulling ahead of Cam, gaining distance.

Kelly lengthened her strides, letting her feet find their own way. The incline became steeper, but she didn't slow down. Along with hearing Cam clomp through the forest, Kelly heard something else in the distance. Something familiar.

A waterfall.

She opened her ears, sensing its location, and headed toward it. Within two dozen steps the woods broke into a clearing, and Kelly stopped abruptly, staring over the edge of a steep cliff. Her eyes dropped, seeing the waterfall in the distance, the double rainbow floating in the mist it created. Then her eyes dropped further, staring at the rocks below, a drop of forty or fifty feet.

Kelly felt like she did while standing on a diving board. Her knees got weak. Her mouth became dry. She hated heights.

But Grandma came to the rescue again.

"What do you think you should trust more, your eyes, or the solid ground?"

The ground. I trust the ground.

Kelly saw a rock ledge, maybe three feet below her. Narrow, but enough to stand on. It looked solid enough to hold her.

She turned when she heard Cam come up behind her.

"You can run pretty fast, Kelly," he said, out of breath.

Kelly took a small step back, feeling her heels teeter over the edge of the cliff.

"But now you don't have anywhere else to go."

You're wrong. I do have a place to go.

"I think, this time, I can finally make the screaming stop."

Cam moved forward, slow and easy, swishing the

scalpel in the air. Kelly waited until he was within striking distance.

I trust the ground, Grandma.

She looked down, then stepped backward off the cliff.

The cuffs were thick leather, brown and stiff with dried blood. Maria fought while Eleanor buckled them on, kicking and punching, enduring jolt after jolt from the cattle prod from Harry as he giggled and drooled. She finally fell to her knees, weak and shaking, unable to resist anymore.

Eleanor opened the latch on the banister, swinging the gate open.

"So feisty," Eleanor said, her bug eyes glinting. "But I think this first drop will take the fight right out of you."

Eleanor began to shove her toward the edge. Maria spread out her feet, grasping at Eleanor's ankles, but the old woman was too powerful and continued to push.

A foot away.

Six inches.

I'm going to drop. I'm going to drop, and the fall will rip my shoulders from my sockets.

Maria closed her eyes and set her jaw, trying to prepare herself for the oncoming agony.

Then there was a crash. A gigantic crash that shook the entire house.

"Go check!" Eleanor ordered Harry.

He loped off, and while Eleanor was distracted, Maria grasped her chains and whipped them straight at the bitch's head.

Eleanor staggered back, and Maria scrambled away, heading for the shotgun propped up against the wall.

The old woman recovered quickly, grabbing Maria's chain, yanking her to a stop. The shotgun was almost within reach. Maria strained for it, kicking out her foot, knocking it onto the floor.

But then she was being yanked back to the railing. Eleanor reeled in the chain, hand over hand, like a longshoreman pulling in a net. Maria stood up, pulling back, putting her whole body into it. But there was no way she'd win this tug of war. Eleanor was too strong. Too heavy.

Inch by inch, Maria lost ground. She tried to shake the chains, but it had no effect. She changed positions, draping the chains over her shoulder, leaning in the opposite direction. But inch by terrible inch, Eleanor brought Maria back to the banister.

"I have royal blood!" Eleanor grunted, grabbing Maria by the wrists. "You can't defy me!"

And then she shoved Maria off the edge.

Kelly dropped down off the edge of the cliff, landing on the ledge a few feet below.

She didn't look down. She had no need to.

I trust the ground is solid. I trust my feet. I'm not going to fall.

She hugged the cliff face, knees slightly bent, and waited for Cam.

"Kelly?" she heard him say, giggling. "You did *not* just jump down there." A moment later, she saw Cam's face peer over the edge.

"Whoa. We're pretty high."

Then Kelly started screaming. She screamed loud and long. Over and over.

"Shut up!"

Cam slapped his hands to his ears. Kelly screamed even louder.

"Why did you kill me, Cam! Why didn't you let me go! I'm your best friend!"

"Shut up! Shut up! Shut up!"

Cam got on his knees, scalpel in hand, obviously desperate to silence her.

Kelly jumped up, snatching Cam's hair, holding on while trusting her feet would find the ledge again.

Momentum took him off the edge of the cliff and right over her head. Kelly's feet landed solidly.

Kelly didn't bother watching him smash into the rocks below. But she heard it. A long, fading wail, ending in a sound like a belly flop.

I did it.

I'm alive.

I'm alive!

Then Kelly chinned-up to level ground and then ran into the woods, anxious to find Mom.

Felix climbed out of the truck. Driving through the front door of the inn had done quite a bit of damage to both the vehicle and the building. He also could add whiplash to his shopping list of injuries.

He looked around the room and felt his heart skip a beat.

This place is a slaughterhouse.

The dead were strewn about everywhere, and a large cloud of flies buzzed about, hopping from one bloody treat to the next.

Is Maria one of them? What happened here?

Most of them looked deformed. Felix wondered if he

should start searching corpses. Then he had something more pressing to deal with.

Harry.

The harelipped man jogged down the stairs, running right at him. Felix backpedaled, but Harry was too fast. His huge hands wrapped around Felix's throat, completely encircling it. Harry giggled, spit and snot dripping through the split in his face, and then began to squeeze.

Felix instantly saw stars. He swatted ineffectively at Harry's face, then made a halfhearted attempt to scratch at the giant's eyes. Harry began to shake him, and Felix felt the edges of his vision begin to dim.

Weapon. Need a weapon.

But he had no weapons. The only thing he had on him was his cell phone. The phone he'd carried with him every day since Maria disappeared. The phone with her last text message to him on it, that he'd read over a thousand times.

The phone.

Felix fumbled for his ripped pocket, digging out the phone with his thumb and pinky.

Choke on it, asshole.

Then he shoved it right down the massive hole in Harry's face. Felix pushed past Harry's squirming tongue, fitting his whole hand inside the split palate, jamming the phone into Harry's throat.

Harry's reaction was instant. He dropped Felix and clawed at his own face, digging his fingers into his mouth. But his fingers were too large, and the phone was down too deep.

Felix picked himself up off the floor, then stared up at Harry as his face turned red enough to match his eyes.

And then Felix saw something else. Something above

Harry. A woman, hanging from the railing up on the third floor, her feet dangling down.

Maria?

Maria!

As the giant Harry keeled over, Felix ran around him, ignoring all of the pain in his body, bounding up the stairs with energy driven by love, flying up the first flight, the second flight, desperate to reach her before she fell.

Save her. Got to save her. Got to—

"Sorry, lover boy. Y'all don't get to be the hero."

Felix stared at Eleanor. Stared at the shotgun in her hands.

The sound was thunderous.

The shot slammed Felix into the wall.

For a moment, he felt a stabbing, white-hot pain.

Then he didn't feel anything at all.

Millard dropped his overalls to his ankles, revealing a pair of filthy tighty-whities. His head was leaking blood like a sieve, but it didn't stop him from smiling. He tugged a packet out of his breast pocket and dusted powder all over his face, making him look like a ghost.

Letti's broken arm hurt like crazy, but she wasn't thinking about herself. She was thinking about Kelly. And Mom.

I'll get him for you, Mom. Maybe not today. Maybe not next month. But I will kill this son of a bitch.

Millard spat out pink clumps of styptic.

"You like eatin' dirt before, whore? Maybe I give you a bit more to snack on."

Millard bent down, reaching for the earth, and then he doubled over in a blur of blood and fur.

JD!

The German shepherd locked his jaws right between Millard's legs, shaking his muzzle back and forth, trying to rip his manhood free.

Two tugs later, the dog did.

Millard rolled around on the ground, holding his crotch with both hands, swearing and moaning. JD went for his throat, but Letti called him back.

"JD, sit! I got this one."

It took Letti a minute to find a suitable rock. Big enough to do the job, but not so big she couldn't lift it one-handed. Once she made her selection, she stood over Millard, whose red eyes were as wide as dinner plates.

"Eat dirt?" Letti asked. "Eat this."

She smashed the rock down onto Millard's screaming face. Over and over and over.

After the tenth or eleventh blow, his head split like a cleaved watermelon.

Letti dropped the bloody rock and spat on his corpse.

JD limped over to her. She could see a gash in his leg. It looked pretty ugly, but Letti vowed right there to get him the best vet in the country.

"Good dog," Letti said, patting his head. "You are one really good dog.

He wagged his tail and licked her face. Then his ears pricked up, and he bounded off into the woods.

"JD!" she yelled.

"Mom!"

Kelly!

Letti hurried after the dog, and found him running

circles around her daughter. Kelly hurried over to Letti, embracing her, and Letti hugged her back despite her broken arm. Love was the best pain reliever in the world.

"I followed your footsteps, Mom! That's how I found you!"

"I love you, Kelly. I love you so, so much."

Kelly buried her face in Letti's neck. "I love you, too, Mom. Where's Grandma?"

Letti gripped her daughter tighter. "Grandma didn't make it, honey."

Kelly pulled away. She looked older. Much older. And Letti saw a glimpse of what her mother told her. Of the amazing woman Kelly would grow up to become.

"She saved me, Mom," Kelly said. "Grandma saved my life."

Letti blinked back the tears. Tears of pain. Tears of loss. But mostly, tears of pride. Pride in her daughter, and pride in her mother.

"She saved us all, baby. Your grandma saved us all."

Hanging from the banister, Maria heard the shotgun blast. And she knew whom Eleanor had shot.

Felix. My Felix.

He came for me.

And she killed him.

The anger in Maria took over, like a monster invading her body. It worked into every pore, every cell, filling her with such all-encompassing rage that Maria felt like she could put her fist through a brick wall.

Maria hooked a leg up on the bottom of the railing, pulling herself onto the third floor. Eleanor swung the gun around, but Maria was already running at her, the chain wrapped tight around her fist.

She punched Eleanor in the nose again, doing even more damage this time. Eleanor moaned, and Maria tore the double-barreled shotgun from the old woman's hands. She aimed at the bitch's diseased head and pulled both triggers.

Nothing happened. The gun was empty.

Changing her grip, Maria brought the gun back like a baseball bat, swinging with everything she had, cracking Eleanor across the head so hard it could be heard in neighboring states. Eleanor collapsed, but Maria's attention was already on Felix, the blood spreading across his chest.

Maria tore at the buckles on her wrist cuffs, using her teeth, and pulled her hands free. She patted down Eleanor's body and found a packet of QuikClot.

Hurrying to Felix, she lifted up his blood-soaked shirt, dumping the powder on him, pressing it into the jagged buckshot wounds on his chest and shoulder.

"Please," she said. "I've waited so long for you. Please don't leave me, Felix."

She put her fingers on his neck, trying to find a pulse, but her hands were shaking too badly.

"You can't die, honey. You can't. Not now. Not after all of this."

She put her ear to his chest, but couldn't hear a damn thing. Not knowing what else to do, she wrapped her arms around him, pressing his cheek to hers, rocking him back and forth.

"I love you, Felix. I love you so much."

This isn't how it's supposed to end. After all of this, it's supposed to end happily.

A whole year I dreamed, prayed, for this moment.
This can't be the end.

And then Felix mumbled something.

"Felix? Oh my God, Felix? What did you say?"

"I love you, too, babe," he said. "God, you're so beautiful."

"I missed you so much."

"I missed you, too. You think you can get me an aspirin?"

Maria began to laugh so hard she wept.

Deb splayed out her arms, trying to palm the sheer face of the rock, but she kept sliding. The metal spikes of her prosthetics skipped across the surface of the shelf, not any better at traction than the climbing shoes she wore years ago when she was in this very same situation.

Above her, the cougar watched her slow descent with narrow, evil eyes, swishing his broken tail back and forth.

It's happening again. I'm reliving my worst nightmare.

And Deb knew, from past experience, that she had only six seconds left. Then she'd be over the edge, and even Mal with all of his good intentions wouldn't be able to catch her when she fell.

Strangely, mixed in with the terror was a bit of melancholy.

Is this what I was meant to do in life? Make the same mistakes?

"Use your leg!" Mal yelled up at her.

I can't use my leg, you moron. They keep slipping. What I need is longer arms to grab onto that outcropping just out of my reach.

Oh, son of a bitch!

Suddenly understanding Mal's advice, Deb reached down and hit the button on her right stump cup. The air hissed out, breaking the suction, and she tugged off her leg.

Only a few seconds left! I have only one shot!

She stretched, using her leg like a climbing pick, holding on to the cup and swinging the foot upward at the outcropping.

It caught!

Deb stopped sliding. She hung there, gripping her prosthetic, the metal barbs in the toe hooked around the protruding rock.

Okay. Now I just need to get to it.

There were no other handholds or footholds, so Deb had to slowly chin herself up. Her prosthetic wasn't secure enough to hang from, but it was enough to hold her on this incline. She raised herself gradually, bit by bit, until she was able to get her fingers on the outcropping.

From there, it was only a few inches to the seam. Once she had a solid grip, she put her leg back on, pressing the button for suction.

This route was trickier than the other one. Steeper. Fewer decent holds. But this route didn't have a cougar waiting for her, so Deb followed the seam, keeping away from the shelf where the creature perched.

After five minutes, she found her rhythm. Handhold. Toehold. Handhold.

Toehold.

After ten minutes, the lookout station was in sight. Deb kept her emotions in check, but she was secretly astonished that she was actually going to make it.

"Deb!" Mal yelled.

Deb looked down. The cougar was a few feet below her, legs splayed out, clinging to the rock face. It thrust its entire body upward, its massive claws batting her artificial leg.

Of course it can climb. That's why they're called mountain lions.

Deb stuck her hand deep in a crevice, gripping the stone inside, waiting for the next lunge.

The lion jumped again, coming up another two feet, its fierce jaws locking around Deb's stump cup.

Deb quickly reached down, hitting the release. Her leg came off.

The cougar, losing its balance, fell from the rock face. It landed a few feet below, on the angled, sheer face where Deb had slid off all those years ago.

Like Deb, the cougar couldn't get a grip on the sheer rock. It spread out all four legs, claws scraping against stone, but couldn't stop its inevitable slide.

"How do you like it?" Deb shouted at the lion.

It roared once—an angry, futile roar—and then the monster that had haunted Deb's dreams for so long slipped right off the edge of the mountain, falling thirty long feet, smashing to the unforgiving ground below in a brilliant explosion of blood.

And it felt pretty goddamn good.

"You okay?!" Mal called to her.

"Yeah! Are you?!"

"I am! But it's raining cats and dogs down here!"

Deb smiled.

Next time I have a chance, I'm going to kiss that guy.

The rest of the climb, even with only one leg, was uneventful. Deb made it to the shelf and crawled to the lookout post. It was unoccupied, but the rangers were kind enough to leave a door open for her, and a fully charged radio.

"Hello, hello? This is Deb Novachek. I'm with Mal Deiter. We called earlier, and there's a helicopter looking for us. Can anyone hear me?"

"This is ranger base three. We read you, Deb. Over." Deb practically wept.

"I'm at a lookout station. The number on the radio is six-four-eight-seven-two."

"Roger that. We'll send the chopper your way."

Deb found a stash of water bottles next to the radio. She twisted the top off one, drank the whole thing in a few gulps, and let out the biggest sigh of her life.

Then she closed her eyes and waited to be rescued.

Eleanor Roosevelt's head hurt. She felt someone patting her cheek, and she opened her eyes, ready to tell whichever son it was to leave her alone.

But it wasn't one of her sons.

"I'm thinking of a number from one to ten," Maria said, staring at her.

"Guess what it is?"

Eleanor looked at her wrists. The strappado cuffs were on her.

No. Not this.

I'm royalty. I have presidential blood in my veins.

They can't do this to me.

"The answer," Maria said, "is fuck you."

Then the man, Felix, kicked Eleanor in the face.

Eleanor fell backward, through the gate, off the edge.

The next thing she knew, her head was hurting again.

She looked around, saw she was on the first floor.

Those fools. They must not have put the chains on correctly.

My head still hurts. But other than that, I'm perfectly fine.

Eleanor reached up a hand to rub her temple.

It didn't work, for some reason.

She tried with the other hand, and that didn't work, either.

Then she felt something drip onto her face.

Looking up, Eleanor saw Maria and Felix, staring down at her. She also saw the two lengths of chain.

Each chain had an arm attached to it. Each arm trailed veins and arteries and tendons and torn muscles that stretched down and were still tenuously attached to the torn sockets of Eleanor's shoulders.

Oh Lordy. Those are my arms.

Then there was pain. There was amazing, excruciating, unbearable pain.

Eleanor screamed through the pain for the entire four and a half minutes it took her to bleed to death. But to her it felt a lot longer.

Felix pulled his eyes away from Eleanor's death throes and turned to look at Maria, but she was gone. Before he had a chance to panic, she walked out of one of the bedrooms, a baby in her arms.

"Her parents are dead," Maria said. For someone who had been through hell, she looked positively radiant. "I want to keep her." The baby was adorable. And Maria was beaming.

But this isn't right.

Felix shook his head sadly. "Don't you think we need to do something else first?"

Maria's smile vanished. "What do you mean?"

Felix took her hand, which hurt like hell for him. Using his thumb and pinky, he placed Maria's pear-shaped engagement ring on her finger, the one he took off Eleanor when he was cuffing her wrists.

"There," he said. "Now we're ready to start a family."

They kissed, lightly, because they were both so injured. Then the three of them held each other until the helicopter arrived.

ONE YEAR LATER

Deb had never been so terrified in her life.

A sea of eyes watched her, judged her. Deb turned and looked at Letti, who gave her an intense stare and a nod. Beside Letti was Maria, who mimicked Letti's gesture.

Deb's throat was dry. Her heart was beating so fast she felt ready to faint.

The oppressive silence hurt her ears.

Then someone sneezed. A child. Deb glanced at the audience, saw it was the baby Maria and Felix had adopted, sitting on Felix's lap. Next to them, Kelly was leaning forward in the pew. Kelly spoke silently, urgently, mouthing the words so Deb could read her lips.

"Say it!"

Deb looked down at her ridiculously expensive dress, the long train covering her prosthetics, making her appear completely normal. She looked at the minister, who was smiling patiently at her. Then she looked at Mal. So handsome in his tuxedo. So much love in his eyes.

And suddenly, Deb wasn't scared anymore. With him by her side, she didn't think she'd ever be scared again.

"I do," she said.

Then she kissed him before the minister even had a chance to pronounce them man and wife.

Franklin Delano Roosevelt sat in the talking booth at West Virginia's Northern Correctional Facility, waiting for his visitor. Franklin missed life on the outside. He missed the food. He missed sex with women. He even missed his job as hotel manager in Monk Creek. But most of all, he missed his momma and his kinfolk.

Prison life wasn't so bad. The state gave him monthly transfusions, though they weren't nearly as much fun as the ones he used to get at the Rushmore Inn. Franklin ran a tiny black market store within the walls, selling cigarettes, drugs, tattoo supplies, candy bars. After the Rushmore Massacre, as the papers had called it, Franklin inherited a tidy bit of money from his many dead siblings. And that didn't count all the money Momma had stashed away. It was enough to hire a hotshot lawyer, who got his charges reduced from *murder* to multiple counts of *accessory*. Franklin got eight years, but would be out in four for good behavior.

Franklin's mood brightened when Chester walked over and sat across from him. Chester B. Arthur Roosevelt was one of only five brothers still alive. The other four were wanted by the police and had to stay in hiding. But Chester had bought hisself a swell fake ID, and the law couldn't touch him.

"You find a place?" Franklin asked.

"Boardin'house. Southern Georgia. Deep in the woods, outta the way. Big ole basement. Perfect for us."

A boardinghouse? That would be easier to run than a bed-and-breakfast.

Franklin never really warmed up to Momma's plan for making the next President. All he really cared about was the fun he had with the women they caught.

At the prison, Franklin learned there was some new-fangled chemical enzyme that turned regular blood into type O negative. That meant they didn't have to be so picky and choosy. Now they could grab whomever they wanted.

"You buy it yet?" Franklin asked.

"Got the deed this week. Should have 'er up 'n' runnin' real soon. Be all ready for you when you get outta here. Have a nice bunch of sweet honeys all tied up and waitin' for you."

Franklin smiled. He'd already done a year of his sentence.

With this to look forward to, the next three would just fly on by.

AFTERWORD

In 2007 I wrote a horror novel called *Afraid* under the pen name Jack Kilborn, and that landed me a two-book deal. My publishers wanted a book similar in tone to *Afraid*, so I pitched them the idea for a book called *Trapped* and wrote the first few thousand words. They placed an excerpt for *Trapped* in the back of copies of *Afraid*, hoping to release the book in the winter of 2009.

Unfortunately (for me), my editors *hated Trapped* when they read the whole thing.

Personally, I liked it. The novel was more intense than *Afraid*, and probably a little meaner and gorier (maybe more than just a little), but I believed it kept to the same theme and tone of the first Kilborn book. Namely, regular people in a dark, confined setting, confronted with an overpowering, horrible threat.

Since I wanted to get paid, I rewrote *Trapped* according to the editorial notes I'd been given. I don't believe it made the book better, but it did make it different. I toned down a bit of violence and sex, added a bit more violence in other areas, changed a few characters, cut a subplot, and wrote a new ending.

My editors hated the new version as well. So I put *Trapped* away, figuring it would find readers eventually, and instead wrote *Endurance*, the third Jack Kilborn book in my two-book contract. My editors liked *Endurance*, but wanted me to make some significant cuts. Having been down that road before, I told them no, and I pulled *Endurance* from publication.

So now I had two intense horror novels, ready to publish. All I had to figure out was what to do with them.

During the eighteen months I'd been working on *Trapped* and *Endurance*, I'd turned some of my older books (written under my real name, J.A. Konrath) into e-books. To my surprise, they sold like crazy. Rather than pursue traditional print publication, I decided to do it alone and release *Trapped* and *Endurance* myself.

I like *Endurance*. So much, that I didn't want to see it diminished by what I felt were unnecessary edits. Though it isn't as horrific as *Trapped* (I don't know if I'll ever write anything as horrific as *Trapped* ever again) there were certain creepy elements to this book that weirded me out. In fact, the whole reason I wrote this book was because of an idea I had while on vacation.

We were renting a cabin in the woods in northern Wisconsin, and I was sitting on the bed when a disturbing thought hit me. *What if the cabin's owners were watching us, right now?*

In fact, if you were a psychotic voyeur, it would be pretty easy to rig your house with hidden passages and peepholes and then rent it out to unsuspecting guests.

I immediately became paranoid and looked at the closet, the bathroom, the stairs, wondering if I was being spied on.

Then I heard something creak under the bed.

Could someone actually be under there?

No one actually was. But I kept thinking about how awful it would be to stay in someone else's house and suddenly realize someone was under your bed.

Of course, what could be even worse than that?

Someone under your bed, and you don't have legs so you can't run away.

I hope you had as much fun reading *Endurance* as I had writing it. If you did, I encourage you to check out *Afraid*, *Trapped*, and my J.A. Konrath books, which also have some good scares in them.

And if you'd like to see a sequel, e-mail me. I may not listen to my publishers, but I *always* listen to my readers . . .

Where superstition ends, true fear begins.
*In 1906, a crew of workers at the Panama Canal
unearthed something that could not be identified or
explained. Something sinister. And very much alive . . .*

One hundred years later, a team of scientists gather at
an underground facility in New Mexico to determine
what this being is—the most amazing discovery in the
history of mankind—and how it has managed to
survive. A biologist will analyze its structure.
A veterinarian will study its behavior. A linguist will
translate its language. But even the greatest minds
in the world cannot answer one inescapable question:
Could this ancient creature, this mockery of
God and nature, actually be the ancient
demon known as . . . the Beast?

ORIGIN

*From bestselling author J. A. KONRATH comes a tense
and thrilling exploration into the mysteries of life
and death, good and evil, and the original source
of our darkest fears . . .*

Praise for **J.A. KONRATH's** *bestselling thrillers*

"Konrath is one of the greatest thriller writers alive."
—Blake Crouch, bestselling author of *Wayward Pines*

"EXCELLENT."—Lee Child

Panama

November 15, 1906

"Where is it?" Theodore Roosevelt asked John Stevens as the two men shook hands. Amador, Shonts, and the rest of the welcoming party had already been greeted and dismissed by the President, left to wonder what had become of Roosevelt's trademark grandiosity.

Fatigue from his journey, they later surmised.

They were wrong.

The twenty-sixth President of the United States was far from tired. Since Stevens's wire a month previous, Roosevelt had been electrified with worry.

The canal project had been a tricky one from the onset—the whole Nicaraguan episode, the Panamanian revolution, the constant bickering in Congress—but nothing in his political or personal past had prepared him for this development. After five days of travel aboard the battleship *Louisiana,* his wife, Edith, sick and miserable, Roosevelt's nerves had become so tightly stretched they could be plucked and played like a mandolin.

"You want to see it *now*?" Stevens asked, wiping the rain from a walrus mustache that rivaled the President's. "Surely you want to rest from your journey."

"Rest is for the weak, John. I have much to accomplish on this visit. But first things first. I must see the discovery."

Roosevelt bid quick apologies to the puzzled group, sending his wife and three Secret Service agents ahead to the greeting reception at Tivoli Crossing. Before anyone, including Edith, could protest, the President had taken Stevens by the shoulder and was leading him down the pier.

"You are storing it nearby," Roosevelt stated, confirming that his instructions had been explicitly followed.

"In a shack in Cristobal, about a mile from shore. I can arrange for horses."

"We shall walk. Tell me again how it was found."

Stevens chewed his lower lip and lengthened his stride to keep in step with the commander in chief. The engineer had been in Panama for over a year, at Roosevelt's request, heading the canal project.

He wasn't happy.

The heat and constant rain were intolerable. Roosevelt's lackey Shonts was pompous and annoying. Though yellow fever and dysentery were being eradicated through the efforts of Dr. Gorgas and the new sanitation methods, malaria still claimed dozens of lives every month, and labor disputes had become commonplace and increasingly complicated with every new influx of foreign workers.

Now, to top it all off, an excavation team had discovered something so horrible that it made the enormity of the canal project look trivial by comparison.

"It was found at the East Culebra Slide in the Cut," Stevens said, referring to the nine-mile stretch of land that ran through the mountain range of the Continental Divide. "Spaniard excavation team hit it at about eighty feet down."

"Hard workers, Spaniards," Roosevelt said. He knew the nine thousand workers they had brought over from the Basque provinces were widely regarded as superior to the Chinese and West Indians because of their tireless efforts. "You were on the site at the time?"

"I was called to it. I arrived the next day. The . . . *capsule*, I suppose you could call it, was taken to Pedro Miguel by train."

"Unopened?"

"Yes. After I broke the seal on it and saw the contents . . ."

"Again, all alone?"

"By myself, yes. After viewing the . . . well, immediately afterward I wired Secretary Taft . . ." Stevens trailed off, his breath laboring in effort to keep up with the frantic pace of Roosevelt.

"Dreadful humidity," the President said. He attempted to wipe the hot rain from his forehead with a damp handkerchief. "I had wished to view the working conditions in Panama at their most unfavorable, and I believe I certainly have."

They were quiet the remainder of the walk, Roosevelt taking in the jungle and the many houses and buildings that Stevens had erected during the last year.

Remarkable man, Roosevelt mused, but he'd expected nothing less. Once this matter was decided, he was looking forward to the tour of the canal effort. There was so much that interested him. He was anxious to see one of the famed hundred-ton Bucyrus steam shovels that so outperformed the ancient French excavators. He longed to ride in one. Being the first President to ever leave the States, he certainly owed the voters some exciting details of his trip.

"Over there. To the right."

Stevens gestured to a small shack nestled in an outcropping of tropical brush. There was a sturdy padlock hooked to a hasp on the door, and a sign warning in several languages that explosives were contained therein.

"No one else has seen this," Roosevelt confirmed.

"The Spaniard team was deported right after the discovery."

Roosevelt used the sleeve of his elegant white shirt to clean his spectacles while Stevens removed the padlock. They entered the shed and Stevens shut the door behind them.

It was stifling in the small building. The President immediately felt claustrophobic in the dark, hot room, and had to force himself to stand still while Stevens sought the lantern.

Light soon bathed the capsule sitting before them.

It was better than twelve feet long, pale gray, with carvings on the outside that resembled Egyptian hieroglyphics to Roosevelt. It rested on the ground, almost chest high, and appeared to be made of stone. But it felt like nothing the President had ever touched.

Running his hand across the top, Roosevelt was surprised by how smooth, almost slippery, the surface was. Like an oily silk, but it left no residue on the fingers.

"How does it open?" he asked.

Stevens handed his lamp to Roosevelt and picked up a pry bar hanging near the door. With a simple twist in a near-invisible seam the entire top half of the capsule flipped open on hidden hinges like a coffin.

"My dear God in heaven," the President gasped.

The thing in the capsule was horrible beyond description.

"My sentiments exactly," Stevens whispered.

"And it is . . . alive?"

"From what I can judge, yes. Dormant, but alive."

Roosevelt's hand ventured to touch it, but the man who charged up San Juan Hill wasn't able to summon the nerve.

"Even being prepared for it, I still cannot believe what I am seeing."

The President fought his repulsion, the cloying heat adding to the surreality of the moment. Roosevelt detected a rank, animal smell, almost like a musk, coming out of the capsule.

The smell of the . . . *thing*.

He looked it over, head to foot, unable to turn away. The image seared itself into his mind, to become the source of frequent nightmares for the remainder of his life.

"What is the course of action, Mr. President? Destroy it?"

"How can we? Is it our right? Think what this means."

"But what if it awakens? Could we contain it?"

"Why not? This is the twentieth century. We are making technological advancements on a daily basis."

"Do you believe the public is ready for this?"

"No," Roosevelt said without hesitation. "I do not believe the United States, or the world, even in this enlightened age, would be able to handle a discovery of this magnitude."

Stevens frowned. He didn't believe any good could come of this, but as usual he had trouble going toe-to-toe with Roosevelt.

"Speak your mind, John. You have been living with this for a month."

"I believe we should burn it, Mr. President. Then sink its ashes in the sea."

"You are afraid."

"Even a man of your standing, sir, must admit to some fear gazing at this thing."

"Yes, I can admit to being afraid. But that is because we fear what we do not understand. Perhaps with understanding . . ."

Roosevelt made his decision. This would be taken back to the States. He'd lock it away someplace secret and recruit the top minds in the world to study it. He instructed Stevens to have a crate built and for it to be packed and boarded onto the *Louisiana*—no, better make it the *Tennessee*. If Mother found out what was aboard her ship she might die of fright.

"But if the world sees this . . ."

"The world will not. Pay the workers off and have them work at night without witnesses. I expect the crate to be locked as this shed was, and the key given to me. Worry no more about this, John, it is no longer your concern."

"Yes, Mr. President."

Roosevelt clenched his teeth and forced himself to stick out his hand to touch the thing—a brief touch that he would always recall as the most frightening experience of his life. He covered the fear with a bully Roosevelt *harrumph* and a false pout of bravado.

"Now let us lock this up and you can show me that canal you are building." Stevens closed the lid, but the smell remained.

The twenty-sixth President of the United States walked out of the shed and into the rain. His hands were shaking. He made two fists and shoved them into his pockets. The rain speckled his glasses, but he made no effort to clean them off. His whole effort was focused on a silent prayer to God that he'd made the right decision.

Chapter 1

"*You have reached Worldwide Translation Services.
For English, press one.*

"*Por español . . .*"

BEEP.

"*Welcome to WTS, the company for your every translation and interpretation need. Our skilled staff of linguists can converse in over two dozen languages, and we specialize in escort, telephone, consecutive, simultaneous, conference, sight, and written translations. For a list of languages we're able to interpret, press one. For Andrew Dennison, press two. For a . . .*" *BEEP.*

The business phone rang. Andy glanced at the clock next to the bed. Coming up on 3:00 a.m. Chicago time. But elsewhere in the world they were eating lunch.

If he didn't pick up, it would be forwarded to voice mail.

Unfortunately, voice mail didn't pay his bills.

"WTS, this is Andrew Dennison."

"Mr. Dennison, this is the President of the United States. Your country needs you."

Andy hung up. He remembered being a kid, sleeping

over at a friend's house, making prank calls. It seemed so funny back then.

He closed his eyes and tried to return to the dream he'd been having. Something to do with Susan, his ex-girlfriend, begging for him to come back. She'd told him that would only happen in his dreams, and she'd proven herself right.

The phone rang again.

"Look, kid. I've got your number on the caller ID, so I know you're calling from . . ."

He squinted at the words white house on the phone display.

"Mr. Dennison, in exactly five seconds two members of the Secret Service will knock on your door."

There was a knock at the door.

Andy jackknifed to a sitting position.

"Those are Agents Smith and Jones. They're to escort you to a limousine waiting downstairs."

Andy took the cordless over to his front door, squinted through the peephole.

Standing in the hallway were two men in black suits.

"Look, Mr.—uh—President, if this is some kind of tax thing . . ."

"Your particular skills are required in a matter of national security, Mr. Dennison. I'll brief you in New Mexico."

"This is a translation job?"

"I can't speak any more about it at this time, but you must leave immediately. You'll be paid three times your normal rate, plus expenses. My agents can explain in further detail. We'll talk when you arrive."

The connection ended. Andy peered through his peephole again. The men looked like Secret Service. They had the blank stare dead to rights.

"Do you guys have ID?" he asked through the door.

They held up their IDs.

Andy swallowed, and swallowed again. He considered his options and realized he really didn't have any.

He opened the door.

"As soon as you're dressed, Mr. Dennison, we can take you to the airport."

"How many days should I pack for?"

"No need to pack, sir. Your things will be forwarded to you."

"Do you know what language I'm going to be using? I've got books, computer programs . . ."

"Your things will be forwarded."

Andy had more questions, but he didn't think asking them would result in answers. He dressed in silence.

The limo, while plush, wasn't accessorized with luxuries. No wet bar. No television. No phone. And the buttons for the windows didn't work.

Andy wore his best suit, Brooks Brothers gray wool, his Harvard tie, and a pair of leather shoes from some Italian designer, which cost three hundred dollars and pinched his toes.

"So where in New Mexico am I going?" Andy asked the agents, both of whom rode in the front seat.

They didn't reply.

"Are we going to O'Hare or Midway?" No answer.

"Can you guys turn on the radio?"

The radio came on. Oldies. Andy slouched back in his seat as Mick Jagger crooned.

Chicago whipped by him on both sides, the streets full of people even at this late hour. Summer in the city was around the clock. The car stopped at a light and three college-age girls, drunk and giggling, knocked on his one-way window and tried to peer inside. They were at least a decade too young for him.

The limo's destination turned out to be Midway, the smaller of Chicago's two airports. Rather than enter the terminal, they were cleared through the perimeter fence and pulled directly out onto the runway. They parked in front of a solitary hangar, far from the jumbo jets. Andy was freed from the limo and led silently to a Learjet. He boarded without enthusiasm. He'd been on many jets, to many places more exotic than New Mexico.

Andy was bursting with curiosity for his current situation, but sleep was invading his head. It would probably turn out to be some silly little international embarrassment, like a Pakistani ambassador who hit someone while drunk driving. What was the Hindko word for *intoxication*? He couldn't remember, and since they didn't let him take his books, he had no way to look it up.

At a little past 4:00 A.M. the pilot boarded and introduced himself with a strong handshake, but didn't offer his name. He had no answers for Andy either.

Andy slept poorly, on and off, for the next few hours.

He awoke during the landing, the jolt nudging him alert when the wheels hit the tarmac. After the plane came to a stop, the pilot announced they'd arrived at their destination, Las Cruces International Airport. Andy rubbed some grit from his eyes and stretched in his seat, waiting for the pilot to open the hatch.

The climate was hot and dry, appropriate for the desert. The pilot informed Andy to remain on the runway and then walked off to the terminal.

Andy waited in the powerful sun, the only human being in sight, his rumpled suit soon clinging to him like a close family. A minute passed. Two. A golden eagle rode a thermal in the distance, circling slowly. Andy wondered when his ride would arrive. He wondered why this town was called The Crosses. He wondered what the hell was so important that the leader of the free world woke him up at 3:00 a.m. and flew him out here.

From the opposite end of the runway an army Humvee approached. Andy noticed the tags: Fort Bliss. The driver offered him a thermos of coffee and then refused further conversation.

They drove west on Interstate 10 and turned onto highway 549, heading into the desert. Traffic went from infrequent to nonexistent, and after they passed the Waste Isolation Pilot Plant—a large complex fenced off with barbed wire—they turned off road and followed some dirt trail that Andy could barely make out.

The Florida Mountains loomed in the distance. Sagebrush and tumbleweeds dotted the landscape. Andy even saw the skull of a steer resting on some rocks. This was the authentic West, the West of Geronimo and Billy the Kid. Andy had been to several deserts in his travels: the Gobi in China, the Rub‘ al-Khali in Saudi Arabia, the Kalahari in South Africa . . . . but this was his first visit to the Chihuahuan Desert. It left him as the others had—detached. Travel meant work, and Andy never had a chance to enjoy any of the places he'd visited around the world.

The Humvee stopped abruptly and Andy lurched in his seat.

"We're here," the driver said.

Andy craned his neck and looked around. Three hundred and sixty degrees of desert, not a building nor a soul in sight.

"You're kidding."

"Please get out of the Humvee, sir. I'm supposed to leave you here."

"Leave me here? In the desert?"

"Those are my orders."

Andy squinted. There was nothing but sand and rock for miles and miles.

"This is ridiculous. I'll die out here."

"Sir, please get out of the Humvee."

"You can't leave me in the middle of the desert. It's insane." The driver drew his pistol.

"Jesus!"

"These are my orders, sir. If you don't get out of the Humvee, I've been instructed to shoot you in the leg and drag you out. One . . ."

"I don't believe this."

"Two . . ."

"This is murder. You're murdering me here."

"Three."

The driver cocked the gun and aimed it at Andy's leg. Andy threw up his hands. "Fine! I'm out!"

Andy stepped out of the Humvee. He could feel the heat of the sand through the soles of his shoes.

The driver holstered his weapon, hit the gas, and swung the Humvee around. It sped off in the direction it had come. Andy watched until it shrank down to nothing.

He turned in a complete circle, feeling the knot growing in his belly. The only thing around him was scrub brush and cacti.

"This is not happening."

Andy searched the sky for any helicopters that might be flying in to pick him up. The sky was empty, except for a fat desert sun that hurt his eyes. Andy couldn't be sure, but the air seemed to be getting hotter. By noon it would be scorching.

He looked at his watch and wondered how long he

could go without water. The very idea of it made his tongue feel thick. A day, maybe two at most. It would take at least two days to walk back to the airport. He decided to follow the truck tracks.

"Andrew Dennison?"

Andy spun around, startled. Standing twenty yards away was a man. He wore loose-fitting jeans and a blue polo shirt, and he approached Andy in an unhurried gait. As the figure came into sharper focus, Andy noticed several things at once. The man was old, maybe seventy, with age spots dotting his bald dome and deep wrinkles set in a square face. But he carried himself like a much younger man, and though his broad shoulders were stooped with age, he projected an apparent strength. *Military*, Andy guessed, and upper echelon as well.

Andy walked to meet the figure, trying not to appear surprised that he'd just materialized out of nowhere. The thoughts of vultures and thirst were replaced by several dozen questions.

"I'm General Regis Murdoch. Call me Race. Welcome to Project Samhain."

Race offered a thick and hairy hand, which Andy nervously shook. It felt like shaking a two-by-four.

"General Race, I appreciate the welcome, but I think I've been left out of the loop. I don't know . . ."

"All in good time. The President wants to fill you in, and you're to meet the group."

"Where?" Andy asked, looking around.

The general beamed. "Almost a hundred years old, and still the best hidden secret in the United States. Right this way."

Andy followed Race up to a pile of rocks next to a bush. Close inspection revealed that they'd been glued, or maybe soldered, to a large metal plate which spun on a hinge. The plate swiveled open, revealing a murky stairwell leading into the earth.

"Cutting edge stuff in 1906, now kind of dated." Race smiled. "But sometimes the old tricks are still the best."

Race prompted Andy down the sandy iron staircase and followed after closing the lid above them. The walls were concrete, old and crumbling. Light came from bare bulbs hanging overhead every fifteen steps.

Only a few hours ago I was asleep in my bed, Andy thought.

"Don't worry," Race said. "It gets better."

After almost two hundred steps down they came to a large metal door with a wheel in the center, like a submarine hatch. Race stopped in front of the door and cleared his throat. He leaned closer to Andy, locking eyes with him.

"Three hundred million Americans have lived during the last century, and you are only the forty-third to ever enter this compound. During your time here and for the rest of your life afterward, you're going to be sworn to absolute secrecy. Failure to keep this secret will lead to your trial and inevitable execution for treason."

"Execution," Andy repeated.

"The Rosenbergs were numbers twenty-two and twenty-three. You didn't buy that crap about selling nuclear secrets, did you?"

Andy blinked. "I'm in an episode of The *X-Files*."

"That old TV show? They wish they had what we do."

Race opened the door and bade Andy to enter. They'd stepped into a modern hospital. Or at least, that's what it looked like. Everything was white, from the tiled floors and painted walls to the fluorescent lights recessed into the ceiling. A disinfectant smell wafted through the air, cooled by air-conditioning. They walked down a hallway, the clicking of Andy's expensive shoes amplified to an almost comic echo. It could have been a hundred other buildings Andy had been in before, except this one was several hundred feet underground and harbored some kind of government secret.

Andy asked, "This was built in 1906?"

"Well, it's been improved upon as the years have gone by. Didn't get fluorescent lights till 1938. In '49 we added the Orange Arm and the Purple Arm. We're always replacing, updating. Just got a Jacuzzi in '99, but it's on the fritz."

"How big is this place?"

"About seventy-five thousand square feet. Took two years to dig it all out. God gets most of the credit though. Most of this space is a series of natural caves. Not nearly the size of the Carlsbad Caverns two hundred miles to the east, but enough for our purpose."

"Speaking of purpose . . ."

"We're getting to that."

The hallway curved gradually to the right and Andy noted that the doors were all numbered in yellow paint with the word yellow stenciled above them. Andy guessed correctly that they were in the Yellow Arm of the complex, and was happy that at least one thing made sense.

"What's that smell?" Andy asked, noting that the pleasant scent of lemon and pine had been overtaken by a distinct farmlike odor.

"The sheep, over in Orange 12. They just came in last week, and they stink like, well, sheep. We think we can solve the problem with HEPA filters, but it will take some time."

"Sheep," Andy said. He wondered, idly, if he'd been brought here to interpret their bleating.

The hallway they were taking ended at a doorway, and Race ushered Andy through it and into a large round room that had six doors along its walls. Each door was a different color.

"Center of the complex. The head of the Octopus, so to speak. I believe you've got a call waiting for you."

In the middle of the room was a large round table, circled with leather executive-type office chairs. Computer monitors, electronic gizmos, and a mess of cords and papers haphazardly covered the tabletop as if they'd been dropped there from a great height.

Race sat Andy down in front of a screen and tapped a few commands on a keyboard. The President's head and shoulders appeared on the flat-screen monitor, and he nodded at Andy as if they were in the same room.

"Video phone, got it in '04." Race winked.

"Mr. Dennison, thank you for coming. You've done your country a great service."

The President looked and sounded like he always did: fit, commanding, and sincere. Obviously he'd had a chance to sleep.

"Where do I talk?" Andy asked Race.

"Right at the screen. There's a mike and a camera housed in the monitor." Andy leaned forward.

"Mr. President, I'd really like to know what's going on and what I'm supposed to be doing here."

"You were chosen, Andy, because you met all of the criteria on a very long list. We need a translator, one with experience in ancient languages. You've always had a gift for language. My sources say you were fluent in Spanish by age three, and by six years old you could also speak French, German, and some Russian. In grade school you were studying the Eastern tongues, and you could speak Chinese by junior high."

Only Mandarin, Andy thought. He couldn't speak Cantonese until a few years later.

"You graduated high school in three years and were accepted to Harvard on scholarship. You spent four years at Harvard, and wrote and published your thesis on giving enunciation to cuneiform, at age nineteen.

"When you left school in 1986 you lived on money left to you by your parents, who died in a fire three years before. After the money ran out you got a job at the United Nations in New York. You were there less than a year before being fired. During a Middle East peace talk you insulted the Iraqi ambassador."

"He was a pervert who liked little girls."

"Iraq was our ally at the time."

"What does that have to do with—"

The President held up a hand, as he was so accustomed to doing with reporters.

"I'm not sitting in a seat of judgment, Andy. But you're entitled to know why you were chosen. After the UN fired you, you started your own freelance translation service, WTS. You've been making an average living, one that allows you to be your own boss. But business has been slow lately, I assume because of the Internet."

Andy frowned. In the beginning, the World Wide Web had opened up a wealth of information for a translator, giving him instant access to the greatest libraries in the world. But, of course, it gave everyone else access to those libraries too. Along with computer programs that could translate both the written and the spoken word.

"So you know I'm good at my job, and you know I could use the money."

"More than that, Andy. You're single, and you aren't currently seeing anyone. You don't have any relatives. Business is going poorly and you're behind on your Visa and your Discover Card payments, and you've just gotten your second warning from the electric company. Your unique mind, so active and curious years ago, hasn't had a challenge since college.

"You didn't talk to the media after the incident at the UN, even though reporters offered you money for the story. That's important, because it shows you can keep your mouth shut. In short, by bringing you in on this project, you don't have anything to lose, but everything to gain."

"Why aren't I comforted that the government knows so much about me?"

"Not the government, Andy. Me. No one else in Washington is aware of you, or of Project Samhain. Only the incumbent President knows what goes on there in New Mexico. It was passed on to me by my predecessor, and I'll pass it on to my successor when I leave office. This is the way it's been since President Theodore Roosevelt commissioned construction of this facility in 1906."

Andy didn't like this at all. His curiosity was being overtaken by a creepy feeling.

"This is all very interesting, but I don't think I'm your man."

"I also know about Myra Thackett and Chris Simmons."

Andy's mouth became a thin line. Thackett and Simmons were two fictitious employees that Andy pretended to have under salary at WTS. Having phantom people on the payroll reduced income tax and was the only way he'd been able to keep his business afloat.

"So this is a tax thing after all."

"Again, only I know about it, Andy. Not the IRS. Not the FBI. Just me. And I can promise you that Ms. Thackett and Mr. Simmons will never come back to haunt you if you help us here."

"What exactly"—Andy chose his words carefully—"do you want from me?"

"First you must swear, as a citizen of the United States, to never divulge anything you see, hear, or learn at Project Samhain, under penalty of execution. Not to a friend. Not even to a wife. My own wife doesn't even know about this."

Not seeing an alternative, Andy held up his right hand, as if he were testifying in court.

"Fine. I swear."

"General Murdoch will provide the details, he knows them better than I. Suffice it to say, this may be the single most important project this country, maybe even the world, has ever been involved with. I wish you luck, and God bless." The screen went blank.

"It's aliens, isn't it?" Andy turned to Race. "You've got aliens here."

"Well, no. But back in '47 we had a hermit who lived in the mountains—he found our secret entrance and got himself a good look inside. Before we could shut him up he was blabbing to everyone within earshot. So we faked a UFO landing two hundred miles away in Roswell to divert attention." Andy rubbed his temples.

"You want some aspirin?" Race asked. "Or breakfast, maybe?"

"What I want, after swearing under the penalty of execution, is to know what the hell I'm doing here."

"They say an image is worth a thousand words. Follow me."

Race headed to the Red door and Andy loped behind. The Red Arm hallway looked exactly like the Yellow Arm; white and sterile with numbered doors, this time with the word red stenciled on them. But after a few dozen yards Andy noted a big difference. Race had to stop at a barrier that blocked the hallway. It resembled a prison door, with thick vertical steel bars set in a heavy frame.

"Titanium," Race said as he pressed some numbers on a keypad embedded in the wall. "They could stop a charging rhino."

There was a beep and a metallic sound as the door unlocked. The door swung inward, and Race held it open for Andy, then closed it behind him with a loud clang. It made Andy feel trapped. They came up on another set of bars fifty yards farther up.

"Why two sets?" Andy asked. "You have a rhino problem here?"

"Well, it's got horns, that's for sure."

Race opened the second gate and the Red Arm came to an abrupt end at doors Red 13 and Red 14.

"He was found in Panama in 1906, by a team digging the canal," Race said. "For the past hundred years he's been in some kind of deep sleep, like a coma. Up until last week. Last week he woke up."

"He?"

"We call him Bub. He's trying to communicate, but we don't know what he's saying."

Andy's apprehension increased with every breath. He had an irrational urge to turn around and run. Or maybe it wasn't so irrational.

"Is Bub human?" Andy asked.

"Nope." Race grinned. The general was clearly enjoying himself. *Didn't have visitors too often*, Andy guessed.

"So what is he?"

"See for yourself."

Race opened door Red 14, and Andy almost gagged

on the animal stench. This wasn't a farm smell. This was a musky, sickly, sweet-and-sour, big-carnivore smell.

Forcing himself to move, Andy took two steps into the room. It was large, the size of a gymnasium, the front half filled with medical equipment. The back half had been partitioned off with a massive translucent barrier, glass or plastic. Behind the glass was . . . "Jesus Christ," Andy said.

Andy's mind couldn't process what he was seeing. The teeth. The eyes. The claws.

This thing wasn't supposed to exist in real life.

"Biix a beel," Bub said.

Andy flew past Race, heading for the hallway.

"I promise not to tell anyone."

"Mr. Dennison . . ."

Andy met up with the titanium bars and used some of his favorite curses from several different languages. His palms were soaked with sweat, and he'd begun to hyperventilate.

Race caught up, placing a hand on his shoulder.

"I apologize for not preparing you, but I'm an old man with so little pleasure in my life, and it's such a hoot watching people see Bub for the first time." Andy braced the older man.

"Bub. Beelzebub. You've got Satan in there."

"Possibly. Father Thrist thinks it's a lower-level demon like Moloch or Rahab, but Rabbi Shotzen concedes it may be Mastema."

"I'd like to leave," Andy said, attempting to sound calm. "Right now."

"Don't worry. He's not violent. I've even been in the dwelling with him. He's just scary-looking, is all. And that Plexiglas barrier is rated to eight tons. It's as safe as visiting the monkey house at the zoo."

Andy tried to find the words.

"You're a lunatic," he decided.

"Look, Andy, I've been watching after Bub for over forty years. We've had the best of the best in the world here—doctors, scientists, holy men, you name it. We've found out so much, but the rest is just theory. Bub's awake now and trying to communicate. You're the key to that. Don't you see how important this is?"

"I'm . . ." Andy began, searching his mind for a way to put it.

Race finished the thought for him. "Afraid. Of course you're afraid. Any damn fool would be, seeing Bub. We've been taught to fear him since we were born. But if I can paraphrase Samuel Butler, we don't know the devil's side of the story, because God wrote all the books. Just think about what we can learn here."

"You're military," Andy accused. "I'm sure the weapons implications of controlling the Prince of Darkness aren't lost on you."

Race lost his friendly demeanor, his eyes narrowing.

"We have an opportunity here, Mr. Dennison. An opportunity that we haven't had since Christ walked the earth. In that room is a legendary creature, and the things that he could teach us about the world, the universe, and creation itself stagger the imagination. You've been chosen to help us, to work with our team in getting some answers. Many would kill for the chance."

Andy folded his arms. "You expect me to believe not only that the devil is harmless and just wants to have a chat, but that the biggest government conspiracy in the history of the world has only good intentions?"

Race's face remained impassive for a few seconds longer, and then he broke out laughing.

"Damn, that does sound hard to swallow, don't it?"

Andy couldn't help but warm a bit at the man's attitude. "General Murdoch . . ."

"Race. Call me Race. And I understand. I've been part of the project so long the whole thing is the norm to me. You need to eat, rest, think about things. We'll grab some food and I'll show you your room."

"And if I want to leave?"

"This isn't a prison, son. I'm sure you weren't the only guy on the President's list. You're free to go whenever you please, so long as you never mention this to anyone."

Andy took a deep, calming breath and the effects of the adrenaline in his system began to wear off. Race opened the gate and they began their trek back down the hallway.

"The world really is going to hell, isn't it?" Andy said.

Race grinned. "Sure is. And we've got a front-row seat."